On Her Master's Secret Service

Masters and Mercenaries, Book 4

Lexi Blake

On Her Master's Secret Service
Masters and Mercenaries, Book 4
Lexi Blake

Published by DLZ Entertainment LLC

Copyright 2013 DLZ Entertainment LLC
Edited by Chloe Vale and Kasi Alexander
ISBN: 978-1-937608-13-2

Acknowledgements

I want to say a special thanks to the people who make this series work. Chloe Vale, you're the best editor in the business and I can't think of anyone I'd rather have on my side. To my other editors and betas – Kasi Alexander and Riane Holt – this series wouldn't be the same without you. To Sheri Vidal and Lexi's Doms and Dolls – thanks for all the support, ladies. And to the amazing Liz Berry. You know this book would be so much poorer without your input. And I would be less without your friendship.

But in the end, this book is about a marriage, about long term love and commitment, so I have to dedicate it to the man who taught me what love really is. This is for my husband, Richard.

Prologue

Georgetown, Virginia
Six Years Earlier

Alex McKay's feet pounded against the concrete as he raced into the hospital. A week. She'd been in that monster's hands for a week. All he'd been able to do was pray, and he wasn't fucking good at praying.

He nearly slid on the slick tile of the ER floor, his heart beating a rapid rhythm in his chest. For seven days, two hours, and seventeen minutes, his heart hadn't beat at all it seemed. From the moment his wife went missing, he'd been in a nauseating purgatory of guilt and fear.

Please let her be alive. Just alive. I'll take living and breathing.

Because he knew damn well she wouldn't be whole, and it was all his fault.

All he could see was the way his living room looked. That sight seemed to be imprinted on his brain. The room where he and Eve made love and cuddled and watched TV had been desecrated, their pictures cracked and broken, their belongings treated like rubbish. He'd hated that.

He'd really hated the bodies that had been strewn around that room. Bodies and blood.

"Alex!"

He stopped on a dime. God, he didn't even know where he was going. He'd gotten the call that she'd been found and he'd just driven like a madman toward the hospital without

5

asking a single question. His partner was up ahead. Right in that instant, Warren Petty looked like an ocean of calm. He'd been right at Alex's side since the moment he'd walked into the home he shared with his wife and found it violated, their whole lives in pieces as surely as their possessions had been vandalized.

And Eve had been gone.

"Alex, she's alive."

He nearly fell to his knees. "Where?"

Warren didn't seem to need more than that one word. They'd been partners for years. His face grew grim, and Alex felt himself flush with fear. That was the face Warren used when he told people bad news. As FBI agents working the worst of crimes, he and Warren had been forced to deliver bad news more than once. But Alex never thought he would be on the receiving end of that look.

Warren had been standing beside him when he'd discovered that the guards he'd left behind were dead and his wife was missing. Warren was the one who'd told Tommy and Leon's wives they weren't coming home again.

"The cops found her walking along 29."

Alex took a long breath, processing the information. She'd been in the area? God. He'd been searching every hour of every day and she'd been close. "Did she escape?"

"Evans dumped her on the highway. Alex, I talked to the doctors." Warren's eyes closed briefly. "They're going to run a rape kit when they can, but they need to deal with her injuries first. I'm so sorry you're going through this. You have to know that I'll do anything to help you and Eve. She's strong. She's going to come through this. I believe it. If anyone can survive this, it's Eve."

His wife. His sweet, smart, precious wife needed a rape kit. A million memories splashed across his brain. The first time he'd kissed her. His hands had been shaking because he'd known she was the one. The first time they'd made love. He'd had sex before, but he'd never worshipped a woman until he'd moved inside Eve, her body becoming his temple to love and protect.

They'd been trying to have a baby. Two months. Two months without condoms or birth control. God. What if she was pregnant now? How the hell would he deal with that?

Alive. She's alive and you will take it. She is alive and that is all that matters.

"Can I see her?" He needed to see her, to be in the same room with her. All he'd wanted for seven days was one more minute with her.

Warren shook his head, glancing down the long white hallway. "No, I'm sorry. She's in surgery. They couldn't wait. Stay calm. She's going to be fine. He pushed her out of a moving car. She's got a little internal bleeding and her left arm has to be reset. Most of the surgery they're going to do is cosmetic. He cut her up, Alex."

Alex was well aware of what Michael Evans was capable of doing to a woman. "Oh, god."

Warren sat down, his body slumping as though he couldn't stay standing a second longer. His head fell forward. "Alex, if I'd only…"

"This is not your fault. This is mine. She told me what would happen." His wife was a brilliant profiler and what had he done? He'd ignored her work because he'd been so much smarter. He'd arrogantly told her she was wrong on this one. "She told me not to do that interview. She told me to keep this little war between us private, but I thought I could get him to come out of hiding."

He'd been an idiot, going on a national show and basically calling the man out as a coward. He'd been

7

tracking Evans for years, and after the last clinic bombing took the lives of four people, Alex lost all patience. Evans's latest target was in Alex's backyard, right in DC. He'd felt impotent, useless, so he'd tried to call the man out. He'd been willing to try anything.

"He came out of hiding all right." Warren shook his head, his face pale.

"I thought he would come after me, damn it. He was supposed to come after me." His hands were shaking. He couldn't stop shaking. He needed to get himself under control. "Michael Evans was supposed to want to kill me. I was the bait."

But Michael Evans, homegrown terrorist extraordinaire, hadn't gone for Alex's throat. Oh, no, he'd gone for something much worse. The man Alex had been hunting for the majority of his FBI career had raped his wife and tossed her to the side of the road like garbage.

Evans is likely to play with his prey. He prefers to cause the maximum amount of pain to his enemies as evidenced in the brutal deaths of several men he believed to have betrayed him, but there is a certain honor to the games he plays. Up until now, he hasn't come after you personally because you've kept this in the Bureau. If you do this interview, he's very likely to come after you. He'll see it as a declaration of war. Please don't do this. You can find another way to catch him.

He could still hear her pleading with him. She'd been terrified that Evans would kill him. She must have been scared when she realized Evans hadn't come for him. He'd come for her.

Warren turned his head up. "I've called Eddie. He said if there's anything he can do, any way he can ease the way for the two of you, he won't hesitate to call in a couple of favors. We can get her the best room in the hospital. We can make sure the press stays off her. We're here for you."

Warren's brother was a senator. He had serious pull. There was talk of him going for the nomination during the next election cycle. But none of it mattered. Warren's political pull wouldn't make Eve's pain go away. Nothing could. Alex felt his fists clench. "How long before she's out of surgery?"

"An hour or so. Sit down, man. It's going to be a while." Warren gestured to the chair beside him.

He shook his head. He couldn't sit. He couldn't wait. He'd been waiting for days. He couldn't do it anymore. He pulled out his cell. There was exactly one person who could put him at ease. "I'll be back. I have to make a call."

He stepped away. He felt calmer now. Sitting and waiting would only make him crazy. He needed to do something. He dialed a familiar number.

A low voice came over the line. "This is Taggart."

His best friend. His rock. Ian had flown in the minute Alex called. He'd dropped everything and been in DC before dawn. He'd used his high-level contacts to get Sean a leave of absence as well. Apparently it paid to work for the CIA. Ian kept his connection to the Agency quiet, even from his brother, but Alex knew that Ian worked as a spy. He needed Ian now more than ever. "Ian, I have to find him. I have to bring him in."

"Did you find Eve?"

"Evans tossed her out of a moving car. She's alive, but she's in surgery." He would know all the gruesome details later. "Ian, you know I have to find him."

He needed to start making up for his mistakes. He needed to make sure Eve was safe.

"I'll help you." Ian's voice didn't falter. Like the man

9

himself, it was steady and firm.

His hands stopped shaking as Ian started to talk about his plans. This, at least, was something he could control.

* * * *

Eve opened her eyes. The world was still groggy, hazy. She stiffened immediately, waiting for the next blow.

"Eve, you're home. You're here. It's Alex. I'm here with you, angel." Alex's voice brought her out of the last vestiges of her panic.

How long had she been with Michael Evans? According to the police, it was only a week. Seven days of pain and humiliation. One hundred and sixty-eight hours. It wasn't so long when compared to a whole life, so how was it those hours felt like an eternity?

She'd been in the hospital for two days. She forced herself to count the time. It brought her back to reality. This was day three, the third day of the rest of her life, and she was home.

"Can I get you anything?" Alex shuffled his papers around. So many papers and phone calls. It was all he did anymore. He shuffled papers around and talked to people on the phone and sat by her bedside.

He wouldn't get in bed with her. She was too fragile, he claimed. He didn't want to jostle her in his sleep so he didn't seem to sleep anymore.

"No." It was too early for another pain pill. She glanced at the clock. She had an hour's worth of steadily increasing agony before she could take another one and find some brief moment of relief.

Alex settled back down. He stacked his file folders. "I have a good lead going. There's a reliable witness who puts him in Memphis six hours ago. Ian is already on the road."

"I don't want to talk about Evans." He only seemed to want to talk about the case. She understood why. He was in control of the case. He could do something about the search for Evans, but couldn't he see that she needed distance? "I don't like all these papers and computers around me."

She felt like she couldn't breathe. Every piece of paper was another link to the man who raped her. She just wanted some normalcy. Being back in her home actually gave her a sense of comfort. She'd worried it would bring back memories of the initial attack, but all she'd seen was her house in perfect order. From what she understood, Ian and Sean Taggart had made arrangements to put the house back together. Alex's childhood friends were home on leave from the Army and they were trying their best to make things normal for her again, but Alex kept bringing all those files in. She just wanted a minute where she could fool herself that things were ordinary. Just one moment.

Alex scrambled, pulling the papers off the bed. "I'll move them to the nightstand. I'm sorry."

It was a king-sized bed, but more often than not, they ended up cuddled together right in the center so there was always plenty of space.

She moved gingerly, trying not to shift her left arm too much. It ached, a deep throb in her muscles. Every single movement pulled at her as though her skin was now too tight for her body. "It's late. You should get some sleep. Come to bed."

He ran a hand through his hair. He looked so much older than he had a week ago, his mouth turning down in a perpetual grimace. "I don't want to hurt you."

He wouldn't jostle her. Maybe she would get some sleep if he were in bed with her. "You won't. There's plenty of room."

He shook his head, picking up the papers and holding them to his chest like they were something precious. "I move too much. I would end up next to you."

"Would that be such a bad thing?" He hadn't touched her since before the incident, nothing beyond the merest brushing of his hands across her as he settled a blanket around her or helped her out of bed.

He sighed, a heavy sound. "Eve, you flinch when I touch you."

Because she could still feel Michael Evans violating her. She could still feel his hands slapping at her as he tied her down, feel the knife he'd used to carve her up.

I think you perverts call this knife play. Play. I like to play, too. Tell me something, whore, does your husband play like this?

She shivered.

"You see," Alex said, turning away. "You can't even think about it."

"I wasn't thinking about you, Alex." The whole time she'd been in that room Evans had kept her in, all she'd been able to think about was getting home to Alex. He was right there. He was six feet away. Why did it feel like a chasm had opened up between them?

"I can be patient, angel," Alex said quietly. "It's going to be okay, but for now it's probably best that I don't get into bed with you. You've been through so much. I can't stand the thought of causing you more pain."

But being apart from him was a different kind of agony. She was just about to argue when she caught sight of herself in the mirror. The bandage around her neck had come slightly undone, and there was no way to miss the stitches that ran down her skin. She looked like Frankenstein, newly stitched together and unleashed on the world. Her face was a mass of bruises and her lip was just beginning to deflate.

Maybe Alex didn't want to sleep with her for different reasons.

For years she'd been his submissive and he her proud Dom. He would take her to the club they belonged to and gain great pleasure from showing off her beauty.

She wasn't very beautiful now. She was battered, and she wasn't sure she would ever be the same again.

"What if I can't get into slave pose?"

She found it comforting. Since he'd introduced her to D/s, she'd greeted him at least once each day by falling to her knees and allowing them to splay wide, her head bowed and palms up on her thighs. She kept a perfectly straight back even though she was bigger than many of the girls. She'd tried to diet, but Alex always stuffed her with sweets.

Her legs were scarred now and one of her ankles had nearly broken. What if she couldn't be his partner? What if her days as his submissive were over?

He reached out for her, but then drew his hand back. "You don't worry about that right now, Eve. Angel, I would understand if you never called me Master again."

His words didn't make sense. He was her Master. They'd made an agreement. They had a contract. They'd sat in bed one day shortly after they'd met and spent the day discussing what their contract would be. When they'd gone over hard and soft limits, they had kissed and played. When they discussed their duties to each other, he'd been deep inside her. Their contract was intimate and real. They were married. They talked about everything. A contract could be cold. Ian wrote up cold contracts because he didn't love the submissives he took. But their contract had been warm and happy and it connected them.

What if he didn't want her now that Michael Evans had used her?

She'd changed her whole life to be with Alex. She loved their life together. What if it was all over?

"I can't have a baby." Maybe that was what had put that dark look in Alex's eyes.

He shook his head. "That is not what the doctor said."

No. He'd been very clinical about the whole thing. He'd talked about damage to her uterus and losing one of her ovaries in the accident. He'd nearly performed a hysterectomy. The internal bleeding had been worse than he'd thought at first, but one of the nurses fought for her. It had been touch and go for a while. "It's unlikely."

"Unlikely isn't never. And I don't care about that. I'm just happy you're alive."

He didn't seem happy. He seemed grave and grim. The only time he became animated was when he was running down a lead on Evans. Then his face was flush and a passionate anger would seep into his eyes.

"It's going to be all right," he promised. "You'll see. I'm going to catch him and you'll feel safe again."

She might never feel safe again. "I don't want to talk about him. I want to forget him."

She knew she couldn't forget, but she needed to try to find some normalcy again and she couldn't do that without her husband. She caught another glance of herself in the mirror and the deep need to argue with him fled. She couldn't help but notice the way his eyes slid away from her. He didn't want to be here.

He didn't want to look at her.

Suddenly the ache inside her had nothing to do with her bones.

Alex hung his head as he grabbed his laptop. "You'll

see. You're going to feel so much better when you know he can't hurt you again. I'm going to give this to you. I screwed up and you paid the price, but I'm going to make this right."

She reached out to him, but he was already at the door. She pulled her arm back before he turned. How could she tell him that he couldn't make it right again? She wasn't sure at this point that she could even come back from what she'd been through. It was so close. Every time she closed her eyes, she could see that face looming over her. She needed Alex to take those visions away from her.

"I need you." She hated how small her voice sounded.

"I'm here, angel." He set the papers down and moved toward her. He crossed the space between them. The space between. There'd never been space between them before. Even when they were miles apart, she could feel him. They were married in every way—their hearts and minds and souls melded together. But now she felt every inch of air and distance that separated them.

He reached out, his fingers brushing her, and she flinched because every piece of her skin was still sensitive.

Alex nearly jumped back, his whole face flushing with horror. "I'm sorry."

She was making it all worse. "Please give me some time."

She couldn't lose Alex. She would heal. She would work. She would make her way back to where she'd been before.

Alex was at the door again. "I'll give you all the time you need. I'm going to find him. I'm going to get him for you."

"I don't need that." She didn't want him out in the field now. Tears streamed down her face, making the world a blurry mess. "I don't want you out there with him. Please,

Alex. Stay with me."

"I will if you need me to." He hesitated, his fingers curling around those files that meant so much to him. "Warren can handle it. And Ian's looking into things on the side."

But he wanted to handle it himself. He wanted it so bad. It was right there on his face. Her heart fell. He wanted his revenge. He could say it was all for her, but it was really because he could control this part of his life. Chasing after Michael Evans was active. Sitting at her bedside and hoping she healed was not.

"I'll be fine." Maybe when the scars were gone, he could forget that she'd been such a victim. Maybe she could forget. Maybe they could find normal again.

"Are you sure?"

She wasn't sure of anything. Nothing. Her world had flipped, and she hated where she'd landed. She'd learned so much about herself. She'd learned that she could break, that she was fragile.

Now she was learning that her marriage was fragile, too.

"You should go and help Ian." Perhaps being with Ian for a few days would be good for him. Ian would watch out for him.

She trusted Ian with Alex's life. Though Warren had been his partner for the last few years, she preferred knowing that Ian was watching his back. Perhaps Ian could talk to Alex. Ian hadn't hesitated around her. Ian had reached for her and when she'd flinched, he'd growled at her. He'd told her he wasn't that "motherfucker who hurt her" and he demanded that she accept his comfort.

Ian didn't feel the guilt Alex did. Maybe he could help Alex.

She needed her husband. God, she needed her Dom so badly.

"I love you, Eve." He whispered the words. "I'm so sorry."

She closed her eyes as though she was going back to sleep. She heard the door close.

She didn't need his sorrow. She didn't need his guilt. She needed his strength, but she couldn't ask for it because she'd changed on a fundamental level. She wasn't his sweet little innocent sub anymore.

Time. She needed time.

She let her hand find the bandage over the spot where he'd nearly split her throat.

Did time heal all wounds? Perhaps not. Perhaps it just brought scars that proved she'd survived on a physical level.

But she might have lost her soul because she wasn't sure her marriage had survived at all.

Eve closed her eyes and prayed for dreams of yesterday.

Chapter One

Dallas, Texas
Present Day

Alex McKay felt his stomach churn as he stared at the projection in front of him.

"Do you know how dangerous this could be?" Ian Taggart asked.

The conference room was quiet. Not one sliver of early morning light made it past the tightly drawn shades. The sun was coming up. He knew it because of the time, but in the dark conference room, it still felt like night, utterly dark, the only illumination a series of slides that depicted his life in tragic photos.

He sighed and simply clicked to the next slide. The last thing he needed was Ian telling him how dangerous Michael Evans could be. He knew that up close and personally. Michael Evans had cost Alex McKay just about everything he cared about in the world. His job. His future. But most of all the fucker had cost Alex his wife. And that was why he was going to find him no matter the cost.

"The last time I had a source contact me, they believed Evans was in Argentina, but that was over a year ago. This is the first time he's surfaced since then." He kept his voice moderate, like he was just going over another Tuesday morning case file and not the most important events of his life.

Adam Miles slipped into the room, sliding into the seat to Alex's left. "Is there a reason we're having a meeting at six in the morning? I don't think I should have to be awake before the sun is."

Jake Dean rolled his eyes as he followed his partner. Jake and Adam always worked together, but then they pretty much did everything together—including their wife, Serena. "He's bitching because I refused to let him wake up Serena this morning."

"I don't do well without a good-bye kiss," Adam said, sulking a little.

Ian groaned, sitting back in his massive leather chair. Dressed for business, the early morning hours did not seem to faze Ian at all. Unlike Alex, who was still in sweat pants and a T-shirt, Ian had come into work in a designer suit. It would make most men look civilized, but Ian just looked like a well-dressed gangster, the kind who could kill a man and never even wrinkle his clothes. "Adam, dude, get out from behind Serena's skirts."

"I spend all my time trying to get into her skirts, boss," Adam shot back.

"If you're all done here, I would like to continue." Alex really didn't have time to sit and listen to how fucking happy Adam was. "Or we can just close this thing up right now and I can handle this on my own."

"What crawled up Alex's butt and died?" Jake asked in a whisper that absolutely everyone in the building could probably hear.

"Shut up, Jake." Ian leaned forward. "Michael Evans seems to have surfaced."

"Fuck." Jake looked up, and even in the dim light of the predawn conference room, he could see the solidarity in Jake's eyes. "Anything you need, man. We're here. Where's

Li, by the way? Tell me he didn't kill the English asshole?"

"Like he bloody well could." Simon Weston was damn quiet. He'd slunk into the room without anyone noticing. As the newest member of the McKay-Taggart Security Service's team, the former MI6 agent hadn't much tried to fit in with anyone past Ian. Ian seemed to have taken the man under his wing despite the fact that Simon had nearly blown up their last assignment. He'd been fooled by Eli Nelson, and didn't Alex know that feeling. Despite his surly attitude, Alex felt a bit of a kinship with Simon. He knew damn well what it was like to get his ass handed to him on an operation. "Liam had other plans this morning, and this is just a friendly little info share. I can fill him in later."

He'd pointedly not invited Liam this morning, and he'd lucked out because this was Liam and Avery's weekly breakfast with Eve. Liam and Eve had gotten close over the years, and she adored Li's new wife, Avery. They were the perfect distraction. Eve usually came in early, but Tuesdays were spent at a local café.

"Who's Michael Evans and why does everyone look like their best mate just got run over?" Simon asked. He stood in the back, not bothering with one of the four seats left.

Alex directed his attention to the projection on the wall. It was a picture of a man he knew far too well. "This is Michael Evans, thirty-seven. He's a homegrown terrorist. He ran a small commune in the northern section of Idaho. No name. Just two hundred acres and a belief that the United States government has grown corrupt. I'll admit, it's not just the US government Evans has a problem with. It's mostly all of society. The FBI didn't pay much attention to him until we discovered his ties to jihadist leaders in Mexico. Between 2001 and 2005, Evans made over fifty trips to

Central America. The CIA marked him as a potential stateside contact for the Taliban and Al-Qaeda and other associated groups."

Simon nodded. "Yeah, I remember him now. He was all over the news a couple of years back. I was actually in the States when he was arrested. He grew drugs on that land of his and funded small cells. They bombed low profile sites, if I remember correctly. I found it rather odd that they didn't choose high value targets."

"Evans considered them to be very high value targets. Allegedly, he was the money behind fifteen clinic bombings across the US," Alex murmured. Evans had managed to kill doctors, nurses, and patients, most of whom had only walked into the clinic for routine exams, but they made Evans's hit list because the clinics were government funded and offered family planning. "He also targeted domestic abuse shelters. He liked to set those on fire. Evans isn't really big on women's rights."

"He specifically targeted clinics where women got routine care and could procure birth control. In twelve of the clinics he targeted, no abortion services were provided," Ian continued. Ian knew the file as well as Alex. It was this very case that had brought Alex to Dallas to found the company with his best friend. Ian was a head case half the time, but Alex owed him everything, and that was his only reason for having this briefing. If it weren't for Ian, he would be on his way to the meet site right now.

"What's his motivation?" Jake asked. "I know the case files, but I never really understood what he wanted. Obviously he's a misogynist pig, but terrorists usually have a point they're trying to get across."

"Evans is a deep believer that modern America has stripped men of all their god-given rights. He wants to go back to the times when a man owned everything. When a man had full rights to his property and could enforce his own laws on that property, and part of the property included a man's wives. Yes, I said wives," Alex explained. "He had several wives across the country. He killed one when she turned state's witness against him. He left behind the corpse of another woman when he fled his Idaho compound. Wherever he is now, we should be prepared that he likely has a wife or two and he won't hesitate to throw them in the line of fire."

"Charming," Adam muttered.

"Yeah, well, he's no prince." Alex clicked through to the next slide. It was the one of Evans being hauled in. Evans was smiling at the camera, his handsome face looking more like a movie matinee idol than a mass killer. Those good looks had brought him hoards of women who wrote to him in prison or did an enormous amount of his dirty work.

Evans is a charismatic killer, Eve had written. *He uses charm to draw his victims in, but in the end, he can't consider himself a winner unless he beats a male he considers of equal worth.*

God, if he'd just listened to Eve. "Evans was placed in prison awaiting trial. He had excellent lawyers, naturally. They managed to push the trial out almost two years and to have Evans held at a medium security prison to await trial."

"He escaped in a mattress, right?" Simon finally moved in, sitting down and starting to glance through the material in front of him.

"Yes, right before the state was set to present opening arguments. He had a long-term issue with his lungs. They were damaged from a fire in his childhood, and he was on oxygen therapy from time to time. He had a breathing episode, very likely faked or purposefully brought on, and, not only did the prison doctor give him a small oxygen tank, he prescribed new, allergen-free bedding. Almost two years to the day that he was arrested, Evans was smuggled out in the bedding. It had been hollowed out. One of his most loyal followers took his place in jail with a duplicated oxygen tank. Because of the mask over his face, no one noticed until almost twenty-four hours later, not even his cellmate. They took him in for questioning, but he wouldn't say a thing. He'd been taken out of the cell at the time, so the authorities couldn't link him to the escape. As far as we know, Evans joined his jihadist friends in Central America shortly thereafter."

"You said the FBI arrested him? Don't you mean you arrested him?" Simon asked, his icy blue eyes coming up from the file folder.

"Yes, I was the arresting agent." He said the words through clenched teeth.

"You were the Special Agent in Charge? I believe that's the local lingo," Simon said. "How long after this case was it before you quit?"

"It doesn't matter," Ian pronounced.

But Simon had a right to know. "I quit two months after Evans was arrested. That was five years ago. I packed up my life and I moved here. Ian and I started this company. Make no mistake. This is personal for me. This isn't a payday, and anyone who doesn't want to volunteer time should feel free to walk away. I'm not going to ask for much beyond some behind-the-scenes support, and even that will be in an informational fashion. I don't need muscle on this one."

He usually was the muscle.

Simon frowned, obviously unwilling to give up. "Why isn't O'Donnell around? I can't imagine he would willingly miss this meeting. Is he already working on the case? And where is our lovely shrink? I suspect she would be helpful in this case. She used to be in a behavioral analysis unit, correct? Did she work on the Evans case with you? Could we see her files on him?"

A tense silence filled the room. They were all perfectly valid questions, and Alex resented the shit out of them.

"Yes, Eve used to work with the BAU. She was a profiler, but she doesn't need to be involved in this case." None of them really needed to be involved. Just him and Evans and whoever the hell this mystery contact was. He glanced at the clock. Four and a half hours. Just four and a half hours before he could meet his contact and start up the nasty game he and Evans hadn't quite finished.

"What do I not know?" Simon asked. He looked around the table, studying every man there. "I obviously am the only one not in on the joke."

"It wasn't a joke, asshole," Adam said. "And Eve should be here. She has a right to know if the man who raped and brutalized her is back in the States."

"Eve isn't coming anywhere close to this case," Alex stated flatly. "And if I get even a hint that Evans is close to us, she'll be on her way to a safe house and under twenty-four seven cover."

"Ah, no, not a joke at all." Simon closed the folder. "I assume this is of absolutely no use. It's going to be sanitized. I'll research it myself. I'm rather surprised they allowed you to stay in charge."

Simon was right about the file. He'd sanitized the thing because he couldn't stand the thought of anyone knowing what had happened. The Bureau had kept things very quiet and the press had only gotten the merest hints of what his wife had to go through. They had enough other evidence on Evans to burn the fucker five times over.

24

"I was taken off the case, but I didn't stop working," Alex admitted. The Bureau had granted him a leave of absence, but he'd simply used it to track down Evans. He often wondered if Warren resented him for that. Warren Petty had taken over for Alex, but Alex had gotten the arrest.

"Do you think he's going to come after her again?" Simon asked.

He lived in terror of that very thing happening. He dreamed at night of her being gone and the days that passed until she'd been discarded like a used up tissue, tossed on the side of the road in the middle of the night. She'd had to make her way to a gas station, her body naked against the snow and frost.

Had Evans intended for her to live? Alex thought he had. Eve was supposed to be a reminder of everything Alex had done wrong, of how much he'd lost and how much more powerful Michael Evans was.

Don't push him this way, Alex. Keep this private. If you go to the press, I think he'll lash out and he'll strike at you.

He could still see her eyes pleading with him to change his plans, but he'd known what he was doing. He'd known he could take Evans down.

But Evans hadn't come for him. Oh, no. That would have been too easy.

"I don't think he's coming after Eve. I have no evidence that he would. It's been almost six years since he had any contact with her, and we all know damn well that he likes to play with his prey." Ian stood up, turning on the lights and flooding the room. "There's also the fact that they've divorced. That had to give Evans an enormous amount of pleasure, and I'm sure he knows that it happened. I'm sure he kept track of you after he fled the States. But when you left the FBI, you very likely went off his radar. A man like

Evans would no longer consider Alex to be a real threat. And he wouldn't care about Eve at all at this point."

Alex couldn't take that chance.

"I want her kept out of this. It's why I didn't contact Li. Li is close to Eve. He would tell her," Alex admitted. He wasn't bringing Eve into this. The less she knew the better off they all would be. He couldn't take her back into that hellhole. He couldn't.

And he also couldn't allow anyone else to handle this.

"Why do you think he's surfaced?" Jake asked.

"I received an e-mail from a woman named Kristen six weeks ago. According to the e-mail, she's an investigative reporter and she's been tracking Evans since his jailbreak. I'm supposed to meet her later this morning. It's a public venue. Right out in the open." The woman in the e-mail had insisted on it. He'd been told flatly that if she saw someone other than him, she would walk away. He couldn't let that happen. "I need someone to have eyes on Eve while I make contact. I can't take the chance that this is his way of getting at her."

"I'll keep eyes on Eve, and Jake and Adam can handle your backup," Ian stated.

This was precisely why he hadn't wanted to have this little session. "I can't. If she sees anyone but me, she'll run. That e-mail was very plain. She will deal with me and only me. I don't know what she looks like. I have no idea. I have to talk to this woman, Ian. I can't let her slip past me. The meet up is totally public. There's nothing to worry about."

"She won't know we're there," Jake promised. "Believe it or not, we've done this a time or two."

"You two handle close cover. I'm the shadow. I'm the expert." He was damn fine at blending into the shadows. It was a complete reversal of the first ten years of his career.

He'd been the FBI's golden boy, a shining star. The last five years he'd made a goal of never sticking out, always being the behind-the-scenes guy. He'd become a ghost, excellent at watching and waiting in the wings and almost never acting.

"I think I'm fairly decent at distance coverage," Ian said with a frown. He'd been a long-term CIA operative. He knew distance cover. "Jake and Adam can handle Eve and I'll back you up."

There was only one problem with that.

"No. You're too conspicuous. I can't risk it."

"Could we clear the room, guys?" Ian crossed his arms over his massive chest and started to pace.

The guys were out in a flash, Adam giving him the evil eye. Yeah, he was on Team Eve for sure.

Ian stopped in front of the window, pulling the blinds open and staring out at the early morning light. The city was starting to wake up, pinks and purples on the edge of the horizon. There were tall buildings framing the distance, the city a massive landscape in front of him, like a watercolor painting, so beautiful and slightly unreal.

He remembered one perfect day. Hawaii. He and Eve had gone to Kauai on their honeymoon, and they hadn't slept at all one night. He'd taken her out to the beach and made love to her in the waves, and they had sat there and watched the sky come alive—nature's great show. He could remember the way she felt in his arms, her back to his chest as they watched the sunrise. The whole world had been alive then, full of promise. They had been young. So fucking young. Strong.

Neither of them had known how broken they could be, how easy it was to take a life and snap it like a twig until nothing remained but meaningless pieces.

"What are you doing, Alex?" Ian asked, not bothering to turn around.

That should be plain. "I'm trying to catch a killer."

Ian's shoulders slumped forward as though that was the last thing he'd wanted to hear. "You're trying to correct a mistake, but you're making the same one again."

Frustration welled. Fuck, yeah, he was trying to correct a mistake. It had been the mistake of a lifetime. Of course he wanted to correct it. "I'm not going to let him get close to her again, man. You can't think I would ever let that happen, but you, of all people, should know damn well that I can't just let this go."

How was he supposed to sit around knowing Evans was out there? He'd spent the last several years of his life following leads down every damn rabbit hole he could. He'd wasted countless hours talking to people who said they'd seen him, spending money on witnesses who led to nowhere. This could be the same thing all over again, but he had to keep trying. He would stop trying when he was fucking dead.

"That's not the mistake you're making." Ian finally turned around, leaning back against the window and looking like he hadn't slept in days. He'd been this way ever since they'd gotten back from London, as though just being in that city again had aged him, forcing him to remember the wife he'd lost.

"Going after Evans is the mistake? You think I can't take him down? My mistake the first time was pure arrogance, Ian. Trust me. I was humbled. I'm not looking for glory this time." He'd been trying to make a life for himself and Eve and fucking everything up because he didn't believe he could be wrong. He'd been on a fast track, but now he knew how fast the worm turned.

"No, this time you're looking for revenge."

Yes. He wanted revenge. He felt his jaw tighten, his vision focus in. "For Eve."

Ian's eyes narrowed. "Really? Are you sure about that?"

He was sure, and he fucking well deserved revenge. Evans had torn them apart. "How can you say that? You've known me for twenty-five freaking years. How can you question me like this? You don't have to help me. I'll take a leave of absence. Maybe that'll make it easier on everyone."

It would be for the best anyway. He'd only let Ian know because they were family. They had a deal, him and Ian. They'd had it since they were kids growing up in the same low-rent trailer park with exactly two ways out—prison or the US military. Ian had stayed in the Army and Alex had gotten out the minute they would pay for his college. The friendship had survived years and distance.

The deal was simple. They didn't go off half-cocked until the other knew what kind of shit was going down. Ian would watch out for Eve. Hell, if anything happened, Ian would watch out for her for the rest of her life. They had that deal, too. Ian watched Eve and Alex took care of Sean and now Grace and Carys. God, Sean had a kid.

How was he almost forty and single, with no prospect of a family on the horizon?

A ghostly image on the wall answered the question. The lights were on, but he could still see Michael Evans grinning at the camera.

He couldn't fix his problems with Eve. He'd ruined her life. He'd been directly responsible for all that pain. Days. She'd spent days with that monster, and Alex would spend a lifetime trying to make it up to her.

Ian's voice broke through his thoughts. "I wasn't talking about going after Evans. I was talking about leaving

Eve out of it."

Alex felt his eyes go wide. "You can't possibly expect that I would bring Eve into this. You of all people should know how dangerous it is to have your wife involved in a case."

He wanted to take the words back the instant he said them. Ian didn't move an inch. There was nothing in his stance that let Alex know he'd hit him hard except his skin paled. They never talked about the woman Ian had married and lost five years before.

"Charlotte has nothing to do with this. And she was always involved in that particular case. Hell, I *was* her case, and she did a spectacular fucking job. I laugh a little at the irony since her job was to fuck me. Charlotte married me knowing exactly how dangerous the job was, and she got burned. Eve, on the other hand, was perfectly innocent. If anyone deserves revenge, it's Eve, and you want to take that from her now, too."

Alex placed his hands on the conference table, palms down, just trying to hold on. "How can you say that? I was her husband. It was my job to protect her."

"And you couldn't possibly have known that the man you were tracking would come after your wife." Logic. Ian loved to come after him with logic, but Alex knew the truth.

He should have fucking known. He should have read Eve's damn case study, but he'd been so sure that he was right, that he couldn't possibly be wrong. "Yeah, well, if I'd paid any attention to Eve's profile, I would have. She knew. But I was far too smart. I thought I had the fucker down."

"And you didn't," Ian agreed. "And Eve paid the price and she continues to pay it every single day because neither one of you can let go for a second."

"If putting Michael Evans back where he belongs gives

30

her a minute of peace, I'm going to do it. I'm her husband. I have to do this for her."

Ian shook his head, his eyes grim. "You're not her husband anymore, Alex."

"Fine, then I'm her Dom."

"Are you? You don't act like it."

Alex felt his back get tight, like a dog that just figured out he was about to get kicked. "Wow. Do you have something to say to me? Don't fucking pussyfoot around, brother. You want to call my rights into question? You want to take a look at my contract?"

He hated the fact that all he had left with Eve was a cold contract between them, one they'd renewed every year for five years now. Ian knew damn well what was in that contract because he was the one Eve had turned to when she'd asked for it. A contract that delineated everything he was allowed to do, everything he couldn't do, everything that sat between them. A contract that allowed sex but not love, discipline but no compassion.

Life without the possibility of parole.

"That contract is everything that's wrong between you and yet you just keep signing it, man."

Because if he didn't, he was pretty sure Eve would drift away from him, perhaps even find another Dom. He couldn't handle it. Just fucking couldn't. He would very likely sign that contract for the rest of his life because no matter how angry he got, how alone he felt, he couldn't live without her. "She needs to scene. It's the only way she can cry. Do you think I haven't been over this with her? Do you think she hasn't been to therapy?"

His wife—ex-wife—was a brilliant psychologist. She'd done her time on a couch.

Guilt plagued him. He hadn't taken the same time.

Before the divorce, he'd cut out on counseling sessions, skipped on her dinners, spent nights away from home, and all in the name of catching Michael Evans.

"I know she's been, but it hasn't helped. Oh, Eve looks fine on the outside, but she hasn't gotten back to her old self. She laughs, but it never reaches her eyes. She'll let people hug her, but she doesn't hug back. God, Alex, I remember when Eve was the touchiest, feeliest sub I'd ever met."

"He raped her. He abused her. She can't go back," Alex said. "We can't go back."

"Then Evans wins. He did his job, and you should just hang it the fuck up. Why bother hunting the man down? You're already dead. You just forgot to tell us to bury the fucking body, man."

He thought seriously about putting his hands around his best friend's throat, but he backed off. Ian couldn't understand. None of them could. He should have done what he'd thought was best in the first place and just handled it on his own. "Whatever. I'm going to get ready to meet the contact."

"You're not going without backup. Take Jake and Adam and that's an order."

But Ian had forgotten one tiny truth. "You're not my boss. You're not my CO, and if you want me to walk, this is the way to get it done."

He started for the door. There wasn't anything left to say.

"Alex, please take Jake and Adam."

Fuck. Ian almost never asked politely. "I can't. If she spooks easily, I'll lose the chance."

"All right. Don't you dare go in unarmed."

Like he would do that. "I'm good."

"Alex?"

When the fuck had Ian gotten so chatty? "Yeah?"

"She needs you. She needs you to be her Dom more than she needs someone to avenge her. She needs you to take the reins because she can't let go of this on her own. She needs her husband."

But he wasn't her husband anymore. He was her part-time lover and full-time therapy session. He wondered if she even saw him now or if all she saw was how he'd failed her time and time again. Alex let the door close behind him.

Revenge was all he had left.

* * * *

Eve stopped at the front desk. Grace wasn't around, but there was a massive bouquet of flowers taking up most of the space. Gorgeous calla lilies.

Eve whistled a little. Those must have cost a fortune. What the hell had Sean done?

And then she saw there was a card attached.

Ian Taggart

She rolled her eyes. Some sub was trying to get in good with the Master. Whoever it was, they were barking up the wrong tree. Flowers wouldn't impress Ian. No. If you wanted to impress Ian Taggart, you better have a six-pack in your hand or a shiny new gun.

Those poor subs at Sanctum didn't really have a chance with Ian. He needed a woman who could physically put him on his ass. She was pretty sure that was the only way to bring down the man. A woman who could outthink him, out manipulate him, outplay him. That was the only way to nab Big Tag.

"Eve, I thought you were going to breakfast with Liam." Alex stood in the doorway of the conference room.

His eyes widened on her, and he shifted the stack of folders from one hand to another.

And immediately Eve was suspicious. "I had some reports to file and some personality profiles to complete. Ian's looking to hire some office personnel. Li is coming to pick me up in about twenty minutes."

Alex nodded. "That's good. Traffic is rough right now."

Traffic was always miserable, but even if it had been light, she knew Alex would rather someone drove her. Not because she wasn't a good driver, but Alex preferred that someone watch over her.

It just couldn't be him.

Because she was stubborn and couldn't find a way out of the corner she'd put them both in.

He stood there staring at her. When he looked at her like that, like she was the only woman in the whole world, she wanted to walk into his arms and pretend like the last six years hadn't happened.

"Was there a meeting I didn't know about?" She tried to catch a glimpse of the name on his folders, but they were blank.

He moved them, sliding them under his arm. "I wanted to go over a few things with Ian. Just bouncing around some ideas I have on an open job."

Work. They could talk about work. Sometimes she suspected they both came up with the thinnest of reasons to ask each other for advice. At least she knew she did. It was an excuse to be in the same room with him.

Do you need an excuse? You said you needed time. He gave you time. How long can this go on?

"Do you want to run it by me?"

He shook his head. "No. I think I can handle this one. What the hell did Sean do?"

He stepped up and looked at the flowers.

"They're not for Grace," she said.

"Phoebe? Phoebe is dating someone? Phoebe barely talks. I can't imagine her dating someone."

Phoebe Graham was the accounting girl. She typically hid in her office. She was terrified every time she found herself in a room with Ian or Alex. Sometimes Eve thought the only reason Phoebe had taken the job was because Ian had told her she was hired and she was afraid of not showing up for work. "Nope."

Alex's eyes narrowed. "Someone's sending you flowers?"

Well, she was the only other woman in the office. It was a decent bet. "No. They're for Ian."

Alex laughed a little, his shoulders relaxing. "Should have sent him a six-pack." He walked over and his free hand briefly touched the blooms. "They remind me of our wedding. We had white flowers, too."

They had been all over the church. She'd stood at the end of the aisle and looked up. Alex and Ian and Sean had been giant predators dropped into a dainty white garden. She'd been so proud, so fascinated with her groom.

God, she still was.

Alex McKay was still the most beautiful man she'd ever seen. And lately, it was so much easier to forget all the reasons she had for keeping her emotional distance from him.

Unfortunately, she remembered another incident where she'd received white flowers. "I don't like them now. They remind me of my hospital room."

He'd filled her hospital room with white flowers, giving her gifts, but turning away from her.

"Eve," Alex began. He cleared his throat. "I'll make

35

sure Ian gets them, though he'll probably just throw them out."

He picked up the vase and card, juggling them with his file folders.

"Do you want me to take the folders?"

He backed up. "No. I'm fine. You have a good time with Liam. Speak of the devil. Hey, man, how's it going?"

She turned and sure enough, Liam O'Donnell was walking up behind her. He nodded Alex's way. "Morning. Evie, are you ready to go?"

She nodded as she watched Alex struggle with everything he was carrying, but she didn't offer to help again. He would just say no. He would rather drop everything than admit he needed help. She sighed and turned to Liam.

Twenty minutes later, Eve looked at Avery and wondered if she'd ever been that young and in love. Though Avery was only ten years younger, that was just a number. Avery's innocence couldn't be measured by years. It went deep into her soul. Avery had lost everything at a young age and still her eyes were bright as she turned to her husband.

She often wondered how Avery would have handled being in Eve's position. Avery wouldn't have broken the way Eve had. Avery likely would have walked away with a bruised body, but with her heart still capable of love. Avery, it seemed to Eve, was indestructible.

Eve was deeply aware of how fragile her own soul was.

"I want pancakes." Avery set down the menu she'd been studying.

"You always want pancakes, girl. Ya never try anything else. Why do you waste your time looking at the menu?" Liam's voice was gruff, but his eyes were lit with laughter. He loved his wife. The connection between them was a palpable thing. Li winked Eve's way as he set down his own menu. "What about you, love? Are you trying something different?"

She never tried anything different. "No. I'll stick with what I know."

Half a grapefruit, two scrambled egg whites, whole-wheat toast, no butter. No indulgences for Eve St. James. Discipline. It was what her life had become. And now she could fit into those designer dresses that had been out of reach all those years ago because Alex liked to stuff her with chocolate and rich foods. He used to order in from the most decadent of restaurants and feed her while she sat in his lap and they cuddled.

"Order for me, will you?" Liam was pulling out his phone, checking the screen. "I have to take this. And for god's sake, woman, order your own bacon this time. You always say you won't eat it and then you steal mine."

He brushed his lips across his wife's as he scooted from the booth.

The waitress chose that moment to take the orders and refresh their coffee. When she was gone, Eve forced a smile on her face. Coffee. Her only real indulgence, well, besides all the BDSM and the soulless sex.

"How are you feeling?"

Avery smiled. "Good. This is actually a far easier pregnancy than my Maddie."

Eve froze. Madison. Avery's child. The one who died.

Avery's hand came out, covering Eve's. "It's all right."

That summed up Avery to a *T*. Avery had lost a child and she reached out to comfort Eve. Eve pulled back, reaching for her coffee mug. "I'm sorry. I'm always a little shocked that you can speak about her so easily."

Loss was something to be hidden. God, she was glad

she wasn't her own patient.

Avery just gave her a gentle smile. "I miss my baby every day, but it would be wrong to pretend she didn't exist. Do you know what Liam gave me as a housewarming gift when we bought our place here?"

She hadn't been to their big house in North Dallas. She hated that part of town because it reminded her so much of the sleepy, upscale Virginia neighborhood she and Alex had moved into once they could afford it. Those houses were all lovely, with signs of life and children on every lawn. An overturned bike here, a massive fort there, a man washing his prized car in the driveway.

Her apartment was sterile. Lovely, but sterile. Rather like herself.

She shook her head. "No, but I suspect it wasn't a houseplant."

Avery's eyes teared up. "He had a painter do a portrait of Madison from her baby pictures. Of Maddie and Brandon. He put it up next to the pictures of us from our wedding. He said it was because they were a part of our family, and he never wanted this baby to forget that he or she had a big sister once. And I cry when I look at that picture. I do. I cry when I think how I lost Maddie and my first husband, but I would dishonor them if I tried to forget. They were a real part of who I was, of who I am today. So I'll talk about her because she's still here with me. I would hate it if she wasn't. Sometimes pain can be sweet if we let it. It can remind us of all the good things. Just because something bad happened, it shouldn't erase the sweetness that came before it. Maddie died. But that doesn't mean I can't remember how she smelled when I held her against me, how she'd cuddle her little head to my breast. Brandon died, but that doesn't mean I don't think about how funny he was and how he asked me to marry him, but only after he'd thrown up because I told him I was pregnant." Avery laughed, the sound bright and happy. "It was not the most romantic of proposals."

Eve couldn't help it. Avery could be infectious. It was why she'd come to deeply enjoy these mornings with them. She'd always found it easy to be around Liam, but it was a joy to be around Avery. Avery made her wonder why she'd stopped hanging out with girlfriends. She used to love her girls' nights out. Now she always came up with an excuse not to join Grace and Serena. "He really threw up?"

Avery nodded. "Oh, yes. We were only eighteen, and we'd only had sex once and it hadn't been that great. We'd kind of gone back to holding hands because he'd been so embarrassed about it. And then whoops goes the pregnancy test. He was a little surprised. How did Alex ask you?"

Without even thinking about it, Eve snorted a little at the memory. It was the day he'd placed a delicate collar around her throat. He'd snicked the lock into place and then boldly told her that he wasn't satisfied with just a collar. He wanted her to wear his ring, too. "He didn't ask, the bastard. He told me I would marry him. Doms."

"Nice. So you two were in a D/s relationship before you got married?"

"Oh, Alex was born a Dom. We met in college and Ian had already introduced him to the lifestyle." God. What was she doing? She was gabbing like a schoolgirl, like a woman who was still married, telling her girlfriends how they met. Eve clammed up. She wasn't a girl and she wasn't like Avery. She cleared her throat. "But that's a boring story. Did you find out if the baby's a boy or a girl yet?"

"We won't know for another couple of weeks," Avery said, her eyes focused on Eve as though she was trying to

39

decide just how far to push. "But it doesn't matter. We'll be happy either way. I heard Serena's having a boy."

Jake and Adam had done nothing but talk about their future son. Everyone was moving on with their lives. It was just she and Alex and Ian who were stuck, and Ian couldn't help it. He hadn't found the right woman.

Eve knew she'd found the right man. Alex was still here. He was still in her bed some nights. She could reach for him, hold him tight.

Lately she'd been wondering if they shouldn't try again. Lately the memories had started to fade and she found herself reaching for Alex again. She'd started remembering things fondly. Their wedding day. She'd found photos in a box in her closet, and she'd stared at them for the longest time, thinking how handsome he'd been. He didn't smile in the pictures. No, not Alex McKay. He smirked in the sweetest way, those upturned lips a testament to how satisfied he'd been with the day. In the picture she'd finally placed on one of the bookcases in her office, Ian and Sean had been standing beside Alex, all three of them so arrogant she had to laugh.

And her momma and dad had been beaming out.

It couldn't hurt to pull that old picture out, she'd told herself. It was just a nice memory. But placing that picture where she could see it had her thinking.

Hell, Avery and Liam had her thinking.

What if they could start over?

"How long did it take you after Brandon died to want to try again?" The question was out before she could really think it through, and she wished immediately that she could take it back. It was rude. It was intrusive. "I am so sorry. We're not in a therapy session. That was uncalled for."

Avery reached out again. Eve got the feeling she would

just keep right on trying even after Eve pushed her away, so she should just give in, let Avery hold her hand. "Hey, I know you're a professional, but you should remember that sometimes friends are therapy, too. And it was a long time. I had a lot to work through. I had a lot of rage and anger and bitterness."

Somehow she couldn't see Avery being bitter for a second.

Avery seemed to sense what she was thinking. "Hey, I'm human, too. I hated the world for a while, but one day I woke up and I realized I didn't want to live my life that way. I had to make a choice. I could be angry about the past or I could try to find a future. It sounds simple."

Eve shook her head, surprised at how emotional she was getting. She never cried, but the tears were right there, threatening and somehow sweet. "No. It's not simple at all."

It was a decision she had yet to make.

"A divorce can be like a death," Avery said gently.

Eve took a long breath. "It wasn't the divorce that hurt me. I mean, it did, but something else happened and I don't think I've gotten over it." That was a lie. She knew damn well she hadn't gotten over it. "I've done all the therapy, but I'm just now starting to think that I want to move on with my life."

Her grieving process had been long and painful for them both, but she was finally at the point where she might be able to accept that Alex had changed. He'd been so distant after Michael Evans had nearly killed her. He'd said all the right things. He'd told her he loved her and that nothing had changed, but he'd left her alone when she needed him most. He'd gotten obsessed with revenge.

"I need to make a choice. I need to try again or let Alex go." Saying it out loud was a huge weight off her chest.

God, she actually felt lighter.

"Are you joking, Evie?" Liam asked. *Damn.* She hadn't heard him return. He slid into the booth, placing his hand over Avery's and hers, lending his support. "Because you can't imagine how much better we would all feel if you were serious. I worry about you, girl."

It had been years since she'd led a real therapy session. Not since her college days. She'd left counseling for profiling, but she hadn't forgotten one truth about therapy. Sometimes it took the right words to reach a person. A therapist could say the same thing a hundred different ways, but only one of them would reach inside the subject and plant a seed. It was why a therapist shouldn't give up.

She thought about her wedding day picture. What did she owe that girl in the picture? What did she owe the Eve she had been? What did she owe her parents, who still loved her?

What did she owe the husband she'd loved from the moment she'd met him?

"I want to try. Li, do you think you could help me with something? I want to surprise Alex at Sanctum tonight. I think I might want to renegotiate that contract of ours."

Liam smiled and promised to help as the waitress brought their food.

Avery, who had promised she didn't want bacon, stole her husband's.

And Eve thought about the future with a smile on her face for once.

Chapter Two

Alex looked around the space, trying to judge just how many ways he could get screwed here. The sun gleamed into the elegantly appointed mall. NorthPark Center was a testament to Texans' love of all things shiny. It was exactly the type of place Eve used to adore when they couldn't afford to buy a damn thing. They would browse through stores like Versace and Gucci, and she would complain about her weight. He would point out that they couldn't afford the clothes anyway and then feed her a cupcake because she loved chocolate and he loved her every curve. She was thin now, and she dressed beautifully, but she never smiled. Naturally, now that he could afford just about anything, she wouldn't accept a gift from him.

Alex glanced around the large walkway that had been designated as his meet spot. He didn't like it. There were too many ways in and out. He counted at least seven ways a person could come up on his back. Two of the stores in this section had both interior and exterior exits. Of course someone might notice an armed crazy walking through Williams-Sonoma or Tiffany. And hell, he had the ducks to protect him. He was standing by an interior duck pond, waiting on intel about the most dangerous man he knew.

What the fuck was he doing? He should walk away. If he met with this contact, one of two things would happen. Either she would be working for Evans and he was screwed, or she was on the up and up and he would be drawn right back into the world that had cost him his marriage. He knew it all intellectually and yet he stood there, watching and waiting.

A little girl was squatting down not five feet away from him, her big blue eyes studying the small ducks who called this indoor pool their home. Her mother was talking on a cell phone as she twirled her multitudinous shopping bags around and complained about her latest round of Botox. As far as Alex could tell, she shouldn't complain. The Botox was totally working. Her expression never once changed even as she bitched about her nanny requiring a day off to attend a funeral. Welcome to the wealthy side of Dallas.

He glanced to his right. Neiman Marcus was up ahead. To his left was a long line of shops and not a single sign of his contact. He was stuck here with Momma Frozen Forehead, a young woman in a suit and nametag eating her lunch, and two dudes in smart suits showing each other what they'd bought at Brooks Brothers.

Fifteen minutes. He'd been waiting for fifteen minutes, and now all he could think about was the cake pop stand near the exit. Eve would love that. They used to joke about food on a stick. Everything was better when it was on a stick. Now she just ate yogurt and salads. Her eyes never lit up over a salad.

Ian was right. His head wasn't in a good place for this. Five more minutes and he would call it fate.

He glanced up at the shop girl. Woman. She was probably thirty-five, but she had a sweet smile that made her seem younger. She kept talking to the little girl who was studying the ducks, her face shining as she did. Only the small creases around her eyes gave her away as older than thirty.

Damn. He was actually thinking about how pretty she

was. It had been a long time since he'd noticed another woman. Even as he realized how her strawberry blonde hair caught the light, it was an intellectual study. His cock wasn't engaged at all. She was just a pretty girl with a brilliant smile.

He only wanted one woman.

And then Red looked up and winked at him.

Fuck. What did he do about that? He got hit on at Sanctum a lot, but that was an easy thing to deal with. He just gave the subs a decisive shake of his head and they melted away. He had no idea how to deal with a woman who wasn't a trained submissive. Did they follow orders? He rather thought not. The wives of his friends were all subs, and half the time they didn't follow orders. Grace was known to laugh when given an order she didn't want to follow, and Serena had a potty mouth. Avery just smiled and agreed and did whatever she damn well pleased.

He wasn't even wearing a ring to prove his off-the-market quality. He didn't have a ring. Well, he had it, but he felt like a freak when he wore it now. Maybe he should still wear it.

Would the contact run when she saw he was being hit on by a cute redhead?

She waved his way.

Damn it. He was trained to kill, to track, to run large investigative units, but he hadn't flirted in almost twenty years. He didn't even want to.

She rolled her eyes and sighed and then pointed to her nametag.

Kristen

Yeah, he hadn't really been trained to profile. She was his contact. This whole thing was more Ian's speed. Alex had been a cop at his heart. He felt himself flush as he

45

walked toward the pretty woman who was only interested in his connections.

She moved her sandwich out of the way as he joined her on the bench.

"Sorry about that." Her voice was husky, and he noticed that she was solidly built. He would bet when she stood up that she would have an hourglass figure. There was nothing fragile about this Kristen. "I wanted to make sure we were alone first. You seemed to have been a very good boy."

"I told my boss we were meeting across town." In the West End, to be precise. With its shops and numerous restaurants, it would take Jake a while before he realized he'd been had. Because there was no way Ian hadn't sent someone along to shadow him. He knew his best friend. Besides, it was what he would have done in the same place. "We're alone. So talk."

"Wow, you are all business, aren't you? Come on. We're here and it's beautiful." She turned her face up to the sun that was streaming through the skylights. "Shouldn't we enjoy the day a bit? I was really having a nice time sitting here and reading. And this chicken salad sandwich rocks, let me tell you. Got it off a street vendor named Carlotita. She knows chicken salad. Oh, yeah."

Alex shook his head. He'd expected this meeting to be dark and ominous and she just kept grinning. "What do you want? Because you're obviously not serious. Is someone playing a joke on me?"

She frowned. "I am so sorry. This is completely serious for me, Alex. Trust me. I've been working on this particular case for a very long time. I can see the finish line now. I'm just…happy to be here. I always wanted to come to Dallas. I have some history here." She pulled a small envelope out of the trade paperback she had been holding. It didn't look like her reading habits were any more serious than her demeanor. *Surrender to Me.* Yeah, she was very literary. She caught him staring. "Hey, Mister. Don't turn your nose up. This is one hot book. And I've been using Ms. Shayla for some research. Open the envelope. It's got some important information about Michael Evans."

He opened the envelope and pulled the neatly folded papers free. He looked over the information she'd typed up. It was a list of locations and dates. And a photocopied passport that plainly showed Michael Evans. He was thinner and his hair was blonde instead of dark, but there was no way to mistake those eyes. "Is he still going by Andrew Johnson?"

She shrugged a little. "I suspect he has several passports from a couple of different countries."

"How did you get this?" She might look like a sweet little ball of fluff, but she'd been close to Michael Evans if she'd gotten a copy of his passport.

A little smile tugged her lips up, and her eyes nearly slid away from his for a second. The minute she'd heard the command in his voice, her hands had turned palms up on her thighs. If they had been alone, she likely would have sank to her knees. Sub. Very well trained. Too many coincidences were racking up. "I didn't copy it myself. I followed him for almost a month until he finally went to a bank. He was moving around a lot of money and they made a copy of his passport. Honestly, he probably dumped this ID after that, but I needed to prove to you that I'm serious."

"You broke into the bank?"

She shook her head. "Oh, I totally could have, but I didn't have to. Also, the bank gets freaky about records and they would have contacted him if they thought his records had been compromised."

"Then how?"

"I dressed up as the copy repair person. The manager was all like, what? But then I let him get a glimpse of cleavage and a fake work order and I was totally in. All I had to do was copy the hard drive and I had what I needed. Oh, and I fixed that little wheel that was squeaking and causing all the paper jams. It just needed some WD-40."

She could really talk a mile a minute. Not everything she was saying made sense to him. "Copy machines have hard drives?"

"Oh yes, and they are so totally helpful when you want to get information but you don't want anyone to know you have it. Really, it's awesome. So the hard drive on a copy machine actually takes a picture of everything the copy machine scans." A look of satisfaction came over her face, like a cat who had licked up all the cream. She was submissive, but she would likely be a merciless brat from time to time. "Do you know the kind of information on copy machines? Records of all kinds. Medical records. Banking records. Prison records. Military information. All that lovely information and all I need to get it is a thumb drive. That's power for you. No one ever thinks about the fact that a copy machine is really a computer."

There was far more to the woman in front of him than a cute smile. "Are you really a reporter?"

He had to ask because she was starting to sound more like a supervillain. He had to admit she would be even more effective than that fucker Eli Nelson because very few people would suspect the curvy redhead had a brain in her head unless she wanted a person to know it.

She reached into her bag and pulled out a set of credentials. "Here you go. This is my real name. Kristen White. I'm going by Priest for my undercover, but I've discovered it's better to not screw with my first name. It would look awfully silly if I didn't answer. Feel free to look me up. I'm freelance, but I've worked all over the world. I've had articles in everything from *The New York Times* to *National Geographic*. I picked up on Evans while I was working on a story about jihadist infiltrations into Mexico and South America. I read up on his case and thought it would be an interesting story. Two years later and I'm still following him."

"You've been following him full time for two years?"

She shook her head. "No, I've been researching when I had time, but six months ago I got a lead I couldn't pass up. I'm a little obsessed, you see. When I figured out I was in the right place, I decided to reach out to you."

"Why me? I'm not with the FBI anymore." But his old partner still was. Warren Petty was in charge of a whole unit now. He'd moved right into the place Alex had left behind and continued on the career path. "Special Agent Petty is in charge of the case now. I'm just a civilian."

The thought didn't rankle the way it used to. He had come to a point where he could deal with his new career. The money was damn good and he wasn't held back by bureaucratic crap, so he could actually do some good, too. And when it came to resources, he would put Ian up against just about anyone, including the US government, but if he was Kristen White he would want FBI contacts.

"No. You're the man I want to talk to," she replied with an amount of gravity he was surprised to see in her. "You're the one who'll stick with me. Special Agent Petty has other cases, but I suspect you'll focus all your attention on this one. Besides, you can work in a way the feds can't. Bureaucracy moves slowly. We need to be fluid."

All very good points. He couldn't argue with her logic.

"How much do you know?"

"I know Evans went after your wife. I'm sorry about that. There wasn't much press coverage, but I can read between the lines. Evans used her as a trophy to lord over you. I can only imagine how he would have degraded her. I want to help you, Alex. I know what it's like to have someone you love used cruelly. My own marriage fell apart because someone needed to use my husband. I wasn't in a position then to help him. I had to watch it all happen, so I know where you are and I want to help."

She sounded so damn sincere, but he needed to take a step back. She was too good to be true. "I need to check out your credentials."

She sat back. "All right, but why don't I tell you what I need so you can make an informed decision. I'll be waiting for the next twenty-four hours and then I'll have to find someone else."

"Someone else?"

"Yes. I need backup, and I've figured out a way to bring another person into the inner circle. I've worked for months to get into a place where they trust me enough that I can bring someone else in."

"They?"

"I'm working at a club run by a man named Chazz Breyer."

That name rang a bell. "He was in prison with Evans for six months. He was Evans' cellmate. He did time for armed robbery. Five years."

"Yes. And he's running a club now. I believe it's a club that launders the money from Evans' drug-dealing business. He's been running drugs all over the Southern US, and he's busy amassing a fortune. I've estimated what he's made at somewhere in the hundred million vicinity. Even if he's kicking most of it back to his South American connections, he's still got some serious bank going. What do you think he's going to use that money for? He's planning something. I know it."

Evans had killed plenty of people with the chump change he'd made before. What could he do with serious connections and millions of dollars? "What's your plan?"

"From what I've been able to figure out, there's a network of these clubs across the US, each one keeping the business small so they don't attract too much attention from the authorities, but when you put them together, they're significant. Evans visits from time to time to pick up money or information or to just keep everyone in line. I've been working at Cuffs for six months and Chazz trusts me."

"Cuffs?" Alex felt his blood pressure tick up a notch.

"It's a nightclub with a fetish theme. They all are." She started to reach for his hand and then pulled back. "I believe it's another way of him insulting you. You were his greatest nemesis."

The motherfucker. "Evans found out about my lifestyle. He paid some people at the club my wife and I went to in Virginia. He used it against her."

"He likes to hold a grudge. I'm sorry. Should I not have brought you into this?"

He shook it off. Evans would want to desecrate anything that was sacred to Alex, and staying away from him wouldn't change that. "No. I want in. You're working for him?"

"I'm tending bar, but I convinced Chazz that what he needs is a Dom in Residence. He doesn't really understand the whole lifestyle thing. I took him to an actual club in Miami and showed him how they run. He wants someone to come in and run scenes, for entertainment. I've convinced him that this is the way to get the big boss to notice him. He's got some contacts coming next week and he wants to run the idea by them. He's trying to move up in the organization. From what I understand, all of the men are somewhat curious about the lifestyle. A person who could give them information would likely be quite popular."

"I'm not going to counsel a bunch of tourists. Especially drug dealing, very likely terrorist tourists."

"Just run some hot scenes and give the crowd something to talk about."

Her plan fell into place. "I'm the new Dom in Residence."

"You're also my brother," she said with a grin. "I'm bringing you back with me from Austin. I have all the information for your cover on a thumb drive if you're interested. And I told them you would bring your own sub. I thought that would make it easier. The more people we can bring in, the safer we're all going to be."

Who the hell would he take in as a sub? "Why didn't you just say I was your old Dom? That would have been simpler."

Her face screwed into a mask of horror. "Oh, no. You're going to be expected to have sex with your sub. I can't have sex with you. That's just horrible."

He wasn't that bad looking. Not that he would have sex with her. "I'm not exactly chopped liver."

"They think I'm a sweet little lesbian. It was easier that way. Until I met a Domme. She was scary and very aggressive, so now I'm a celibate lesbian because my lover died in a car crash and I can't get over her."

That didn't seem fair. "So you don't have to have sex, but I do? That's nice for you."

She shrugged. "Hey, what can I say? I'm saving myself

for someone special. Come on. I've done my research on you. You've been a Dom for over a decade. You can handle it. And you regularly attend a club called Sanctum. Very private. Very selective."

"Yes, my partner Ian Taggart and I founded the club when we moved here and started our company. We're serious lifestylers. The idea of a bunch of tourists playing at D/s in a bar scares the shit out of me."

Kristen seemed tenacious. "This is the best way to get you in and you know it. Chazz doesn't need a new bouncer. He needs something different. None of the other clubs have tried this. It's going to get Evans's attention. Come on, Alex, you know you want to."

Alex shook his head. "I don't know that I'll be willing to do this. I need to take a look at your research."

"Of course, you're careful. But in the end you'll come back to Florida with me." She sat back, her smile that of a woman who knew the outcome was certain.

"Florida?"

"St. Augustine to be precise. We're set up in the Old City. You'll like it. I've got a nice-sized condo in Palm Coast that will function as our base. I've been staying in a craptastic apartment in order to look like I need a bartending job, but I can sell you as a wealthy man who just enjoys his kink. But you really do need to bring a sub with you, preferably someone trained in both investigative techniques and the lifestyle. There are a lot of people in and out of that club, and they're a bit on the scary side. I would be happy to have a couple of people watching my back."

He was not going there. He was not taking her with him. Fuck no. "I'll see what I can do, but it might be hard to find a sub who meets your demands."

She frowned and then looked at him as though she was

trying to figure him out. "You work with her every day, Alex. I don't know that this can happen without your ex-wife."

He stood up. "Then we're done here. If I can't come up with someone and I can't go in alone, then the whole op is off."

She held up her hands in supplication. "Whoa, there, big guy. Let's not jump to conclusions. Take a look at the research and my plan and then make a decision." She reached into her big bag and pulled out a thumb drive. "Here it is. I'll be in town all weekend. I would love to bring you back to St. Augustine with me. I promised Chazz I would try to fill the empty positions. He trusts me, but if I don't he'll do it himself and I'll lose out on the chance to put my own people into place."

She picked up her sandwich and dropped what was left in the trash before shoving her book into her bag. "I sincerely hope you'll reconsider. I think Evans is going to move soon, and I don't know that I can do it alone."

"Why not bring the feds in?" It was the only thing that made sense. If she really had all the information she said she had, then they would be all over the case.

She was quiet for a moment, as though trying to decide just how much to say to him. "The minute we bring the feds in, we lose control of everything. Don't get me wrong. I've studied all their case files. I have them back at my place."

"Those files are confidential." And wasn't it interesting that she had them?

Kristen grinned and shrugged a little. "Nothing is confidential if you have the right skills. I need those files. They're important. I keep studying them because they might tell me what Evans is planning next. I also worry that Evans maybe had someone on the inside. Maybe at the prison, but I can't discount that he might have had someone in the government, too. His prison break had to be expertly timed."

His brain rejected the notion immediately. Evans was smart. He could have handled everything on his own. He had a legion of crazy minions willing to do just about anything to please him. He could have talked to other prisoners. One of them could have known about the routine maintenance.

"Think about it," Kristen said with a grim nod of her head. "Call the feds if you like, but I have zero use for them. They'll just muddy things up and then I won't get a story out of this. You caught him once without their help."

It had been a little more complex than that. "I still had access to the case files and the databases. I don't anymore."

She winked. "Then aren't you lucky you have me? You can reach me at the e-mail address I gave you."

"Why can't I just call you?"

She wagged a finger at him. "No, no. This girl doesn't just give out her number to any guy who comes along. It's best we keep things nice and easy until you decide if you're in or you're out. And even then, I don't want to meet with anyone but you and your sub. I don't want to be exposed to the rest of your team. I understand you'll bring backup with you, but they're yours, not mine, and I can't risk getting in close contact with them. This is a dangerous story I'm working on."

"All right, but it would help if you would come in and meet the team. You don't have to be involved once we get there, but they would feel better meeting you."

"I'm not here to make your guys feel better. No contact with anyone who isn't working in the club. That's a deal breaker." She nodded and started to walk off before turning back abruptly. "I'm going to be waiting for that e-mail,

McKay. And in the meantime, I'll try to find the last member of the team. Cuffs is down a cook. I don't guess you know anyone who can play chef? Chazz is trying to spruce up the kitchen staff. The last guy barely knew how to work a fryer. I think it would be great to have someone in the kitchen. Those guys love to talk."

Alex felt a smile slide across his face. Oh, he would feel so much better with that backup. Little Tag was retired from active duty, but he bet Sean would come back for a brief reappearance. "Yeah, if I go in I think I can work something out for you."

She gave him a thumbs-up, and he watched her walk away, her hips swaying. She was a complete enigma. If he had to guess just from looking at her, he would say she was likely married with a couple of kids and a career doing something that involved service to the people around her. The minute she opened her mouth, he was pretty sure she was capable of taking over the world and not batting an eyelash. She bought a cake pop from the vendor and winked as she disappeared from sight.

And he was left with a problem. Could he trust her? Did it matter? He was so hungry to go after Evans, he might not care if she was trustworthy or not.

"She's very attractive," a clipped British voice said from behind him.

Damn it. Simon was better than Alex had given him credit for. He hadn't gotten even a hint that he was being followed. "How long?"

Simon straightened his tie. He normally stood out when he was in one of his suits, but here he just looked like he was taking a break from work. "Have I been following you? Since you left the office. Don't worry. Jake and Adam finally gave up and went to lunch. They were right where you told them to be. Such good lads. Not me. I know a desperate man when I see one. I also know your tell. I've only played poker with you three times, but you tap your left hand when you're bluffing. You slapped your leg when you told Ian where you were going. I was watching through the glass."

Alex turned to him. "And you decided to follow me why?"

"You need backup. You're far too close to this. What did she offer you? A way into Evans's inner circle?"

"Not exactly, and I would never be allowed into his inner circle. He knows me. But I might be able to work at the outer edges of his organization. And the minute I see him, I'll kill him, so it's all cool."

Alex started to walk toward Neiman Marcus.

Simon followed along. "You can't be thinking of actually doing this. You're too close to this case. If you need to send someone in, I'll do it."

There were several things wrong with that scenario, including the fact that Simon taking over his responsibilities made him want to punch something. He decided to go with the most obvious, least emotional reason. "The job is for a Dom in Residence. You don't even have Master Rights at Sanctum yet."

Simon shrugged as he walked. Somehow the Brit made the gesture look elegant. Alex didn't miss how every woman they passed stopped and stared at Simon. If the job had called for a manwhore, Simon would have been perfect. As far as Alex could tell, the Brit had a different woman every night of the week. "Ryan passed me on the primary courses. I haven't passed Ian's ropes tests. I've been practicing on that little sub, what's her name? Sonya? Sasha?"

"Sondra," Alex corrected. Sondra was a nice young

woman in nursing school. Simon had been sleeping with her off and on for weeks, but he couldn't remember her fucking name. Yeah, that was classy.

Simon snapped his fingers as though the name had fallen into place. "Right. Sondra. I'll pass next week. I'll be fine. I'm new to the lifestyle, but I rather enjoy it. I like being in control for a bloody change."

Alex liked being in control, too, and he wasn't about to give it up. "It's not happening. If I decide to take the job, you would be backup, nothing more. Evans is mine."

Evans had destroyed him. It would be nice to return the favor.

"Well, it certainly sounds like he has your number. One hint of the man and you're lying to your friends. I called Ian, by the way. He thinks you called me when the meet changed at the last minute and you realized I was closer. I think Ian has enough on his mind without worrying about his best friend lying to him."

Ian should understand. He was obsessed with finding Eli Nelson. Alex had caught him on several occasions staying up late at night at the office going over and over every piece of information they had, all of it laid out on a conference table like the pieces to a puzzle he just couldn't make fit.

"Thanks." Guilt gnawed at him. He wasn't trying to lie to Ian, but this was important. *And what about Eve? How is she going to take it, you asshole?*

Lately his inner voice had taken to calling him all manner of names. He strode through the door and a blast of heat hit him. The Texas sun had been turned up to full blast. He looked out over the well-manicured landscape of North Dallas. Northwest Highway was in front of him, cars jammed into the lanes like sardines moving slowly toward some unknown destination. Traffic in Dallas always sucked, but construction was making it utterly unbearable. He strode toward his truck, wondering how his reception would be back at the office. He didn't believe for a minute that Ian would buy Simon's story. Ian knew him way too fucking well. He was in for an ass kicking the minute he got back to the office.

And he would take it because the truth of the matter was he needed his team.

"Mate, that's a terrible look. What's going on in your head?" Simon was a douchebag when it came to women, but he was astute. And he was the only one who didn't have a personal relationship with him and his wife. Ex-wife. Eve. Simon didn't know the intimacies of the case. Maybe he would be a good sounding board.

That traffic really did look like hell. And there was a great sushi place inside. "What do think of raw fish, man?"

Simon turned a little green. "I think it sounds perfectly horrible. We Brits believe in frying our fish, thank you very much."

"You're not in England anymore, buddy." He would learn. "Come on. Lunch is on me."

They walked back inside, Alex's brain turning around and around the whole time.

* * * *

Alex picked up his cell, hitting a number he hoped still worked. Simon was sitting at the table, a pint in front of him. The Brit didn't have a problem drinking his lunch, but he actually had a fairly cool head when it came to business. They'd spent an hour and a half discussing the upcoming op, and Alex was feeling better about it.

"Petty."

Alex couldn't help but smile a little. Petty sounded every inch the FBI agent. Serious and just a little bit pompous. He'd sounded that way at one time. "Hey, Warren, how's it going?"

There was a little pause. "McKay?"

"Yeah."

"Holy shit. Alex fucking McKay." A little slap came over the line. Warren had always smacked the nearest hard surface when he was surprised. "What the fuck? How long has it been?"

So freaking long. "At least three years. How is the wife?"

"Alice is good. And Janelle is about to graduate from high school. Can you believe it? I have a damn eighteen-year-old kid." There was a little pause and a sigh. "How is Eve?"

Alex stared out of the window. He could see the parking lot from here. The day was sunny and bright, with busy shoppers walking by. Eve was likely in her office by now. "She's good. We're both busy working."

"Yeah, I've heard a lot of good things about that company you started with Taggart. You have some serious contracts. Is it true you're working with the Secret Service?"

They had been consulting on certain details of travel, but they'd signed a metric shit ton of non-disclosure agreements. "I have no knowledge of that."

A knowing chuckle came over the line. "Got it, man. I told Eddie he should call you when the campaign heats up in a couple of months. You know he's going for the nomination."

Edward Petty. Senator from Oklahoma. Warren's brother had his eye on the White House. He'd been in the senate for the last six years. Alex remembered when Eddie was just a fresh-faced kid who had lucked into a congressional seat. "We're close enough. We can certainly handle his security and run background on everyone surrounding him. He can't take that seriously enough, you know."

A low chuckle came over the line. "Oh, I know. I think Eddie has learned that lesson along the way. Everyone wants something from him. Alex, it's so good to hear from you."

Because he hadn't called his old partner in forever. Their friendship had been one more victim of Evans. "Well, I have a favor."

"Anything."

"Have you got new information on Evans?" He hesitated to mention what Kristen had discovered. He didn't know her yet, couldn't trust her.

Warren sighed, a low sound. "Man, you need to let that go. I know how much you want this guy. God, no one knows more than I do. I know what happened, but I promise, I'm doing everything I can to find Evans. The fucker seems to have disappeared. I've gotten some CIA intel that he's working somewhere in South America with a cartel."

Narcoterrorists. It fit with what Kristen had told him. "I can't let it go and you know why. I have some connections now. I might be able to give you some insight. Could you just let me look at the new intelligence? I know it's not protocol."

"I could bring you on as a consultant, Alex, but do you really think that's a good thing to do? You're still with Eve, right? Does she know you're looking into this?"

He didn't want to talk about this shit. "Eve and I are fine. She isn't particularly interested in this case. I'm just looking around. I'm curious. You would be, too. If this happened to Alice, you would always want to be in the loop. You know it."

A long pause came over the line. "I know. I don't want this case to go cold. It eats at me."

"I know, man." Warren had been by his side after Eve had been taken, staying up late helping to look for her. "I just want to look at the new information."

Maybe there was something in there that would jump-start his brain and put him in the proper mindset. He had the original files practically memorized, but there was five years of information he hadn't been privy to, including all the files on Evans's escape. He'd been out of the loop by then because his wife had become a victim.

"Things have tightened up around here. I have to get you clearance. I'm sorry, but I'm about to be under a lot of scrutiny because of Eddie."

Damn it. Bureaucratic red tape. And Warren was right. The minute Eddie threw his hat in the nomination ring, the press and Eddie's opposition would scrutinize every member of his family, especially his FBI brother. "Do what you can. I understand."

It could be weeks or months before he got the information. He was more dependent on Kristen than he liked.

"I'm sorry, but, damn, man, it's good to talk to you. Any chance you'll be in DC soon?" Warren asked.

"Probably not, but I bet you'll come out to Oklahoma City in a couple of months."

"Absolutely, can't miss little brother's kick-off speech. I'll be sure to stop in Dallas. I would love to see your operation. See how the other half lives. Maybe I'll even get out of government work one of these days. You know the pay is shit."

The pay at McKay-Taggart was much better and they could choose the cases they worked. Warren was a longtime agent, and he had deep political connections thanks to his brother. He would be a welcome addition. "Any time you want to talk, my door is always open. And anything you can do to get me those files would be appreciated."

He didn't want to trust Kristen's hacked files. He wanted to look at the same thing Warren looked at. It might not tell him anything he didn't know, but maybe studying them would keep his head in the game.

"I'll see what I can do. Hey, is Evie...I don't know, how is she really doing? You know I think about her a lot. I just...I wish I could catch him, man."

Warren had been the first of his friends to get to the hospital. Ian had been on a plane the second he found out, but Warren had been there when Eve had come out of surgery and the doctor had informed them of all the damage. He'd been the one to stand outside the room while Alex cried over his wife's body. Warren had kept everyone off him. "We're still standing."

It was the best he could say about them. And they might not be standing when Eve found out where he was going and why. He wasn't sure what would be worse—Eve being pissed or not caring at all.

"All right. Give her my love. We all miss you, man."

A knot sat in his chest. He'd really loved working with those guys. For a long time it had been him and Warren and Tommy and Leon. Tommy and Leon were gone now. They'd been a tight-knit little family, but when the chips had fallen, he'd come back to Ian and Sean.

Simon stepped up, his cell in hand and a frown on his face.

"Give me a second, Warren." He muffled the phone

against his shirt. "What's going on?"

"Ryan just left me a message looking for you," Simon explained. "He's been trying to call you."

He'd noticed and Alex had let it roll to voice mail because Ryan Church managed Sanctum, and right now Sanctum was at the bottom of his priorities. Besides, Ryan's next call would likely be to Ian. "Why didn't he call Ian?"

"I think Ian is the problem, McKay. He didn't say exactly what was happening, but he said Ian's in trouble. With traffic we're at least forty minutes away."

Alex held the phone back to his ear. "I have to go, Warren. Just e-mail me the files if you can. Thanks for everything."

He hung up and they took off for the parking lot. No matter what was going on in his world, he would drop it all for Ian.

Chapter Three

"What do you think this is about?" Liam asked, pulling his SUV into the parking lot at Sanctum.

Eve shook her head. She'd gotten a phone call from Ryan almost thirty minutes before. He'd been a bit cryptic, asking her if she wouldn't mind coming down to the club and dealing with an issue they had.

Alex was stuck in traffic. Ian was nowhere to be found, and Jake and Adam were apparently somewhere in the West End eating chicken wings. That left Liam driving her to the industrial-style building where Sanctum was housed. She'd argued that she could drive herself. She was perfectly capable, but Liam had professed a sudden and deep desire to visit the club he loved during daylight hours.

Yeah, like she couldn't figure out what that was about. The men of McKay-Taggart were all alpha-male, protect-the-women types. When Grace went out for a coffee run, one of the men inevitably decided that he needed to go, too, and she either found herself with an escort or an errand boy. It was just the way they were. These men had seen all the crap that could happen to a woman on her own and had made a conscious decision that it damn straight wouldn't happen to one of theirs.

"Did Ryan say anything?" Liam asked, peering out the front window at the unobtrusive exterior of the club. Eve knew exactly why he was asking. He was debating just how much ammo to take. She wasn't foolish enough to think he

65

was questioning whether or not he should take a piece with him. Oh, no. He always had a gun on him. He just needed to know if he should carry an extra clip or two.

"Well, sweetie, he called me so I don't think the club's under siege. I think we can safely bet this is a purely therapeutic visit." Sometimes Ryan called her in to interview potential members. No one got into Sanctum without a thorough screening. It was the same for new employees.

But he'd been awfully evasive about this visit. And she never did emergency interviews.

"Just stay close to me," Liam said. He never bothered to hide that thick Irish brogue anymore unless he was undercover. Liam was finally comfortable being Liam.

Could she be Eve again?

She slid out of the SUV, her heels hitting the pavement. She loved the black and gold Givenchys, but maybe the first thing the new Eve should do is buy a pair of flip-flops. She was pretty sure the new Eve wanted some comfy shoes. Not anything horrible. She could find designer flip-flops, surely. And maybe the new Eve could ease up on the diet a bit. Once a week. Twice. Maybe a little chocolate every now and then.

Maybe she would let Alex order for her. He always knew what she liked and when he'd really been her Dom, she could relax and enjoy it. She had…issues. She'd had them all her life, but those years when she'd been married to Alex, they had been under control because he'd been in control.

Wouldn't it be nice to have permission to enjoy her life again? Some of her peers would say it wasn't healthy to seek another's permission, but Eve had learned long ago that it didn't necessarily matter how a person found happiness so long as they did. And it was beyond healthy to acknowledge one's weaknesses and to seek a remedy to them.

"Earth to Eve?"

She couldn't concentrate today. "Sorry. I was thinking about something."

He gave her a grin. "You were thinking about that bugger again, weren't ya?"

"I've been thinking about a lot of things." She looped her arm through his because while the parking lot was well taken care of, it was still a minefield when it came to five-inch heels.

"Do you have any idea how far you've come in the last couple of months?" Liam modified his walk for her, giving her balance against the slight uphill grade. "When I first came on, you wouldn't touch anyone, not for any reason."

"Hey, I've learned to trust you guys." She wasn't sure when it had really started, but she thought it might have begun with watching Sean fall in love. And then Adam and Jake, and now Li. She grinned up at him. "I figure if you idiots can get your shit together, I should probably get mine."

Liam laughed. "See. There you go. Ya never used to joke. It looks good on ya, darlin'. We love you, Evie. There's nothing we want more than for you to get your shit together."

She gave his arm a squeeze. Having these men around had been a wonderful thing, but she really thought it was their women who were bringing her out of her shell. They'd all been through hell, and they were still standing. Eve was still here, still kicking. They found their strength. She was going to find hers, too.

It was time. Alex had changed. She had changed. The question was could they still be together?

The door to Sanctum opened and Ryan Church stepped

out. Eve could hear loud music blasting from inside just for a moment before the door closed again.

"Are you having a party?" Eve asked. Sanctum didn't open until eight or nine o'clock at night, depending on the day. It was just a little past two in the afternoon. No one except staff should be here, and from what she understood, Ryan ran a tight ship. He was a former CEO who had run into hard times. He'd taken the job of Dom in Residence and manager of Sanctum after his business had gone under.

Ryan had a grim handsomeness to his face. She pegged his age at somewhere around forty. He'd been in the lifestyle most of his adult years, and she'd heard a rumor that he'd even kept a permanent submissive at one point, but she'd left when his fortunes had turned. "Yeah, I guess you could call it a party. A party of one. I'm sorry to call you, but we don't know how to deal with him. I've tried talking to him, but he just ignores me. I tried sending him a couple of subs, thinking maybe they could change his mood, but he just scared the fuck out of them. I now have three crying subs and my bar manager just quit on me because he says he can't handle Guns N' Roses. Does he do this often?"

Eve looked at Liam, who shrugged. Obviously he didn't know what the hell was happening. "Does who do what often?"

"Ian. He was here when I got to work an hour ago. None of us were supposed to be here until six this evening, but I wanted to go over the scenes for the weekend. There's a really complex one Jake wants to do and with Serena pregnant, I wanted to make damn sure every piece of equipment is in full repair. I brought the subs in so we could test everything, but there was already a scene playing out on the stage. Ian has got that Scotch bottle in complete submission, I tell you."

"Ian Taggart is here, and he's drunk at two o'clock in the afternoon?" Ian was always in control. She'd never once seen him out of it.

"As far as I can tell. He's not exactly talking much. He growls a lot. Cusses. That man has a mouth on him. And it's a good thing he's the boss because he's worked his way through a bottle of Macallan thirty-year-old Scotch. Do you have any idea how much that costs?"

A whole lot. What the hell? She looked to Liam. "Do you know of anything that could have set him off?"

Liam shook his head. "No idea, but he won't want me to see him like this. He might be able to handle it with you."

Because she was a sub and his longtime friend, but Li was right. He would be horrified at anyone but her and Alex seeing him in less than perfect control. He might still lash out at her, but she could handle it.

"Should I call Sean?" Li asked, looking a little helpless. None of them wanted a world where Ian Taggart wasn't Superman or at least a growling, foul-mouthed equivalent.

That would be the worst thing he could do. Sean and Ian had a complex relationship. Over the last year, their relationship had been strained because of an operation where Ian chose to save his brother's life over Grace's. Grace had survived, but Ian wouldn't make the same mistake again. Sean, however, was slow to forgive. "Don't you dare. Just try to get Alex here as fast as possible. I'm going to go and just reassure myself that he's all right."

"I don't think he's okay," Ryan said, opening the door again.

"Sweet Child O' Mine" blasted through the club. The guitar riffs reached a crescendo and then went silent. Eve breathed a sigh of relief. "Thank god. That's way too loud."

"Oh, wait for it," Ryan said.

The song started again. "Does he have it on autoplay?"

"Yep, and he's threatened to shoot me if I turn it off. I haven't seen a gun, but I don't doubt he has one hidden somewhere." Ryan sighed. "I'll be honest, I have no idea what to do. I would leave him be, but the rest of my staff is going to be here in a couple of hours to start setting up. Should I cancel the scenes for tonight?"

And be forced to explain why? "No. Let me talk to him. Can you turn it down a little? Just a smidge. He might not notice."

They walked through the lobby, and she caught sight of Ian. Well, the back of him. He'd taken a chair and placed it in the center of the stage. He was directly facing the St. Andrew's Cross, his back to the rest of the club. He'd taken off his jacket, and she could see that he'd rolled up his sleeves. A glass with a couple of fingers of amber-colored liquid was in his right fist, the bottle on the floor beside him.

And the energy coming off him was righteously bad.

Yeah, he wasn't okay.

Ian had been Alex's best friend most of their lives. He wasn't a big talker. She'd never had a therapy session with him. Ian's version of therapy was very different. He wouldn't talk about what was wrong. He would drink and apparently listen to metal ballads.

But in the end, she couldn't treat him like a patient. She had to treat him like a friend, or better, a Master. Those other subs had probably tried to offer him sex. He didn't need that. Half the time she wondered if there was an actual submissive bone in their bodies.

Sometimes a Dom needed a sub for way more than sex. Maybe it was time to start getting that part of her life back, too.

She kicked off her shoes and shrugged out of her jacket,

folding it and putting it on a table. She pulled out the pins in her hair as she stared at Ian.

Ryan was watching her with his arms crossed. "The other subs tried."

"The other subs don't love him. That man has basically been my big brother for most of my adult life. I'm not going to offer him my body, Ryan. He would vomit. But I can offer him something else. Now get them out of here. You should leave, too."

Ryan frowned. "I don't know about that. He might be the boss, but I'm the Dom in Residence and I'm responsible for the safety of every sub here."

And sometimes she just couldn't be submissive. "And I own a piece of the club. It might not be the biggest chunk, but I'm still a founding member." She softened a little. "Ryan, I appreciate it, but Ian Taggart, for all his bluster, wouldn't hurt a sub. Never. And he definitely won't hurt me. Please. You called me here for a reason. Let me do my job."

He gestured to the three women huddled together, and they moved toward him like a small herd of baby chicks. God, they were young. When the hell did everyone get so young?

One of the girls was crying, her mascara in streaks down her face. "I'm sorry, Sir. I tried."

Ryan shrugged. "I guess he wasn't in the mood for a lap dance."

"But the music really lends itself to dancing," the blonde said. "I just wish every Dom was as nice as Master Alex. He would never call a woman a skank."

"Well, in Master Ian's defense, he had asked you to stop and then you took off your top," Ryan argued.

"I was just trying to help." She turned her eyes to Eve. "I don't know what the Ice Queen is going to do that I can't."

"Amanda!" Ryan shouted over the music.

Amanda, who might look like a baby chick, but who obviously had kitty claws, pouted. "Well, everyone knows how she uses Master Alex when he's the best Dom in the world. One day he'll wake up and he'll see he needs a real sub."

Eve took a long breath. She should be patient. The girl was young and obviously handicapped by her innate skankiness. Ian had nailed it. It was just part of her personality. "It's all right, Ryan. Just take her out of here, please."

Amanda walked past, a sullen look on her pretty face.

Did Alex look at the young subs and wonder what he could have if he wasn't saddled with her? He was known as the huggy Dom. He was the Dom all the whiney subs went to when they needed a cuddle. And he gave it to them because she wasn't willing to take comfort from him. Alex needed to give comfort. It was his primary purpose as a Dom, and she hadn't accepted a hug from him in years, much less allowed him to kiss her. Sometimes she wondered if guilt and need was all that was left between them.

No. She wasn't going to think that way. They were moving past that. Years separated them from the time after her kidnapping. Alex was a different person. He'd stood by her through everything. He wasn't looking for some twenty-something playing at submission.

Axl Rose started wailing again, and she prayed Ryan managed to get the subs out and turn the volume down.

She stepped up the three elegantly placed stairs that led her to the stage. The music volume went down by roughly twenty-five percent.

"Hey, turn my fucking music back up!" Ian shouted.

"Axl Rose called. He wants his record back, babe." Ian was one of very few men she felt perfectly comfortable calling by pet names. Ian had been at her wedding. Ian had done his damnedest to save her. Tears blurred her eyes briefly because she realized just how much she loved him. He was a friend. No. He was her family.

"Go away, Eve. I'm in the mood to tear someone up, and I don't want it to be you. I've made enough subs cry today."

She stepped in front of him. He was the very picture of decadent beauty. Ian Taggart was a Viking of the first order. He was roughly six foot five and had not an ounce of fat on him, but she could see the weary set of his brow. Blond hair and startlingly sharp blue eyes didn't make him any less of an actual man. He still had his sorrows. He still needed comfort. He just didn't always take it. Ian Taggart was practically a demon, and even demons needed friends. "Well, if one of them was that little skinny blonde, I'm okay with it."

He chuckled a little. "I wondered when you would notice that Mandy has a thing for your ex." He shook his head. "You go and defend your Dom. And if you wouldn't mind doing it in a vat of Jell-O while wearing a bikini, that would really liven up the day."

She sank to her knees before him, a sign of respect. "I can't leave you, Sir."

"Fuck." He took a long drag from his glass. "I didn't expect anyone to be here. Church is too serious about his job."

But Ian's pride wouldn't let him retreat. She totally understood that. "Want to talk about it?"

"Want to talk about what happened between you and Alex?" It was a challenge.

"If I don't, I'll have to walk away, right?" This was the way Ian played things. He was a great believer in making bargains. She was sure he thought she wouldn't live up to her side.

"Yeah. So just go now."

"But if I do talk, you'll tell me why we're reliving the eighties?"

His eyes narrowed. "You don't talk about your shit."

She didn't before, but he severely underestimated how much she cared about him. "I was raped."

His gorgeous face went tight. "Don't do this to me. I already know the story."

But it was what he needed. He needed to open up and the only way she could make it safe for him to be open was to be open herself. Ian might know the facts, but he'd never heard her say them. "I was raped, and Alex couldn't handle it and he turned away from me. It nearly killed me, Ian."

He closed his eyes, but his hand came out as though it had a mind of its own. He touched her hair, drawing her closer.

"I thought he cared more about punishing the man who hurt me than he wanted to be with me." The words were nearly stuck in her throat, but it was easier because she'd made the decision to give them another chance. She had to talk about it.

"Eve, he loves you."

But he might love revenge more. It didn't matter now. Michael Evans was a million miles away. "I'm thinking about renegotiating our contract. Now, I've talked. Why are we listening to hair metal?"

He frowned, those full lips turning down. "Because I like it."

"It doesn't seem to be making you happy."

74

"Can you leave this alone?"

She laid her head down on his lap. She knew just how to manipulate Ian Taggart. What the other subs didn't understand was that Ian responded to tenacity, gentle, loving tenacity. "Yes, I can leave it alone."

She gave him a couple of seconds of quiet. She knew he would make the right decision. He would never leave her hanging.

"Manipulative little brat. You know me far too well. Fine." His hand soothed back her hair. "I had a woman I...cared about."

Well, of course it was about a woman. And he wouldn't talk about it normally. He would hide it. She was catching him in a vulnerable moment, but she thought he needed to talk. She didn't know about any woman he'd really cared about except his high school girlfriend named Holly. From what she'd been told, they'd been engaged, but Holly had broken it off during his first stint in Iraq. As Alex explained it, one day he'd had a fiancée and the next he had a Dear John letter.

That was right about the time he'd discovered BDSM. Had he been mourning her loss for all these years? As long as Eve had known him, he'd always been surrounded by subs. He was a sub magnet, but she'd never seen him fall for a single woman. If he said he'd cared about a woman, then he had very likely loved her with his whole damn soul. "Is this about Holly?"

He snorted a little. "Holly? No. I thought Holly was the queen bitch of the world. Then I met Charlotte. No. I'm not pining over Holly. I wish Holly and mid-level lawyer husband number two all the fucking best in the world."

Charlotte? She didn't know a Charlotte, and she couldn't very well push him. "Charlotte is a nice name."

She could only soothe him. Any aggression or outright curiosity at this point would send him into his shell.

"Yes. A lovely name for a lovely woman. But she was a crazy bitch."

For Ian, that was practically a term of endearment. He was a man who appreciated a righteous bitch. She softened her voice and hoped she wasn't going too fast. "What happened to her?"

It couldn't be good.

His expression never changed. It stayed a careful blank. He took a long drag off the Scotch. "I can't make her leave. She's in my head. I can't get her fucking out. Never met anyone with skills like Charlotte. She could make me run in circles and I liked it. Do you know what's it like to not be able to get a woman out of your head?"

So he'd been in love. God, Ian in love was probably a sight to see. "Why don't you call her?"

There was a long pause. She couldn't imagine that a woman wouldn't fall madly in love with Ian Taggart. He was gorgeous and had that crazy, impossible wall up that seemed to call to most women.

He took a long breath before answering. "No point. If you and Alex can't make it, there's no hope for a dumb shit like me. You two had it all. You were what I was aiming for."

She felt tears blur her eyes. Ian never talked like this. Just looking at him, she wouldn't really guess he was plastered. His hands were steady and his voice was perfectly controlled, but the words coming from his mouth proved it. When Ian was sober, he would very likely never admit he wanted more than sex from a woman. "Well, we're just human, Ian."

"Nah. You were more. You were happy, and then shit

happened and it all died."

It was a little more than shit. She'd been brutalized, and Alex couldn't handle it. "Yes, but that doesn't mean you can't find a good relationship."

He laughed a little, but there was nothing humorous about it. "Good? You think I can find a healthy relationship with some nice woman out there? Maybe raise a few kids? Hey, we could find a four bedroom with a white picket fence and a dog named Cuddles. Who the fuck do you think I am, Eve?"

It was then that she noticed the envelope on the floor next to him. She recognized it from this morning. It had been delivered along with the flowers. "I think you're one of my oldest friends and you deserve some peace."

His eyes darkened. "That's only because there's so much you don't know about me, honey." His mouth flattened, and he let his head drift back. "I really do care about you, Eve. And not simply because you were Alex's wife." He took a long breath and looked back down at her. "Are you sure you're done with him?"

She could answer that honestly. "No. I don't know that I'll ever be done with him, but I also don't know that we can live together again. I've changed since we got married."

"You got stronger. I actually thought you weren't a good match for Alex. You were too submissive in the beginning. Alex needed a challenge. It's one thing to have a sub in the bedroom, quite another when your partner, the woman you rely on, is utterly dependent on you for every decision."

She felt her eyes narrow. "I certainly was not."

"He picked out your clothes every morning, Eve."

It had started out as a game. He would pick out her clothes for their dates and he always selected her lingerie.

Somewhere along the way, they had fallen into the habit of him laying out her clothes and admiring her. "It was just for fun."

"Was it?"

"I wasn't completely dependent on him." She said the words and she meant them to some extent, but looking back, she knew she had been far more dependent on him than she was really comfortable with. And yet those were some of the sweetest times of her life. "I can't be that girl again. I don't know that Alex will accept anything less."

"Alex has accepted the crumbs you've given him for years. He'll take anything. If I met you today, I would say you're too cold for him. Back then you were too submissive."

Ian didn't pull punches. Damn, hearing that hurt. "So you think I should let him go."

Let him go to the likes of the Amandas of this world? Younger women or subs who weren't damaged and set in their ways? Women he could settle down with into a happy, congenial partnership where he made most of the decisions?

"I think you need to take all the sweetness of the woman you were and merge it with the strength you have now. I think you should stop fucking lying down and fight. We're all fucked up, Eve, but at least the rest of us are walking wounded. At least we're trying to get somewhere."

A little kernel of anger lit inside her. "Oh, really? Just where are you going, Ian? Because from where I'm sitting, you've been in one place for a really long time, or are you trying to tell me that you go through a sub a night because you're looking for 'the one'?"

He snorted, a sound sure to be ridiculous on a lesser man, but Ian made it sound elegant. "Yeah, that's my story. No. I already found 'the one' and she's dead and I think Eli

Nelson had something to do with it."

She felt her mouth drop open. She'd known Ian and Nelson had a history, but how far back did it go? "What?"

"Fucker sent me a card. I already tossed the flowers out. I nearly hit Phoebe in the head. She's going to quit one of these days." He nodded toward the envelope at his feet.

Eve pulled the card out. It was all hearts and flowers, sappy and sentimental, and it announced Happy Anniversary. It was unsigned, but the mailing address was London, England, Eli Nelson's last known whereabouts. The rogue CIA agent had been causing trouble for the entire group since he'd attempted to use them to steal industrial secrets for his Chinese handlers. A few months ago, they'd all learned that their ties with Nelson went back much further than they had known. He'd ruined the operation that cost Liam years of his life and then tried to kill both him and Avery after running off with the information he'd been willing to kill for.

And Ian had struck back, rendering that information useless. They were two titans taking massive swings at each other.

"Why would he send this to you?"

Ian shrugged. "He wants me emotional. He wants me off my game. And he definitely wants me to think he killed my wife."

Eve felt her eyes go wide and her heart drop into her stomach. His wife? Ian had been married? "How long has she been gone?"

Maybe he'd been right when he'd said there was a lot she didn't know.

"Years. Minutes. Sometimes I think I still see her. What am I doing? She played me. She was working for Nelson all along, and she got burned. This is stupid. I need to be working on a case and I'm sitting here like some fucking teenager listening to music and crying over a girl."

He wasn't crying. His face was a block of stone. Eve had about two million questions, but it seemed wrong to intrude. He was so private. He would regret every word he said later, and she couldn't stand the thought of anything humbling him. She laid the envelope down and moved to her feet.

"I'm going to hug you now."

Ian's eyes came open and a wary look crossed his face, as though she'd just warned him something terrible was about to happen. "Why?"

"Because you need it, Sir, and you can't accept it from one of the other subs because they all want something from you. I only want something for you."

"Everyone wants something, Eve."

She made the bold play. She sat in his lap and put her arms around his neck. He was the brother she'd never had, and she couldn't leave him sitting here like this. "I want you to be happy. And I think I finally want to be happy, too. You're right. I've been a zombie for years, and I need to start living again. And you need to figure out what you want."

His voice was a low rumble. "I want to tear Eli Nelson's balls off and shove them down his throat and then, when he's gagging on his own testicles, I want to hang him with his large intestine."

Well, at least he had a goal. "Can I do anything for you?"

He was silent for a moment, and then his voice was deeply weary. "You can sit with me. Do you know how long it's been since someone just sat with me? Since someone touched me and didn't want a damn thing except to make me feel better? It's been five years. Not since she died."

She let her head rest against his broad shoulder, taking comfort from the closeness. There didn't have to be anything sexual about it. "It's been five years since I let Alex kiss me. I miss him, Ian."

"And I miss Charlie. And if you ask me when I'm sober, I'll pretend she doesn't exist. I'll pretend I never married her. I'll pretend I didn't hold her dead body in my arms."

She felt tears fill her eyes for the second time that day. Something seemed to have opened up. "I am so sorry, Ian."

His hand drifted to her cheek, and he swiped at a tear with his thumb. He held it up and stared at it. "Eve, you're crying. You never cry unless it's a scene."

She pulled back and looked at him. "Yeah, well, apparently now that I'm walking wounded instead of zombie girl, I can cry again. Just a little."

His lips curved up, and he was so beautiful when he smiled. "There's my Eve."

The music stopped entirely, the whole place going dead quiet in an instant. Then a cold voice spoke. "Your Eve? Is there something I don't know about?"

She damn near jumped out of Ian's lap at the sound of Alex's voice, but she stopped herself because she hadn't done anything wrong. It was her place as a submissive to offer kindness. Hell, it was her place as Ian's friend to offer him comfort. How many times had she caught Alex snuggling with some sub whose Dom had left her or who'd had a bad day? They were touchy-feely people, but the way he was looking at her now made her want to cringe.

"I think you should move now." Ian's hands were held up and away as though showing Alex he wasn't trying anything funny.

Eve moved off his lap, turning to face her ex. "Calm down, Alex."

"Why don't you two run along and fight this out in private. I have things to do." Ian poured himself another Scotch. "And someone better turn my fucking music back on."

"I'd like an explanation." Alex practically growled the words. "I was told there was trouble at the club and I walk in and the only trouble I see is that you two didn't get a room. There are privacy rooms in the back, though I do know that Ian doesn't mind fucking in public."

Ian stood, his big body still moving with grace despite drinking the majority of a bottle of Scotch. "You know I don't, buddy. And you and Eve like to keep things private. Maybe then no one will see that you're just like the rest of us when it comes to sex. It's just a bodily fucking function, huh?"

"Is that what's going on here? Are you scratching my wife's itch?"

God, he was so gorgeous, but he could act like such an idiot when he got jealous. "Yes, Alex. After more than ten years of friendship, Ian and I have decided to become lovers. I couldn't resist him. He's so tender."

Ian's hand shot up in the air, his middle finger extended.

Eve stalked toward Alex, her voice a harsh whisper because Ian needed something more than Alex's caveman act. "He's upset and I bet you know the reason why. Does this date have a particular meaning? Is there a reason Eli Nelson would send him an anniversary card?"

The way Alex's face paled told her everything she needed to know. He knew about Ian's marriage. He knew that she'd died. "Yeah. I know what today is. I got a call and I forgot. I usually make sure he's not alone today. I remembered the minute I walked in here and heard that fucking song, but then you were sitting in his lap. Damn it." He turned around, yelling out. "Simon, get that music back on."

Guns N' Roses started wailing again, and Ian sighed and settled back down.

"We need to tell Ryan that the club is closed tonight. He'll know who to call. Damn it. I have to work tonight."

"I'll baby-sit." Liam put a hand on Alex's shoulder. "This about his wife?"

Alex nodded. "This is the day she died. He goes a little crazy once a year. I've been handling it. We usually go out to his place and get trashed and keep it out of the public eye, but I was involved in a case."

Liam knew. Everyone knew but her. It hurt a little, but Ian was so private, she couldn't hold it against the men for keeping his confidence.

Liam sent her a tight smile of encouragement. He knew what she was planning to do tonight. "I think you have something more to handle tonight, mate. Go and talk to Evie. I'll make sure he gets home in one piece. If you like me at all, take the Brit with you. Please."

Alex frowned. "I don't know. All right. Just watch out for him. I really do have something I need to get done. Call me if you need me. And have Simon drive Ian's car back to the office. You'll have to take him home with you tonight. Eve, do you need a ride home?"

"I actually hoped we could talk." He had just been an asshole, but he'd always been possessive. She was willing to give him a little leeway. The first time she'd caught him hugging another sub, she'd wanted to snatch the woman's hair right off her head. "Do you have time for dinner?"

He stopped, his eyes widening. "You want to have

dinner with me?"

"Yes. I think we should talk." They rarely spent time together that they weren't working or doing exactly what Ian had accused them of—having empty sex. It had been a very long time since they just sat down and talked, and she knew that had been her fault. "How about Thai? My treat."

His jaw squared and a stubborn look came into his eyes. "I have to work. I really want nothing more than to take you up on that and I will eventually, but I have a case I'm looking into and timing is of the essence."

"You need me to run the background check on the girl?" Simon asked. She hadn't noticed him leaning against the bar. "I can certainly handle finding out if the girl is who she says she is. Now making sure she's got the connections to Evans is another story entirely."

Eve felt like the ground shifted underneath her. "Evans?"

It was a common name. It could be anything because there was no way Alex would get involved in any case having to do with Michael Evans without letting her know what was going on. He wouldn't do that to her. Not again.

The flush on his face told her a different tale. His whole stance stiffened as though he'd just gone on the defensive. "It's nothing for you to worry about, Eve. I'm going to Florida for a couple of weeks. I'll talk to you when I get back."

He walked out of the dungeon toward the lobby, and Eve sank into a chair, her hands shaking. She'd been ready to start again, but nothing had changed.

Nothing at all.

Chapter Four

Alex stalked out of the dungeon, cursing under his breath. Why the fuck had Weston felt it necessary to mention Evans's name? He was a fucking idiot who had just screwed up everything.

"Hey!"

Alex stopped in the middle of the lobby but didn't turn around. He knew exactly who was coming after him. Weston wasn't the only idiot Euro he had to deal with. "I don't need to hear from you, Liam."

"I bloody well think you do," Liam shot back, rounding on him. "What the fuck was that about?"

When Liam was angry, his Irish got up and his statement sounded more like "wha de fook was dat aboot?" Yeah, he was pissed. Alex filled his lungs with air and prayed for a little patience because he was the one who had handled that poorly. Weston had spoken out of turn, but had he really expected that Eve would never find out? He ran a frustrated hand through his hair. Eve had picked the worst possible time to decide to relax the rules a bit.

"Would it do me a damn bit of good to point out that it's none of your business, O'Donnell?"

"She asks you to go and have dinner with her and you turn her down over a case?" Liam shook his head. "I'll handle the bloody case. Just give me the details and stop acting like an ass. Eve's got some things to talk to you about."

"It doesn't matter. She won't talk about it now." What the hell did she want to discuss? Was she finally going to tear up their contract and split them up permanently? Bitterness welled up. It would just have to wait.

What the hell was he going to do if Eve finally let him go?

Liam calmed a bit. "She will if you just apologize. Just walk back in there and talk to her, mate. You can't imagine how hard it was for her to do this. Just walk back in and take her out to dinner. You can still make this right."

But he couldn't. He'd lost that chance a long time ago. "I can't, Liam."

Eve walked by them. She'd replaced her shoes and put her jacket back on. Just for a brief moment, she'd been as soft as she was all those years ago. It was why he'd nearly taken his best friend's head off. She'd looked soft and sweet in Ian's arms. There had been none of the coldness of the last few years, and he'd ached that the warmth hadn't been for him.

Except it had been there when she'd asked him to dinner. Her eyes had lit up with a spark he hadn't seen in forever. Had she met someone? How would he take that? Could he watch her be happy with someone else?

"I would like a ride home, please." Eve didn't look back, merely went to stand by the door. It was obvious that all of her softness had fled the minute she'd heard Evans's name. He'd been right to keep her out of this. He just wanted to protect her. Why couldn't anyone see that?

Liam stepped up. "I'll run you back to the office then, love. Alex, stay with Ian until I can get back."

Eve held a hand up. "I would like Alex to take me." She turned, and he'd been right about the softness. There was none of it now. Her face was a careful, perfect blank. "I think he can manage to drop me at my car before he goes back to work. You are going back to the office, aren't you?"

She didn't wait for an answer, merely stepped out into the afternoon light, moving toward the parking lot.

"I'll handle her," Alex said.

"She was going to ask you to revise your contract," Liam said with a frown. "Why would she be so upset about you working? Can't you put if off for a couple of hours?"

She was going to ask him to revise the contract? How? To give them more freedom? Or less? *Fuck.* She wouldn't answer him if he asked now. There was nothing to do except plow ahead. "I've got a lead on Michael Evans."

Liam cursed under his breath. "Were you going to tell her?"

"No. She can't do anything, and she'll only worry." It could bring her nothing but pain to talk about this again.

Liam shook his head. "But it's her worry, Alex."

Liam didn't understand. He'd been through a lot, but he'd never seen his love torn apart by a monster. "I'm going to ask you something and I want you to answer me honestly. If some man had raped and brutalized Avery, would you want revenge?"

"Hell, yeah, I would."

At least someone understood. "Good, then."

He had his hand on the door when Liam spoke again. "But I would want my wife more. If it came to a decision between the two, I would always pick her."

"Yeah, well, I don't get that choice." Revenge was really all he had left, and even if Eve wanted him back, he wasn't sure he could give up looking for Evans. As long as he was out there, Eve wasn't really safe. He remembered the way Evans had looked at him when he'd been hauled into the courtroom for his bail hearing. He'd smirked and mouthed the words, "We're not through."

No, if Evans was out there, it was only a matter of time before he came after Alex, and the only way to come after Alex was through Eve.

He turned and walked to the lobby door, the music still pounding through the club. He'd thought Ian had some closure. He knew Charlotte was dead, had held her body in his arms. He knew nothing else would come from it, but it seemed he was still haunted. Every year, Alex hoped he wouldn't hear that fucking song and every year on this day, it was all Ian played until he passed out and showed up to work the next day with red eyes and a closed mouth. They would spend the next three hundred and sixty-four days pretending she had never existed.

But Alex's ghost stood at the passenger door of his truck, a frown on her gorgeous face. He strode out into the heat of the day and opened the door for her.

"Liam said you wanted to renegotiate our contract." He had to try.

She settled into the seat. "That doesn't really matter now, does it?"

"What did you want to negotiate, Eve?" Hell, it might be easier on him if she wanted to cut him off entirely. At least he could focus on the job at hand.

Her eyes shifted toward him. "I want to see the file, Alex."

"There isn't a file yet. Warren is going through the proper channels to try to get it to me." He closed the door and walked around to the driver's side of the truck. He got in and fired up the engine, grateful that the drive wasn't a long one.

"Fine. I want to know what you've discovered. Is he in the States?"

This was the last conversation he wanted to have, but she had to know at some point in time. "I think he's a regular visitor. He seems to be setting up some kind of business connections here, a series of clubs that he's using to sell drugs through."

"He's probably using the clubs to launder the money, too," Eve said, her eyes on the road ahead of them. "And he would also see them as another form of the commune he had built up. He very likely has a female in every one."

She sounded like they were talking about a regular case, but every time he glanced over at her, he could see the scar on her neck. It was the worst of her scars. That cut had been deep and was still thick on her skin, but there were more scars on her back and belly. They were faint now, faded to whispery white lines, but he remembered them fresh and bloody.

"Eve, you don't have to do this. I'm checking out the source tonight. If she checks out, I'm going to Florida to see this club for myself."

"She?" The question was coated in ice.

At least she could still feel a little jealous. "Yes. Her name is Kristen, and she's an investigative reporter. She's just a source, angel. She's tied Evans to narcoterrorists in South America."

"Why doesn't she call the feds?"

"Because they can't work as quietly as I can and they don't have the same stake in this."

"Oh, so the people with stakes in a case should be the ones working it? Excellent. I'll be going to Florida with you then," she explained, her mouth in a stubborn line.

"Absolutely not." He didn't want her on the same continent with Evans much less the same city. "Eve, be reasonable. It's probably nothing. I'll go to the club, check it out for a couple of days, and report back."

But something told him this lead wasn't nothing. Every instinct in his body told him that this was the lead he'd been waiting for and Evans was close. He just needed to get into the right place to lay in wait. Adam could bury faked records so Alex could pass any background checks. He would change his hair color and wear colored contacts. Most of the time, he would hide behind sunglasses. He was older now and his body bigger than it used to be. He spent more time in the weight room now than he used to. He could pass for long enough to get in the same room with Evans and after that, it wouldn't matter if the fucker recognized him.

"Would it change anything if I asked you not to go?" Eve asked in a perfectly calm voice, as though the outcome didn't mean a thing to her.

He pulled up to a stoplight. "Why would you do that?"

"Because we can't move on if you keep bringing Evans in between us."

"What?"

She smoothed down her skirt even though it didn't have a wrinkle on it. "He's always there."

"Because you can't forget," Alex replied, his voice low and sympathetic. "I understand that, angel. You'll be able to sleep at night if I can take him out."

She laughed, a deeply bitter sound. "I'm not the one obsessed with Michael Evans."

He felt his jaw clench, his fists tightening on the steering wheel as he eased the truck forward and turned onto the freeway. Downtown was in front of him, the Omni hotel blinking its symphony of lights as day began to turn to evening. They were surrounded by concrete and facades and lights. He glanced at the sidewalks with their small patches of perfectly kept grass in neat little boxes. The late-afternoon commuters hustled to get to their train stops or parking lots. They were moving, but Alex felt like he was stopped. He and Eve hadn't really moved in years. They were still having the same old argument. "He's kept us apart for five years. If that's not obsession, I don't know what is."

"I admit that I was hurt in the beginning," Eve began. "But he isn't the one who kept us apart. We both had a hand in it, and until we acknowledge what we've both done wrong, we can't even think about being together again."

She was dangling the only bait that might be able to lure him away, but he had to be strong. They hadn't been able to make it with Evans between them. The only way to move forward was to end Evans permanently. "You're trying to stop me from going after him. That's the only reason why you're saying any of this."

Her fingers tightened on the handles of her purse. "I don't want you to investigate him. Let it lie, Alex."

"I can't. He'll come after you again." He saw it every night in his nightmares. Evans would come after her, and she would be alone and vulnerable.

"No. He won't," Eve replied, her voice tight. "He has no reason to. He's moved on to bigger and better things. You're the one who's still playing the game. Give the information to Warren."

"No." He couldn't trust anyone else to handle it. Kristen was right. This required a small, very quiet team on the inside. Warren couldn't put that together in time.

"Then we're done, Alex. Drop this or we're done completely."

His stomach turned over. "We've been done for a long time, Eve."

She went silent. The only sound in the truck was the smooth running of wheels on concrete and the muted sound of traffic beyond the closed up windows. And it struck Alex that this might be the last time they were alone together.

"What did you really want to talk to me about tonight?" Alex asked. The office was straight ahead. He only had another few minutes with her, and he thought seriously about just taking off. Just driving away, away from the office and the case and Evans and both of their lonely apartments.

But he couldn't drive away from their problems. They were always with them, an anchor dragging them down.

"I wanted to discuss the dissolution of our contract. It's cruel for me to keep using you like I have been." She was stiff in her seat, her eyes on the office, her hands folded together.

"That wasn't what Liam made it sound like." Liam had sounded hopeful.

"Would it change your mind if I said I wanted to try again?"

She was trying to keep him out of harm's way. That was all. "No. If you want to try again, you'll wait for me."

"And if you want to try again, you'll let this lie."

They were at an impasse, but that had been the way they'd lived for years now. Neither one of them had been able to give up or give in. They had wasted years. "Eve, I don't want to lose you."

She sighed. "Then don't."

The car behind him honked, and he had no choice except to turn into the parking garage. The first car he saw was Eve's immaculate white Mercedes. He stopped in front of it and prayed for just a little more time.

She was out of the truck the minute it stopped rolling. She looked up at him, her brown eyes weary. "You're going to go, aren't you?"

"Yes." He had to.

She nodded. "You're not doing this for me, you know."

"Of course I am. I'm doing it for us." So they could feel safe again.

"Of course you are," she murmured. "Because you always make the right decisions, don't you, Alex? You always know best."

Except the time that he'd ignored her warning and ruined their lives. "Can't you see I'm trying to make this right?"

She slammed the door, but not before Alex heard Adam yelling.

"Eve!"

She turned and walked toward Adam, a smile on her face. For years she hadn't smiled at her own husband. Hadn't let him kiss her or hug her. She had kept him at arm's length because he'd screwed up, and now she was trying to keep him from correcting the mistake.

Adam opened his arms, and Eve walked in for a hug.

She gave so much to the other men in her life but nothing for the man who had loved her, who had waited for her.

But he would do one last thing for her. He would take Michael Evans down and then she would be safe.

Then the game would be over, but Alex already knew he'd lost.

* * * *

Eve glanced up at the clock. How many hours had gone by since she'd told Alex they were through? Eighteen? Nineteen? It seemed like forever and yet she could still see the look on his face.

93

She leaned back in her chair. The conference room was full, and she was the only woman there. Grace was working half days for the time being, and Eve felt her loss.

Ian walked in, dropped the folder he was carrying, and slung his massive body into the chair at the head of the table. "Who's presenting today?"

"Just me," Alex said.

"Fine. Give me updates before Alex goes." Ian glanced around the table. Alex had been right. If she hadn't known to look for the slight reddish tint to his eyes, she wouldn't be able to tell anything had been wrong with Ian.

Jake passed him another file, this one thick with paper. "We cleared up the McConnell Systems case. Adam nabbed one of the vice presidents for selling the latest software upgrades to a rival. So the good news is, we're free for a few weeks. We're evaluating security for a firm in Houston, but that job doesn't start right away."

"Weston?" Ian asked, never looking up.

Simon looked absolutely perfect in his Brooks Brothers suit. "I've got two cases running, and I'm working security for Lyle Benson's trip through Dallas. I'm just coordinating, of course. He has his own small army of bodyguards, but I'm checking his routes and the places he's planning on staying."

Ian frowned. "Yeah, well, keep the billionaire happy. He keeps us on retainer, and we train that small army of his. So, let's get on to the non-moneymaking portion of my day."

"I told you, I'll handle every bit of this." Alex stood, his eyes not quite meeting hers as they moved past her and focused on Ian. "I just need a short leave of absence. As I've never actually used a vacation day in the last five years, I think I'm due."

"Oh, and if I thought for a second you would go and hang out on a sunny beach, I would happily send your ass on its way," Ian grumbled. "But you're not going to do that, so I'm left with helping out. What's the setup?"

She'd done nothing all night long but worry about the setup. What exactly had Alex found out and what was he planning on doing about it? And why the hell should she care? He was picking his own revenge over her again.

When would she learn that she would always come second? That what had happened to her mattered more than who she was?

She just prayed this was a distance job. Maybe he would just watch the club from a distance and wait to tag Evans. She could handle it if he was out of harm's way.

"I'm going to work for a club that we suspect is a front for Evans's business. It's all in the packets." Alex looked tired, like he'd stayed up all night working. She suspected that if she looked in his office, she would find his clothes from yesterday. He always kept a spare set in his desk in case he pulled an all-nighter.

She slowly sipped her coffee, careful not to give away the fact that her heart pounded at the thought of him going undercover.

"How are you gaining access to the club?" Ian asked, opening the folder. "Did you follow up on the reporter?"

Simon nodded. "I pulled up everything I could on her last night. She graduated from Columbia with a Master's in Journalism. She worked at two small papers and then started doing some freelance work. She hit a couple of big stories, and now she works freelance full time. Comes from money as far as I can tell. She's the only daughter of a couple of wealthy socialites. When they died a few years back, they left her everything. I tried to find a good picture of her, but all I could get is this grainy shot of her in Pakistan when she was reporting on the Kashmir district."

"Odd. You couldn't even find a Facebook picture?" Adam asked.

"Nope. She's very private. No social media. Her driver's license is in there, but she's due to renew next year."

Alex shrugged. "Looks enough like her. Anyway, Kristen has been working there for a couple of months, and she thinks Evans is going to show up soon."

"What proof does she have of that?" Eve asked.

"She's heard word that he comes in every six months to check on operations and keep his flunkies in line. He's due in anytime. I'm hiring on as the Dom in Residence."

She felt her skin flush. Evans was a bastard. Maybe Alex was right that Evans hadn't forgotten about them. There was only one reason to use BDSM as a theme and that was to send Alex a giant middle finger. "He's set his new network up as BDSM clubs?"

"They're fetish themed nightclubs," Alex replied tightly.

Well, Michael Evans always had a sick sense of humor. "Why can't Ryan go in? He runs Sanctum."

"Ryan isn't trained. If I need someone to pose as a CEO, I'll send Ryan in," Alex shot back.

"Whereas it's so much better to send in someone who's emotionally involved and who could be recognized at any moment. Yes, that's a much better idea," Ian said with lazy menace. "Would you like to explain why I'm not going in?"

Alex got his stubborn face on. His brows furrowed and those massive linebacker shoulders of his squared off. He was acting like a five-year-old with a toy he didn't want to share, so why did she find him so damn attractive? "The source is only willing to work with me."

Ian shrugged. "Then make her willing to work with me."

Alex leaned over the table, his hands flat on the top. "You don't know how hard it's been to get her to let anyone but me in. I've been talking to this woman online for six weeks. I've finally gotten her to agree to meet, and last night I managed to negotiate to bring a couple of people in. I thought she was going to walk. She will if we change out leads. I'm going in, Ian. And you know damn well why, and you would do the same thing in my position."

Ian groaned and let his head fall back. "Fine. I very likely would, but then you would be in my shoes pointing out how fucking stupid all of this is. We don't know anything about this woman. She could be working for Evans for all you know."

He'd thought through that scenario, too. "Then I'll get to see him sooner than I thought. But I don't think she's working for him. Her credentials check out and this would be just the type of story she usually does. I talked to two of the editors she's worked with and they said she's one of the best in the business, but she disappears for long stretches because she goes undercover. I know I'm taking a chance, but it's my chance to take."

Ian ran a frustrated hand through his hair and seemed to concede. "So, how many other people can we get in there? If you think you're going in alone, you're insane."

Alex's eyes found his file again. "Like I said, I negotiated with her, but she's stubborn. I can bring three people with me. I need Adam on call."

Adam nodded. "Sure. Do I need to go to Florida? Make it quick. Serena can still fly for about six weeks. After that

I'm stuck here because I'm not leaving her behind while she's pregnant."

"Yes, because god knows I can't take care of her," Jake said with a long-suffering sigh.

"Well, you forget her marshmallows. She's carrying our baby and you expect her to drink hot cocoa without marshmallows."

"Dear god, you would think she's the queen of fucking England," Ian said with one of his patented eye rolls.

"Not at all," Simon replied drolly. "Her Majesty would never touch anything so lowbrow as cocoa. Now, my cousin on the other hand will, and William definitely prefers marshmallows. Harry pretends his Irish cream is cocoa, and even then he'll spike it with whiskey. Funny fellow, Harry."

Simon was connected.

Liam made a vomiting sound. "Get back to Buckingham, you prat. And that's complete shite. You're like third cousins and your brother's the heir."

Simon leaned forward, obviously willing to prolong the argument, but Eve had other things on her mind. "Evans knows what you look like, Alex."

All eyes shot to Alex. At least she wasn't the only one with concerns.

"I'm bigger than I was back then. I've put on thirty pounds of muscle. I'm going to wear colored contacts, and I'm taking my hair down to a buzz cut. It's a fuckload grayer than it was back then, and I used to keep it much longer and perfectly styled."

Because appearance meant something in the Bureau. Alex had been climbing the ladder, and Eve had encouraged him. She'd loved the way he looked in a terrifically fitted suit. And he was right. None of those suits would fit him now. He was far too muscular. "I think it's a risk."

"One I'm willing to take, but you know as well as I do that attitude and perception are more important than actual looks. I don't carry myself the way I used to. On a cursory glance, Evans likely won't notice me, and the people running his club won't know me at all. Even with the press coverage, the Bureau made damn sure pictures of the unit didn't get out. I'll be fine."

She wasn't so sure, but it was obvious he couldn't be talked out of it. And another problem crept into her brain like a weed she needed to pull. "Dom in Residence? So you'll be running scenes and handling subs?"

She'd placed careful emphasis on the word "handling."

"Are you asking if I'm going to have to fuck the subs?" Alex asked.

The rest of the men were watching them like they were a really well-played tennis match, their heads swinging back and forth between them.

"Is it too early for popcorn?" Adam whispered to Jake.

"Shh," Jake hissed back.

Well, she'd started it. And they were a weird little family. If she wasn't the one on display, she would have been sitting right next to Adam watching the scene play out. She was kind of used to doing her therapy in public and half naked. It was the way of their little world. "Yes, I'm curious about whether or not you're going to screw half of Florida."

Oh, she'd scored a hit with that one. A muscle in Alex's jaw twitched up, a sure sign he was pissed. And his eyes narrowed and she just knew whatever was about to come out of his mouth would hurt like hell. "No, Eve. Just one. I'm going to be running very specific scenes with one sub. I'm taking a sub from Sanctum in with me. She's a police officer so she understands undercover. I talked to her last night and she's agreed to use her vacation time to come with me. I'll only have to fuck her."

Wow. Getting kicked in the gut would be way worse.

He frowned. "Eve, I shouldn't have told you like that."

She shook her head. "No. I was vicious and you responded. I understand."

Getting Michael Evans was more important than anything. It always had been, and he wouldn't share it with her. She stood up. She wasn't needed here. Not at all. "I'll let you finish up without me since I'm not involved in this op. I've got psych profiles to work up anyway. If you'll excuse me."

She got up, taking her coffee with her. Low-fat latte, no cream. That was her life now. Yep. She'd chosen this. If she was going to work up a profile on herself, she could write page after page. PTSD. Control issues. Just on the right side of OCD.

The subject is mired in the tragic events of her past. The subject is unwilling to even think about moving past her own pain and is content to remain passionless because she is afraid her passion was what cost her in the first place. She fears another loss of self though she can't stand the person she's become.

Subject will now die and be found in her spotless apartment weeks after her lonely demise without so much as a cat to witness the event because they shed on her pristine rugs.

In this therapist's opinion, subject needs to get her shit together.

Yeah, she probably shouldn't evaluate herself. She got damn snarky when she did that.

"Eve."

She'd almost made it to her office. She didn't turn around because she was pretty sure those pesky tears were starting up again. "It's fine, Alex."

She tried to step into her office, but he followed her, slamming the door shut behind him.

"You don't really have a right to complain about where I sleep."

She turned, no longer caring what he saw. "You're on the wrong side of that door."

"I don't want to leave like this," he said. His fists were clenched at his sides.

"Then don't go. Let Ian handle it. He can play this role."

"I can't do that."

There was another solution to the problem. "Then take me as the sub. If it's going to be so easy to fool them, then I can put on a dark wig, and we both know how much weight I've lost and that I certainly carry myself differently."

His face went stony. "I will not take you."

She could be stubborn, too. Anger lit inside her. "Then you've made this decision and you should leave my office. You should also know that I won't be here when you get back. I'll find another job. Hell, I'll find another city, and then neither one of us has to go through this again."

His hands came out, reaching for her arms and dragging her close. "I don't want you to leave."

"And I don't want you to go." She needed to push him away. *Right now. Just shove out at him and get him out of this office before you do something stupid. Insanely stupid. And stop looking at his lips.*

Her eyes weren't listening. God, he had the most gorgeous lips. They were full and sensual, and when he smiled, he could light up a room. Alex loomed over her, every inch of his six and a half feet a testament to pure male beauty, from his golden brown hair to those deep green eyes, to a body she wanted to touch but couldn't allow herself to.

He pulled her closer. "I don't want any other woman. You're the only one who does this to me."

He rubbed his cock along her belly, and she nearly groaned. He was so hard. Long and thick, his cock was as perfect as the rest of him. She couldn't help it. She moved against him. No matter what came between them, she could never hide her response. She could control the interaction, but she craved him. Every minute of every day, she wanted Alexander McKay inside her.

Even though they were standing in her office and the rest of the team was just a couple of doors away, her whole body had softened, preparing to welcome him inside.

"Let me kiss you." He dipped his head toward hers.

She turned away. This was one of the things she'd wanted to change about their contract, but she couldn't do it now. Every reason she'd had the contract written in the first place was back in play. He was bent on pursuing revenge and leaving her behind.

"Damn it." His hands shifted, one arm moving under her legs. He lifted her up easily, his face harsh as he looked down at her. "Then I'll take what you'll give me. You'll allow me to kiss you somewhere else, won't you, Eve?"

He laid her out on her desk. He didn't have to move anything because she kept her desk as pristine and free of clutter as she kept her life. Everything had its place and she kept it there with a brutal proficiency.

Her back was settled against the desk and she knew she should protest, but he was already moving, shoving her skirt up and pulling at the thong she wore.

"I fucking hate these things, but that's why you wear them, isn't it?" He growled the question as he ripped the little silk thong off her.

And she couldn't deny it. It wasn't really because she knew he hated them. It was more a case of needing to take her identity back. Alex had forbidden her to wear underwear when they'd been married, and for a long time after they had divorced, she hadn't been able to stand the feel of them against her skin. She'd been filled with a perverse need to prove she was in control of what she wore, the same way she'd been with food. Alex had demanded she indulge, so she took control and portioned out what she was allowed.

He pulled at her ankles, forcing her down the desk until her ass was almost hanging off. He forced her legs apart, but then he knew damn well what that did for her. This was the only way she could allow herself to submit anymore. She'd thought, just for a moment, that they could have something more, but if this was all there was between them, then she would take it.

"Ask me."

She closed her eyes. He always demanded this of her. It was the one thing he'd held hard on. He'd been willing to give up kissing her, sleeping cuddled close, but she knew he would never give up this.

"Alex, will you touch me?"

"Not good enough."

He wanted to hear her talk dirty. "Alex, will you put your mouth on me?"

He flipped her over so fast she could barely register the movement. One minute she was flat on her back and the next she was face down on the desk, her legs scraping to find the floor. A hard *smack* blasted through the office, and she felt her eyes tear up. He slapped at her ass five times in succession, and every inch of her skin lit up with just the right amount of pain. God, she needed this. She had no idea how she would ever get through a day without the possibility of his hands on her.

Even with everything they had been through, she couldn't stop wanting this man. It had been this way since the moment she'd laid eyes on him, and she was damn sure she'd go to her grave with him in her heart.

He leaned over, one hand tangling in her hair. He pulled gently, but every nerve in her scalp came alive. The bastard knew just what pulling her hair did for her. Her pussy started to pulse, just begging for release. She could feel his erection along the seam of her ass. Years. It had been years since he'd taken her there, since he'd shoved that massive dick inside and made her scream his name. "All right, angel, here's the truth. You're going to give me what I want. You might have me so hamstrung with rules that I can't see straight half the time, but I am the Master of this. You will say the words I want to hear or I'll walk away. No more spanking. No sex. You'll feel achy all day long, and you'll wish you had just said the words."

He tugged on her hair, proving his point as she gasped with pleasure.

"Please, Alex, please eat my pussy. Please lick me and bite me and fuck me with your tongue."

She could feel his breath on the back of her neck, his mouth hovering there. He ran his nose through her hair, breathing her in before he stood back up and gave her another ten quick hard smacks that left her breathless. He turned her back over.

"Spread your legs wide." His voice was dark chocolate and full of command.

Eve did as he demanded, placing her heels on the edge of the desk, her pussy wide open to his view. Her heart was racing, blood pounding through her system. She hadn't been this spontaneous in years. She'd put Alex in his place and she'd kept him there. Her bedroom, once a week, no kissing, no sleeping over.

But she couldn't turn him away now. She felt greedy and desperate to get his mouth on her. If he'd given in, even the tiniest bit on the Evans situation, she would probably be kissing him for the first time in years, devouring his mouth and hoping for the future.

Alex loomed over her. "If this is all I can get, you know I'll take it."

He dropped to his knees, and she felt his nose right where her labia parted. He always seemed to love her smell. She'd been so self-conscious at first, but Alex had broken her of the habit and of so many self-defeating insecurities. He'd loved how she looked and smelled and simply was, and somehow it had been enough for her.

She let her eyes roll back as he took that first long swipe with his tongue. Just for a few moments, nothing mattered. Not the past. Not the future. For these brief moments, they were just Alex and Eve again.

This was heaven.

As Alex pressed his tongue against her, it was all she had not to beg him for more.

Chapter Five

Alex wanted to give her so fucking much more. He wanted to rip every stitch of clothing off her and kiss her from head to toe. He would sink his hands into her soft hair and tug on it. He would spend at least an hour on her mouth, learning it again, sucking on her lips and her tongue, rubbing them together and holding her head to his so he could eat her up.

He would use his hands to worship her, not leaving an inch of that porcelain skin untouched, unloved. He would take all day, and no one could stop him. He would tie her up, using an intricate Shibari design. He could spend hour after hour lovingly winding silk rope around her body, creating a dress to show her off in.

But he had to settle for this. He had to follow her rules now. No kissing. She only was willing to be touched all over when he got her so hot she forgot her inhibitions. This was the only way she could accept affection now. Every touch and caress, every word, had its place and its boundaries.

And he still needed her. He loved the way she smelled and how wet she got for him. Her pussy was pink and hot with arousal, her cream already making the walls slick and ready for his cock. He swiped at her pussy, letting his tongue go from her tight cunt all the way up to the jewel of her clit. He could hear her little moans and cries, each one going straight to his cock.

She was the perfect picture of a satiated female, with

her skirt shoved around her waist and two buttons of her blouse undone. He could see the mounds of her breasts peeking through her lacy bra.

A knock on the door jarred him. He nearly growled as he heard a familiar voice. "Eve?"

Liam. Damn it. His Irish accent grated as did the worried tone of his voice. He knew they weren't involved, knew that Liam was a good friend to her, but he hated the fact that she spent so much time with him, giving him her advice, her soft smile, and her laugh. He sucked her clit into his mouth, biting down gently. He wanted to make sure Liam didn't think he was hurting Eve. Oh, no. He wasn't hurting her at all.

She groaned, the sound loud and sure.

"I'll come back later then." He could hear Liam chuckle as he walked away.

"Bastard, you knew I would nearly scream," she whispered as though she could still keep what they were doing a secret.

He knew exactly what to do to get her to scream, and he didn't care if everyone in the office knew that they were making love. "I'll make you do more than scream, angel. I'm going to make you come."

She was the only woman he'd touched in a sexual way since he was fucking twenty-three years old. She was the only woman he wanted to touch for the rest of his life. The thought of having to have sex with Amanda made him queasy, but she was the best sub for the op. He'd gone over every possibility, and she was the only one who made sense. She was a cop. She had some experience, and she'd always been obedient. He would find a way around the sex. He would fake it. Hell, he wasn't even sure his dick would work without Eve. He could make up some shit story about

107

withholding his cock because of his sub's bad behavior. All that mattered was staying true to his wife so he could come home and try again.

Once he'd freed her from Michael Evans's power, they could start over.

"Please, Alex." She looked down her body, licking her lips as she watched him lick her pussy.

He pushed her thighs farther apart, spreading her wide for his delectation. He suckled on her clit, not enough to make her come, but just enough to send her hips moving against his mouth. This was what he lived for. He dragged the flat of his tongue all through her pussy. The flesh was soft and hot, like butter drizzled with honey.

He fucked into her, his tongue diving deep. He pulled her close so he could go as far as his tongue would let him. He rubbed his nose against her clit, pressing down hard so he was stimulating both parts of her gorgeous pussy. Over and over he fucked and rubbed until he felt her letting go, her hands finding his hair and pulling him close.

She was on the edge, right where he wanted her to be.

He kissed her, sucking each side of her labial lips into his mouth as he let a finger find her cunt and fuck deep. He put his tongue right on her clit again as he curved his finger up into her pussy, seeking that spot that always got Eve going. She was so responsive, so easy to take to the edge. When she was squirming against his tongue and fingers, he felt about ten feet tall. He was surrounded by Eve. Her scent, her taste. The silky feel of her skin became his whole world.

His cock was dying, but he liked it that way. It fucking meant he was alive, and she was still with him. Every pulse and play of her flesh licked along his spine. He would have her soon. He could revel in pleasuring her because he knew his time would come.

He slid his free hand under her ass cheeks. Even though she'd lost weight, her ass was still curvy and lovely. His favorite thing in the world was smacking it over and over until it was a gorgeous pink. He loved everything about it from the sounds—the hard smack and then her sweet little gasps and moans—to the way her skin got hot and pink, signaling her readiness. When he saw that rosy sheen to her backside, he knew her pussy was soft and wet and ready for him.

He'd tugged on her hair, wanting her as wet as he could get her. Eve loved it rough. She was the perfect sub for him. He wasn't a complete sadist. He didn't want to hurt her, but he wanted his sex nasty and dirty and hard, and Eve responded to that.

He fucked two fingers high into her cunt as he sucked on her clit, biting down. With his free hand, he held her steady, his fingers sinking into the sweet flesh at her hips. Her tangy taste filled his mouth as he curled his fingers up, and he felt her start to shake and moan.

Her honey coated his tongue as he felt the little muscles of her pussy clenching his fingers tight. She kept quiet as she came, the only sounds little harsh gasps and sighs.

He pulled his fingers out, licking the cream from them before he tore open the fly of his slacks. His erection was thick and pulsing, desperate to get to her. He shoved his boxers down and took his cock in hand. He looked down at her. She was a gorgeously decadent sight with her satiated eyes and wanton pose. Her chest was moving up and down, her nipples straining against the thin material of her bra and silk shirt. With his free hand, he reached down and palmed a breast. Like the rest of her, they were smaller than before, but he loved their shape and how they swelled in his hand.

"Alex, we should talk." She was coming out of the haze

of lust. He could see that plainly. He only had a couple of seconds to bring her back in or she would shove him out of her office, and they would part with nothing solved between them.

"You're going to leave me like this?" He stroked his cock knowing damn well she wouldn't do it, but a little kernel of resentment was stoked inside him. She wanted to talk after he'd given her what she needed, but taken nothing for himself. "I've followed all your rules. Are you through with this, too?"

"Alex," she whispered his name and for the first time in a long time, he saw some emotion on her face. "I don't want to fight."

He wanted to take her in his arms and carry her home and take care of her all over again. "I don't want to fight either, but if you're not going to let me have you, you should tell me now so I can find a shower and get the water as cold as possible."

She sat up, and he was sure she was going to straighten her clothes and turn him away. He hadn't done what she wanted him to and that seemed to be the dynamic of their relationship now. Her eyes turned down, and she watched his cock. "That looks painful."

"Yep."

A little smile curled her lips up, and every word out of her mouth was a throaty seduction. "I'm a therapist. I can't leave a person in pain."

She reached out and touched him. He damn near came right then and there. It had been forever since she'd touched him for anything but balance and support during a scene or very vanilla sex. She licked those sultry lips as she stroked him up and down.

Her palm was soft, and she held him with a sure grip,

her white-tipped nails forming a fist around him. He let himself enjoy the feel of her gripping his dick until a big problem occurred to him. *Damn it.* He wasn't prepared for some afternoon delight in her office. "I don't have any condoms."

He kept a box at her apartment because that was the only place they had sex anymore. Maybe he could just let her stroke him to orgasm. It might be heavenly to watch as her small, perfectly manicured hands stroked him over and over.

A wicked grin crossed her face. "You also don't have lube, and in a couple of minutes this is going to get rough on you." She gently swiped a thumb across his cockhead, gathering the fluid that beaded there. She was right. It wouldn't be enough. A good hand job required lube.

He pulled away. *Fuck all.* Now he was sexually frustrated on top of everything else.

Eve lay back on her desk, her legs parting again. "It's all right. We both know neither of us has a disease."

They'd only had sex with each other for over a decade.

A sad look came over her face. "And we both know the other problem is very unlikely to occur. Make love to me before you leave. One last time."

It wasn't the last time. It couldn't be the last time. He wouldn't let it be. She would see that once he'd finished this chapter of their lives, they could start a new one.

"I can't let you go, Eve," he reached down, taking charge of his cock and placing it right on her entrance. Heat threatened to overwhelm him as the head slipped just inside. Every muscle in his body tensed as he forced himself to hold still. "I just can't do it."

He surged in, and her eyelids slid closed as she took a long breath and adjusted to his cock. "You can't let go of a lot of things. That's our problem. But this isn't our problem. God, you feel so good."

She never talked during sex anymore. How pathetic was he that five little words from her were all it took to make him feel ten feet tall? He felt good to her? Well, he could give her more. A lot more. He gripped her hips, hating the clothes between them. He wanted her naked and laid out for him, but the situation was far too urgent. He needed her right now.

So tight. He had no idea how she stayed so fucking tight. Years and years had gone by. They'd made love more times than he could count, and every time he got inside Eve felt like the first time. And there wasn't anything in between them. He'd been using condoms for years, telling himself it wasn't so different. He'd been wrong. This was primal. He was connected to her. She could put all the rules and walls between them, but for these few moments, they were together.

The heat threatened to curl his spine. His cock was surrounded, engulfed in her. He had to force his way in, inch by glorious inch. Her legs came up, circling his hips. The feel of her heels pressing into him made him groan. Those heels of hers could leave marks on him for hours afterward, and he loved it. Days later he might feel a twinge of pain and remember just how hard she'd come.

This was where he wanted to be. This was where he always wanted to be.

He let his head loll back, his senses taking over. He rolled his hips, trying to get as deep as he could go. He let his hand drift to her clit. He wouldn't last long. He could already feel a tingle along his spine as his balls drew up, ready to shoot off and fill her up. There was no way he could last when she was so wet and clamped so tight around him.

He fucked into her, letting his instincts lead him. All the way in and then back out before sliding in and up, seeking her G-spot. Over and over he pounded his flesh into hers as though he could mark her and force her to stay with him, to never leave him.

Her heels dug into his backside as she held them tightly together. It was a fight to pull out far enough, but the sweet friction was doing its job and quickly. He pressed down on her clit, circling it with his thumb until he heard her gasp, felt the tension of her orgasm on his dick, and he couldn't hold back a second longer.

He poured himself into her. Come bubbled up from his balls, shooting off in waves of pleasure. He dragged oxygen into his lungs as a sense of peace settled over him. He fell forward, his chest against her breasts.

"Alex." She held still underneath him. "Alex, you should move now. I can't breathe."

He was heavy, but she used to love having him on top of her. He forced himself to move, to leave her. His head was reeling, but he knew one thing. This wasn't over. His hands shook slightly as he pulled his boxers up and refastened his slacks. "We're going to talk when I get back. Don't think I'm going to let the situation stay this way forever."

Ian was right. He'd let her drive the boat for too long. If they were going to have any kind of shot at staying together, he had to start pushing her boundaries.

She sat up, trying to straighten her clothes. She didn't meet his eyes. "Then don't go."

She was still trying to control everything, but he couldn't let her this time. If Evans was out there, it was only a matter of time before he came after them again. "I have to, but I'll be back."

Her voice was shaking a little as she hopped off the desk and pulled her skirt down. He wanted to reach out to her, but she turned away. "If you go back into his world, you're going to start another war."

The war had never ended. It had just been put on hold. She should know that more than anyone else. "I love you, Eve."

He turned and walked away, trying to put his mind to the task at hand.

* * * *

"Eve? Do you want a glass of wine?"

Grace's words pulled Eve out of her misery. She plastered a smile on her face and looked up. "Sure. That sounds nice."

Why the hell had she decided to come here tonight? She should have sent a gift with Avery and locked herself in her apartment for a few days. She wasn't exactly in the mood for a dinner party, but she'd promised Grace. It had only been a few hours since she and Alex had parted. She could still feel him inside her. There was a pleasant ache in her bones because he'd been so rough. It had been years since he'd manhandled her the way he had today, like she wasn't made of glass, like she was a woman.

Grace sank down next to her, handing her a glass of ruby-red wine. She had the same in her hand. A little smile crossed her face and she sighed as she sipped. "God, it's been so long since I had a glass of wine."

Eve took a sip of the wine. It was rich with cherry overtones. "I'm not sure I could go too long without a glass."

114

Serena laughed as she sat down opposite Eve. She was wearing jeans and a flouncy top that successfully hid what Eve knew was a little baby bump. Both Serena and Avery were pregnant. Grace's daughter was only six weeks old. Everyone was having babies, moving on.

She looked out at the patio where Ian was sitting in front of the pool, talking to Simon. Everyone was making a life for themselves except her and Alex and Ian.

"She's going to pump and dump," Serena said with a nod. "I'm totally doing that after baby boy is born. I never realized how much of my creativity is dependent on vodka."

Grace took a drink, her eyes closing in apparent pleasure. "Carys has plenty to eat. I froze some breast milk for just such an occasion." Grace turned Eve's way. "So, I heard you and Alex got busy today."

Serena rolled her eyes, her hand fiddling with the iced tea at her side. "I thought we decided you were going to be subtle."

Grace shrugged. "I'm not good at subtle. Ask Sean. I very subtly told him how mad I was that he was getting back in the business by screaming at him and throwing a fit. After a nice long spanking, he convinced me he was right."

"Getting back in the business?" Eve asked. Sean was out of security. He'd finished culinary school and was working with local chefs to perfect his menu for a restaurant he was going to open next year.

Grace frowned, but there was sympathy in her gaze. "He's going to Florida with Alex."

She practically sighed in relief. She could trust Sean to watch his back. Then she realized why Grace would be upset. Sean had a baby to worry about. "I'll talk to Alex. He can't take Sean with him."

Despite how much better she would feel, she couldn't

allow him to drag Sean and Grace into their trouble. It was bad enough that Adam was going.

Grace shook her head. "Absolutely not. Do not talk to Alex. Besides the fact that my backside is really sore because a disciplinary spanking isn't as much fun as the erotic ones, I understand why Sean needs to go. I got scared for a minute, but I married a military man. Oh, he might be a chef now, but he'll never not be a soldier and he's never going to let a man he loves like a brother go into battle alone if he can help it."

"I'm sure he can find someone else."

"No. Sean needs to do this. Carys and I will just have to settle in and wait for him. I've always known that he would drift in and out of the dangerous stuff. It's a part of who he is." Grace certainly seemed at ease with the decision now. "Besides, he really wants to learn how to cook Cuban, so he's going to do some research while he's there. Now, what was this about office sex?"

This was why she didn't come to dinner parties. This was why she didn't hang out with other subs. Because other subs were nosy. "It was a mistake."

Serena and Grace exchanged a long look as though they were having a silent conversation about how to proceed. If she didn't shut this down, they would end up talking to her about her non-existent relationship.

She definitely didn't want that. "I really don't want to talk about it. I hope you can respect my privacy."

"We have privacy? Why do we need privacy?" Avery sat down next to Serena, a glass of tea in her hand. She looked at all of them, her mouth open a little. "Oh, y'all started the Alex talk, didn't you? I told you it was a bad idea."

Eve felt her face flush. It was time to go. She set her

wine glass down and stood up. "I think I'll just skip the dinner, Grace. I'm feeling a bit tired."

A frown passed over Grace's face. "And I'm going to ask you to stay."

That was a deeply aggressive move for someone like Grace. "Like I said, I've had a long day and I'm tired."

"He's taking Amanda with him."

That stopped her in her tracks. She sat back down, trying to process the new information. Alex and Amanda?

Avery leaned over, whispering Grace's way. "You didn't have to tell her like that."

"Yes, I did," Grace said. "Eve doesn't respond to subtle. She would walk out of here in a heartbeat if I let her because she's more than willing to listen to every single one of us and help us with our problems, but she won't have the decency of returning the favor."

A shitty day had just turned worse. "I'm a therapist. I'm supposed to listen and help. If I'm not doing a good enough job for you, I can certainly refer you to someone else."

Grace stood up, facing her down. "And I'm family. I'm your sister and that's not going to ever change. And I can't refer myself or find someone else."

Serena stood up beside Grace. "What she said."

Adam walked up carrying a tray of appetizers, a big smile plastered on his face. He stopped as every single female looked at him. Without a word, he backed away.

"Well at least the men won't come in now." Avery shook her head as the kitchen door swung behind him.

Eve had to ignore everything except what Grace had said. "What are you trying to tell me?"

"I'm going to ask you this and if you want to tell me to keep my nose out of your business, then I will, but we're family now and I happen to care a great deal about you.

You're more than willing to help me out any time I'm in trouble. Can't you understand that I want to do the same for you?"

"Me, too," Serena said, reaching for her hand. She stopped as though realizing she was about to do something rude.

God, when had she made the conscious decision to shove everyone away? Maybe that decision hadn't been conscious. Maybe it had been born from her pain and misery, but she'd done it all the same. She was surrounded by these amazing women and they were right. They were family. She grabbed Serena's hand. "I'm worried about Alex."

Grace sank back into her sofa, a long sigh coming from her chest. "Thank god. I hate doing the tough-chick thing."

Avery smiled. "I advised that we should just get you drunk and have a sleepover. I always talked too much at sleepovers."

Serena snorted a little. "Yeah, that would totally work. Avery and I would be snoring by nine and Grace would be up all night with Carys. Nope. This is better. So talk and tell us how we can help because I hate Amanda."

"Is she the one who's always so sweet around the Doms and then tells all the subs in the locker room that they're fat?" Avery asked. "Yeah, I hate her, too. I told her I wasn't fat, I was pregnant and she said 'same difference. If it moos like a cow...'"

Grace gasped. "She called you a cow?"

Avery nodded. "Apparently she was very interested in Li before we got married. He admitted to sleeping with her a couple of times, but then he slept with most of them. Why did I get the manwhore?"

"Reformed manwhore," Eve said, getting a little angry

at the thought of Amanda trying to undermine everyone around her. "Now she's after Alex."

"Well, I think Ian would be her first choice, but he sees right through that kind of crap," Grace said.

"Alex is softer than Ian. He wants to believe the best of people, so when Amanda pulls her doe-eyed routine, he buys it. Come on. It's an age-old tale. Men are dumb. Like eighteen seasons of *The Bachelor* haven't proven that," Serena said. "They always pick the nasty one and then they're all like, 'What? I didn't see that coming.' Dumb ass."

Amanda was awful. She got that. It didn't explain everything. "Why would he take her? He needs backup. He pretends like this isn't dangerous, but this guy he's going after…"

"Is one of the worst terrorists in the world and has hurt all of us very deeply," Grace finished.

Eve shook her head. "I don't understand. You know Evans?"

"I know that he hurt you and that means he hurt every one of us, and we all have to pitch in."

A deep well of emotion surged. There were things she knew intellectually, but hadn't put into practice, holding the truths close to her heart. One of those truths was the fact that she didn't have to be alone. She didn't have to hide or cover up. If she were on the outside looking in on her own case, she would tell herself that talking about it, opening up and sharing the burden where she could was the only way to heal. "Can I be honest?"

"Of course," all three said at the same time.

Eve couldn't help but laugh. "I don't want him to go."

"I wouldn't either," Serena said. "It's scary to send them off."

Eve shook her head. "It's not totally about the danger. Alex is making the same mistakes all over again. He's opening wounds that might finally be healing."

"I don't think they're healing for him, sweetie." Grace looked out to the patio where the men had gathered. "They're tough men. They like to pretend they don't feel things, but it's an act."

"I think I understand," Serena said. "You want him to focus on you, on your relationship."

Finally someone got it. "Serena, after it happened…" *God, be brave, Eve. Just fucking say it.* "After I was raped…"

"After you were tortured," Grace prompted. It was obvious to Eve that Grace was taking the big-sister role, and she wasn't about to let Eve sugarcoat a damn thing. She should be annoyed, but she only felt a deep sense of gratitude.

"After I was tortured, Alex shut down. He said all the right things, but he wasn't there for me. I'm not saying he didn't sit with me and hold my hand."

"He pulled away," Avery concluded. "Yes, I do understand that, but not the way you would think. I understand where Alex is coming from."

Eve sighed. "Of course, I know that it's a typical reaction for the loved ones of a victim to pull away due to an overwhelming sense of guilt and a fear that the world won't be the same again. I've seen it in a lot of people."

Avery wouldn't let up. "But you haven't felt it, Eve. I know you're smart and you're so educated and experienced when it comes to people's motivations, but you can't know what it feels like to be the one who didn't die."

But Avery did. "I didn't die, Avery. It wasn't as bad as that."

"No, she's right," Serena argued. "A rape is something traumatic. The only thing I can think of that's worse than it happening to me is knowing that it's happening to someone I love and not being able to stop it."

"He was helpless, Eve." Avery's eyes closed and opened again as though she was briefly reliving what she'd had to go through. "I was helpless. I was trapped in that car and I listened to my daughter die. I watched my husband bleed to death. Alex didn't have to watch, but I can imagine that it was horrible for him. He had to sit there knowing that you were hurting. Can you imagine the scenarios that played through his head? Have you told him what happened? Have you really talked about it?"

"I didn't want to burden him." She'd talked to her therapist but only in general terms. She'd told the police, but that was a clinical thing, divorced utterly from the emotions she'd felt. "It should have brought us together. I thought we were strong enough that it would bring us together, but he drifted away from me."

"And you're so angry about that," Grace said. "I would be. I would feel abandoned."

"He didn't want me anymore. I wonder if he thinks I'm dirty, Grace." She'd never said it out loud. "He wouldn't touch me for the longest time and then it was different. I hated how different it was, like I wasn't the woman he'd married anymore but he was too honorable to leave. So I divorced him, but we fell into this stupid contract and we haven't been able to move on. Just when I thought I could, Michael Evans pops back up."

"He was always going to come back." Serena sat back, her face thoughtful. "That's what Jake and Adam said."

"I don't think so. I know Alex has it in his head that Michael Evans is out there plotting against him, but I disagree. Evans was satisfied with the revenge he had against Alex."

"But Alex isn't satisfied that the threat is gone." Grace took a sip of her wine. "He can't be until Evans is in jail or dead. Eve, you think this is about revenge, but I think you're wrong. You're too close to the situation. You both made mistakes, but the first one is not talking about this. I know it's hard, but you've both tried to find ways around the situation. You didn't divorce Alex because you're not in love with him."

Eve let her eyes close, unwilling to look at them while she admitted her sins. "No. I did it because I needed him to notice me again." A hand slipped over hers. She looked down. Grace. The words seemed to come more easily now. "I wanted him to fight me, but he didn't. He told me if that was what I needed, then he understood."

"Dumbass," Serena said under her breath.

They'd both been stupid. "But I don't know that I'm willing to jump back into this with him. I think we might have made too many mistakes. It might be best to just let each other go and start over again."

"You can't until you sort some things out," Avery argued. "And I don't know how you do that from here when he's in Florida."

"I've tried to make him stay." It was the first time she'd asked for anything in years, but she had to acknowledge that it might be too late.

"Oh." A little gasp came out of Serena's mouth. "Oh. Now I don't hate that idea at all."

Grace leaned forward. "She just got a plot idea. When she says she doesn't hate something, it's usually really good."

Serena got very animated as she talked about her

writing, her hands fluttering as she spoke. "Look, sometimes when you're writing, a good plot is right in front of you, but it's in these weird little pieces. So, Alex needs backup, but he's afraid to take Eve. We all hate Amanda, and let's face facts, I don't care that she's a cop, she's a ho-bag and she'll throw him under a bus if some hottie comes walking by. Our men are involved in this potentially dangerous operation and wouldn't we feel safer if there was a sister on the inside? There's one solution to this problem. You have to kill Amanda and take her place."

"I'm not killing Amanda." But the rest of the idea had a tantalizing efficiency to it. She should be the one watching over Alex. He'd said no when she'd run the idea by him initially, but did that mean she had to obey him? He wasn't thinking. She was the only one who could really do this. She had the training to handle it. She knew Michael Evans better than anyone did. She'd practically written the book on the bastard.

Serena leaned forward, a beseeching look on her face. "Oh, I wish you would. I caught her trying to get Jake to help her with suspension play. She shook her thong right in his face and then I overheard her talking about how sad it was that he was saddled with someone like me. Of course, I then wrote her into my next book and brutally murdered her there, but this would be like research for me. We would all help you bury the body."

Eve felt a smile slide across her face as she looked at the women around her. They would. They would be right there with shovels and flashlights and alibis, and a nice bottle of wine for afterward because they were a sisterhood. They might not share blood, but they shared a life.

"No bloody death, Serena, but she's definitely not going to Florida. I already asked Alex if I could come and he said no, but he's wrong about this. I need to make sure I'm the one he introduces as his sub. Did Adam do her cover?"

"Oh, yes. He booked the tickets and everything, but none of this works unless we spring it on Alex when he can't back out," Serena mused. "We need Sean in on it, too. He knows where the meet site is."

Grace gave the room a peaceful smile. "I think Sean is going to have to leave a little later than planned because Carys has some sort of emergency. Just a couple of hours. Long enough that he has to meet Alex at the club and take Alex's sub with him. Yes, I think that can be arranged. Sean can't stand Amanda, and he's got the very same fears the rest of us have. She won't watch his back. She'll be too busy trying to get into his pants. He'll hop on board."

"I need to change my hair color." Her heart thumped in her chest, adrenaline starting to flow. Was she really going to do this? Alex was going to be pissed, but she couldn't let him go without proper backup. And in a club, she might be more effective than he was about gathering information. Women gossiped. A lot. He had to have a sub the other women would trust or it wouldn't work.

"Makeover! Oh, this is going to be fun." Avery clapped her hands. "I think you would look gorgeous with a nice walnut shade. It would totally contrast with your skin."

"Is it safe to come in yet?" Adam poked his head out of the kitchen. "Because the hors d'oeuvres are getting cold. Sean is going to be pissed if I serve them cold, but you ladies looked like you were talking about men, and not in a happy, fun way. I refuse to be the dude who gets his balls kicked in because he was stupid enough to walk in at the wrong time."

Poor Adam. Stuck with the ladies. "Yes, I think your balls are safe. And besides, I need a favor from you. We've been plotting, you see."

Adam was in the living room in a flash, a wicked grin on his face. "Oh, I love a good plot. Count me in."

She took one of the canapés off the platter. She actually had an appetite for once.

One way or another, she was going to make sure her husband came back from Florida in one piece. And then they could finally have closure.

Chapter Six

Alex glanced down at his watch and silently cursed.

"They're going to be here, right?" Kristen cast a nervous glance toward the stairs and the door at the top where apparently the great Chazz Breyer was going to eventually make an appearance.

It was the door to the office he would eventually have to get into. Alone.

"Sean texted me. His flight landed an hour ago. They should be here any minute."

"I don't like last minute changes in plans," Kristen grumbled. She was dressed casually in jeans and a V-neck T-shirt that showed off a nice rack. Her strawberry blonde hair was in waves across her shoulders, but he couldn't get the sight of Eve spread out on her desk out of his head. He'd thought of nothing else for the last twenty-four hours. He'd tried to call her, but she wouldn't answer her cell. He'd skipped the dinner party where he'd been sure to see her because he'd wanted to get packed and ready, and now he wondered if that had been a mistake.

He shouldn't have left things that way between them, but she hadn't given him a choice.

"So, what do you think of the place, Anthony?" She dropped his fake name casually. For now he was Anthony Priest, known to most as Master A.

He had to pull it together because they weren't alone. Several young women were currently milling about either cleaning tables or restocking the bar. As far as he could tell, the club was a repurposed industrial warehouse. Sanctum was the same, but Cuffs had maintained much more of its former identity than Sanctum. The floors were concrete and the walls, for the most part, were still metal and girders. There was a bar area and what appeared to be a roped off VIP-type area. The VIP area looked like someone had ordered a bunch of BDSM equipment off the Internet and tried to approximate a play space, but nothing was set up properly. He hoped no one actually tried to play here. "It looks like crap."

"Yeah." Kristen frowned as she crossed her arms over her chest. "They would have been better off hiring a decorator, but Chazz decided he would save the money. You have to understand that most of the regulars who come here are just tourists who read a couple of books and decide they're in the lifestyle. Then there are the college kids who just want to drink, and the guys who come out because our cocktail waitresses are dressed in fet wear. No one knows what they're doing."

"But you do." He'd been studying her from the time they'd met at DFW through the hours on the plane. She was odd. Totally competent one minute, he was halfway intimidated by how smart she was. She had been talking about trying to map out Evans's organization and the methods she'd been using to track him, and then the flight attendant had brought around the wine and she'd clapped like a little girl and claimed that first class was "the bomb." And the girl seemed deadly intent on drinking her share. She'd had five glasses of wine, but he couldn't tell she felt a thing. She was perfectly steady.

He'd sat beside her on the plane, studying the files she'd hacked into while she'd read something on her e-

127

reader that made her fan herself more than once.

She was a complete enigma.

She shrugged a little. "I've been around. Look, brother, I know it comes as a shock that I've taken to the lifestyle, but we need you here. And can anything be worse than my coming out? Mom nearly had a heart attack because I had disrupted her perfectly good plan to marry me off to the doctor next door. You know how a really good plan can slip up, don't you, Anthony?"

Yeah, and he was out of practice. He needed to save the questions about her past for the condo because he was supposed to be her big brother here. And a nasty, badass Dom. He had the temporary tats to prove it. Kristen turned out to be quite the artist with the airbrush. "Yes. Well, I'll have to make some plans for this place because that equipment looks like shit, and it's going to get worse if it isn't properly taken care of."

"Well, that's what I'm hiring you for, isn't it, Master A?" The door to the office had opened and a man with a medium-sized build and a longish, dark ponytail began to walk down the stairs. He was dressed in a T-shirt and running pants, his sneakers squeaking on the metal stairs. A heavy gold chain hung around his neck. Alex pegged his age at fortyish, though it was obvious he was trying to look like he was twenty-one and fresh off the Jersey Shore.

"I wasn't aware you had hired me at all yet."

His heavy Jersey accent flooded the room. "Hey, any family of Kris's is family of mine. Ain't that right, sweetheart?"

Kristen gave him a bubbly smile. Yeah, she looked like the perfect picture of innocence. "You know that's true, Chazz. We're all one big freaky family here. Anthony, I told you the interview is a formality. There's nothing to worry about."

"Nothing at all. We're very happy to have you, Master A. I'm afraid we're trying to find our feet." Chazz looked him over as though sizing him up. "You're a big guy. Did Kris tell you I might need you for some bodyguard work as well as being our resident expert?"

The bodyguard work was something he was terribly interested in. According to Kristen, Chazz went off on mysterious meetings at least once a week and took some of the bouncers with him every time. She'd tried to talk to a couple, but they were all closed mouthed about what they were doing. Then there was the night once a week where the club was supposed to be closed, but she'd seen the lights on and cars in the parking lot. She'd tried to get in, but found security on the doors, security she didn't recognize. "I've done a little muscle work in my time."

"Yes, you have. A very impressive résumé. So you've worked in a couple of clubs?"

According to the résumé Adam had created, he'd worked in clubs in New York, DC, and Houston and was a trained security guard. The résumé had been uploaded to the web, and to the casual viewer, it looked like Anthony Priest had been looking for work for about three months. He had résumés at several websites, a FetLife account, and all the various footprints he would naturally leave behind in cyberspace.

"I've worked in actual BDSM clubs. This is my first experience with a nightclub."

Chazz nodded. "I need to get myself a membership to one of those clubs."

Alex didn't bother to mention that the private clubs tended to screen out idiots like Chazz. "So what exactly do you expect from me?"

"Kris here had a great idea," Chazz explained. "She thinks instead of just having themed tables and cocktail waitresses, we should differentiate ourselves. We want to run actual scenes. You know for entertainment and shit."

He forced himself not to shudder. "And you expect me to use this equipment? On my sub?"

"I have a whole collection of whips and paddles and some canes and stuff. I got them secondhand. They're all over the walls, just like a real dungeon. All you'll have to do is walk up to one and pluck it down, my man," Chazz argued.

Chazz wouldn't know a "real" dungeon if it bit him in the ass. It was obvious Chazz either didn't practice or didn't care about his subs. "Secondhand? And they just sit on the wall? I'm not using those. They have to stay purely decorative. Humans sweat and bleed, and there are various other bodily emissions I won't even get into. You're going to get your ass sued. I'll bring my own kit and I'll make sure everything is sterile."

"Whoa, so we're like infection central here," a deep voice said. "I always knew it."

Alex turned and saw a young man, probably somewhere around twenty-five. He was wearing a muscle shirt that showed off a single tat on his arm. Army.

"I don't need your sarcasm, Jesse." Chazz shook his head. "I swear if he wasn't so good with a gun, I would have fired his ass a long time ago. That's my lead bouncer, Jesse Murdoch. He also functions as my bodyguard and I haven't died yet, so he's not a complete idiot."

Jesse gave a sarcastic salute. "I aim to please, boss. Hey, Kris. So this is big brother."

There was something about the way the younger man eyed him that made Alex wary. He'd spent too long in the

FBI to not be able to size people up. He wasn't on Eve's level, but something was off with Jesse Murdoch. His eyes quickly went to every single place where Alex might be packing. He was looking for guns. Smart kid, but Alex wasn't strapped yet. Even the great and mighty Ian Taggart hadn't found a way to get a gun through public airport security.

"Don't pay any attention to him. He plays here from time to time, but only with the regulars. He's not a true Dom," Chazz said, puffing up a little.

What the fuck was a "true Dom"? *Idiot.* Alex simply nodded as though Chazz was obviously a member of the "True Dom Club." If that asshole was a Dom, Alex would eat his shoe.

"So, I heard you were also bringing a cousin along?" Chazz asked.

Sean. "Yes, Kris mentioned you needed someone to run the kitchen."

He shrugged. "Yeah, my last guy kind of sucked."

"He gave everyone food poisoning," Jesse added.

If he couldn't take down Evans for drug dealing and terrorism, at least he could call the health department in on the fucker. "I can assure you my cousin won't give anyone food poisoning."

Real poisoning was totally on the table, however. That hadn't slipped his mind. He would prefer to strangle the fucker, but the purpose of this whole exercise was to take Evans out, and he would do that any way he could. If he decided that the best path to a successful operation was a portion of deadly French fries, then that was the way he would go.

Fuck. He might have to think of something else because Sean had become a horrible food snob. He likely wouldn't

lower himself to make French fries. Alex had to hope that
Michael Evans liked foie gras.

Chazz leaned against one of the tables, his eyes
narrowing. "Your cousin did some time."

According to all his Adam-approved records, Sean
Reilly had spent time in prison for armed robbery and
assault. "He fell in with a bad crowd. We've all done that
from time to time."

"Yes, I did my own time, so I understand. You did a
little time, too."

That told him something. Chazz had a halfway decent
hacker on the staff. Adam had suggested a juvenile record
for Alex, something he could bury under a couple of layers
of bureaucracy. It was a little test, Adam had explained. He
wanted to know just how savvy these guys were so he
wouldn't underestimate them. As Adam was listening to
everything that was being said thanks to the micro wire he'd
placed on Alex's belt buckle, he was very likely formulating
his tech plans right now.

Alex frowned, acting surprised. "That record was
expunged."

If he could convince them he was just a dumb grunt,
they would trust him faster, speak more freely around him,
see him as no kind of threat.

Kristen put a hand on his arm and gave Chazz her own
frown, looking every inch the protective sister. "He was
seventeen, Chazz. You can't hold it against him."

Chazz held his hands up, a superior smile on his face.
"Hey, I don't hold nothing against nobody. But there's no
such thing as buried these days, not records or anything else.
You would do good to remember that. Big guy like you is
good to have around, if you know what I mean."

Alex damn well knew what he meant. He meant that it

was only a matter of time until he was in. He nodded. "Yeah, I want to be helpful, but my first order of business is to get this club in shape. Do I have any kind of budget?"

"Write it up and let me know what you need, but don't throw anything out without talking to me. Now, where are your other friends? Because Kris promised you were bringing along a sub of your own who can help train these dumb bitches. We have some bigwigs coming in a few weeks. They're very interested in 'playing' as we call it in our little world." He waved his hand at the women who were currently cleaning his club.

So they were basically using their subs as prostitutes. Nice. One more strike against the fucker, but it would fit with Evans's philosophies. It made for a problem though. "I don't share my sub."

He wasn't going to put Amanda in harm's way. She was simply here as backup. The last thing he needed was to worry about her being raped because these guys didn't take care of their women.

"Kris told me," Chazz said, holding a hand up. "She said you were a one-sub Dom. I don't get it, man. There's so much trim in the world. I couldn't hold myself to just one, but, hey, to each his own. I was a little surprised you let her off the leash long enough to fly here by herself."

Only because he seemed to be under a mistaken impression about how D/s relationships worked. "It was easier for her to fly in with Sean. I trust him. He'll take care of her."

"Yeah, you gotta have someone to keep an eye on your bitch," Chazz said.

Kristen squeezed his arm lightly. "Amanda is on her way. You're going to love her. She's practically the perfect sub. She'll have these women trained in no time."

Alex smiled. If Chazz kept calling what seemed like perfectly pleasant women bitches, he was going to strangle the fucker. Though he'd laughingly called Eve a bitch from time to time, it was with deep affection, the same way she would call him a righteous asshole. Still, the whole idea of Amanda walking through those doors and greeting him with a kiss put his gut in a knot. He should have played gay and brought Adam in. It would have been easier on him to kiss Adam than Amanda.

The door opened and a stream of late-afternoon light filtered in making a shadow of the woman walking in the door. She was followed by a big, bulky shadow. Sean. Alex released a long breath. He felt better with Sean here. His back was much safer than before.

Amanda walked through, and it looked like she'd followed his instructions to the letter. Her hair was longer than it had been before. He didn't know if it was a wig or extensions, but it would change her in a subtle way. And that was what he wanted, for her not to look exactly like Amanda King.

She moved out of the shadow and he caught a look at the new Amanda. He felt the smile slip off his face because she really didn't look like Amanda at all.

He blinked to clear his vision because he hadn't seen Amanda. He'd seen Eve, with chestnut-brown hair that brushed the tops of her breasts. She was dressed in the skimpiest clothes he'd ever seen her wear, a mini skirt that couldn't possibly cover her ass. It looked like someone had wrapped a bandage around her hips and called it a skirt. Her tank top molded to every inch of her torso, stopping roughly an inch above the skirt, giving him a glimpse of skin every time she moved.

And her freaking legs looked a million miles long in

what had to be five-and-a-half inch platforms. She was wearing the thin leather collar that should have been around Amanda's neck.

Eve. Eve was here, and she looked like sex in stilettos.

Kristen didn't miss a beat. She greeted Eve like they were the old friends they were supposed to be. "Hey, Mandy. How was the flight?"

"Great. Couldn't have been better." Eve smiled up at him.

Sean held out a hand in greeting. Nothing in his expression gave away the fact that the operation had just gone to hell. "Hey, brother." He looked around the club. "This is a shit hole."

"Nice, Sean." He forced himself to stay calm. "This is Chazz. He runs this shit hole. This is my cousin, Sean Reilly."

Chazz snorted a little. "Well, Reilly, that's why I'm hiring you and Master A. I want to class the place up a little before our big meetings. You're going to have to work fast because we have three VIPs coming in next week. It's what I like to call a dry run for the major meeting coming up in a couple of weeks. We're going to have to make this place classy for the big boss." Chazz's beady rat eyes took in every inch of flesh Eve was showing off. He didn't seem capable of hiding the leer on his face. "Though you already class the place up, sweetheart. I take back what I said, Master A. If I had that fine piece of ass in bed with me, maybe I could let the others go."

He started to see red, but Eve was right next him, a hand on his arm. She giggled. She actually giggled at that fucker and looked like a bubblehead who thought it was flattering to be called a piece of ass. "I think I'm going to like it here, Master."

Chazz winked and took another look at her legs before nodding toward his office. "I'll make sure you like it here. Now, let's get down to business. I think Kris can show Mandy around. Why don't we go upstairs and talk about what I need from you all over the next couple of weeks? Master A, if you'll join us."

Chazz didn't wait around, simply started up the stairs.

Sean put a hand on his shoulder, his head leaning in close. "Save the punishment for later, man. Don't blow the op because you're pissed."

Oh, but he was super pissed. And terrified. And volcanically angry at being maneuvered into a place where he had to allow her in or give up everything. And Sean was right. He had to think about this for two seconds. He glanced back at Eve.

"Here, sub."

Her eyes flared. Yeah, she wasn't used to him commanding her, but she was the one who had decided to blow all his plans to hell, so she would just have to handle the big bad Dom. And the big bad Dom wasn't about to play nice. Oh, no. He'd played things her way for far too long, and she wasn't going to come out of this unscathed.

Eve walked over, a tight smile on her face. "Yes, Master?"

He gripped the back of her neck. Even in those fuck-me shoes, she couldn't match his height. He forced her up on her toes. He brought his voice low. "We will discuss this in a few hours, sub. If you want to play, angel, we're going to play it my way. You want to take on the role of my slave? You better think about what that means. It means I'll have you the way I want you. I'll fuck you when I want, where I want, how I want, and I won't listen to your protests. You belong to me. Mine. You're fucking mine for however long

136

this lasts."

"Alex," she started.

He tightened the hand on her neck in warning. "That's Master, sub. And you'll feel the flat of my hand on your ass tonight right before you sink down to your knees and suck my cock. That's right. You're going to sleep in my bed tonight with my come in your belly. Still happy you walked through that door, Mandy?"

He let his mouth hover right above hers, but he wasn't going to let their first kiss in years happen in this place. Oh, it was going to happen, but not here and not when he was thinking about punishment that wasn't anywhere close to erotic.

There was a fire in her eyes he hadn't seen in forever. "Yes, Master."

He turned on his heels and forced himself to walk away, his brain warring between anger at her being in danger and a savage thrill that he had her where he'd wanted her for years.

In his power. In his bed.

* * * *

Eve watched Alex stalk up the stairs. Her hands trembled just slightly, but she had to get that under control. She couldn't give them all away now. She hadn't seen that much passion from Alex in years, and it scared the crap out of her.

It also got her heart fluttering, and all of her woman parts had responded in a way she'd forgotten was possible. She was standing in the middle of a dangerous operation, and she was a little worried her panties were damp. *Damn.*

The redhead was in front of her again, reaching for her

hands, taking them in her own. "I'm so happy you're finally here."

This must be the mysterious Kristen. "Me, too."

Kristen was good. She covered the shaking of Eve's hands with her own. Eve gave her a small smile and wondered if Kristen even knew she wasn't the woman who was supposed to be here.

"Hello." The man who hadn't followed the others up stared at her with a charming smile on his face. The minute Alex and the men had gone up the stairs, he'd switched from dark and broody to playboy.

He was gorgeous and far too young for her. She put him at twenty-five tops. Nope. He was a baby, despite his broad shoulders and bedroom eyes.

"Hey, Murdoch, get your ass up here," Chazz yelled from the top of the stairs.

Murdoch winked at her. "I guess the formal intros can wait. Later, babe."

He turned and ran up the stairs, and Eve managed not to roll her eyes. He could use a couple of seduction classes.

"Idiot. Come on, Mandy," Kristen said. "I'll show you the locker room and we can talk."

Eve glanced around the space. It had potential, but no one had taken it past very utilitarian. Two women were cleaning, one pushing a mop across the floor and another wiping down tables. The one running a cloth across the table was roughly thirty, with bleached blonde hair and far too much eye makeup. She frowned Eve's way, her painted lips turning down.

So she wasn't welcome by everyone.

She followed Kristen along the hallway to a small room.

"That's the men's locker room," Kristen said, pointing to a door on the left. "And this is us."

She pushed through an opaque glass door and into a very bland locker room. There was a row of old school lockers and a single bench seat.

Kristen flipped her strawberry blonde hair back and sat down on the bench, crossing her very long legs. "It's nice to meet you, Eve. I'm glad it's you and not that bratty ho-bag. What's up with guys? All they see is a bright smile, and they never look past a woman's tits until they get married and then they wonder why Mary Sunshine got replaced with Sally Yells a Lot."

Eve glanced around, trying to figure out if this Kristen person was about to get them in serious trouble.

Kristen waved a hand negligently. "No bugs in here. I check every day when I come in. Now the men's locker room is a different story. I bugged that myself, but don't warn your husband. We can listen in on him and the blond hottie talking about all sorts of things. Men totally gossip more than you think. We can talk freely in here as long as we're alone."

"How do you know who I am? And how do you know I'm not the bratty ho-bag?" Eve asked. She had to hand it to the girl. Her description was dead to rights.

She sat back and looked Eve up and down. "As to how I know you're not who Alex thought you would be, well, I'm a smart girl. I do my research. You are Dr. Eve St. James, only child to Donald and Jennifer St. James. You were the star of your high school debate team, on the swim team, and the editor of the Madison High Examiner. Busy girl. You graduated from Yale with top honors and everyone was sure you would go on and start a private practice. How upset were your parents when you joined the FBI's Behavioral Analysis Unit instead?"

She wasn't sure she liked how much Kristen knew

about her. "They were horrified, of course."

"Of course," Kristen said with a perfunctory nod. "Your father is one of the most respected therapists in the world."

And she'd been a profiler, a woman who dealt with the worst of the worst, the types her father didn't really believe in helping, and she couldn't make him understand that by catching criminals, she helped out everyone. He'd expected her to fall in line and take over his practice, but the idea of listening to overly privileged men and women complain about their nannies and kids and the horrors of being left off the maître d's list at the latest overpriced restaurant bored her to tears. She was happier profiling for Ian and having sessions with the people who needed her most. "Yes, he wasn't thrilled I chose the Bureau."

"Was he happy that you married Alexander McKay? He wasn't in your social class. Far from it, actually."

Eve held a hand up. "Is there a reason my father's reaction to Alex is relevant to this conversation?"

It was starting to annoy her. She felt like she was behind the redhead by more than a few steps.

Kristen gave her a bright smile. "I'm sorry. I'm going on and on. It's just that I've been studying you all for a while now. I'm afraid it's a little like meeting characters from a book you really enjoy reading."

Eve felt her eyes narrow in suspicion. "Why have you been studying me?"

"Because I knew I would need Alex McKay if I wanted to break this story. I couldn't go to the feds because I'm not sure that Evans doesn't have someone on the inside. McKay only has one side to work here and that's to take Evans down."

Eve got the gist. "He wants revenge for what Evans did to me. You're using that to your advantage."

"I simply prefer that the people I surround myself with have open motives that dovetail nicely with my own," Kristen explained. "To that end, I would advise you to keep an eye on Jesse Murdoch. I haven't figured out what he wants yet, and that makes him dangerous in my book. Actually, you could help me with that."

Eve let her lips curve up. "Yes, well, I think we can safely say he has an Oedipus complex."

Kristen snorted a little, shaking her head. "You're not old enough to be his mother. You're barely older than me, and I'm not willing to play the cougar yet."

"What do you get out of this, Kristen?" Eve never took her eyes off the other woman. She was usually quite good at detecting lies, and she wanted to see if Kristen had any tells.

Kristen stood, walking right up to Eve and offering her hands, proving once again that she was smarter than Eve had suspected. She held her arms out, palms up. "It's okay. Feel my pulse. Watch my eyes. I'm not going to lie to you, but I want you to feel perfectly safe with me."

Eve was game. She placed her fingers on Kristen's wrists, finding her pulse quickly. "What do you get out of this?"

"I get to put on the white hat for once. I get to help out some people who I truly believe need helping out, and I might just get a little redemption. I had a job go bad on me a couple of years back and I lost someone I love very much. I want to honor his memory by being better than I was before."

Her pulse stayed perfectly steady. There was no dilation to her eyes, and she never blinked or looked away. "Why Alex?"

"Because he always wore the white hat. And because I knew damn well he wouldn't pass up a chance to avenge you. He's trustworthy, and I know I can count on exactly what he will do. He's a known quantity. You're the unknown. Why are you here?"

Eve let Kristen's hands go. Either Kristen was a sociopath or she wasn't lying. Sociopaths could often pass lie detector tests because they simply didn't feel enough to show physical signs when they were lying. "I'm here to watch Alex's back."

"You're not here for Evans?"

She felt a shudder go through her. "No."

"Not even a little?"

"No."

"Now that does surprise me." Kristen walked to one of the lockers and worked the wheel of the lock there.

It was odd. She actually thought the other woman sounded a little disappointed. "Why is that?"

The locker came open, and Kristen pulled out her bag. "I guess I thought you would be the type of woman who would want to go after Evans."

"I don't want revenge." She never really had. She'd just wanted it to be over and then she'd wanted everything to be normal.

"I wasn't talking about revenge. I thought you would go after him so he could never do it again. So no other woman would have to go through what you went through. I guess I read too much into it. I didn't think you would want to hide from it."

Eve bristled a little. "I'm not hiding."

"But you're also not here to take out Evans. It's okay, but you should understand that is my goal. I'm going to make sure he can't hurt women anymore. Because it's the right thing to do and I do the right thing now."

"I'm not hiding." She wasn't hiding from anything. She

142

was trying to rebuild her life. "I'm just here to make sure Alex doesn't kill himself."

"Well, as long as we understand each other. I'm sure we can get along. You watch Alex's back and I'll handle the investigation part on the girl end. Was that really Sean Taggart?" She glanced back toward the door. "He's Ian Taggart's younger brother, right? I thought he would be bigger."

Sean was six foot three. "He's only small compared to Ian. There's a reason they call him Little Tag."

"Big Tag and Little Tag. That's cute." She settled the bag on her shoulder. "You have to watch out for Sienna and Sage. They're twins and they're mean-girl subs. They'll very likely be all over Master A as soon as they lay eyes on him. Chazz tends to use them as arm candy when he entertains. That can happen in or out of the club, which is precisely why I needed someone on the inside. He always takes bodyguards with him, but I can't trust any of them. It was a lucky thing that his last two bodyguards ran off. No idea where they went."

Now Kristen's irises flared just the tiniest bit. A lie. She'd done something to force the guards to leave. Very interesting. "Yeah, I'm sure that was a lucky happenstance."

"Hey, a girl does what a girl has to do." Kristen shrugged and got back to her rundown. "The waitresses run the gamut from dumb but well-meaning to annoying. Bunny is exactly what she's named for. Fluffy and sweet. Karma is all right. I think she's probably the most self-destructive of the group. Azure is the one who gave you the evil eye as you walked in. But the one you really have to watch out for is Chazz."

"What's he capable of?" Eve asked.

"I think he's capable of anything, and I'm lucky he has

143

a thing for me or I would be screwed. The key with Chazz is to pretend like he's the shit. The minute he knows you think you're above him, he'll slit your throat without a single thought. Never drop the submissive routine. He talks like a dumb shit, but he's serious, and in his head, you're a slave and he's the ultimate Master and he controls everything. If he decides it's easier to kill you than keep you, he'll do it."

He sounded like he had a lot in common with Michael Evans. "How has he gotten away with this?"

"I think he's got someone on the inside who's protecting him. A couple of cops come to the club from time to time. Chazz has his connections. Remember that. This isn't Sanctum. This is Hell, and we all just have to try to survive. They should be done soon. I'm going to go make sure the car is ready. Meet you back at the bar."

Kristen walked out and Eve deflated.

What was she doing? She wasn't a field operative. God, had she made a terrible mistake?

She sat down on the bench, trying to process everything the other woman had just told her, but all she could do was think about the fact that "the big boss" would be here in a few weeks. That was what Chazz had said. If Kristen was right, Michael Evans was the boss, and he would breathe the same air as her in a matter of weeks.

You're just a little whore. That's all any of you are.

She shivered in the cool of the room and closed her eyes, thinking soothing thoughts. It was the only way to make the bad images go away. She deserved her peace. She deserved to have a life that wasn't filled with the man who had raped her. She was a damn psychologist. She wasn't some warrior princess. She'd taken plenty of self-defense classes, but she hoped she wouldn't have to use them.

She wasn't hiding. She was helping out. She was here

because she was the best person for the job and because Alex was her responsibility.

Her brain floated back to the day she'd told her parents she was marrying Alex. She hadn't told Kristen what their response had been. They'd been all smiles on the day she and Alex had married, but they hadn't been happy about it. Her mother and father had planned on her marrying a doctor or a lawyer, not an FBI agent. Alex had been too rough for them, too possessive, too real.

Her parents hadn't known about the life they'd led. She'd hidden it from them. They still didn't know.

She wasn't hiding.

Eve stood up, straightening her clothes. Well, what there was of her clothes. Damn it. Why had she come here?

To make sure Alex survived. That was why she was here. That was why Sean was here. No matter what that Kristen girl said, she wasn't hiding and she had a purpose.

She glanced at the mirror, smoothing back her hair. Evans didn't matter. Alex was the only thing that mattered.

She turned. She would figure it out later. Right now, all that mattered was getting through the next couple of hours until she could talk to Alex and make him understand that nothing had really changed between them. She'd thought about changing their contract, but that had been a mistake.

I'll fuck you when I want, where I want, how I want, and I won't listen to your protests. You belong to me. Mine. You're fucking mine for however long this lasts.

Nothing had changed? He seemed to think so. He seemed to think she had a real role to play. His sub. His slave. His.

His to command. His to control. His to fuck and love and satisfy.

It was like a drug she'd managed to kick long ago.

Submitting to Alex had always been a high. She hadn't needed to think about anything when Alex was in control. She only needed to feel, to give over.

And that hadn't gone well. That had ended in pain and misery.

No. She wasn't going down that path. Nothing had changed between them. They were still divorced. They still had all of the same problems that had been between them since the incident with Evans. This was just a job.

She walked out the door, determined to put a good face on things, and ran straight into a nicely cut chest. She just about fell back, but two hands gripped her arms, balancing her so she didn't fall.

"Hello again." Jesse Murdoch loomed over her, his handsome face staring down. Sandy blond hair and ice blue eyes. He really was perfection with his sensual lips and a strong jaw, but no one had moved her since the moment she'd caught sight of Alexander McKay. No other man would ever make her heart race. No other man would ever force her pulse to pound through her body. She could appreciate them on an intellectual level, but there was no man for her but Alex McKay.

But she had to play a part now. She smiled up at him. He was the one Kristen couldn't figure out. If there was one thing Eve could really contribute to the team, it was her instincts for the human psyche. But she needed him to trust her first. "Hi. Is my Master finished with the meeting?"

She wasn't going to lead him on. He needed to know she was the "good girl." Men would do a lot for a woman they seriously considered to be innocent and pure. Jesse had that look about him.

He smiled, but there was a sadness to it. "So you're pretty much into him, huh?"

She put a hand on the collar at her throat. "He's my Master. I would hope I would like him."

"Sometimes that's not the case around here." He was still standing close, but something had changed. The tension was gone. He was just friendly now. "Sometimes a woman stays with a man because they don't have anywhere else to go."

She took particular note that he'd called her a woman and not a sub. He hadn't followed her lead. It could mean nothing or it could mean that he wasn't as invested in the lifestyle as he wanted them to believe. Jesse Murdoch wanted to be the white knight. He wanted to charge in and save someone. Unfortunately for him, she didn't need saving. "I love him."

He sighed a little. "Fine. All the pretty ones love someone else. Anyway, if you need anything, you call for me. If your man isn't around, you call for me. Can you do that for me, sweetheart?"

"She isn't going to do anything except to step away from you and get her ass to my side."

There was that voice that had a direct line to all her pink parts. Alex stood in the hallway, his big body taking up all the space. Jesse was just as big, just as broad, but somehow he didn't fill the space the way Alex did.

Eve stepped away, and the minute she came within arm's length of Alex, he pulled her close and forced her behind him as though there was a threat just waiting to take her out.

"I don't know how this club has worked up until this moment, but I just officially became the Dom in Residence here, so this just became, for all intents and purposes, my club. So I'm going to teach you the first rule of this club. Don't you fucking touch my sub. Mine. That collar on her neck was placed there by me. She belongs to me, and this isn't some happy little office where there are civilized rules and I have to put up with you hitting on my woman with a smile and hope that she doesn't reciprocate. This isn't the civilized world and the next time I find you alone with my submissive, I'll make sure you never do it again. Am I clear?" He was a caveman, a Neanderthal, a freaking possessive maniac, and she kind of wanted to do him hard right then.

"Clear as crystal, boss." But there was a grin on Jesse's face.

"It better be."

Eve wanted to say something, to protest, but this wasn't the place. Alex turned, grabbing her hand and starting down the hall.

She practically ran to keep up with him. Nothing had changed? She was fooling herself because from the moment she decided to get on that plane, everything had changed.

She just needed to figure out how to deal with the fallout.

* * * *

Jesse Murdoch watched the ridiculously titled Master A walk away, his shoulders squared off and a possessive arm around his...what did they call her? Submissive? Why did they have to fuck things up with different names for shit? He wasn't sure he got the whole BDSM thing.

Scratch that. He was damn sure he didn't get that shit. It seemed an awful lot like a way to abuse a woman to him.

The first few times he'd had to watch Chazz take a whip to one of the girls had sent him straight to the bottom of a bottle. He still wasn't sleeping, but fuck, he never slept.

Every time he closed his eyes, he could see the dirty cell that had been his home for so long, smell the shit and piss and blood that had been his life.

The brunette turned slightly, her eyes trailing behind, finding him.

He had to admit, she was a looker. A little thin for his tastes, but there was an almost innocent appeal to her. He gave her a smile and she turned away, disappearing down the hallway with her psychotic boyfriend.

Was Master Asshole the one who had given her those scars on her neck? Fucker.

The new Dom and his pretty punching bag were more than just a curiosity for Jesse. They were a complication he didn't need.

He glanced once and then twice down the hallway. Empty. By nightfall, the whole place would be buzzing and a mad sort of chaos would take over, but, for now, all was quiet.

Like he liked it.

He slipped inside the women's locker room. He had to use the women's locker room because some asswipe had bugged the men's. No prying eyes or ears in there this time of day. He gave the whole place a quick lookie-loo. No one in the stalls or the showers. He shoved a trashcan in front of the door. It wouldn't keep anyone out, but it would let him know if someone was coming in.

He moved back to the shower stalls and pulled out his cell phone, the one he kept in his boot along with his knife. He had two cells. This one was utterly untraceable and had only one number programmed in. Jesse hit the button and waited.

"You have something for me?" His contact was always succinct.

"A couple of new players."

"Names?"

"Anthony Priest and Amanda King. I just met them. Chazz brought them in to, I don't know, I think they're supposed to fuck in front of a crowd or something." He was still a little hazy on what the dickwad was supposed to do. "He's forty or so. Buzz cut. A couple of tats. She's a brunette with some scars. Nice tits. She's less mouthy than Kris. The dude is Kris's brother."

"Really? Because as of three months ago, she didn't have a brother."

He should have known. "Fuck."

"Calm down. There's a reason you leave the intelligence work to me. You're a useful vessel, Murdoch, but you're a soldier."

He wasn't anymore. He'd lost that as surely as his honor had been stripped away, along with his humanity. "Who the fuck is he, then? And why did he show up now? If Kris is pulling some shit, what does she know that I don't?"

It sat in his gut—this feeling that she was on top of him. She wasn't what she said she was. He knew that even before he'd been told to watch out for her. But his contact didn't want her touched. Not yet. Somehow, it had been there in the back of his head that maybe she played for the same team as him, and he'd been brutally surprised to discover it wasn't true.

He didn't want to kill her, but he would if he had to.

"Just lay low for now." His contact had a deep voice. He'd never met the contact, only been given a phone number along with living expenses and the keys to a rathole loft he'd quickly turned into his little hidey-hole, but he'd seen pictures of the man. "I want everything in place when it's time for me to come in."

That was his job. Make things right. "What do you need from me?"

"Well, I seriously doubt that Anthony Priest is anything but an alias. I need pictures. I want pictures of him and the woman who's with him. Do it quietly. I don't want them to suspect a thing. You've gotten close to Chazz?"

"I'm in the inner circle. He's a loyal employee from everything I can tell."

"See that he stays that way. I want reports on anything out of the ordinary. And if it comes to it, I might need you to take out the new guy."

Jesse took a long breath. This was kind of what he'd been dreading and hoping for since the moment he'd decided to move to the dark side. What his father had done was all pure and white hat, but this was something different. It was all he had left. "Yeah, I can snuff him if I need to."

"And the girl?"

He'd never killed a woman before. He swallowed once and then again. He wasn't sure he could, but he knew what he had to say. "Yeah. I'll do her, too, if I have to."

His contact chuckled over the line. He seemed to have a dark sense of humor, but then that wasn't so surprising. "It's good to know I can count on you."

The line went dead, and Jesse shoved the phone back in his boot. He moved quickly, exiting the locker room before anyone came in. He shoved the trash can back into place and found the hallway empty. He made his way back out on the floor just in time to see Kristen leave with her so-called brother and the pretty brunette he might have to kill.

His stomach turned a little at the thought. Not that he would have to kill her, but that he might like it. He might like it a lot. He was an addict. Oh, he wasn't addicted to anything so cheap as liquor or meth. He'd become a little addicted to violence, to spilling blood, and he'd been off his own personal sauce for a while now. He was worried that this time, he might not be able to come back.

But he would do it because it was his job, and it was the only fucking thing he had left. Maybe he was still a soldier deep down, and a soldier didn't falter when the job at hand was a little nasty.

He watched as the big guy shoved out the front door, holding it open for his woman. She was so small compared to him. She had scars that proved her life wasn't that great. Maybe he would be freeing her in the end.

It didn't matter. He had to keep his head in the game. Amanda King didn't matter. Kristen Priest would go, too. Hard decisions would be made, and he would carry them out. He steeled himself.

Anything for the mission.

Chapter Seven

Alex pulled the SUV into the underground parking garage, his every movement a precise response to nearly going out of control. He'd been on autopilot since the moment he'd realized Eve was here and in danger and had actively attempted to wreck his plans.

It was a betrayal. It burned in his gut. She was sitting behind him, but he kept glancing back at the rearview mirror, looking at her, trying to make eye contact. His brain was working overtime trying to figure out exactly what she was doing. His heart and head had been racing ever since she'd walked through the door.

Watching her smile up at that far too young for her himbo had done nothing to calm him down. Too young for her? Was Jesse Murdoch really too young for her? Or was Alex getting too old? He'd thought seriously about choking the fucker when he'd walked in on Jesse looming over Eve. The younger man had her practically pressed against the wall as he talked to her. Did Jesse think he'd invented that move? Dumb fuck.

"What floor are we on?" Sean asked from the passenger-side seat, his voice pulling Alex back into the here and now.

"My place is on three, but the whole building is protected. There's a security guard at the gate to the island. Once you're here, you have to have a key fob to get into the building from the front or side doors. Even if someone can get into the building, the elevators are protected. You have to put a passcode in to get to the right floor," Kristen said, leaning forward. She was sitting in the back with Eve. "I see Adam is already here."

The spot beside them was already taken by a non-descript sedan. Adam had been given everything he needed to set up his equipment. "Do we only have the two slots?"

The parking was assigned.

"Yes," Kristen explained. "When Sean's car is delivered, one of us is going to have to park in front of the building. There's a side door that takes you straight to the elevator. There's one on each side of the building, so in all there are four points of entry, the garage, two side doors, and the main entry where guests have to go."

It seemed fairly secure, better than he would get if they were at a motel. "The last one in parks outside. How many bedrooms do you have?"

"I have three. Adam is already set up in one. I thought Eve and I would share."

No fucking way. "Eve stays with me."

She'd made her bed and she was definitely going to lie in it with him.

"Alex, we don't need to play games outside the club," Eve said in a far too patient voice. She'd been the calm one, the easy one to deal with. She hadn't been snippy with anyone and everyone who asked a question or had a comment. And it was pissing him off. He was a volcano waiting to go off, and she was an ocean of calm.

He put the car in park, slammed out of his side, and hit the button to release the trunk. He stalked around to the passenger side of the back and had Eve's door open before she could do it herself. He turned his back because if he laid a hand on her at this point, he just might have her over his knee right then and there. Getting the luggage was easier than dealing with Eve.

Even from the parking garage he could smell the salt in the air, hear the sound of the Atlantic hitting the shore. It was a soothing sound that did nothing to ease his anxiety.

What the hell was he supposed to do?

Sean walked up beside him and leaned in, grabbing his suitcase and a rolled up piece of luggage that he'd explained contained his knife set. He'd checked it at the airport but had been carrying it around ever since. "Don't do something stupid. You need to think about this for two seconds."

"I don't think I have to do something stupid. You already did that for me." Sean should have made sure Eve was safe at home. It was what he would have done for Sean.

Sean shook his head. "You're my friend, but she's my friend, too, Alex. If I had stopped her, she would have shown up anyway and then everything would have really gone to hell."

"Yeah, I think that was her plan. She tried to talk me out of this. She couldn't get her way so she manipulated the situation until I had to make a choice. I could give up looking for Evans or place her in danger. I'm either doing her bidding or I'm the bad guy, but that's the way the last few years of our relationship have been."

"I never made you the bad guy, Alex," Eve said, her voice as steady as when she talked to her patients. He was getting her shrink voice. Awesome. She stood there, her grave eyes staring him down, and he felt like the bad guy. He was the asshole who always let her down.

He didn't want to have this conversation here with witnesses. Hell, he didn't want to have this conversation at all. He nabbed his bags and shoved Eve's on top of his and started to follow the arrows that led to the elevators.

He was such an idiot. She was topping from the bottom and here he was still carrying her fucking bags around because he couldn't stand the thought of not doing it. Because a long time ago, he'd promised her father that he would treat her like a princess for the rest of her life, and she was still alive so he was still held to that vow and that meant Eve St. James didn't carry her own bags or open her own doors.

And she sure as fuck wasn't sleeping alone tonight. There was a limit to his generosity.

"This is fun. All we need is some popcorn because this is a whole lot of drama." Kristen gave him a wink as she walked through the door he held open. The elevator was immediately to his left. The door between the garage and the elevator was open, but the garage itself had a gate and a remote entry and security on site. Eve walked through next and then Sean.

Alex looked around. He needed to get his head out of his ass and start assessing their situation. This was going to be their home for the next couple of weeks. He needed to figure out the weaknesses.

"I count two CCTV cameras. One right behind you." Sean held up his middle finger with a smile. "Hello, Adam." He shrugged. "You know he's already watching. It probably took him like five seconds on arrival to cut into the feed."

Eve and Kristen were standing next to the elevator, just out of range. He lowered his voice. He just couldn't fucking let this go. "Why would you do this to me? Adam, I get. He's always been closer to Eve, but I didn't expect it from you."

Sean frowned. "I did not betray you, and Kristen is right. You sound like a drama queen. Eve is not some girl off the street. She's Eve St. James, and she's smart and more capable of doing this particular job than anyone else. I brought her here for the same reason I came here myself. To watch your back because you are not capable of being reasonable about this. So calm yourself down before you do something truly stupid. Every single one of us walked away from something to be here to back you up, and we did it because we're a family. Every one of us except that girl you're placing so much trust in. She's hiding something."

He didn't like looking at himself through the filter of Sean's eyes. "I wouldn't have brought Grace into this. Never."

Sean's eyes rolled. "Grace isn't a trained agent so no, of course, you wouldn't have brought my wife here. It's a completely different scenario. I'm going to give you a piece of advice and you can take it or leave it. This is your last shot with her. If you bungle it, I think she's going to leave permanently, and there is no way you recover from that. You can think that the last few years have been bad, but nothing is going to be worse than not being able to watch over her. She's here because she loves you whether she can say it or not. So make sure she can say it. She placed herself in your hands, in your complete control."

Alex huffed at the very idea. He knew exactly how this would go. He had been playing this game for five years with her. "Eve thinks she can play the role at the club and then do what she likes outside of it. It's the way she's worked ever since the divorce."

"This isn't Sanctum, man." Sean reached out and gave his arm a brotherly smack. "This is an op. What's the first thing Ian taught all of us?"

"Live the op so the op can't die." Don't break cover. Live and breathe the cover. It was the only way to survive. Eve's cover was to be Master A's sub.

157

His submissive.

"Are you two going to stand around holding the door open forever or do you want to come see my party pad?" Kristen asked. Eve simply stood by the elevator, a wary look on her face.

He kind of liked that look. She was always so sure of him, so sure she could handle him. It was good to know he had her off-kilter for once. "We're coming."

He crowded her, forcing her to the back of the elevator.

"Do you have to stand so close?" Eve asked, her eyes turning up.

It was time to start laying out some ground rules. "You're my sub. There's no such thing as personal space for you. Not when it comes to me. You act like this out in the field and you're going to give us away."

"We're not in the field. We're in the elevator." She didn't sound quite so calm now. She spoke in a breathy, slightly shaky voice, the one that let him know she was off her game. She stared at a place just below his chin, as though she couldn't quite look him in the eyes.

He forced her chin up, bringing those chocolate brown eyes to meet his own. Thank god she hadn't covered up her eye color. "We're always in the field, pet. I'm going to call you pet most of the time because I just can't bring myself to call you Mandy. It doesn't fit. Pet is so much better. It's more descriptive of just what role you're going to play."

Her jaw firmed and those perfectly waxed eyebrows climbed up in a stubborn expression. "If you're trying to scare me off, it won't work."

"I can't scare you off, pet. You took that choice away from both of us. If I do that then I have to leave the whole operation behind, and I'm not going to run home with my tail between my legs. Sean seems to think you're competent.

Tomorrow you can prove it. You're back on training sessions."

Her eyes flared. "I don't need training sessions, Alex. I've been your sub for a long damn time. I think I can handle myself at the club."

He let a little smirk cross his mouth as he pressed her further against the wood panels of the elevator cab. "Not that kind of training. Self-defense. Exercise. If you want to be in the field with me, you'll be trained by me."

"This place comes equipped with a full workout room. It's really nice," Kristen added helpfully as the elevator dinged and opened, the doors revealing some sort of private entry hall.

Eve frowned up at him. "I don't know that training sessions are necessary."

"Well, then it's good you're not in charge, isn't it? I'm in charge of this operation and you're going to follow my command or we can have a very quick breakup and I can find another sub." He felt marginally better having taken control. Or maybe it was the Asian waterfall that greeted him. The small entry hall was decorated in dark reds, the focal piece a lovely stone water fountain that ran from the ceiling to the floor and gave the whole space a serene feeling.

And let Alex know that Kristen had serious cash.

Maybe Sean had a point. He needed to stop thinking about Eve for two seconds and get his head in the op.

Eve followed after him, those hooker heels she was wearing clicking along the marbled floors. The skirt she was wearing hugged her ass and made his mouth water. He'd had that woman a thousand different ways and he still couldn't wait to do it again, couldn't stop counting every second between now and when he could be inside her again.

The minute Kristen opened the door, Eve strode right by him, not bothering to look back. She brushed by Adam, who was waiting for them, and Alex heard her asking Kristen which room was theirs. At least she wasn't going to fight him on that. Kristen followed her, leaving the men to themselves.

"Dude, she is pissed. Tell me the op isn't off," Adam said, turning to watch Eve as she talked to Kristen in what seemed to be the dining room.

"I believe she's pissed because the op is still on," Alex replied. "Either that or she's not looking forward to our daily workouts. So let's get on with it. What do you have for me, Adam?"

Adam's hands went up in sheer defeat. "Let's clear some things up before we move on. I would like to have it on the record that I am merely here as the tech guy. No workouts required. I'm a married man. I can totally let myself go now. Speaking of letting myself go, Sean, my man, you're here. What's for dinner?"

Sean snorted a little. "I don't know. I'll have to check out what Miss Mysterious has in her fridge. I'm going to go unpack and call my wife. Let me know if you need me, but I think this really is Adam's expertise."

Adam's eyebrows raised in question. "Is he asking about the work-up on Jesse Murdoch that I already have done? Because I know everything, of course."

Adam could be a pain in the ass, but he was damn good at his job. "Give me the story on him."

Adam walked up to the table in the living area and slapped a folder on it. The table looked like the rest of the condo. It was a rich, dark wood and had Asian influences, though with all the computer equipment and wires covering it, Alex could only think that it was from an Early Nerd

Period.

The folder Adam opened contained a picture of Jesse Murdoch and what looked to be a hefty dossier. "Jesse Murdoch. Age twenty-seven and some change. Born in the wilds of Wyoming. Mom was a waitress. Dad was a cop. Shot in the line of duty three months before Jesse was born. Apparently, mom couldn't handle it. She dropped him off at granddad's place one day and never looked back. Now she managed to get her shit together later, but she married some wealthy guy and never even sent the kid a birthday card from what I could tell. He has three half siblings, but I don't think he's met them. Tough breaks. Anyway, he helped out on his granddad's ranch until it went belly up. Granddad dies, and where does a kid who has absolutely nothing end up?"

Alex knew that story well. "Prison or the military."

Adam touched a finger to his nose. "He was in the Army. Lucky, lucky us. I spoke to some of my contacts there while you were driving in from the club. The word was he was being recruited for special ops when he was taken prisoner. He spent a couple of months as a guest of one of the jihadist armies. Most of his unit died in the ambush. Nasty IED. Took out the Humvee they were in. He was taken in with three other soldiers from his unit. He was the only one to survive."

Alex whistled as he looked through the pages of documents Adam had already assembled. "Shit. Was this the incident where they beheaded three of our soldiers?"

It had been a big story a couple of years back. The government had tried to keep it off the mainstream media, but no one could stop the Internet. The group had beheaded good, honest soldiers to further their political interests.

"They executed everyone but Murdoch, including a

female sergeant. When the extraction team found him, he was still alive. He was immediately relieved of duty. The official word was for PTSD."

But Alex knew there was more to that story. "They were worried he'd turned. They couldn't trust him with intel. I saw it on the news, but he almost immediately went into hiding and the story died down. Poor bastard."

Adam frowned. "Unless he actually turned and gave up his teammates."

There had been times when Alex's name and reputation were all he had. He couldn't imagine a whole country questioning him. What had Jesse Murdoch really been through? And how had it twisted him?

He was definitely someone Alex wanted to keep his eye on. "So what's he doing here? How long has he been in Florida?"

"About three months, from what I can tell," Adam replied. "He's been doing odd jobs up and down the coast, keeping a low profile. He did some security work in Virginia for a while, but he drifted down this way and, as far as I can tell, he was hired on at the club ten weeks ago. Other than the fact that he works for a criminal prick, he doesn't have any kind of a record. Not so much as a parking ticket."

But he was working as a heavy for a nightclub that almost certainly laundered money for a terrorist. And he'd been held by terrorists for three months, more than enough time for a man to be indoctrinated into radicalism. Brainwashing was just another tool in a terrorist's kit. Was Jesse Murdoch a sleeper? "Keep working that angle. I might need you to do some surveillance on him. Is Jake in town?"

He asked the question very quietly. Kristen didn't need to know every single player he had on the board. He was willing to trust her, but only so far.

Adam nodded. "Jake and Serena are set up in a rental two buildings down from us in case we need him. Why doesn't Kristen want the whole team here? Why does she want to split us up?"

"She thinks too many new faces around might cause some questions to be asked, but she doesn't know how good my team is. Just keep it quiet. From what I understand, the crowd at the club is quite rowdy most nights. They'll blend in nicely. I want someone to have eyes on her."

Adam nodded. "Will do." His voice came back to normal as Kristen walked into the living room. "You'll be happy to know your place isn't bugged."

"Checked for that, did you?" She shrugged. "I expect you to be thorough, Adam. I'm an open book. Check any records on me you like."

Adam crossed his arms over his chest as he studied Kristen. "I did. There aren't a whole lot of them. I read a couple of your articles, but I was surprised you didn't put pictures with the byline. Most big reporters do these days."

She sank down onto a formal-looking couch, her shoes already tossed aside. If she was deeply disturbed by the fact that her place now looked like Hacker Central, she didn't show it. "The celebrity ones do, yes. They don't usually do deep-cover reporting. I'm part reporter and part investigator. I can't do my job if I'm on the news every night showing off my designer duds. I'm careful about pictures getting out. Did you read the story about a Peruvian cartel working with the government there? I worked on that one for over a year. Don't you think they would love a picture of me to hang on their offices? I cost a bunch of high-ranking officials their jobs. I don't smile for the camera, but then neither do you, Mr. Miles. I didn't find a Facebook page on you with five thousand friends and pictures of your pregnant wife."

Adam's whole body got tense. "How did you know she's pregnant?"

"Because I traffic in information and I am damn good at my job. If I just wanted to connect Evans to the club, I could probably do that on my own, but I think there's something more happening here. Beyond that, Evans is a very bad man and if I have to choose between a great story or justice for the people he's killed and the women he's torn to shreds, then I will choose justice, and I can only get that through men like you. So run all the little bug hunters through the house that you like. Tap my phone. Snoop through my computer and tell Little Tag in there he can give me all the nasty looks he likes. I'm not going anywhere, and he can't intimidate me. I've been in shark-filled waters and managed to stare them all down." She stood back up, gesturing to her left. "The kitchen is that way. Alex, I'm giving you and Eve the master suite because I'm such a romantic at heart. Sean and Adam can share the room with the twin beds and I'll be next to them. There are balcony entries from every bedroom. Make sure the security system is off before you take a stroll. Goodnight, gentlemen. Tomorrow's a long day. And, by the way, tell Sean that he's nowhere near as hot as his brother. And if you want to ask how I know that, it's because my eyes work."

"It's a nice speech." Adam was still looking at her with suspicious eyes. "I hope you are who you say you are."

She shrugged. "If you decide I'm not trustworthy, shoot me in the gut because it would be a real loss to mar my boobs. They're real, by the way. Night."

She walked off, not looking back.

"Holy shit, I think she scares me a little." Sean edged back in the room having obviously heard everything. "You've pissed off every woman on the team today."

Alex stared after her. She was interesting. "I didn't piss her off. It was Adam."

"I don't like not being able to find the information I want on someone. Two grainy photos were all I could find of her," Adam admitted. "Still, I can understand why she wouldn't want her face out there. She took down a whole local government in Peru. I also read an article she wrote that linked the Russian mob to art theft in New York. Apparently because of her, several masterpieces that were lost during World War II have been recovered."

He believed her. There was something deeply sincere about her. She could be playing them all, but he didn't think so. "That had to piss people off. The Russian mob doesn't like to have their schemes revealed. So she's a smart woman. She hasn't lied about anything."

"Yet," Sean said.

"What is your beef with her?" Alex had to admit that he kind of liked her. She was tough.

Sean frowned, looking at the hallway she'd disappeared down. "I don't know. It's the way she looked at me. Like she knew me. I just have a feeling, but then I've been out of the game for a while now. I'm going to go start dinner. Hopefully she has something I can fix. And I'm so much hotter than Ian. The woman obviously needs to have her eyes checked."

Sean walked off toward the kitchen, and Adam moved back to his room.

Alex stared at the ocean in front of him. The entire back wall of the condo was floor to ceiling windows. Because of their height, from where he stood it looked as though there was nothing but endless ocean in front of him. The sun was starting to set, the sky turning orange and red.

Such a lovely sight.

He heard a shower start up. Eve. He had every right to walk into that room and watch her shower. He had every right to join her.

"Hey, she has excellent taste in Scotch, man." Sean was grinning, holding out a couple of tumblers and a bottle of Glenlivet.

"Pour me a double, man." Alex took his liquid gold and let himself out on the balcony. Warm wind brushed against his skin. He stepped up to the railing and could see the roll of the dunes and green palmettos that covered them.

There was plenty of time to figure out how much danger they were all in. Tonight he had to decide how to handle the fact that he was going to sleep next to Eve for the first time in years.

If he slept at all.

* * * *

Eve moved out of the bedroom to the balcony. The master suite was located on the ocean side of the condo, and she could see the moonlight glimmering off the waves. The sound of the surf was methodical and soothing, but she couldn't find a way to calm herself.

Alex hadn't spoken more than two words to her at dinner. He'd talked to everyone else, but ignored her except to see that she had what she needed.

He'd made sure she had the choicest cut of steak and had put a large portion of truffled mashed potatoes on her plate before getting his own helping.

And she'd eaten it even when she knew she shouldn't. Damn Sean. She couldn't pass up his artistry. Maybe she would need those training sessions.

"Go back to bed, Eve."

She'd already been to bed, and there was no way she could sleep in that big bed while waiting to see what Alex was going to do. She'd half expected him to walk in and demand every right she'd denied him for the last five years. She had to make him see that she hadn't betrayed him. "I knew you wouldn't call off the op."

He had a glass in his hand. She couldn't tell exactly what was in it, but she would bet it was Scotch. All the men in her life seemed to turn to Scotch. "Did you?"

He'd shrugged out of his shirt when he'd walked through the room ten minutes before. She'd rested there in bed, waiting for him to come in and start laying down the law as her Master, but he'd simply turned off the security system and slid out onto the balcony wearing nothing but a pair of jeans that hugged his ass.

"Yes, I knew there was no way to stop you, so I came with you. Amanda can't handle an op like this. You were being reckless when you chose her to watch your back."

He took a long sip from the glass before answering. "I have Sean to watch my back. I just needed Amanda to look pretty and keep her mouth closed."

She took a long breath and prayed for a little patience. "Which just shows that you don't know her at all. Amanda isn't known for keeping her mouth shut. She likes to insult every single female around her. She also has a deep-seated need to please whoever she considers to be the alpha male of a group. What happens if she decides Chazz is the alpha male?"

Alex turned, an arrogant look on his face. "Really? That little weasel?"

He wasn't thinking at all. "Just being the biggest and the best looking doesn't make you top dog, Alex. Chazz has power, and Amanda would be attracted to that."

He frowned and ran a hand over his nearly non-existent hair. There was maybe a quarter inch of his dark brown hair left. He'd buzzed it, and he'd been right to do it. It changed his features, making him look harder, leaving nothing to detract from the stark, masculine lines of his face. "Fine, I should have vetted her better, but you had no right to replace her without consulting me. This is my op. I don't want you here."

Well, he couldn't put that any more harshly. He didn't want her. Fine. She could handle that. She was tough, and he was stuck with her now. "I can do the job, Alex. It's not my first rodeo. I will grant you I don't have the field experience that Ian does, but until Ian decides to hire another couple of females, you're stuck with me. You needed a woman for this job and you needed one you can trust."

"I needed one who wouldn't fuck everything up."

Hurt flared through her system. "Are you calling me incompetent?"

He sighed and turned around again. "No. I would never call you that. I'm calling you a distraction I don't need. I need to be sleeping or working on this case, but my dumb ass is standing out here thinking about the fact that I haven't kissed you on the lips in five years and I feel like a stupid kid hoping I don't fuck it up."

Her heart softened immediately. God, she hadn't thought about what it would mean to really be here with Alex. They'd been on plenty of undercover operations before, but never one that forced them together with such intimacy. Somehow, the thought of kissing Alex scared her far more than the operation. She'd been able to hold herself apart from him because she'd only allowed him sex and discipline. Kissing was different. Kissing was intimate.

She'd never forgotten the way Alex had kissed her—

like she was the only woman in the whole world and he couldn't get enough of her.

Kissing was dangerous.

"Alex, maybe we should talk about this."

"All you ever want to do is talk. I'm not your patient. I'm your husband."

Just the word could make her ache. "We're divorced. We have been for a long time."

He laughed, a bitter little huff. "I'll always be your husband. Just because you chose to sign a piece of paper and forced me to sign it too doesn't mean I don't feel like your husband."

"I didn't force you to sign anything." And in her calmer, more reflective moments, she could even admit that the divorce had been a drastic measure. She'd wanted to jar Alex out of the angry place he'd been in and force him to see her again.

He'd simply signed the papers and continued to look for Michael Evans.

"I asked you what you wanted and you said you wanted a divorce, so I gave it to you, but I didn't even move out of our house, Eve. It wasn't until we moved here that we didn't share a house."

But he'd moved from their bed the night she'd come home from her ordeal. He'd sat up in a chair beside the bed, watching over her, but he hadn't slept beside her because she couldn't stand to have anyone touch her at the time. The trouble was, even after a few weeks, they had still been sleeping apart. "It was obvious to me that our marriage was over. You didn't sleep with me. You barely touched me."

His free hand gripped the railing of the balcony, clenching around it. "You had been raped. I was trying to give you time."

She shook her head. "I don't think so. I don't think you really wanted me because he'd had me. All the rest was just physical impulses and a measure of guilt from you. Do you want the truth? I didn't really want the divorce, but you didn't seem to want me anymore so I gave you an out."

He turned to her, the glass crashing to the ground. He didn't seem to care that he'd just broken a glass. "I never wanted an out. I wanted you. I tried to touch you and you flinched every single time. You couldn't stand to have my hands on you because deep down you blamed me for what happened to you. Don't you dare deny it."

She was suddenly so damn tired. She moved to the side, well away from the glass. "I don't deny it. You refused to listen to me. You thought I was wrong about Evans. Hell, you still think I'm wrong otherwise you wouldn't be here. This is ancient history. Why are we talking about it now?"

Now both fists were clenched at his sides as he followed her. "Because it's still here. I'm sorry. I'm sorry I didn't listen to you. I'm sorry I was an arrogant prick who fucked up his job so badly that he could never go back. And I can't tell you how sorry I am that you're the one who got hurt because of it. Don't you think I would change places with you if I could?"

Which only proved that he didn't know her at all. "I wouldn't want that. Did I blame you? Yes. Was that fair? No, of course not. Do I still blame you? I don't blame you for what happened, but I blame you for everything that happened afterward. I blame you for trying to be some kind of vigilante when I needed you to be my husband."

And he would never understand that. She turned, but his hand was on her arm, pulling her back. He loomed over her, his face shadowed by the moonlight. His mouth was turned down, but his eyes roamed every inch of her. "I didn't know how to reach you. I didn't even think I had the right to. What he did…"

"Is over, but you won't let it be over. It will never be over for you, and that's why it can't work between us." Tears made the world a blurry mess because it really came down to that. He wouldn't be able to let go. Not now. Not even if he found Michael Evans and somehow managed to kill him. For Alex, it would never really be over.

Their marriage had broken as surely as the glass on the ground, and neither of them had swept up the pieces. They kept trying to pick them up and fit them back together, but some pieces had shattered utterly and would never fit again. All they got for the effort was bloody hands and frustration.

"Do you want me to walk away now?" Alex asked, his voice tortured. "If I packed up everything and left with you tonight, would you give us another chance?"

She reached up and touched him, her palm to his cheek. He turned into her hand like he needed the feel of her skin against him more than his next breath. "We can't leave because, at the end of the day, Kristen is right about one thing. Michael Evans has to be brought to justice so he can't hurt anyone else. And that's your job."

It was why she loved him. It was also why he would never be able to forgive himself.

"I want to go back, Eve. I want us to be whole again. I want it more than anything." He touched his forehead to hers.

"We can't, baby. We can't go back. I wish we could, but I can't be that girl again. Whether I want it to or not, what happened changed me, and I can't be that sweet submissive thing you loved so much. I can't let you pick out my clothes and make all the choices. I think I would have outgrown it anyway. I wonder all the time what would have happened." It was the very thing that haunted her—the idea that no matter what had happened, she and Alex could have still broken up. "We were very young when we got married. I was already changing before Evans took me. It's inevitable that people grow and change, and distance tends to follow."

She felt his head shake. "No. We would have grown together. We would have changed and evolved because I would never have let it fall apart. We were stupid kids when we got married, but it was real and true and it should have been forever."

But it wasn't. It had been ten years of the contented happiness that came with a good marriage and then five years of aching loneliness, even when he was in bed beside her. It should have been forever, but there had been no happily ever after for them and there never could be until she let him go. "It broke. We broke and we can't come back from that. We can't pretend to be the kids we were before. We can't have the marriage we had, and until we stop looking back, neither one of us can move forward. I've done this to us."

"No. Eve, don't," Alex whispered. She could hear the pain in his voice.

Tears streaked down her cheeks, emotion rolling over her. She still loved him. She would go to her grave loving him, but she was right about this. They were broken and pieces were missing and couldn't be replaced. "I'm so sorry, baby. I should have let you go a long time ago. We should have separated and allowed each other to heal. I've kept us in this corner because I was so scared of a life that didn't have you in it. I was willing to keep both of us in hell instead of just letting go."

"I don't want you to let go. Can't we just hold on? We can just hold on. We can get through it, angel."

But they couldn't. They had been trying for five years. "We're different human beings now. I've changed on a fundamental level, and I hate that. I don't think I can find a new me until we stop trying to get back to a place that doesn't exist anymore. I'm going to stand beside you now, but when this is over, I'm leaving and I'm going to wish you all the best in the world because you deserve it. You deserve the woman who can be everything you need her to be. Someone whole."

She'd been unkind for years because the only way she could keep him was to bind him to her with a contract that was a sort of half-life where they could pretend to still be together, where the past was still between them like a tantalizing dream of what once was.

But it couldn't be again, and she had to let go. She'd accused Alex of not letting go, but she'd been holding the same broken pieces, too. She'd held them hard and fast despite the fact that she was bleeding every minute of the day.

The only way to move on was to let go. She'd been an anchor around his neck, dragging him down, taking what should have been the best years of his life.

His hands moved to her waist, his forehead settling against hers, and she felt the soft drop of his tears on her cheeks. They mingled there with the ones she shed, a final proof that once they'd been together.

She lifted her face, the moonlight illuminating him, showing her the pain in his eyes. The sound of the ocean was a bittersweet irony. They had begun their marriage on an island paradise, and they'd made love on the beach and watched the sun come up. She'd looked out and the ocean had seemed as endless as her love for him. The waves never ended, their potential infinite, and she and Alex had seemed the same way.

Her love was still there, but their potential had died in a fury of blood and pain and guilt. They were shattered. Nothing could take them back to a time when they weren't, and she'd finally realized that if she loved him, she had to let him go.

She brought her nose to his, rubbing their skin together. When they'd been happy, they would lie together in bed for hours, just cuddling and exploring and touching. They would laugh and talk and end up making love, but not until they had teased each other into a frenzy. Most couples they had known would go home and watch TV together, but Eve and Alex had shed their clothes the minute the door was closed, and they had spent those precious hours naked and wrapped around each other.

She knew his body better than her own, knew every muscle, every hollow and valley and inch of his skin. She knew that kissing the back of his knees got him hard and he hated having his feet tickled. She knew how strong his heart was and how when he'd loved her, she'd been the queen of the world.

And whomever he loved next would be the luckiest woman on the planet.

"Don't leave me, Eve." His mouth hovered above hers. The heat of his body warmed her.

"We have to. We're not the same people. I'm not the woman you loved. Please, Alex. Let me go. It hurts too much. I want what we had, but I can't have it. We can't be those kids who were wildly in love and knew they could take on the world. I'm still in so much pain. Staying in this place, wishing for what I can't have, it's an ache inside me."

"Angel." His breath hitched. His hands shook as he touched her face, cupping her cheeks and looking into her eyes. "I don't want you to ache. I love you so fucking much. I never thought you were dirty. You were always innocent, and I'm so sorry I failed you. I fucking failed you and that was the last thing I wanted to do."

"Let it go." She could barely talk, but she forced the words out. This was the last gift she could give him. His freedom. "Please, let it go. You want to know how you can make me happy? You can be happy, baby. You can let go of all this pain and I will, too, and we can start over. We won't be together, but we can let go of those kids we were. They died. And we can mourn them, and we can try to find the new people we are. Please. Let go."

"I love you, Eve." His lips brushed hers, tears flowing freely now.

Soft, sweet. He pressed his mouth against hers and they held for a moment. Eve let it wash over her, memorizing every second. His hands moved to her hair, gently tangling there as he pulled her closer.

She hugged him to her, wishing this moment never had to stop. They could stay here. They could stay suspended in this moment and they wouldn't have to move forward. They wouldn't have to find new lives.

Please let it all stop right here. Let this be it. Forever. Forever with his lips on mine and our hearts beating in time. Alex and Eve. Together.

But time didn't stop. It never did. No matter how she prayed and fought and tried to force the world to stand still, it just kept moving.

Alex broke the kiss, his arms wrapping around her, holding her so tight she could feel his heart pounding. "Will you let me hold you tonight? No sex. Just let me hold you. Let me say good-bye."

She nodded. He wouldn't kiss her again. God.

175

Somehow she hadn't thought this kiss would be their last. How could it be over? And yet she knew it had to be. And she owed him a night of everything she'd denied him for five years. "I'll hold you, too."

He took her hand and led her back to bed.

She clung to him, praying the dawn would never come.

Chapter Eight

Eve could hear the group talking in the kitchen. Sean said something in a low tone and Adam laughed. A feminine voice groaned, and Alex told them all to be serious.

She hugged her robe and hoped she looked somewhat presentable. Kristen had knocked on her door five minutes earlier and told her to wake up because Alex had called a meeting and he wanted her in there pronto. No time to shower or get dressed. Alex was having a meeting and they were all supposed to fall in line.

She'd touched the side of the bed where Alex had lain. It had been cold, proving he'd left their bed a while before. Sometime before dawn, she'd fallen asleep, her tears dried up because she simply had no more to shed, and she'd woken alone.

She felt different, a little less burdened, but the sadness of letting Alex go was still an ache in her heart.

And she had to work with him now. God, how was she going to get through this? How was she going to sit in the same room with him and pretend like everything was normal when a wealth of pain sat between them?

The early morning light streamed through the big bay windows, illuminating the whole dining room.

"Eve? I'm glad you could join us. There's coffee if you would like some." Alex sat at the head of the table. He stood, holding a mug in his hand. He was dressed simply in sweat pants and a T-shirt that clung to his every muscle.

"I'm getting some for myself. Cream and sugar?"

She shook her head. He knew very well she drank it plain. "Black, please."

He looked her up and down. His eyes caught on her breasts for a moment, and she wished she'd worn less leisurely leisurewear. "Huh, I would have thought you like it sweet. I will note your preferences for the future. You should know that we meet every morning at seven sharp for discussion and breakfast. I'll wake you myself tomorrow morning. I know you've worked with Ian and Liam as leads, but I like to run a very tight ship."

So he was going to go the professional route. She could handle that. It might be for the best. "All right. I'll be here on time."

Alex nodded and gestured to the table. "Good. Now, we're bonding over Kristen's excellent homemade cinnamon rolls, and I want reports on the day."

Kristen grinned as she sank into her chair. "And they're totally not poison or anything. Little Tag thought they were."

Sean rolled his eyes. "God, no one calls me that anymore. And I have to admit, they're actually pretty good. You should try one. If she's put poison in it, at least she's going to die with us."

She might have to have a talk with Sean. Even in the small time she'd spent with Kristen, she would trust the woman. She might be hiding something, but Eve would be surprised if she was capable of truly cold-blooded betrayal. The redhead seemed passionate and stubborn, but there was a moral streak to her that was blatantly obvious to Eve.

Adam snorted a little as he pulled off another cinnamon roll. God, they smelled heavenly. "I still call you Little Tag. So does Jake."

Alex returned with her coffee. He set it down in the chair opposite his and settled a plated cinnamon roll with a bowl of fruit in front of where he obviously expected her to sit. "Little Tag, why didn't you make cinnamon rolls?"

Sean's middle finger made an appearance. "I'm not a fucking pastry chef. Tomorrow I'm making frittatas, and they will put these to shame. I also slept through the alarm. I was up half the night talking on the phone with Grace because Carys has her days and nights mixed up. This was way easier to do when I didn't have a baby."

Eve sat down in her chair, pulling the coffee into her hands, warming them. The bay windows showed a spectacularly beautiful morning outside, and the rest of the people at the table were joking and laughing like they were a longtime team. Even Alex was jovial, though his eyes found hers from time to time, and that was the only time their light dimmed.

She felt so odd. He was fine. She was a mess on the inside, and he looked like a man who had been completely unburdened. She hadn't seen him smile so genuinely in years. He even looked younger this morning, as though the night before had released him.

He'd said good-bye to her and it looked good on him.

Her nose was still red from crying, her eyes puffy. But she'd done the right thing. She wanted Alex to be happy. She truly did. She just had to suck it up because she hadn't thought he would be happy quite so fast.

"So, I want to make sure everyone has their assignments for the day. Eve and I have to be at the club by eleven thirty this morning. Sean?" Alex asked, looking every bit the leader of the team.

"I'm going in earlier than you. I've got to go in and make a list of the upgrades I need. Chazz mentioned there was a luncheon in a couple of days. I need to prep for that. After breakfast, I'll head in and see if that dumbass sous-chef followed my instructions."

"What else?" Alex asked.

"I'm going to get a look at the kitchens and see what I can find out about the staff in there. I'll very carefully plant a couple of bugs and take some surveillance shots so we know all the entrances and exits to the club in the unlikely case we get made and have to get out of the place before someone takes our balls off. You should know that my wife expects me to keep my balls. She doesn't want Carys to be our only child. I'm also going to try to get a full list of the kitchen staff. I'm going to assume they're not all on the payroll," Sean said with a knowing grimace.

Kristen shook her head. "Oh, no. Most of those guys are paid under the table. I would suspect half of them are illegal, so good luck with the IDs."

Adam groaned a little. "Just get me names and, if you can, pictures. I'll figure it out. I've got some damn fine facial recognition software. If they're in criminal databases, I should be able to find them."

"You are the computer wizard. Once we set up our bugs, I want you to start listening in," Alex said, looking through some papers. "Kristen?"

She swallowed what looked like half a cinnamon roll. Eve couldn't help but notice that Kristen was one of those women who wasn't bothered by her weight. She wasn't small by any means. She had an hourglass figure and the confidence of a woman who knew she was sexy. And she was actually quite lovely. From her full breasts to her long strawberry blonde hair, she was a bombshell. Was Alex smiling at her just to be friendly? It suddenly occurred to her that Kristen was pretty perfect for someone like Alex. She would understand his work and she had a free-flowing smile that fairly lit up a room. "I am going to use my boobs to distract the kitchen staff so Little Tag can take his pictures. They think these are lesbian boobs. It's like the ultimate forbidden fruit."

"Oh, god, don't send me in with her." Sean let his head hit the table, but not before Eve saw him smile. Maybe she wouldn't have to have that talk. Apparently, Kristen had charmed him, too. "I take back what I said. I figured out what's bugging me about her. She's the obnoxious little sister I was blessed to not have."

Kristen sighed as though deeply satisfied. "I'm totally writing that into my story. If I live long enough to write the story. I'll mention you in my Pulitzer acceptance speech."

Alex's eyes found hers. "You should eat, Eve."

"I'm not a big carb fan." She loved them. Adored them. Craved them. They went straight to her hips, and she had to stay in control. Now more than ever. If she gave in, she would end up eating a gallon of ice cream and crying while watching old movies that made her think of Alex. Sometimes it felt like what she ate was the only thing she had control over.

Alex frowned. "We're having lunch with Chazz and the bouncers. We're supposed to go over what we'll need when we run a scene for the investors who are coming in and then we're going to walk the floor of the club all night so I can get a feel for it. I think you're going to need your energy."

That sounded horrible. Positively awful. And it was what she'd signed up for. "I brought along some protein bars. I'll eat one in a little while."

"All right." Alex put his hands on the table and frowned. "Eve, could I speak with you privately? On the balcony, perhaps? The rest of you, get to work. Tonight,

181

after we get back from the club, I want to hear some plans about how to get a little alone time in Chazz's office. It's isolated. I need a way in and a way to not get caught. I want his computer files, his cell phone duped, his apartment and car bugged. Get me solutions, people. I want to be ready when Evans makes his move. Chazz said he had some big plans in the next few weeks. I think that means Evans is coming for a visit. We need to be ready."

He pushed his chair back and walked out to the balcony without looking back.

It was a different part of the house, but her stomach turned at the thought of being on the balcony with him again. The night before had been so emotional. How could he just walk out there? Was he going to talk about what had happened? Worse, was he going to act like nothing had happened?

She was so damn confused.

But she had a job to do, and Alex was running the op. She owed him the courtesy of following his lead. She took a long breath and forced herself to move. She should have set an alarm so she would be going into this little meeting after a shower and with full armor on. She hadn't even put on makeup. It had been forever since Alex had seen her without the full Chanel treatment. She hated feeling so damn vulnerable.

"What did you want to talk to me about?" She tried to close the door behind her. Hurricane glass. It was so heavy.

Alex shut it with one hand. "We have to talk about how this is going to go, Eve. You haven't been in the field in a long time. We haven't worked together in this capacity before, and I want it to be smooth and easy."

He was so calm, so professional. Somehow, she'd thought they would both be awkward, trying to find their

182

way, but Alex seemed perfectly content. He looked cool and collected as he sat down on one of the rattan chairs with deep red cushions.

The waves crashed against the shores, soft morning light making the whole world seem gauzy and romantic. Why couldn't they have been in a city somewhere without all the romantic trappings of the damn beach?

She was going to have to pull herself together. "All right. So, we're going into the lion's den today, huh?"

His fingers tapped against the arm of the chair. "Yes. And that's what I'm worried about. We're supposed to be a long time D/s couple. I worry that when it comes time to obey me, you're going to flinch."

It was a legitimate worry. She couldn't blame him for it. "I promise I won't. Alex, I can do this job. I know what to do."

"I asked you to eat the cinnamon roll and you wouldn't. I need to know that you're going to play this part every minute of every day we're here. You can't pick and choose what you want to do." He sighed and leaned forward. "I know how the D/s works at your club. It's the same way I view it. The submissive is ultimately in control. She can choose to obey her Master or to use her safeword, but I can't have you safewording me over a cinnamon roll. Go and get one and bring it out here."

She wanted to tell him where to shove his cinnamon roll, but he was right. *Damn it.* She could complain all day long, but she knew she should stay in her cover. If he'd brought Amanda with him, she would sleep in his bed and be his sub twenty-four seven because it was so much easier to stay in character than to figure out when and where to act. This was why longtime undercover officers had trouble. The role became their lives because it had to.

Alex easily opened the door again, and she slipped inside. Adam was standing by the table with a plate in his hand.

He gave her a smile and a shrug. "It was an easy bet, sweetheart."

She frowned and took the plate. "I'm never listening to your wife again."

"Hey, Serena knows how to find a happy ending, honey. Maybe you should trust her." Adam gave her a wink and turned away.

But her happily ever after had ended the night before. She was not going to cry, damn it. She was going to do her job. She walked back out into the warm morning air.

"One cinnamon roll. Fine. I'll eat it."

He sat back on a deck chair. "I'll feed it to you. Sit on my lap."

"Alex." Was he going to torture her?

"We're supposed to be lovers. I have to know you can play the part." He patted his lap.

Her heart fell. He was going to torture her. She'd forced him to say good-bye, and he was going to get his payback. She hadn't expected that from him. She'd been trying to do right for them both.

His expression softened. "This is about the mission. You can't expect me to let you go into this without knowing you can do the job. If you can't obey me here where it doesn't matter, how can I be sure you can do it in the field? You're a very independent woman. It's why I originally chose someone different for the job."

He knew just how to kick her in the gut. She'd screwed up. She should have found him a proper operative, but no, she'd thrown herself into the mix. She was being a damn brat over a few carbs. She lowered herself into his lap.

His arm went around her waist. "That's better. Relax. You have to look like you're very comfortable in my arms. Like this is where you belong. Put your head on my shoulder. You don't have to do anything, pet. Just follow my lead. It's easy if you just embrace the part."

He was killing her. Her heart threatened to pound out of her chest. She could smell him. He'd taken a shower, unlike her. He smelled clean and perfect and masculine. His skin was warm where it touched hers. It was cruel, but maybe once she proved she could play the part, he would ease up when they were alone.

"Open, pet." He'd torn off a chunk of the soft roll, creamy icing dripping onto his hand.

The sweet smell wafted all around her. Cinnamon. Like home. She opened her mouth and nearly groaned. The taste hit her like a freight train of pleasure. Sweet, so sweet it melted on her tongue. She hadn't tasted anything like it in years.

"You missed some icing, pet." Alex put his finger to her lips. "Lick it off."

Without a thought, she opened her mouth and sucked his finger inside. She just wanted some more of the splendid connection he was offering her. She let her tongue rub the underside of his finger, drawing the cream inside.

"Perfect. Again." He offered her another piece and she took it. "Coffee. It complements the sweet." He held his own mug up to her lips and she drank.

Just like that, she was practically in fucking subspace. Her breath had slowed, her eyesight dimmed until she could only see him. And all he'd done was offer her a damn cinnamon roll. This was what she'd been afraid of. Alex was a drug. Her drug. The minute he used that dark voice on her, she lost her mind.

"Very good." His approval rolled over her like some crazy endorphin that made her smile. "I was worried, but I think you'll do nicely. Don't break cover, pet. For the next few weeks, I want you to think of yourself as pet. You belong to your Master. You're his to command. You're still brave and oh so smart. You still have your mission because nothing will please your Master more than completing your mission, but know that your Master wants you safe above anything else. The most important thing is for Master's pet to be safe and whole at the end of the mission."

This was all that was left between them, and his words were still so sweet, they almost brought tears to her eyes. Since she'd let go, every damn thing brought tears to her eyes. She'd spent years bottling up her emotions, but now they were always at the surface. "I'll be careful, Alex."

"Master," he corrected gravely.

She had so little time to call him that. "Master. I will obey. I will fulfill my mission to please my Master."

Eve let her head rest against his chest. They only had until the end of the operation. Alex was trying to give them some time. Maybe this was a good thing. Maybe it was a way to make their parting sweeter. A few more memories.

"Spread your legs for me."

"I'm following your orders, Master." He couldn't still mean to get intimate with her. "I'm not wearing any underwear."

"I didn't ask a question. I gave an order. What's your safe word?" His words came out accompanied by a low growl that sort of rumbled along her flesh because they were so close.

"Red." They had always communicated using red, yellow, and green during scenes. Red meant stop. Green told Alex that she was fine, and yellow meant she was feeling some anxiety. She was really, really yellow right now, but that wasn't what he'd asked. If she kept pushing him, she would only find herself in more trouble. Alex was testing her, pushing her boundaries to see if she could really do the job she'd signed up for. They would have to do some scenes, and those scenes would involve intimacy. He wasn't asking for anything truly unreasonable.

Eve relaxed and let her legs fall open. They were facing away from the glass doors. No one could see what Alex was doing. And, again, it wasn't like most of the people in the condo hadn't seen her naked at one point in time.

She shivered a little as his big hand cupped her knee and started to make its way up her thigh. He was so warm, so big and safe.

"You need to really think about that safe word, pet." His breath played along her skin. He was whispering, his lips brushing against the curve of her ear. "While we both agree on how to practice, we're not going into this club as Alex and Eve. I have to be rough. I have to be completely in control. I have to play into what these men think D/s should be, and these are not nice men."

He moved his knees apart, forcing her legs to spread further. A cool breeze hit her pussy, reminding her how nice it could feel to be completely naked. She wasn't able to focus on all the reasons why it was wrong. Alex would keep her safe. Alex would watch their back while she got to relax and simply feel.

How easy it was to fall back into old habits.

"Don't tense on me. I mean it, pet. If I have to retrain you, I will."

Which meant spankings and not the erotic kind. She didn't particularly want to spend the whole day with a sore backside. Alex meant to have his way, and when he got that tone of voice, there was no negotiating. She forced her muscles to relax, her brain to give over.

"Very nice. Such a good little pet. Have I told you how pretty you look today?" His fingers skimmed her labia, and she had to remind herself to breathe.

"No, Master." Every word from his mouth just got her hotter. She could feel her pussy softening, getting slick and ready.

His fingers slid easily across her flesh, scraping her clitoris with erotic intent. "That was a mistake on my part. You look lovely, all soft and tousled. I like you like this. And I have to admit, I think the longer hair looks lovely. It isn't a wig?"

How did he expect her to think when he was rubbing her clit in tight little circles? Except that was probably the point of this exercise. He was forcing her to think through the pleasure, to not forget that they were playing a part. "No. Serena had a friend of hers open her salon early, and she dyed my hair and gave me extensions."

"Can I pull on them? You might like having your hair tugged on."

He knew damn well it turned her on, but he seemed intent on pretending he didn't. And she was close, so close. The tension was building deep inside.

"Do you like what I'm doing to your pussy, pet? Do you enjoy having my fingers on you? This is why I can't have my sweet little pet wearing panties. I want access. I want to know that I can stroke you anytime I like. That's the way this is all going to go from here on out. My way. I'll have you when I want you, how I want you, and you will thank me sweetly for it at the end of the day."

"Yes, Master." She bit her bottom lip to keep from crying out.

"That's right. Keep quiet. I'll tell you when I want you to scream for me." His thumb stayed at her clit, but a finger slipped inside her, massaging her vaginal walls, stroking her in just the right place. "Today is going to be a learning experience for both of us. Let's set some ground rules. No talking to the other men. I'm going to be very territorial about you. They'll figure out quickly that I'm a possessive freak with violent tendencies and they should stay away from my sub. I need you to study everyone very carefully. Be submissive. Cling to me, but keep those ears open and your brain working. That's what I need from you. If I need to leave you alone, I expect you to go to the kitchens and stay with Sean. Is that clear? You are not to be alone unless you're in the women's locker room, and even there I would prefer you take Kristen with you. Say 'yes, Master.'"

She would say anything he wanted her to. "Yes, Master."

A second finger joined the first. She could feel the thick line of his erection against her ass. Was this what he was planning on doing for the next several weeks? Was this his idea of keeping her in line? Because it was totally working.

"Come for me."

Three words said in that low, gravelly voice of his and she went off like a shot. The orgasm rolled over her and Alex shifted, hugging her tight, his tongue licking the shell of her ear as she rode out the pleasure.

She sagged against him, every muscle soft and relaxed. Maybe this was his new version of working out.

"That was excellent, pet. You can get up now." His arms came out from around her, and she felt the loss of his warmth.

With wooden legs, she moved from his lap. She'd kind of expected him to turn her around and order her to ride his cock. She smoothed out her robe and hoped she wasn't too disheveled. "All right. I'll go and get ready for the day."

She sniffled a little as she moved toward the door. She'd tried to be kind, but she was confused as to where he was. He'd been professional, but then he'd gotten so intimate. Intellectually she understood the point of the exercise, but her heart was racing and her hands shaking and she just wanted to be held again.

"Eve?"

She turned back, every nerve wary. "Yes, Sir?"

"Master," he corrected, his voice firm.

He obviously wouldn't give her an inch. "Yes, Master?"

"I know we haven't worked together in this capacity before and that might be a problem."

He seemed intent on beating a dead horse. She huffed a little. "I'll fulfill my duties."

"That's not the problem."

God, what was he going to throw at her now? She just wanted to run inside and take a shower and put her armor in place again. Control. She needed to get back into control. "What is the problem, Master?"

He moved behind her, his front to her back and she could feel the erection he pressed to her ass. "I find you very attractive. I'm struggling to keep the relationship on a professional level. It's going to be hard for me. We're going to have to live together, to sleep together, to have a D/s relationship. I can tell you it's going to be very difficult for me to remember where the operation stops and reality begins."

She turned, anger rising. "Alex, what the hell kind of game are you playing?"

His hands came up, cupping her face the way he had the night before. She could smell her own arousal on those fingers. Yes, they were getting very intimate. More intimate than they'd been in years. "You told me to let go. I let go. We have a problem, angel. The new me is just so fucking attracted to the new you. You're so fucking gorgeous. I want you. I thought you should know. I'm going to do exactly what you asked of me. I'm going to find the new me. I already know one thing about the new Alex McKay. He wants Eve St. James."

He hadn't really listened to her the night before. He'd placated her. "This isn't going to work."

He backed her up, giving her no space. He very deliberately sucked his fingers into his mouth, tasting her, his tongue working to gather every bit of cream she'd left on his hand. "And you taste like heaven."

Just like that her pussy started tightening again. Control. She had to find some. "You can't just pretend like we don't know each other."

"It's what you wanted. New you. New me. New start." His mouth hovered above hers. "And if last night was a kiss good-bye, then I want my hello kiss. And I'm going to have it."

This was no sweet brushing of his lips against hers. Alex pressed his mouth to her with deadly intent. He forced her jaw to open and his tongue surged inside, sliding alongside hers. He cradled her close, rubbing that big erection against her belly as he took her mouth again and again. One of his hands came up and tugged on her hair, fisting it.

"Yeah, I like the longer hair, pet. I'm going to love to hold onto it while I fuck your ass," he whispered along her cheek. "Oh, did you think I would forget the fact that you haven't let me inside your ass in forever? I'm the Master again, and I'm going to have you every way a man can possibly have a woman. You want me to get to know you all over again? I'll be thrilled to. Now go and get ready. Meet me in the weight room in ten minutes. If you're not there, it's twenty smacks. Every minute you keep me waiting is another ten. So be late, if you like. I would love to see how the new Eve handles my discipline."

He stepped back and opened the door wide, holding a hand out for her to enter first. She forced herself to move.

What the hell had just happened?

"Ten minutes," Alex announced again as he walked past her. She could only stare as he strode back into the kitchen, his shoulders straight and proud.

"Wow," Kristen said. "The boss looks like a whole new man. Whatever you did to him last night really worked."

"Yeah," Eve muttered. A whole new man. A dangerous man. She wasn't sure she could handle the new Alex.

She rushed to the bathroom to get cleaned up because she was pretty sure she was running out of time—in more ways than one.

Chapter Nine

Five days later, Alex looked over the men assembled in the VIP section of the club and felt a sense of satisfaction. At least one thing had gone right with this damn operation. Almost a week had gone by and he still hadn't found a chance to slip into Chazz's office. Security was lax around the club—everywhere except Chazz's office.

But Alex had a plan for that and Jake was right where he should be, his eyes bloodshot and his normally pressed suit just the slightest bit wrinkled. His eyes slid over Alex and then back to Eve. He leaned over to the man seated to his left and whispered something in his ear.

Chazz laughed and leered a little Eve's way before shaking his head. Alex could just catch the last of the conversation. "I don't think he's the sharing type, buddy."

The VIP section of the club had been transformed into a dining area. Only the kitchen staff was around at this time of the day. The rest of the club was quiet. Chazz and Jake sat while three other men were gathered together talking quietly.

He slid his fingers through Eve's, completely satisfied with the connection. God, he'd gotten to touch her more in the last several days than in the years that came before. Even though they were in the middle of an operation, he allowed himself to revel in the way her hair smelled. She'd changed her shampoo. She used to favor floral scents, delicate rose and lilacs. Now, her hair smelled like grapefruit, sharp and alive.

He dropped his head close to hers and whispered, "Don't give away Jake, angel. He's here for a reason."

"Yes, Master."

He was almost disappointed with the blank doll look on her face. He'd gotten used to bratty Eve. He would never admit it to her, but when she'd said she was worried that they hadn't been as solid as they'd seemed back when they were married, he'd agreed. He hadn't told her that he'd worried their life had become a dull set of never-ending protocols, and he'd actually resented having to select her clothes for her toward the end. That look on her face now was the one she used to get when she simply agreed to everything.

Maybe they'd both lost themselves somewhere along the way. He'd had five days of getting to know her again. Five days of holding her. Five days of completely withholding his cock.

That had to change.

"Although you could have told me in the car," she whispered, her whole face turning stubborn and resentful.

And so cute. She was adorable when she thought he was a dumbass. He leaned over and kissed her. She didn't flinch anymore. She was beginning to openly accept his affection even when they were in private. "I wasn't sure he'd made it in. I found out about this investor meeting thing yesterday afternoon. Chazz mentioned he was going out to party. I wanted to see just how reckless he is. I sent Jake in to party with him. I hadn't heard anything since. Apparently it went pretty well because he hasn't changed his clothes."

It proved that Chazz was a bit reckless. Jake had partied with him the night before. This was supposed to be a serious, rather secretive business meeting and Chazz had invited a virtual stranger in. Now, Jake had been playing a high roller, throwing money around, so Chazz might honestly think he was going to get something out of it, but there was no way the man had vetted Jake.

And it was also the perfect time to bug the little fucker's car. Jake ran a hand through his hair and blinked twice. To the casual observer, he would simply look like a man who was a little tired, a little unkempt, but to Alex those two gestures meant the world. Jake had completed two of his three objectives. He'd bugged the car and Chazz's private residence. Jake sniffed and gave him a little shake of his head. It was a no go on the keys to the office.

Damn it.

He was going to have to find another way in. Every day that went by put them in danger.

"He's going to be obnoxious, isn't he?" Eve asked, proving she knew how these things went.

And that was another reason he'd asked Jake to play a small role. If he needed to learn something about Chazz, then Alex wanted Chazz to learn something very specific about him. "Oh, yes. He's going to prove a couple of points about me as well as getting his hands on some financials for us. But I can't keep him in the game for long."

Eve cuddled close, keeping her voice low. "Because Serena needs him and we need Adam."

He ran his hands through her hair, fisting it gently and forcing her to look up at him. He damn straight liked the new hair. Even the color looked good on her, making her skin glow. She'd been a cool blonde for so long that he'd forgotten how the more natural brown shade brought out a flush in her cheeks. He'd made her leave off most of her makeup, allowing only a little mascara and some gloss. She'd been bitterly angry about that. Apparently, she didn't find the dusting of freckles across her nose and cheekbones as sweet as he did. And someone was walking up behind them. He hardened his voice. "Be a good girl. I need to plant a GPS on one of the fuckers we're meeting with. I would really like to know where some of the strongholds are. If I get a chance, I'm going to try to slip it into a pocket."

The tiny GPS locators were one of Adam's new playthings. He was a tech guru who very likely could have made millions off some of his little toys, but luckily, Adam was damn loyal. The tiny locator was black and would stick to a piece of clothing or a briefcase. He just had to find the right time to tag one of the bastards.

The blank doll face was back. "Yes, Master. I am always a good girl. Not that it does me any good."

He felt a grin slide across his face and quickly quashed it though he couldn't dampen the joy he felt. Withholding sex had been hell on earth, but he had a point to prove. She wanted to start over? He could do that, but it would be his way this time, and part of his way was proving he was boss in the bedroom. He slept with her in his arms every night and then showered with her in the morning, washing every inch of her himself. At first she'd stood stiffly in his arms as though it was something to endure. Slowly but surely, she'd softened, allowing him to touch her and comfort her. Somewhere around day three, she'd started rubbing against him. And this morning she'd been damn sullen about the fact that he wouldn't take her.

His plan was working perfectly. At least the plan with Eve was working. The operation was another story.

"Gentlemen, these are the two I was telling you about. This is Master A and his slave. What should I call her?" Chazz asked.

Mine. He felt a growl start in the back of his throat

because the slimy fucker was practically looking down Eve's shirt. "Slave will be fine in a dungeon setting or one in which we're working in high protocol, like today. In a more casual setting, you can call her Amanda. For the purposes of today, I thought we would be formal."

Chazz nodded. "Absolutely. Everyone is very curious. I've seated you at the head of the table and your slave next to you."

Alex shook his head. That simply wouldn't do. "She doesn't need a chair. She sits in my lap or at my feet. And I'll feed her from my plate. She takes only what I give her."

She would look very nonthreatening and she would be able to make a careful study of every man in the room. Still, her nails slightly dug into the flesh of his hand even though her expression never changed. She kept her head lowered submissively, but she got her point across. He would pay for it later. Or he would spank her ass for brattiness. Either way, he was looking forward to it.

She'd said good-bye on the balcony five days before, and he'd woken up knowing she'd been right. They would never have a clean slate. He didn't want one. He wanted to acknowledge the relationship they'd had before, but he'd made a shrine of it and he'd been forced that night to really look at it. Their marriage had been far from perfect. He'd made mistakes. She'd made mistakes.

They were starting over.

Because he'd realized one thing. She still loved him. Deep down and underneath it all—Eve still loved him. Still needed him.

He wouldn't let her down this time.

But he might piss her off. Since they'd come to Florida, she'd received three disciplinary spankings. She'd been late to workouts twice and mouthed off at him when he'd very politely requested that she perform another set of squats. He'd kept her off-kilter all week long.

And he had no intention of changing that.

He led her to the seat they had offered him. Four men sat around the table besides Chazz and Jake. Jesse, the little fucker, already had eyes on Eve. And he wasn't even trying to hide the fact that he was carrying. Alex could see the round edge of his shoulder holster peeking from under his jacket. The ex-soldier looked a little awkward in a sport coat.

The other three men did not. They were all either South American or Middle Eastern. In the normal course of events, their nationality didn't mean a damn thing. Alex had known plenty of all-American criminal assholes, but they were here "investing" in Michael Evans's club.

These were men with ties to Evans. Evans was quite the terrorist entrepreneur. Alex was almost certain Evans was using the club to launder money, and having control of the money would give Evans a certain amount of power in the cells.

These were either jihadist terrorists or they worked for cartels. And every single one of them was looking at Eve.

He sat down, tugging her into his lap. He wanted her on the floor, safely at his feet where they couldn't see her, but he needed her expertise more than he needed her hidden away. That was what the old Alex did. Damn, but she'd gotten to him that night on the balcony. He'd been thinking about his actions all week.

Had he turned away from her? Had it been easier to focus on Evans than to try to deal with what had happened to them?

And it had happened to them. He'd spent too many years not acknowledging that they were truly in this together. Eve had been the victim and Alex the man who had failed her, but sometime that night, as he held her close and felt her breath on his skin, he'd discovered something important.

They had to survive this together or neither could really survive it at all. Eve was right that they needed to move on, but she was wrong about how they should do it.

She thought he needed someone whole? He couldn't be whole without her.

And that meant allowing her to be the partner she needed to be.

He pulled her into his lap and she immediately responded, allowing her head to find his chest.

The door to the kitchens opened and Sean walked through carrying a plate, followed by several young men who looked like they'd been forced into proper serving attire. Sean had spent his time getting the kitchen staff in order. They were running like a well-oiled machine.

"This is promising," one of the Middle Eastern men said. "The last time I was here, your cook was horrible. If you intend to entertain my associates, you have to be better."

Sean was wearing a perfectly pristine white chef's jacket. "Today's luncheon starts with lobster ceviche. There's a beet and endive salad. Our main course is a rubbed rack of lamb with a celery puree. Enjoy."

Kristen walked by, opening a bottle of wine. "I am the bar manager and sommelier for the club. Hopefully for the clubs. I believe you will find this first offering pairs nicely with the lobster."

Kristen was wearing a black jacket that she seemed to be having a bit of trouble with. She subtlety pulled the sleeves down a couple of times as though they kept riding up and she was trying to maintain a professional air.

She was taking pictures. One of the buttons on her jacket was a camera.

Adam would have some work to do tonight.

She stopped when she got to Jake, and her face tightened. *Fuck.* He had hoped that she wouldn't recognize him, but apparently she'd really done her homework. She finished her job and nodded as she walked off, not sparing him another glance.

He knew an angry woman when he saw one.

Jesse Murdoch looked down at his lunch like he'd hoped for fries and a burger.

One of the investors turned to Murdoch. "You were a soldier, correct? I remember your face."

Alex felt Eve tense. He cuddled her closer. She was interested in a reaction. He could feel it. He shifted her so she could see the younger man whose face had flushed immediately. He wasn't particularly good at hiding his reactions.

"I did my time," Jesse said in a hard voice.

The man next to him smiled, a smooth, practiced expression. "Yes, I rather thought that was you. I shouldn't be too surprised to see you here. Smart man. You picked the right side."

Jesse took a sharp breath and then slammed out of his seat, his chair barking across the floor. "I'm not hungry. I'll be on the door outside."

Jake snorted a little as the door slammed. "He's a pistol, that one."

Chazz frowned. "He can be a hothead, but he's proven to be a loyal soldier."

Eve was staring at the door, her brown eyes curious. She was interested in the young dumbass in an intellectual way. That made Alex interested as well. Was there

200

something to the kid that he was missing?

"I believe our mutual friend would find him intriguing. You know how he loves to corrupt Americans," a second man said.

Now Alex's attention was focused. He maintained a quiet air, paying attention to Eve, feeding her soup as he took his own, but he was all about the mutual friend.

Chazz proved just how reckless he was. "Yeah, Mikey is going to love Jesse. He's a little too soft on the pussy though. We need to teach that boy how to handle his scene. Master A should be able to do that. I think Master A could be good for all my men. He'll get the women in line before the big boss shows up."

Oh, he so wanted to meet the big boss. His heart beat a little faster. Evans was coming and soon. He needed that date. He needed to know where and when.

Eve stiffened slightly.

And he couldn't hold her close because everyone was watching. She was supposed to be a pretty plaything. He couldn't show his softness or they would know he wasn't what he said he was.

She was scared, and he was going to fail her again.

Goddamn it. This was why he didn't want her on this op.

"He seems fairly soft on women." The third man stared at them, his nose wrinkling as though he found the entire thing distasteful.

He was losing them. He didn't change his expression at all. "She's behaving. I like to reward proper behavior."

"Women should know their place whether they are rewarded or not," the second man said. He turned to Chazz. "You said he was going to perform a scene. Is this what you meant?"

"No. A scene is much more involved." Chazz nodded toward the door where Jesse stood. "I've brought in some equipment. If we choose to go this way with the clubs, we would need to invest in better quality 'toys' as we say in the lifestyle. We want everything to look good."

The third man huffed a bit. "I don't need equipment to bring my women in line. I simply need the back of my hand."

Oh, that fucker would feel the back of Alex's hand. Eve snuggled a little closer, her very presence calming him. It struck him rather forcibly that she hadn't calmed him down in years. Since the divorce, since the incident, his blood pressure ticked up when she entered a room whether from guilt or fear of losing her, but after the week before, he felt different.

He was in control again, and she was his partner. It might not last past the mission, but he was going to enjoy it for now.

He had to put on a show because he'd just figured out what Chazz was doing and why.

"Up, pet." He moved Eve off his lap as Jesse reentered the room carrying a whipping bench. The younger man moved easily, hefting the heavy bench like it weighed next to nothing.

"I was told to bring this thing in here." He set it down a good twelve feet away from the table and then turned. He didn't meet eyes with the men at the table, but he stared at Eve like she was a lamb going to slaughter.

The boy seemed to have a problem with D/s, but then if Chazz had been his only instructor, it was to Jesse's credit that he had a problem.

"Thank you." Alex turned to his audience. He got it now. He was the distraction. If Chazz hadn't figured it out yet, he was about to help him along. This was what Evans wanted. This was why they'd come looking for a Dom in Residence.

Sean chose to make a very well-timed entrance with the second course. As the soup course was taken out, he managed to have a few words with him and Sean agreed to the plan.

Alex was about to make himself indispensable.

Jesse took up residence at the back of the room, his eyes squarely on that chair.

"Come, pet." He reached into his well-worn kit and withdrew the silk rope. He'd switched to silk from jute as soon as he'd been able to afford it. In the last five years, these toys were the only presents she would accept from him, so they were top of the line. She was wearing a thin leather collar around her throat, the one he'd picked up for Amanda with little thought past the fact that it was supposed to be part of their cover. He didn't like the look of that cheap thing against Eve's silky skin.

He was going to buy her a new collar. Something with diamonds and maybe an emerald or two. It would look beautiful around her throat.

For the time being, she belonged to him and she would accept his gifts. Ian was right. He'd been a pussy for far too long. It was time to be her Dom again. Eve needed his domination. Without it, she'd become far too strict on herself. She needed to know it was all right to relax from time to time.

And he needed her to give him purpose.

"Why aren't you in proper position?" He growled the words at her, forcing his fingers into all that hair and tugging lightly. Her head came back and a throaty gasp left her mouth.

It was an act. From the outsider's point of view, he would seem brutal, but Eve's easy compliance guaranteed she felt no pain. Eve had always enjoyed "angry Master" scenes, and they had played it out many times in front of an audience. This was a delicate dance they'd perfected long ago. She'd known exactly what he needed the minute he'd growled. He watched her eyes flare slightly and her body relax, sure signs that she was following his lead.

She sank down with him, her every move pure precision and grace. She'd fought so hard to gain her agility again. For the longest time he would wince every time he saw her practicing, a reminder of how he'd failed her.

But he needed to take his guilt out of the equation. Eve sank into a perfect slave pose. The new Alex had a sudden insight. It wasn't a reminder of what she'd lost. It was an example of how fucking strong his wife was. She hadn't let Evans take this part of her life.

They had both had a hand in letting Evans tear them apart. He'd spent years blaming the wrong people for their divorce. He'd allowed it.

He'd forgotten he was the Dom.

He held a hand out, presenting her to the company. "This is how my slave is to greet her Master. It reminds her always of her position. She is to serve me." *To love me. To give me a reason to live. To honor me with her trust.*

But he stopped at serve because these men wouldn't understand the true beauty of the power exchange. But he knew one thing they would understand. They would understand the beauty of his submissive.

"Get on the chair, pet."

He couldn't miss the way her face flushed. She was nervous, but he knew damn well she wasn't going to falter. Her eyes had dilated. She was getting aroused at the thought of discipline even in front of a group of men she didn't know. She'd always been an exhibitionist and unashamedly so.

She kept her head bowed as she moved to the whipping chair. It wasn't up to his standards, but it would have to do. He couldn't exactly stop this brutal little exchange to explain that his sub was far too precious to use a substandard bench.

Still, his cock hardened the minute she placed herself across the bench. It was tilted in a way that brought her ass high in the air. The main part of the chair was a leather flat that ran the length of her torso but still gave Alex access to her pussy as it stopped right in the middle of her pelvis. He'd situated the chair to the side where the audience could see what he was going to do. They would be able to see the curves of her backside, but the sight of her naked pussy was only for him.

Her arms were placed on twin appendages that ran on either side of the chair, mirroring the ones for her legs.

"My pet is well trained," Alex explained. "She will remain where I have placed her until such time as I allow her to move, but I am going to tie her down today for the purposes of this scene. A not so well-trained sub would require this."

One of the "gentlemen" chuckled. "Certainly couldn't have one getting away."

Sean stood at the back of the room. No one seemed to have noticed that he hadn't gone back to the kitchen. No. Not a single man was looking anywhere but exactly where Alex wanted them to look.

"Perhaps you gentlemen would prefer to stand. From your position now, you won't be able to see my lovely pet's skin as she takes my discipline." He needed them standing up to prove his point.

Without hesitation, they rose.

He hated this. It was different at Sanctum. At Sanctum, everyone knew the rules. People knew what was expected of them. At Sanctum, showing off his sub was a thing of great pride for both Master and submissive.

Here, it was a necessity. This was why he hadn't wanted to bring Eve with him.

She turned her face up slightly and gave him a little wink and a wiggle of that gorgeous ass of hers.

She was stronger than he gave her credit for. She knew the job, and he couldn't have a better partner. His misgivings were about his possessive nature and not any damn weakness in his sub. His sub, his love, was the strongest person he knew. A well of strength opened in Alex. They could do this. They could do it together.

He didn't hesitate again. He flipped her little skirt up. She'd been a very good pet. She wasn't wearing any panties. Yeah, now he had their attention. Eve had the most gorgeous ass on the planet. No man could possibly look away.

And if a single one of the fuckers tried to touch her, they would find their hands on the floor and detached from their bodies.

He patted her gorgeous ass before moving to tie her hands. He made quick work. Eve often liked to be tied up. They had struggled with it at first. She'd spat out her safe word every time he'd tried to tie her down, but she'd kept at it. She'd insisted on trying every session until she could stand it again.

Holy fuck. Eve had been trying to tell him. Eve had been working through all her problems, and he'd seen it as nothing but a burden to be borne.

She'd been trying. How had he not seen that?

He paid special attention, making sure there was no way

he could chafe her skin. He heard her sigh as he cinched the silk against her skin.

What the fuck had he been doing all this time? She trusted him. She'd shown him an awesome amount of trust. She'd put her body in his care even after they'd divorced. She had tied him up in a million rules and restrictions, but now he saw that for what it was. She'd been pushing him to see how far he would let his guilt take him. Every rule she'd placed on him had been a plea for him to push back, for him to be her Dom, to be the man she'd married.

And he'd been a complete pussy. He'd let his fear rule him. He'd let his need to give in to his guilt push away the most precious thing in his life. She'd been practically screaming for him and he'd been in stasis.

He wasn't going to fail her again. She talked about some new Alex, but she needed the old one. She needed the real Dom that had been sleeping inside him for so long.

She needed the Dom, but with a twist. He'd tried to shelter her before, but now he knew she was more than a sweet thing to protect. She was a partner.

He smacked her ass with the flat of his hand. His Eve could take a hell of a lot more than what was about to happen here. He let his guilt slide away. They had a job to do, and he was suddenly looking forward to it because she was here with him.

"This is the heart of BDSM, the connection between Dom and submissive. She is here to serve me. Right now, it pleases me to discipline her." He gave her five quick smacks, the sound cracking through the air. A pretty pink immediately flushed across her skin.

Every eye was on them and Sean moved in. He was quiet, moving with a negligent grace. His hands were quick, sliding in and out and moving on to the next man while every single one of them, including Chazz and Jesse, kept their eyes on Eve's ass.

Another quick five slaps before he reached into his bag and pulled out a deerskin flogger. The falls were soft and supple, a work of art, alternating dark brown and flesh colors.

"What exactly is that, Master A?" The second of the men leaned across the table as though trying to get a better look at the toy in his hand. Sean took the time to lift the idiot's wallet.

"This is a flogger." He turned and brutally brought the implement down on Eve's ass.

It was perfect because it made a harsh sound but the deerskin falls were buttery soft. He could strike her all day and she would just sigh at the massaging effect. But there was no way to mistake the men's interest. They believed he was assaulting his slave, and it was doing something for them.

Over and over he brought the flogger down on her flesh, his wrists moving in a familiar pattern. He made a figure eight with his hand, carefully placing each blow though he knew damn well he wasn't hurting her. Eve was very likely getting frustrated. His sweet sub liked more of a bite than he was giving her, but he needed her with him and not lost in subspace. He reached down, sliding his hand under the neck of her blouse to find her nipple. She wasn't wearing a bra so it was easy to tweak her breast and make sure she stayed with him.

There would be time enough for her to slip into subspace later when he fucked her hard. Yeah, he was going to do that and soon. He was done denying them both.

He worked her, going through the motions, the pattern familiar and comforting. This was just a warm up, but it was all he needed for this very vanilla crowd. Eve's ass was a pretty pink, a nice sheen making the flesh slightly shiny. So fucking hot.

His dick was throbbing, just begging him to move on. She was tied down, and he could have her any way he wanted. He could order her to open her mouth and she would. He could force his dick in and out, sliding and slipping against that hot tongue of hers. She would take his come. He was off the fucking leash he'd been on for five years.

But he restrained himself because they were working.

He placed his hand on the globes of her ass. They were warm from the flogging. "This is the beginning of our scene. If we were actually performing, I would move her to a St. Andrew's Cross. Of course, it would be necessary for my slave to wear a thong and nipple covers. We could run into trouble with public nudity."

Chazz frowned, but his eyes were still on Eve's ass. "We can be a private club and then she can be naked."

Chazz was an idiot. Kristen had picked her club well. As far as his research had gone, Evans had clubs like this across the country, but she'd picked this one because Chazz was reckless. He was a small-time crook who'd made some big-time connections, but he didn't have a brain in his head.

"If we're a private club, how the hell are you going to effectively move our friends' product?"

The Jersey boy shook his head as though trying to understand what he'd just said.

Asshole Narcoterrorist Number Two, however, seemed to understand immediately. "We need a crowded club. We need people to sell to, but I still don't see how this is going to work. Why would we need some sex show?"

Number One concurred. "It was quite lovely, and I can

see a whole industry attached to it. The Master could properly train our whores, but I don't see how this helps us move product."

Product being drugs. He was right. They were moving drugs through the clubs and funding their organizations.

"I, uhm, I think it's just a unique idea," Chazz said. "Mikey likes it. It was really his idea to go with the kinky theme."

Alex smiled, showing just a little hint of teeth, a predatory expression. "Gentlemen, if you would please check your wallets."

Quizzical expressions came across their faces and four sets of hands immediately went for their jacket pockets.

The Middle Eastern man frowned ferociously. "You bastard." His expression cleared, his dark eyes rolling. "Ah. Very effective. Could I have my wallet back now?"

Sean stepped forward, placing the wallets back on the table. "Of course, gentlemen. I promise this was for show only."

"Show?" Chazz was getting red in the face as he looked through his wallet.

Idiot. Alex placed a hand on Eve's ass, loving the connection even as he stared down a group of hostiles, Chazz included. The terrorist group seemed to have caught on. They were talking quietly amongst themselves.

"Yeah, boss," Jesse said with a nod, proving he was smarter than Chazz. "You know. It's what you planned all along. You were going to show our guests the power of having a nightly show."

"Unlike your regular nightclub, at least once or twice a night, all eyes will be on the stage," Alex explained. "No one will be able to look away."

One of the South Americans sighed. "I thought this was

210

a stupid idea, but you're right. We can move most of the product very quietly this way, with almost no prying eyes. We could use the…what did you call the cocktail waitresses?"

"The submissives," Alex prompted. "The subs would be able to move through the crowd making your nightly drops. The buyers place their orders with the bouncers and pay up front. The subs deliver the packages during the show."

Chazz nodded as though he'd been in on the idea the whole time. "That way we keep the package and the money separated. And the girls will be trained what to do if they get caught. Master A can make it so they won't ever give up the operation. Yeah, this was always the plan. My plan. I'm pitching the whole thing to the boss when he comes in. He's going to love it."

"The owner of this club is very smart, as you can see." Alex laid it on thick. The last thing he needed was Chazz to think he was going to try to take credit. "It's why I decided to throw my lot in with this club. The scene you just saw was just a teaser. I can make the scene last as long as we need. I hope you can see that this is to your advantage."

"I can certainly see how she's to my advantage," Jake said, leering at Eve's ass.

Maybe Jake was playing his role a little too well. Alex had a sudden need to punch his friend.

Alex untied the ropes that bound her, and Eve slid gracefully to the floor back in slave pose.

"What do you say to your Master, pet?" Alex asked.

"Thank you for the discipline, Master. Your pet is very happy to serve." Her head was down, her voice a soft monotone, but he caught her lips curling up in a seductive little grin. Her long hair hid it from the others. That grin was meant for him and him alone, and Alex's cock pulsed in his slacks.

He reached down and grasped her hand. Eve stumbled a little, her knee seeming to go out on her and she fell against his chest. He forced his expression to go dark. "Go sit down. Your lack of grace disappoints me. On your knees by my chair."

He wanted to lift her in his arms, but everyone was watching. Eve moved to the chair he'd been sitting in and sank to her knees next to it.

Chazz approached, his hand out. "Very nice, Master A. I think that plan went well."

"Yes, I believe you've made your point," the first gentleman said.

Jake was making his move because Alex had more than one point to make. "I know I'm interested in being involved."

"Who is that man?" The second gentleman asked, staring at Jake like he was a bug crawling across the floor.

"He's just a friend. He's in the security business. I'm always looking for decent bouncers." Chazz frowned as though he finally realized that bringing his drinking buddy from the night before into a business meeting was a bad idea.

"And I'm always looking for a pretty whore," Jake said just before he reached down and put a hand on Eve.

Even though they'd planned this, Alex practically saw red. He crossed the space between them in two long strides and then he nearly lifted Jake up by his shirt, his fist coming back and cracking against Jake's jaw.

One punch. The first one had to be good. The rest were all for show. Alex had Jake on the ground, his fists hitting Jake's gut lightly, but the sounds Jake made were pure theater. He howled and moaned and pretended to fight back.

Finally, Sean pulled him off Jake, but his point had been made. Everyone was watching him, their eyes moving from his face to the blood on Jake's.

"You're a complete psycho," Jake shouted, rolling away.

Yeah, that was the impression he'd been trying to make.

Alex stared down at Jake, his voice a low threat. "The next time you touch my property, I will kill you. Do you fucking understand me? I'll take a knife to your gut and you won't go fast. You'll go slow and be in as much pain as I can give you. I protect my property and my friends. You get the fuck out of here. You don't belong here. The boss tried to show you some friendship and this is how you repay him, by screwing up his meeting."

Alex turned and saw red again. Eve was at the feet of one of the fucking terrorists, her arms around his legs, his hand on her head.

It looked like his next fight would be real. No pulling punches this time.

Chapter Ten

Eve planted the device she'd taken from Alex, affixing it to her target's shoe. She'd made a careful study of their shoes. Alex was wrong. Placing it inside a jacket was a bad idea and none of the men were carrying briefcases. The little sticker-like tracking device would stand out on a cell phone, and that seemed to be how these men communicated and kept notes.

A jacket could be easily removed, cleaned, and the tracking signal lost. Most men changed their jackets. But not their shoes.

She leaned over as though the violence was terrifying and she was hoping the man above her would protect her. It gave her a chance to smooth the device down. Of the three men she had to choose from, this one's shoes were well worn. They were black Louis Vuitton loafers that had subtle creases from long wear. The Middle Eastern man's shoes were black, too, but they were new and had an obvious shine to them. They were a no go. A quick shoeshine at the airport would dump the device. The man she'd chosen had dull shoes. He didn't shine them. They were perfect. He wasn't leaving those shoes behind any time soon.

She felt a deep sense of accomplishment even as the man's hand came down on her head.

Damn it. She hadn't thought about the fact that Alex had just pretended to beat the holy hell out of the last man who had touched her. Maybe he wasn't looking and she could move away.

She brought her eyes up. Alex looked like a bull ready to charge. She had seconds before he completely blew up and screwed with their cover.

Eve crawled to him, the wood floors scraping against her knees, but she didn't dare leap to her feet. "I was so frightened, Master. Please forgive me."

She wrapped her arms around his legs. Every muscle in his body was tight with tension. *Please let it go. Please let it go.*

His hand tangled in her hair. "You aren't where I put you. Bad pet. That's fifty. Go through the kitchens to the locker room. Clean yourself up and wait for me. You're obviously not fit for company, you disobedient brat."

She would take it. He was banishing her, but it was probably a good thing. She started to get to her feet. When she was in the kitchens, she could process what had gone on and be ready to talk about her observations later.

"On your knees, brat."

Oh, she was going to give him an earful about that. She kept her face placid and crawled along the floor, well aware that her ass was very likely hanging out. Well, he could just watch her go because after that he wasn't getting any.

She crawled to the kitchens, resenting the hell out of him even as she knew damn well why he'd done it.

The minute she crawled through the swinging doors, Kristen was practically on top of her.

"I need to talk to you and your Master." Kristen kept her voice low. Several servers and kitchen staff were moving around, getting the next course ready.

"I have to go to the locker rooms." And someone so needed to clean this floor. She was going to have to have a serious talk with Sean about the state of his tile. Sure it looked all perfectly clean when one was standing up, but from her vantage point, she could see the dirt. *Ick.* Another reason to be pissed off at Alex.

She was pissed off at Alex. Like really and truly pissed off at Alex and ready to throw a hissy fit the minute she was able to. She kind of wanted to call him a bastard and tell him that if he ever wanted to see the inside of her vagina again, he better come crawling.

She was mad. A little kernel of happiness lit her up. They had tiptoed around each other for years, politeness their refuge against any strong emotion. She'd hidden her irritation with him and he'd been a frustrating well of patience with her.

It wasn't healthy. Couples in love fought. Couples in love got irritated and ranted and raved at each other.

She'd told herself years ago that she'd fallen out of love with Alex. She knew she would always love him, but their real passion had burned away in the aftermath of what had happened. Alex had pulled away and she had gone into a cocoon where nothing could touch her, nothing could make her mad.

Crawling on the floor made her mad.

And she was damn straight going to do it.

"Uhm, is there a reason you're making like a baby?" Kristen asked. "I can help you up if you need a hand."

Oh, no. She was going to crawl every inch of the way. She wasn't going to give her Master any reason to say she didn't comply. It would have been so easy for him to give her a good couple of slaps to the ass, but he'd chosen this. "The Master wants me to crawl to the locker rooms. I am doing my Master's bidding."

"Shit. Wow. Well, I'm coming with you because we have a few things to work out. Can you crawl faster?"

Eve turned her head up, frowning at the redhead before restarting her slow crawl without saying a word. She pushed through the backside of the kitchen and into the quiet hall that led back to the lockers.

"This is dumb." Kristen got to her knees beside Eve, crawling in time.

"You could just go and wait for me."

Kristen's voice went low. "Was that Jacob Dean?"

Eve nodded. "Yes. Alex brought him in for the day."

"And I wasn't told."

"Neither was I. I don't think informing us was high on Alex's list of priorities."

"This is my op, damn it. I laid out some ground rules, the chief one being that I approved every member of the team." Kristen whispered the words, but there was no way to mistake the fact that she was angry. She bit the words out through clenched teeth. She stopped in the middle of the hallway. "This floor is really gross. Is Master A trying to give you Ebola? I think I see some just to the left of you."

Thank god, she was at the door to the locker room. She got up and entered, walking straight to the sink because while she was pretty sure the floor was hemorrhagic fever free, she couldn't say the same thing of staph. She washed her hands. Thoroughly.

Kristen walked around the locker room, checking the stalls before coming back and joining her at the sink. "We can talk. I already did my daily bug check and we're alone now, so it's safe. I want to know why your husband is trying to fuck me over?"

It was an interesting reaction. Kristen seemed so calm, so very patient, but Jake's appearance had her rattled. "I don't think he's trying to do anything to you. This is his op."

She shook her head. "No. It's mine. I mean it's my

217

story. I brought you all in to this."

She didn't understand the way they worked, and this was so much more than a story for Alex. "And Alex has been hunting for this man for years. He's trained. We all are. You have to understand that Alex is responsible for us. You aren't."

"I'm not going to let anyone get hurt. Do you have any idea how long it's taken me to get my ducks in a row? And then Alex McKay waltzes in like he owns the place."

"You did make him the Dom in Residence. He kind of has to act that way. Do you have a specific problem with Jacob?" It didn't make a lot of sense. Kristen had come to them. She'd known they were a team. Why was she trying to pick and choose now?

Kristen dried her hands, her face closing off. "I just don't like surprises. That's all. Who's going to show up next? Is Taggart going to be at my doorstep when we get home?"

"Ian's stuck in Dallas." He'd called late last night. "There's some kind of issue with our bank accounts. He's pretty sure it's Eli Nelson. Some very large accounts got frozen. Ian's having to jump through a bunch of hoops to bring them back online."

Kristen's face was turned away, her voice a little distant. "That's terrible. This Nelson person, who is he?"

Eve shrugged a little. "He's kind of like Ian's nemesis. Let's just say they're on opposite ends of the professional spectrum."

"He should take care of that then. We can handle things here." Kristen took a step back. "I don't like surprises, Eve. I'm willing to share information with you. Hell, I'll open the files I have and let you make copies, but I require the same courtesy."

"Files?" Alex hadn't mentioned files.

She wrinkled her nose a little, looking like a kid who had gotten caught with her hands in the cookie jar. "Yeah. I might have hacked into the feds database and gotten all the files they have on Evans."

"Seriously?" It wasn't the easiest thing to hack into a government database.

It was Kristen's turn to shrug. "It's a hobby. I thought you might like to look at the new stuff and see if you could maybe update your profile. But I get that you're just here for Alex now."

The manipulation was a little blatant. Eve didn't rise to the bait. She was kind of saving all her irritation for Alex. It was a bit disconcerting to realize that she was just waiting for him to walk through that door. She didn't want the peace that came from being alone. She wanted the electric feeling she'd had any time she was near him in the last week. "I'll take a look at the files, though I seriously doubt he's changed his motivations."

Although there now seemed to be a serious money component, as evidenced by the clubs. He'd made small changes before, using his followers to bring in their paychecks and running tiny meth labs. He'd spent everything on his terror campaigns. His bombs had been more sophisticated and deadlier than the usual homemade stuff.

What was he trying to do now? Yes. She would like a look at those files.

Kristen looked down, her eyes catching on something. "I would appreciate it. And I would appreciate if I could be considered a member of this team. I get it. Master Alex is too controlling to give over, but I've been helpful. I want that acknowledged. At the end of all of this, I want everyone to know that I did good, damn it. There's dirt all over your knees. It's probably infectious knowing what goes on in this club."

Kristen turned and walked out, the door sliding shut behind her.

Eve winced. Her knees were streaked with dirt. Someone was so getting yelled at over housekeeping issues. She walked back and started one of the showers. Even if he hadn't told her to get cleaned up, she wouldn't have been able to leave it like it was. She shed her clothes, her brain working on the conversation she'd just had.

Good. It was an odd word. *I want everyone to know I did good.*

It played in her brain, that one sentence looping over and over. Eve groaned a little as the hot water hit her skin. Alex had been easy on her. She barely could feel where he'd spanked her. She liked it harder and he knew it.

I did good.

Kristen was a writer, a good one at that. She'd been nominated for a Pulitzer. Her grammar should be impeccable. Unless she hadn't meant it the way Eve had taken it. I did good could be a grammatically incorrect version of *I did well.*

Or it could mean that she did right, good.

Why was Kristen so concerned with everyone on the team knowing she'd done something righteous? It wasn't the first time she mentioned it. She'd talked about wearing a white hat for once.

But all of her stories helped people. She was a writer who championed the underdog and exposed corruption. So why did she sound like she was seeking redemption?

The stall opened, but Eve didn't scream. She'd known he would be here. She'd known it from the minute he'd ordered her here.

And she'd known that he would be done playing games with her. She'd seen it in his eyes.

Five whole days he'd tortured her with intimacy and no sex. That was done now, and she had the feeling it wasn't going to be a soft and sweet lovemaking session.

Alex stood in the door of the stall, not a stitch of clothes covering his hard body. She glanced over, her eyes taking him in. He glared down at her, his hands on his muscled hips. The big bad Dom was in the house.

He was built like a linebacker, all hard muscle and perfectly sculpted skin. His broad shoulders barely fit in the door of the stall. Those shoulders tapered down to a lean waist and a six-pack that still made her mouth water. His legs were strong, long and thick. And his cock. God, she longed for that damn cock, and she'd had it a thousand times.

So why did it feel new now?

It had to be the whole mission thing. She hadn't been out in the field with him this way before. It was a rush, and being exposed to danger could bring people together. She had to remember this wasn't the real world. They weren't really together.

"You want to explain what you're doing, Eve?" Alex's voice was a low, silky threat. It was the voice he used to employ when he really wanted her to think about what she was going to say to him because a wrong word would bring some punishment.

Fortunately for him, she wasn't afraid of his punishment. His spanking earlier had been more of a tease than anything else. She was still jittery and unfulfilled from those barely there blows and five previous days of sexual denial. "I'm taking a shower because my asshole Master forced me to crawl on a dirty floor."

His expression changed suddenly. "It wasn't dirty. I saw them cleaning earlier. They were mopping."

That was why she'd always trusted him. It took everything she had not to just dissolve into a puddle of goo at his feet. Yes, he was a Dom and yes, he needed control, but the last thing he would ever do was hurt or humiliate his sub. She let a good portion of her irritation go because she was more than his sub right now. She was his partner.

And it was kind of a nice thing to be. *Not the real world.* She forced the words to go across her brain. In the real world, Alex had rarely treated her like a partner. She'd been precious to him, something to take care of, but she couldn't go back now. She'd changed.

She reached out and touched his chest, letting her hand run over all that silky skin and hard muscle. It felt good to be able to reach out and touch him. The minute her fingers brushed his skin, his cock twitched. She still had that power over him. Her anger was dissolving in the heat of longing. She tried to hold on to it. "Your version of clean and mine are quite different, Master."

A hard look came back into his eyes. She was done with her hissy fit, but it looked like his had just begun. "I meant what the hell were you doing out there, Eve?"

Did he really want to have this conversation here? Maybe he wasn't done with his torture. She gestured toward the door. "Master, we might not be alone."

"Don't shake your head at me. I locked the door, and Sean is keeping everyone else busy. So you can answer the question before I start your punishment."

She cocked an eyebrow. "I deserve punishment? You haven't heard the explanation yet."

He crowded her, forcing her back against the tiled wall

of the shower. Her mind got a little mushy when she felt his cock pressing against her belly. He seemed intent on reminding her just how much bigger he was. "I don't need an explanation. You disobeyed me. We had a plan going in. We talked about it this morning."

She hated how breathy her voice got. She had to force herself to fight with him because all she was thinking about now was how good his punishment was going to feel. "You had a plan. You didn't even tell me about Jake until we were here."

"I didn't know he was going to make it, and I don't have to tell you a thing. I'm in charge of this operation. I have to know that you're going to obey me in the field, and you didn't today. You shouldn't have moved from your place. What the hell were you thinking?" He loomed over her, those green eyes of his dark as he stared down.

His adrenaline was still up. He'd been like this whenever he'd come home from a particularly rough case. When his adrenaline was still coursing through his veins, he'd been practically insatiable. In the last few years, he'd exchanged sex for a treadmill from what she'd seen. After nearly losing Sean and Grace to Eli Nelson over a year ago, she'd caught him on mile nine of what turned out to be a twenty-mile run.

He seemed to be falling back into familiar patterns. He'd gotten scared and now he needed to burn off the feeling inside her body.

She should stop him. She should step out of the shower and give them both a chance to calm down. Alex could be crazy possessive, and he'd had to show her off to men he didn't trust. He'd had to watch her get close to a drug-dealing terrorist. He just needed a few minutes and some calm to put things on the right footing.

And it wouldn't hurt for her to tell him the truth.

"I was thinking that you didn't know what you were doing," Eve admitted.

His hand tangled in her hair, pulling on it. He wasn't being gentle with her now. He tugged, lighting up her scalp. God, she'd missed this. "What did you say to me?"

She was pushing his buttons, and she couldn't seem to stop herself. She knew that if she stepped away, he would probably let her. But all she seemed to be able to do was push him further. "I said your theory was flawed and you needed me to fix it for you. I didn't have time or a place to talk to you about it, so I took one of the GPS units out of your pocket when I stumbled into you and I placed it for you. I couldn't exactly call a time-out to explain it all. And you're welcome. In a few hours, when our bad guy leaves, we'll know where he's going."

His mouth dropped open as though that was the last thing he'd expected to hear. "I got the GPS into one of their jackets. I had it handled, Eve. You placed yourself and the mission in danger."

She shook her head despite the fact that he still had a nice grip on it. He seemed to really enjoy her longer hair. "I did what I needed to do. You're not thinking about what could happen. He could drop that jacket at any moment. He probably has several of them. If he has a place here in the States, he'll likely leave it here and then all we'll know is where he likes to sleep when he's in town. But he won't leave those shoes behind. And let's talk about dry cleaning."

She gasped because he turned her and before she could protest, he'd laid ten quick smacks to her ass. The sound cracked through the shower stall. He wasn't playing this time. Her eyes watered, her flesh flaring with pain. It raced on her skin, lighting every bit of her up and making her feel alive. She wasn't sure why this did it for her, but it did. She was just a woman who liked a bite of pain.

She'd fought to get this back, battled to be able to enjoy this again. And Alex had been there with her. Even when she'd treated him like hell, he'd still been there.

"You want to push me, angel?" He had his mouth right against her ear. "It took me a while, but I know this game now. You need this. You need me to take control. You need to play and know that I'm going to give you what you need. But you've opened this door again and I don't know that I can shut it. You might be the smart one. This little play of yours might have been smarter than mine, but know this, the next time you disobey my orders, I will keep you on the edge for hours. You think the last five days have been bad? They will be heaven compared to what I'll do. I will tie you down and your ass will be more than red. I will plug you and spank you and take you right up to the point of orgasm and then sit back and watch you squirm."

That sounded perfectly dreadful. She was a logical woman deep down. There were days when spending an afternoon being edged would be interesting, but not now. Not after the way he'd primed her for days. She needed him.

She needed to take a different tactic. He'd been scared and maybe it was real progress. She'd pushed the mission forward, but he seemed much more worried about the vague possibility that she'd been in danger. Even though she really hadn't. He was trying. He was putting her before the mission. She couldn't help but soften up a little.

"Alex, I don't want that and I don't think you want that, either. We don't have much time in here. We have to get cleaned up and you have to spend the rest of the day with Chazz. Do you really want to spend the little time we have withholding my orgasm? Have the last couple of days really been so easy on you?"

He turned her back around, his eyes on her mouth. He was already wavering. "You know they haven't. But I should spank that ass until you can't sit down and then I should force you to your knees. I should make you suck my cock and take everything I have, and then I should walk away because you need to learn a lesson. I'm in charge when we're out in the field."

He was so frustrating. "I do understand, but I'm right about this, Alex."

His fingers reached for her nipples, twisting them lightly, making her shiver. "I don't care if you're right or not. You have to obey me. He could have hurt you. He could have hauled you away somewhere. He could have…"

She put her hands on his hips, snuggling closer. He needed reassurance. Sometimes it was easy to forget that the Dom needed to feel safe, too. "I'm fine. I promise I will fight like hell if anyone tries to take me again. I'll scream and shout and I will do everything I can to get back to you."

He sighed, his anger seeming to deflate. "Did you fight Evans?"

She didn't want to talk about it. She didn't want to go there. She wanted him to spank her again. She could cry that way. She could let the pain float away.

God, she'd kept it in for so long. She'd blamed Alex, but she was at fault, too. "I didn't. I was scared."

"I know you were, angel." His hands gentled, finding the nape of her neck and pulling her close.

She sighed and relaxed into his strength. His cock was still hard against her belly. He still wanted her. "I couldn't believe it was happening, and I thought I shouldn't fight because maybe he wouldn't hurt me more. I was in shock from seeing them kill Tommy and Leon. I thought maybe he would be easy on me if I complied. I thought he was going to ransom me. I was so stupid. So stupid. I kept thinking he wasn't going to hurt me. He didn't need to hurt me. I was fooling myself but I just wanted to survive. I just wanted to go home."

It was one of the things she regretted most. She'd been so docile, trying to logic her way out of an illogical situation.

He ran a hand across her wet hair, smoothing it out, his eyes so haunted. "I looked for you."

Eve nodded. She was sure of that. "I know you did."

"Ian looked for you. Ian used every influence he had and we couldn't find you and it still didn't work. God, angel, he could have killed you. I didn't sleep for a week. I just focused on finding you. It was the only thing that kept me sane."

And then he'd stayed sane by switching his focus to finding Evans, and she'd gone silent. She'd withheld herself from him because she'd been scared at first, and it had become a habit. "Alex, do you think my scars are ugly?"

She'd never just asked him, terrified that she would get a lukewarm, kind answer. There were so many questions she hadn't asked because she'd been afraid. She knew he wouldn't tell her yes, but how he said it would mean everything.

He tugged her hair, forcing her head back. All tenderness was gone. "What did you say?"

Tears filled her eyes. Relief was a wave that flashed through her system. This wasn't going to be some attempt to placate her. He was pissed. "I was worried that you didn't think I was pretty anymore."

"There is nothing wrong with your body. You are the most gorgeous fucking thing I've ever seen, and I swear if you say one bad thing about the body I adore again, you'll think a little edging is heaven compared to what I'll do to you." A sexy growl came out of his mouth and a fierce desire was on his face. He rubbed his cock against her belly. "Do I have to show you how much I love this body?"

"Please, Alex." She wanted him so badly.

He put his forehead against hers. "No other women, Eve. Not for the rest of my life. If you walk away from me at the end of this, I won't ever want another woman because it's been you since the first time I laid eyes on you. Only you. Compared to my friends, I've practically been a monk. They've had so many women they can't count them, but I was the lucky one because I only needed one. I only need one. I'll show you. I'll fucking show you how gorgeous you are."

He picked her up, his lean muscles easily lifting her as though she didn't weigh a thing. His mouth latched onto a nipple, biting and sucking. The water pounded down on her, but his mouth was hotter. He lashed her nipple with his tongue before giving her the edge of his teeth and making her squirm. He always knew just the right amount of pain to give her, just that little bite that threatened to send her over the edge.

He switched to the other breast, holding her high against the tile. She felt small and helpless, but with her Master that did something for her. She could be helpless against him because he wouldn't hurt her. Not physically.

He played at her breasts, lavishing them with affection before he let her slide down the tile just a bit.

"God, I want you. I won't ever stop wanting you." He pressed his lips to hers, his tongue diving deep.

She had to wrap her legs around his waist and hold on for dear life because his cock knew right where it wanted to go. That big dick of Alex's was already pushing inside, opening her up, showing her how much he wanted to get inside.

"Open up for me, angel. You take me. You take every inch I have. Your pussy is mine, and I fucking want in. You said all you wanted to do was go home. This is my home, Eve. This is my goddamn home, and no matter what happens, it always will be." He shoved her back against the shower wall, his mouth coming down on hers.

His tongue plunged inside while he strained to fit his cock in. Eve softened, opening her mouth to him. Now that he'd kissed her again, she couldn't seem to stop wanting his mouth on hers, their tongues playing, sliding alongside one another. She wrapped her arms around his neck, giving as good as she got.

She couldn't be still now. Later, she would let him tie her up and down and play with her for hours, but this was something more. This was new. She kissed him back, unable to hold herself apart. The water streamed around them, but she didn't notice it. All that mattered was winding her body around her husband's, taking him deep inside. His cock was so big. No matter how many times she had him, it always took her breath away when he started to pierce her. She was deliciously pinned, forced to take more and more of him.

"You feel so good, angel. You get so hot for me."

He'd given her the words she'd needed. She gave him her truth, too. "Only you, Alex. Only for you. I never felt this way for anyone else."

And she never would.

He planted his chest against hers, trapping her between the shower wall and his hard body as he sank home.

So full. He filled her up. Always. He held himself against her, rubbing their chests together as he seated himself to the hilt. He kissed her again as though he couldn't stop exploring her mouth. She ran her hands across his head. His hair was so short now, but it just made him all the more masculine. She held on because she didn't want the moment to end.

There was so much he didn't know. So much she still couldn't tell him. Everything felt new again, but it was fragile, too. She couldn't stand the thought of it dissolving. Not yet. It wouldn't bear the weight of the real world, but she wanted these days with him. For however long they had, she wanted to be with him in every way.

"Please, Alex. I can't stand it. Please."

He nipped at her ear, a little shock through her system. "Please what, angel? Please wash me? Please stand here? You're going to have to be more specific."

He loved to hear her beg. "Please fuck me, Alex. Please fuck me so hard."

"Oh, yeah, you know I want that." He used the wall as a balance as he pulled out and thrust back in hard, making her whole body jump with the thrill of him filling her up again.

Over and over again he slammed inside, his cock rubbing all the right places. She was so primed, her every sense attuned to him. The orgasm built, a cannon threatening to go off. The whole time he pounded his cock inside, he kissed her. His tongue fucked into her mouth in synch with his cock as though he needed to be as intimate as he could. Their tongues slid together in a silky dance. She felt his hands on the globes of her ass, one of them seeking entry there, too. A finger pressed against her asshole, rimming her lightly and forcing the tip inside. She shivered at the dark sensation.

"I want everything, Eve," he whispered against her mouth. "I won't leave an inch of this gorgeous body untouched. I love this body. I loved it when you were heavier, and I still love it now. I love it scarred or perfect. I love it because this skin and bones houses your soul. There is nothing ugly about it. I don't care what he did. This is mine. Mine."

She let her nails sink into his shoulders as he hit the perfect place inside, and she went flying.

Alex fucked deep again, and he shuddered as he spilled his semen inside. His finger slipped back out of her ass, but she knew he wouldn't wait long to take her there now that he'd been let off the leash. He would give her everything he'd promised, total possession. He pressed in for what felt like a pleasant eternity before gently letting her down. He kissed her again, his hand reaching for the soap.

"I'm a pussy Dom. Don't tell Ian. Tell him how rough I was on you, angel." He cleaned off his hands before he started methodically washing her flesh, his hands stroking over her.

She felt weak, stretched and sore. He hadn't exactly been tender, but it had been so good to be close to him, to feel his passion and not his guilt.

"I won't tell." She ran her hand across his scalp, her eyes closing as he got to his knees and started cleaning her pussy.

"That's my sweet pet."

She whispered his name as he dumped the soap and started cleaning her with his tongue.

Eve let everything slip away as she lost herself for the first time in years. She was with Alex, and that was all that mattered.

* * * *

Jesse slipped back out of the locker room, looking around to see if that busybody Kristen had followed him. She seemed to always be around these days. He couldn't have her following him on this errand. He'd set two of the cocktail waitresses on her fifteen minutes before. Sometimes a little chaos was called for. It had been easy. He'd just made up a little rumor that one of the girls was keeping tips from the pool and the rest of them had been all over Kristen.

The cook dude had been yelling at some of the men in the kitchen about proper cooking techniques for lamb and Jesse had managed to slip into the hallway when he should have been enjoying the luncheon. Someone needed to talk to that big blond guy about the fact that the word "beets" and "enjoy" did not belong in the same sentence. He didn't get why they had fired Big Mike. Sure his burgers were a little on the raw side, but at least he hadn't served beets.

Master A had locked the door to the women's locker room, but Jesse had learned long ago that a simple lock couldn't keep him out. A couple of seconds with a pick and a torque wrench and he was in. He had his story all planned out if he got caught. Someone had come by and complained that the locker room was inaccessible. He was just helping out one of the girls.

He hadn't needed a story. Those two weren't about to notice him. He'd followed them hoping he could overhear something, anything that he could tell his boss. He'd gotten exactly what he wanted.

He clutched at his cell phone as he relocked the door and made his way down the hall.

Azure stopped him, her body barely contained in a tiny skirt and a too-tight T-shirt. "Hey, Jesse. Kris is looking for you. And what's with all the VIPs? Chazz said I had to work after hours. What does that mean?"

It meant she would end up fucking one of those men who were here, no doubt. Chazz viewed all the women with the exception of Kristen as convenient whores. But all he could do was shrug. "No idea. Maybe you should tell him you're sick."

She frowned and looked far older than her twenty-two years. "Nah, they look like they have money."

Most of the girls who worked here came from the streets. They saw money as a way out. They couldn't imagine that the streets of Hell were definitely paved with gold. And it wasn't his job to correct her. "I'm sure they do. I gotta run an errand. Tell Kris I'll be back later."

He had a call to make. And he wanted to put himself as far away from that couple in the shower as he could get.

He rushed out into the bright Florida sunshine. Everything was so fucking bright and shiny here. He'd gotten used to the dark.

He could still hear Master Asshole beating his woman. He could still hear the slap of his hand on her flesh and her breathy cries as she took his...discipline. God, what a word. It wasn't discipline. It was fucking abuse, and he hated the fact that it had gotten his dick so hard he could pound nails. He'd just stood there listening to them. He'd seen himself there, smacking that beautiful ass.

He wasn't a fucking pervert. He just wasn't.

He'd heard the way the brutal fucker beat his woman, saw how he humiliated her in the meeting earlier in the day.

So why had it seemed so lovely to him? He hadn't been able to stop watching, and it wasn't just the smacks and how the Master tugged on her hair. He'd watched how she'd curled onto the Master's lap, how she sank to her knees before him and her face had been serene. All the trust in the world had been on her lovely face.

Just for that moment, he'd wondered how it would feel to have a woman trust him like that.

He dragged humid air into his lungs as his cell started to ring. The boss man was right on time.

He answered the phone, looking behind him to make sure no one was following. He started walking down the cobblestoned streets that marked St. Augustine's downtown. "I'm here."

"You haven't sent me the information I requested days ago. I would like an explanation."

Jesse tried to hide his frustration. "There hasn't been a good time to take pictures. I don't want him to catch me. He's gotten in good with Chazz. I think he could cause trouble if he decided to try to get rid of me. So I've been patient. He's actually very observant."

Master A was always watching, Jesse had noticed. The only time the man hadn't been watching was when he was beating the holy shit out of the idiot Chazz had brought with him. Jesse had immediately dismissed the man as one of Chazz's show-off friends and had gone back to concentrating on Anthony Priest.

Who wasn't Anthony Priest. He'd heard the woman call him by another name. And damn if the man didn't move really well. He was supposed to be some sort of professional pervert, but he walked like a cop. And his eyes. They were always moving, always hard. Until he looked at the woman.

Fuck. They were acting. Shitballs. He'd missed it. They were really total perverts, but the Master person wasn't as hard as he pretended. It had been in the way he held her when the others weren't watching. He might have had a negligent look on his face, but Master A's arms had curled around her, making sure there was no way she would fall and he'd settled her in as though her comfort was deeply

234

important to him.

A cop making an appearance could screw everything up.

"Is there any way the local cops are onto this operation?" Jesse asked.

A long pause came over the phone. "I would have heard something. I have contacts there. Why do you ask?"

"I think this Master person is some sort of law enforcement. I don't know why. It's something about the eyes. My instincts tell me he's not what he says he is."

"Your instincts have been off before."

He didn't need to be reminded. There was a reason he was in this position. "Yeah, well, at least I know Anthony isn't his name."

"And how did you figure that out? How did you run anything on him without facial recognition?" The boss relied heavily on high-tech equipment.

Jesse had found out that sometimes it was better to just rely on his eyes and ears.

"His woman called him by another name." While he was spanking her ass. While he was making her groan. How long had it been since he'd had anything but a quickie meant to get both him and the lady off as fast as possible so they could go their separate ways? Half the time he didn't even ask for a name.

"I need to know that name, Murdoch." The boss's voice had gone low, whispering across the line.

"Alex. I didn't catch the last name, but she clearly called him Alex."

Jesse held the phone to his ear as he walked down the crowded street. Tourists were milling around the narrow lanes that offered small restaurants and art galleries and more fudge shops than any town should be able to handle.

They really liked their sweets here. Nothing. He heard nothing for thirty seconds. He stopped, worried the line had gone dead. "Boss?"

"His name is Alexander McKay, and he's an enemy, Murdoch. He's the worst possible person to have walked through that door. He's going to ruin everything."

A cold shiver went up his spine. He'd known there was something wrong with Master A, but he still had to ask the question. "How can you be sure? There are millions of dudes named Alex in the world."

"There is only one who can really fuck everything up. Alexander McKay is going to wreck this operation. He's a man who can hurt us all and he won't hesitate to do it. He is very dangerous."

"How is he involved?" He'd never heard the name Alex McKay before, but then he hadn't exactly studied up. He was a soldier. He was a grunt.

"Do you need me to send you his dossier? Perhaps I should find a more amenable agent."

He couldn't lose this job. It was all he fucking had and besides, he wasn't exactly intelligence here. He was just following orders. It was all he was really good at. "No, sir. Tell me what to do."

"Kill him. Kill him and whoever came with him, but get rid of McKay first."

His gut tightened at the thought of killing the woman. He'd killed men before. That didn't bother him. If McKay was threatening his operation, he had to be eliminated, but the woman was different.

"That's an order, Murdoch. Do you understand me?"

He forced himself to say the words he knew his boss wanted to hear. "Yes, sir. I'll have it done as soon as possible."

"You better because this meeting is going to take place in three day's time. I can't have McKay disrupting it. How much does he know?"

"I don't think he knows about the meeting." Jesse only knew because the boss had told him. At this point, he wasn't even sure Chazz knew what was going to kick him squarely in the balls three days from now.

"Everything rides on this. Everything we've worked for."

He knew what was riding on his shoulders. "I understand."

A long sigh came over the line. "Good. You're a good soldier, Murdoch. You're a good man to have on the team."

"I won't let you down." Jesse ended the call.

The world flowed around him, families with kids, couples holding hands, friends joking around, and Jesse realized just how alone he was. He shoved his cell in his pocket and began the walk back to the club parking lot. He needed to get his shit together because he wasn't going to ever be a part of some happy fucking family.

He had his job, and he was damn lucky to have it. The boss didn't have to trust him. Hell, no one else did. He had one shot at having any kind of a future, and he wasn't going to let Alex McKay, world-class pervert, get in his way. He'd surely been right before. The tenderness he'd seen was an illusion. If the boss said he had to go, then he had to go.

And then Jesse would be in. Then he would really be on the team, a true soldier again.

He picked up the pace, his resolve hardened. He would put the woman down easy, but maybe he wouldn't be so kind to the man.

He had a little aggression to work out after all.

Chapter Eleven

"So you're saying you won't be here any time soon, huh, boss?" Adam asked, his voice clear as day as Alex walked through the front door of the condo. The balcony doors were open and a peaceful breeze came off the Atlantic.

There was nothing peaceful about his best friend's response. Ian's voice cracked through the condo.

"You invited Taggart here?" Kristen whispered, holding back as though the devil himself was in the room.

Well, Ian had quite the reputation. He suspected there was a reason Kristen didn't want Ian around. He would very likely take over. Of course as lovely and soft as Kristen was, Ian would also very likely try to get into her bed. He needed to get her to chill because he'd spent forty minutes listening to her bitch about Jake showing up. "I did not. And since he's talking to Adam through a computer, it's likely he's not on his way."

Ian practically snarled over the connection. "No. I will not be getting on a plane any time soon because some motherfucker managed to get my name on a no-fly list. I swear to god, when I find Nelson I am going to kill him real slow."

Eve gasped a little beside him, rushing toward the dining room table where Adam had a monitor up.

Kristen simply frowned and carefully walked around the mass of tech gear Adam had accrued. She was deliberate about not walking in front of the camera attached to the computer. "Are you sure you weren't going to bring him in, too? I might as well just walk away for all you respect me. I have plans, and you're going to screw them up."

"Oh, Ian. Did they detain you?" Eve asked, her voice sympathetic.

"I didn't ask him to come in," Alex said quietly to Kristen. All her plans had been working, so he chose to placate her for now. The truth was he rather liked Kristen. "And I'm sorry I didn't mention Jacob. The idea came to me late last night. He did his job and he's out of it now. And it doesn't sound like Ian's going to make it out of Texas. I do respect you. I want you on this team. I know Eve respects you, too. She really wants to take a look at those files." She'd mentioned it to him as he'd dried her off from their shower. His gut tightened at the idea of Eve getting deeper in, but he was going to honor her request. And he was going to get back in good with Kristen. He could be charming when he wanted to be. "I'm so grateful that you have the full files. My old partner is a slave to the rules. He couldn't help me."

He could stroke her ego a little.

A little smile curved her lips up. "Warren Petty. I've studied up on him. Interesting guy. His brother is about to be in a tough election fight."

Warren had always supported his brother's campaigns. When they were working together, he'd always been so proud he had a brother in politics. "Hoping you get a story out of it?"

She wrinkled her nose. "Ugh, I hate politics. Talk about mired in scandal. No. I'll stay out of Washington. Yeah, let's not bring the feds in here. I can get us any info we need, though Adam has proven to not be a total nimrod."

"I'm excellent, thank you very much," Adam said. "I could totally have those files in five seconds. Do you want me to prove it?"

Ian's voice came over the monitor. "No, asshole, I want you to prove that you can get my fucking life back in order. Nelson is screwing with me, and I don't like it. I got more than detained, damn it. I got searched by two of Homeland Security's finest, and by finest what I really mean is hairiest and least gentle with the body cavities."

Wow. "Nelson is playing hardball."

Adam snickered. "Or hardballs, as in Ian's case."

Adam should be happy Ian was four states away.

"I'll get the files for you." Kristen walked back to her office.

"Holy shit, did I just hear that big brother got the slow hand from Homeland Security?" Sean wasn't even trying not to laugh.

"Yeah, well wait until Nelson decides to come after you, baby brother. We know he doesn't like you either," Ian said. Alex moved in front of the monitor. Ian was in his office, but somehow he made his presence felt despite the distance. "In the course of a few days, he's managed to blow my whole damn life apart. I just got a notification that someone changed the ownership names on my properties to Hottie McHot Pants. I can't sell those assets or change things or accept rent until I get this fixed. He is seriously fucking with me."

"I can figure it out." Adam hid a smile behind his hand. "I can totally fix all of that for you, but it's going to take a little time. I need everything that's been changed and I can fairly easily change it all back. These are all simple hacks for an expert."

"Can you track him back? Can you use this information

to figure out where he is?" Ian asked.

Adam shrugged. "I can try. He's escalating."

"I'm surprised," Eve said. "This doesn't sound like Nelson. He's never come at us out in the open."

Nelson had been a pain in the firm's collective asses for longer than any of them had imagined. Alex had thought their troubles with Nelson began when the CIA operative decided to sell corporate secrets to the Chinese and he'd tried to use Sean Taggart's wife to do it. But a couple of months ago in London he had discovered that Nelson had been dirty for years and had very likely had a hand in killing Ian's wife and sending Liam on the run. Alex wouldn't put anything past the man, but he seriously doubted that Nelson was out there calling Ian Hottie McHot Pants.

"He's coming after us personally now." Ian sat back in his chair.

"He's coming after the boss anyway." Liam knelt down, nodding toward the monitor. "And I think we might have had a break-in a couple of weeks ago. Ian asked me to go through all the security records. Someone used my security code at 1:51 am exactly three weeks and two days ago. I checked my records. I happen to know I didn't come to the office that night. Avery and I were in Austin for the weekend. The rest of you were working on a corporate case and you were all in Omaha. No one but the accounting girl was in the office, and she certainly wasn't here at that time of night."

Why would Nelson sneak into their office? What could he hope to gain? He'd always tried to stay away from them. "Do we have him on video?"

Ian growled. It was the way he'd communicated since they were kids. "I can't find the things. I'm calling the company that programmed the backup system. I hope we still have the security tapes, but the way the rest of my fucking week is going, I'm sure someone taped soap operas over them. Can I borrow Adam for a couple of hours?"

"Any idiot can run the pics we took today through a facial recognition system," Adam said.

Ian sighed. "Thank god. Then Sean can do it."

Sean flipped his brother off. Ah, brotherhood.

"Fine, Sean can run the pictures. The GPS bugs we planted today will send us reports." Alex wanted to get everything out of the way so he could spend some more time with Eve. He'd realized something today. He really only had the next weeks of this mission to convince her. When they got back to the real world, she would question everything and start putting up roadblocks. He had no intention of going backwards. He needed to use this time to bind her to him again.

Adam slapped his hands together with obvious glee at getting to use his new toys. "I got the reports on the bugs already. I told you they would immediately start reporting back. You got two tagged. Way to go, Alex. I was hoping you could get one. The bad news is one of the bugs tracked right to a dry cleaner and now it's dead. Apparently the dry cleaning process is hell on delicate but brilliantly crafted new technology. But the second one just landed at LaGuardia. It looks like we're getting some movement."

"Well, really?" Eve asked, a satisfied smile on her face. "Now I wonder which one is still giving deeply helpful information and which one is dead?"

"I can still spank you." *Damn it.* She'd been right, but he stood by his rule. She could have gotten hurt. Just because she'd been right didn't prove a damn thing. He'd already known she was smarter than him. Everyone knew it. Hell, he was pretty sure there had been a billboard taken out proclaiming it.

"You like to spank me for no reason at all," Eve said with the most adorable pout.

He did. He would get his hands on her for any reason he could think of. "Get me the information, Adam. I need that information and anything Sean could find. Do we have a workable connection on Chazz's cell phone? Jake gave me the signal that he'd tapped Chazz's cell."

"All I've gotten so far is Chazz ordering pizza with double meat and trying to hook up with two of his servers. Someone named Bambi likes to say ewwww a lot and hang up on him. He's very positive. He just keeps calling back," Sean explained. "Why did I pull baby-sit the douchebag duty? Couldn't Kris do this? She has a way better sense of humor when it comes to two idiots trying to hook up."

He had plans for Kristen. This was his night off so it would look suspicious if he showed up. "Kris is going back to the club tonight. She's going to try to lift Chazz's keys and make a copy of the key to his office."

Ian frowned. "Shouldn't you do that yourself?"

"She's my best shot tonight." They had worked it all out during the drive from St. Augustine to Palm Coast. "I don't have any reason to be in the club until tomorrow night when Eve and I start our nightly performances. The club is closed for a private party for some of Chazz's friends. According to Kristen, he likes to get really drunk. Jake didn't get a shot at it last night, so Kristen is taking hers tonight."

"You're putting an awful lot of trust in someone you don't know," Ian said.

How did he explain Kristen? There was something deep in his gut that told him she was worth trusting. "I think she's the best person to do this job. She's been nothing but helpful up to this point."

"Eve, what do you think?" Ian asked, deferring as he often did to Eve. She knew people. She rarely screwed up.

Eve glanced up, obviously looking for Kristen, but she hadn't reappeared. "I think she's hiding something, but I don't think she means any of us harm. I truly believe she wants to do this job and catch Michael Evans. I don't know if I completely believe her reasons for doing so, but I don't sense anything from her that would make me distrust her. If I had to go off what I know right now, I would say she's screwed up in the past. She's looking for redemption and she goes about it by uncovering corruption and helping people. I would say she probably lives a fairly solitary life. Her parents are either dead or she has a distant relationship with them. She's looking for a family, seeking to cobble together a group of friends to call her own. Earlier today, Alex did something that really pissed her off, but she still got to her knees to talk to me."

"Why were you on your knees?" Liam asked.

The cutest little frown crossed Eve's face. "Alex didn't like how I handled a situation so he punished me by making me crawl across a dirty floor."

He felt himself flush. He wouldn't have knowingly sent her to a dirty floor. "It looked clean to me."

Eve pouted adorably. "Well, you should have looked closer. Anyway, Kristen could have just walked beside me, but she got down to my level. She's a little bit of a puzzle, but if I had to, I would bet that she is firmly on our side."

Ian's eyes widened slightly, and a little grin curved his lips up. "He punished you? Like actual punishment, not something you decided on and manipulated him into?"

Now it was Eve's turn to blush. "It's just for show."

"Like hell it is," Alex muttered under his breath. "She put herself in danger, and she's my sub. I'll punish her as I wish."

Ian slapped his hands together. "Well, hell. At least part of the week is looking up. Adam, please get my identity back and find whatever fucker Nelson hired to wreck my life. I doubt he did it himself. We need to find him and then torture him into giving up Nelson, and then I'll slice his balls off and feed them to him because I'm pretty sure he put my name on a bunch of mailing lists. I'm getting spammed like crazy."

Liam nodded, smiling in agreement. "Damn near took our systems down. He got five thousand ads for male enhancement and two thousand offering him forklift operator training. This is a serious matter, my mates."

Ian rolled his eyes and flipped his computer down, breaking the connection.

Eve shook her head. "Are we sure this is Nelson? It seems so impish. Nelson would just come at him hard."

"Have you ever had a deep cavity search?" Sean asked, shuddering a little. "It's sounds pretty nasty to me."

Eve's eyes narrowed, and she let her sarcasm flow. "No, Sean. I've never had anything shoved into my body parts by some overly enthusiastic Dom. Yeah, no sub ever had to endure that."

And on that note, it was time to take his sub and make a few things clear to her. "You all have your assignments."

Kristen walked in, a stack of files in her hands. She gave Eve a little smile, but held back from the rest, and Alex wondered just how much she'd overheard. "I have the files. It's pretty much everything I could get off the FBI's site. Don't hate me, McKay, but I got the SAC's personal folders on all the victims. I know they were random, but I thought I needed to read their files. You know, they deserve that much."

He nodded and took them from her. "Eve can look through them later, but we're going to have a conversation right now."

After the session in the shower, he knew he had to push through her barriers. She thought they were through, but they hadn't even started yet. In order to let go of the past, they had to face it, finally.

He reached down and took her hand.

"I really would like to look at those files." Eve's eyes strayed to them.

"After." He tugged on her hand, pulling her along.

"Alex." Eve sighed his name. "We really should talk about what's happening."

He walked her into the bedroom. "I don't think so."

Eve pulled away. "We can't just ignore it. We're being truly intimate for the first time in years, but it's not real."

"You're right." It couldn't be real as long as they had so much of the past between them.

Her breath caught just enough to let Alex know she was upset that he agreed. But she smoothed out her expression and was right back to being the logical one. This was the game she'd been playing for five years. It seemed to have become a habit. One he intended to break.

If he hadn't been watching her closely, he wouldn't have seen the truth behind her mask. When had he stopped studying her every expression? When had he become lazy and so scared of losing her that he'd forgotten how to take care of her? "I'm glad you can be reasonable. Alex, we're just holding on to what we know. We're both afraid to let go of the past."

"There were a lot of things about the past that were pretty damn good, you know." He closed the door behind them. This wasn't a conversation that needed an audience.

He placed the folders on the dresser, trading them for something far more important. He zipped open his leather kit, pulling out the lube and a pack of wipes and walking it over to the nightstand.

Eve's eyes widened. "You seem pretty sure of yourself."

He was sure of one thing. She would be underneath him tonight. He would get balls deep inside her and then she wouldn't be able to lie to him—or herself—ever again. "We had years and years of good."

He reached back into the bag and pulled out a length of rope. He had three lengths, each thirty feet. He'd learned that was exactly what he needed to tie up his pretty sub.

Her eyes went to the rope in his hands. "I know we did. We should honor those years by accepting that we've changed. Alex, I don't want to lose you as a friend, but you have to know that once we get back to our normal lives, all our problems are still going to be waiting there. This can't work long term. This kind of passion burns itself out."

He unwound the first length, shaking his head the whole time. "It didn't for me. I've been this passionate about you for fifteen years. I want another fifty more, and I'm willing to fight for it now. I can see where I went wrong. I thought you needed time, and one day blurred into the next until I just gave in on everything because I got confused. I thought I was appeasing you, but I was really appeasing the guilt I felt. Eve, we haven't talked about those days, not really. Seven days. Seven horrible days and we've let them ruin the thousands of good ones."

She stared at the rope, her mouth turning down and her hands flexing, a sure sign that she was getting anxious. "We talked in therapy."

They had spent long hours talking, but it had been

clinical and she'd skimmed the surfaces. After a while, they'd just stopped going and given up. "I hated those sessions. I said whatever I thought would get me out of those sessions as quickly as possible. I didn't do the work to get us through this because it was far easier for me to concentrate on killing Michael Evans. Even after I found and arrested the bastard, I concentrated on his trial and my job."

"I know. I understand why you did it. You could control that aspect."

He'd made some mistakes, but so had she, and she was still making the same ones. "Strip."

"That isn't going to help anything." But she didn't move away from him. Her eyes stayed on the rope and then lowered to his cock. She was watching him carefully and those eyes were a little like a remote. His dick responded immediately.

"I did your therapy. I did it for years. I did it when it made my stomach turn and my heart hurt. I'm asking you for a couple of hours to pay me back for years of topping you on your terms. I need this."

He watched her soften immediately, and then her hands went to the buttons on her blouse. "All right, if this is what you need to get closure, I'll help you. I can't tell you what the last week has meant to me, but they were moments out of time. We were just trying to hold on to something that's gone."

He hadn't been. He'd been trying to build something new, and it was past time she knew that.

He watched in silence as she shed every stitch of clothing. Her blouse dropped and her hands carefully unclasped the bra she wore. It was pink, delicate with scalloped edges that didn't hold a candle in beauty to the flesh it covered. Her breasts were smaller than before, but he loved their shape and the way they felt in his hands. She had perky pink nipples that tightened the instant she was aroused. The areola constricted as he watched, her nipples elongating, preparing for the tug of his fingers and his mouth.

She pushed the tiny skirt off her hips and stepped out of her heels. She bit her bottom lip as though waiting for him to judge her. The perfectly made mound of her sex caught his eyes, and he was almost certain she was becoming wet and soft for him. No matter what else had happened between them, they always had this. All he had to do was think about Eve St. James and he was hard and ready to fuck because she was his mate. More than a wife. More than a sub. She was his other half. They had been hiding behind fear and shame and all those stupid clothes. They didn't need them.

"You're so beautiful. Turn around for me, angel."

She smiled slightly, her anxiety obviously dialed down. She turned for him.

He could see that the curvy cheeks of her ass were still a light pink. Running a hand over those cheeks, he was pleased to see her shiver slightly. "Did you enjoy the flogger?"

It used to be one of her favorite toys. She'd found it relaxing. When she would come home from a rough day at work, he would simply look at the set of her shoulders and order her to the St. Andrew's Cross they kept in the private playroom, and after fifty or so strokes, she would be relaxed and happy and she would curl up in his arms for the night, her day forgotten. God, he missed that.

"It was a very short session, Master."

He couldn't help but grin. "You still started subbing out."

One shoulder shrugged as she turned her head to look at him. "You're quite good with a flogger. We could try it again, you know. That also wasn't much of a spanking if you ask me."

Such a little brat. She had just the tiniest bit of a pain slut in her, but he never let her go too far. That was what he was here for. To give her what she needed while protecting her from going too far.

"Still trying to decide your own punishments?" He sank his hand into her hair and tugged.

She gasped because he knew damn well she liked that pain, too. "Maybe I'm trying to pick my pleasures, Master."

"Your pleasure belongs to me." He tugged her hair again and let his free hand find one of her breasts, twisting it and making her writhe. "Bend over. Grab your ankles."

There was no way to mistake her sigh for anything but satisfaction. Eve bent over, grabbing her ankles and exposing herself fully to him.

"You're already pink, angel." Just the slightest pink, but pink.

"I want more."

It was his call. *Smack. Smack. Smack. Smack. Smack.*

"Where are you?"

"I am so green." Her words were sweet, sultry.

Another quick ten smacks. He could smell her arousal. "I need to talk to you."

"Yes. But touch me first, please, Master. I missed this so much. It's different now."

Because he was giving to her, not because she'd dictated it, but because she'd asked. They were in a sweet harmony. *Smack, smack, smack, smack, smack.*

She moaned, her ass wiggling a little. She needed this, but he needed something, too.

He needed to make sure she understood a few things. "Stand up. It's my fun time now."

Eve's eyes were soft and wide when she obliged him, but her mouth curled up. "Yes, Master."

"Arms folded in a U." He let out a long breath when she complied, folding her arms behind her back, forearms touching, her fingers pointed toward opposite elbows. The position thrust her breasts out. He secured her arms with a double column tie and passed it around her waist. In the low light of the room, her skin practically glowed. He'd missed this so badly. Any time he'd tied her up in the last few years had been strictly for her comfort, but now he could be a little selfish. Now he could take his time, enjoy every knot, revel in the connection.

Do the work it really took to get his wife back.

He worked carefully. The rope was soft, deserving to be against her skin. He secured the rope with an overhand knot in the front.

Eve sniffled a little, a shiver going across her skin.

"Are you all right?" He didn't want her scared.

"I was just wondering."

He started to route the loose ends up her torso, between her beautiful breasts. "About what?"

"If you still think I'm pretty."

He'd dealt with this. "I told you you're lovely. I believe I promised you punishment if you denigrated what is mine again. Are you trying to get more spankings?"

"You said you still wanted me. But you've also mentioned that I'm too thin." Her voice had gone quiet, vulnerable.

He could fix that. He worked another overhand knot halfway between her breasts and throat. He brought the ropes over her shoulders and around her arms, but he started kissing her, paying special attention to those scars that used to make him feel like shit, and now he could see them for what they really were. They didn't have to be a symbol of his failure. They were proof that she had survived. "I think you're gorgeous big or tiny. The real reason I have a problem with your weight is that you never indulge. You never enjoy. I love your curves, but most of all I love knowing that you deeply enjoy the life we share. I adore stuffing you with chocolate."

"I miss chocolate," she admitted in a husky voice.

"I want you to enjoy it again. Now, we're going to talk, angel. We're going to get to the heart of everything." His hands worked slowly, methodically. By the time he was done, she would be wrapped in a beautiful tortoiseshell pattern, and even once he got her out of the ropes, the pattern would be left on her skin for a while, proof of her trust, her love. Because she still loved him. He just knew it.

There was a long pause, her body slumping slightly. "Alex, what do you want me to say?"

He found the rope work so calming. He passed the rope under her arms and back around to her breasts. Her nipples were sweetly puckered. "I want you to stop placating me and talk to me. I want you to stop making excuses and coming up with a million logical reasons for what I did."

He continued to move the rope across her skin, skimming it with his fingers, tightening it just so she would feel it. He made sure it wouldn't cut off her circulation, just leave a pretty pattern on her skin for a while.

Eve remained perfectly still, relaxed under his ropes. "But I'm right about this. That was why you did it. You withdrew from me because it was easier to focus on more active things."

"No," he commanded. This was exactly what he wanted

252

to avoid. "Stop the shrink talk. I want plain English. Tell me what I did. You've danced around the topic for years. This situation we're in is just as much your fault as mine."

He wound the rope around her breasts, forcing them up and out. He knelt down as he moved the rope lower.

Her eyes flared as she looked down at him. "Really?"

She wasn't willing to admit it yet, but he wasn't going to let her get away with it anymore. "Yes, really. Why did you have me sign a new contract, Eve? You didn't negotiate with me. You went to Ian and had him write a contract that outlined how I was supposed to behave in the coldest terms possible. As soon as our divorce was final, you shoved that contract in my face."

And he'd taken it because he'd been so desperate to have any kind of contact with her. He'd lain down during the divorce, giving her everything she wanted, praying she would change her mind. When she'd tossed that contract in his face, he'd signed it before he'd even read it. He just couldn't stand to lose her.

"My behavior was outlined, too." She frowned at him, but it wasn't an angry expression. She seemed more thoughtful than anything else.

"Why did you make me sign that contract? We could have gone on with the one we had before." He should have done this a long time ago. Some people needed to sit in an office setting and talk out their problems with a third party, but he needed this. He needed her naked, his hands working to bring her comfort and pleasure.

"Because we were divorced. We needed to rethink how we acted."

He tied off the design. She looked so fucking gorgeous wrapped up in his ropes. The tortoiseshell design formed a sexy pattern around her breasts, showing them off. Her whole torso was in a gorgeous pattern. If they were at Sanctum, he would spend the next thirty minutes showing her off. She was a work of art. But tonight, he simply made his plea. "Eve, be brave. Please. Don't be logical. Don't be kind. Tell me what I did to you. You were hurting and you needed me, and what did I do?"

He heard her sniffle and looked up. Her brown eyes were sheened with tears. "You ignored me."

He placed his head to her breast because they had finally come to his true crime. A deep sense of peace came over him as he finally admitted what he'd done. He'd been a bastard, but he sensed forgiveness was a heartbeat away. "I ignored you. God, Eve, please forgive me."

* * * *

Alex held her, his head soft against her skin. His words were whispered against her flesh.

She'd always known why he'd done it, but she'd only just realized that she'd punished him. If it had been anyone else, she would have seen it easily. She'd told herself that she wanted that contract to protect them both, but now she could see why it had been important to her. She'd been punishing him, forcing him to see her, to deal with her in the only way he seemed willing to. She'd been like a child who would take any attention she could get. "I never just told you how I felt."

"I want to hear it now, angel," he said. "I need to hear it. I need you to get it all out."

She was tied up, unable to walk out of the room, and that was what she really wanted to do because the truth was so close to the surface and she was afraid to let it out. She'd held it in for so long, terrified of what really confronting that

254

time would mean. "You don't want to hear it all."

He was on his knees in front of her, his head nuzzled between her breasts. "I do. I need to. We need to. I don't want to hear the logic. I want to know how you felt so I can ask your forgiveness. I can't ask for it unless I know. Angel, you had to have been so scared when he kicked the door in."

She closed her eyes. God, she didn't want to do this. She'd told the police and her therapist the bare bones, simply reciting the story over and over again, but the real memories were still inside her. Those moments of terror were deep in her veins, and Alex was trying to pull them out. The problem was she'd held on to them so long, she wasn't sure who she would be when she'd given them all up.

She couldn't be who she was back then. She'd been weak and completely submissive. She'd been dependent and then she'd been so alone. And now she was strong, but she was still so very alone. Could she find a way to be herself and have Alex, too?

"Please. Be brave, Eve. Talk to me." His hands tightened as though he wouldn't let her go.

But he had let her go. He'd agreed to the divorce without a second glance. He'd signed the contract without a word. Could she trust him now? Did she dare to try again? "I thought we agreed to stop doing this. We agreed to move forward and let go of the people we used to be."

His head turned up, his eyes pleading with her. He was so gorgeous, her big bad Dom in a supplicant position, on his knees for his sub. "I can let go of the twenty-three-year-old idiot who didn't realize just how much he could love you. I can. He's gone. I can let go of the man who was so tied up in his own guilt that he didn't really see you for years. But I will never let go of the eighty-year-old man who will hold your hand until the day he dies. I will fight for that old man. I will never let go of him."

Tears blurred her vision, and she knew she was at that fork in the road she'd been terrified of for so many years—that place where she had to finally decide where she was going to go and whether the road would include the love of her life.

And in that moment, she saw him, really saw him for the first time in years. She saw him without the filter of her own pain. She saw him as that young man who had reached for her, who she'd learned with and grown with. She saw the Alex who had been sitting at her bedside when she woke up, his eyes haggard and guilt in every line of his body. She saw the Alex who had given in to her for five years, placating her, giving her only what she told him she needed while his eyes begged her for more. And she saw him as the old man he would be, lined and weathered and still so beautiful to her eyes. He would be there if she let him. He would reach for her hand, their lives so entwined that there was no way to disentangle them.

They had made a mess of things, but he was still here, still reaching out for her. And if she was brave, this time he might never let her go.

If she was really brave, she would make damn sure of it.

"I let him in." She closed her eyes as she said the words, the horror of that day washing over her again.

Alex's arms tightened, an anchor keeping her in the present. "Why would you do that, angel? I left two guards with you. They should have opened the door first."

Alex wasn't the only one who felt guilty. "I thought it was you or Warren. Tommy even told me not to open the door, but I was so sure that I knew who it was. I just wanted to see you. I was scared. And then I was even more scared when Evans was there. I tried to slam the door in his face, but he kicked at it and I ended up on the floor. He had two of his men with him, and then I heard glass breaking and two more came in from the back. I got Tommy and Leon killed."

She could still see them as they fought. They managed to take one of Evans's men but there were too many. They had died in a cascade of bullets, and the last thing she had seen before Evans had shoved a needle in her neck was Tommy, so young. He'd just joined the Bureau and she watched his eyes glass over as he died.

"Eve, you can't blame yourself."

Oh, but she could. Every time she ran a hand over her scars, she remembered the two men who had died trying to protect her. None of them had taken it seriously. Not even Alex, really. He'd left a six-pack of beer to pay his buddies back for babysitting his wife. Warren had been the one to insist on the guard. Alex had been so sure that Evans would come after him.

"I should have been more careful."

"He had four men with him, maybe more. He would have gotten in whether you opened the door or not," Alex said gravely.

She felt hemmed in. She usually loved to be tied up, felt safe. Though now she realized why she loved it. Because Alex never took his eyes off her when she was tied up. He wouldn't turn his back on her. She'd gravitated toward more and more hardcore play because it focused Alex's attention on her. But now it was starting to bother her. She couldn't move. It felt like the walls were closing in and she was alone. She didn't need his ropes. She needed him.

"Keep going. I know he raped you."

"I want out." She couldn't be in the rope anymore. She couldn't. Tears were streaming down her face.

Alex paled, and he was on his feet in a second. He reached into his kit and had a knife in hand. "I'm sorry, angel. I'm so sorry. I won't make you do this again."

He cut through the ties that bound her in quick, economical movements, and she was free within seconds. He took a step back, pain plain on his face, but she couldn't try to soothe him. She needed him.

She threw herself into his arms, wrapping her body around his. She wasn't satisfied with just hugging him. She jumped on him, curling her legs around him and burying her face in his neck. This was home. She breathed in his scent. This was what she'd missed for so many years. The tears came easily now. She wept into his shoulder.

"He hurt me." The words didn't even begin to describe what had happened, but there was more truth in those three words than anything she'd said to him before. He'd hurt her. He'd hurt her so badly, she'd gone into a shell and was only now starting to come out of it.

"I'm so sorry." He moved with her in his arms. "I love you so much."

Now that she was being honest, she couldn't stop herself. "I didn't want to die. I just wanted to get back to you, but after a few days, I started to wonder."

He fell onto the bed, his weight coming down on her. She found it comforting. He was still fully clothed, but it didn't matter. She held on to him because those memories were so close to the surface it felt like she was there again. "What did you wonder about?"

"I wondered if you would want me after what he did." She closed her eyes because it was the question that had haunted her. "It was awful. It was a complete perversion of everything I loved about us. How did he know? How did he know exactly how to hurt me?"

Evans had taken particular pleasure in hurting her with the toys she'd always loved. He'd called her a pervert and a whore as he'd beaten and whipped her. He'd told her she asked for it by going to their club. He hadn't understood at all. Alex would never have harmed her. What she and Alex had was a delicate dance of trust and love and pleasure.

"I wish I could have taken that pain for you. I don't know how you made it through." His voice was tortured, but he kissed her. He kissed his way down the scar on her neck. He didn't let go. He didn't pull away.

She let her arms tighten. It was safe to talk now. "I made it through because you were there with me. I closed my eyes and I pretended you were there. I went crazy. I started to see you when he would walk in and I would go somewhere else in my mind. I played back our sweet times in my head."

"I was with you." He whispered into her ears, his words achingly sweet. "I was with you. I knew you were in pain, and do you know what I wanted more than anything?"

"What?" She was sure he had wanted it to all go away.

"I wanted you alive. I prayed, angel. I prayed that you could take that pain and make your way back to me. I wanted nothing more than to be able to hold you like this. Just fucking like this. I love you. I loved you then. I love you now. I will love you long after we're dead and gone. I love you, and I made the biggest mistake of my life when you came back to me. I should have danced and praised the fucking universe, and all I could do was give in to my guilt. Forgive me."

How long had she needed to hear those simple words? "I needed you, Alex."

He moved along her body, his erection pressed against her core. "Forgive me."

"I tried to get your attention, but you were so far away. I thought that you didn't want me. I thought that you didn't want something that he'd had."

A fierce look came into his eyes and he got to his knee, looking down at her. "You are mine. I don't care what he did to you. You are fucking mine. You've been mine since the day you told me you loved me, and he can't take that away unless we let him." His hands went to his shirt and he tossed it overhead. "You gave yourself to me. You belong to me and nothing will change that except my own mistakes. I should have gotten inside you again the first chance I had. I should have pushed you, even just a little, but I let my guilt keep me away."

His hands were working the fly of his jeans and Eve's whole body softened. She likely looked a mess. She'd never been a pretty crier. She went all out, red nose and blotchy face, but Alex was looking at her like she was the goddess of love and beauty.

"I should have talked to you, but I was afraid of what I would hear," Eve explained. "You aren't the only one at fault here."

He got off the bed with a frustrated growl and shoved his jeans off his hips, toeing off his shoes in the process. He just tossed his clothes to the side and then was back on top of her again. He seemed so hungry for her, as hungry as she was for him.

"I'll tell you how I felt. I felt out of control. I felt lost. I didn't want to make a wrong move with you." He touched the scar on her neck. "I thought you were fragile, and I couldn't stand the thought that I would break you."

"I was fragile at the time." She let her arms drift up to the headboard of the bed, offering him access. "I know I flinched when you touched me, but that wasn't about you."

"I knew that intellectually." He ran his hand down from her neck to her breasts, brushing against the nipples. "But inside I wondered if you blamed me. I certainly did."

She shook her head. "No, Alex."

"You told me I was starting a war."

"I didn't imagine he would come after me. It didn't really fit his profile. I had to change my profile afterward. He was very direct until his attack on me. Don't blame yourself. You did everything you could. You left Tommy and Leon behind to protect me."

His eyes closed briefly. "Only because Warren suggested it. Demanded is more like it. He even picked the guys. It still didn't work."

She needed to bring him back. She'd spent too many years letting him drift in his guilt, but now she knew it was her place to tether him so he couldn't get lost again. "Kiss me, Alex."

He frowned. "Where are we?"

In bed. So he would expect certain protocols. "Please kiss me, Master."

"Better." He brushed his lips against hers before returning to her breasts, his momentary lapse obviously gone. "I love your nipples. Have I ever mentioned that?"

He lowered his head down and sucked one into his mouth.

Eve's eyes drifted closed with pleasure. Yes, this was what she needed. "You might have from time to time. I think Warren blames himself, too. You two were so close and then you haven't talked for years. He called me, you know."

Alex's head came up, and the caveman reared his too gorgeous head again. "He called my wife?"

So possessive. "He called that day to tell me he was going to bring you home. He promised me he would bring you back to me. It's why I thought it was you at the door. I thought he'd talked some sense into you."

"I was stubborn, Eve." He looked up, pulling his body along hers, chest to chest, their legs entangled. "I need to hear the words. I need to hear you forgive me."

She reached for him, her hands cupping his face. It had been forever since they had just looked into each other's eyes. How had she let him slip away? How had she allowed him to drift away when he'd been the only reason she'd survived? "I forgive you, Alex. Forgive me, too."

He kissed her forehead, making her feel precious. "Always, angel. I promise to put you first from now on. I know you don't think this can really work, but I'm going to show you. And I am definitely going to reclaim my sub. Starting now."

Eve gasped a little as Alex moved quickly, flipping her over.

"Hands and knees, Eve. Tonight you're all mine."

Every cell in her body came to life because he was wrong about one thing. She was starting to believe it could work.

They just might be able to start over again.

Chapter Twelve

Alex stared at her for a moment. She was right where he wanted her, on her hands and knees, waiting for his instructions. God, they had wasted so much time, mired in their own miseries when all they'd needed was to reach out and hold on to one another.

"Do you really forgive me?" He knew what her answer was going to be, but somehow he needed to hear it again.

"Alex, I love you."

Something changed inside him. Something fundamental shifted with her words. "I think we should go home. I'll call Warren and turn this whole thing over to him."

His wife was more important than anything else. His wife was the end all, be all of existence.

"We can't." Eve turned her head back. "We're close. I need to see this through. Once we figure out when and where he's going to be, then we can call in Warren, but we're in the best place to find him. I need to follow through, not for revenge, but just for some peace. I need to do what I can to make sure he can't hurt another woman. I need to do this."

This was a completely perverse fight. He ran a hand down the length of her spine. "We're here to observe and gather intelligence only. The parameters of this mission have changed. I'm not willing to lose any of you to him. Is that understood?"

If he could take Evans down without endangering Eve

in any way, then he would. If that wasn't an option, then he would give up his revenge.

"Yes, Master." There was a sweet satisfaction to her words.

Holy hell, they were on the same page for the first time in years. Oh, it was a completely different book, but they were finally together. His cock surged, lust threatening to overtake him.

"Spread your knees. Let me in. I want to taste you first."

"Master, please, can we taste each other?"

His whole body tensed. "Are you sure, angel?"

She hadn't taken his cock in her mouth since the rape. "More than anything. I want this part of us back. I want to serve my Master, my lover. I want to give something back to you."

He twisted his body, lying down flat on the bed. "I want to give you everything you need this time. Come on. Take me."

Eve moved quickly, her body graceful, her eagerness lighting up his heart. She settled her knees on either side of his head. Alex fucking loved that view. Her pretty pussy was creamy and ready to be taken by him any way he wanted it, and he wanted it in all ways.

He pulled on her hips, not willing to wait another second to dip his tongue in.

And then it was his turn to groan because he felt a little whisper across his flesh. Eve's tongue dashed and darted along his cock, licking and playing with the head. It was all he could do to not shudder and shake as she drew him into her mouth in light, sucking passes. Her hands were on his thighs, balancing herself as she played with his cock.

He rubbed his nose in her pussy, reveling in the unique scent of her arousal. He wouldn't wash his face. No. Not tonight. He would be able to smell her all night long.

Over and over he speared into her pussy, using his tongue like he would his cock, fucking deep inside and gathering all her cream. He pulled apart the sweet petals of her sex and sucked them into his mouth one after another. He left no inch of her untouched by his lips and tongue. All the while, she forced his cock deeper and deeper into the hot recesses of her mouth, enveloping him in her heat.

He could feel his cock pulsing with pre-come. A low groan burst from his chest as he felt Eve lick at the slit of his cock, drawing his saltiness onto her tongue before sucking the head in again. She brought one hand up and cupped his balls, rolling them and making him damn near lose control.

But that wasn't going to happen. No. Not tonight. Another night he would let her lick and suck and play until she'd drawn every ounce of semen he had into her mouth, but tonight, he wanted something more.

His tongue spearing deep again, Alex found her clit with the pad of his thumb. He pressed that little button hard, and she began to shake. The muscles of her pussy tightened as she came and her orgasm coated his tongue. She surrounded him, his whole being enveloped in her smell and taste and the sound of her pleasure.

All through it, she never drew her mouth off his cock. She groaned and moaned around it, the vibrations threatening to unman him.

He had about two seconds before she managed to get him to the back of her throat and then he was done for. Using every ounce of his willpower, he flipped her off him.

Eve landed on her back in the center of the bed, all that wild hair flowing around her. It curled around her breasts and damn near reached her hips. So fucking gorgeous. Everything about her called to the primal male inside him.

265

She was always so prim and proper in the workplace. Even in the club, there was a certain reserve that his Eve always kept about her. But here in the privacy of their bedroom, she was simply his, a woman with no inhibitions. His mate.

"Hands and knees again." The command came out harder than he'd meant it, but if it frightened her, she didn't show it.

She simply sighed, her whole body moving with languid grace as she did as he commanded. She turned and positioned herself as though she could see what he wanted without him having to ask. Her ass was high in the air, her forearms flat on the bed making a perfect plane of her back.

His hands found the globes of her ass. "Do you know what I'm going to do to you, Eve?"

Her breath hitched, but the position she'd placed herself in told him the answer before she spoke. "You're going to take my ass."

Oh, hell yeah. "I am. I'm going to take it again because it's mine."

His whole body was taut with desire. The time he'd spent in her soft mouth had his cock primed and ready to go off. He'd had her more in the last few days, more intimately and deeply than in the five years that preceded them, but all he wanted was more. Now that he had her again, all he could think about was more time, more love, more of her.

He kissed her back, running his lips along her spine and paying attention to the scars she had, lavishing affection on them. He ran his hands up her sleek body, finding her breasts again and palming them as he kissed her everywhere he could. Shoulder, neck, down to her waist. His lips dipped into the dimples in the small of her back, and he carefully kissed her sweet cheeks. They bore the mark of his discipline. The sight tightened his cock further.

He slid his hands down, over the flat of her stomach to her pussy. Eve's head bowed, a sure sign that she was willing to surrender everything to him.

His cock found her pussy and he sighed. The orgasm he'd given her had made her juicy and ripe. She was more than ready for him.

"Tell me something, Eve." Now that they were in a good place, he had some questions for her, some things he'd wondered about. And she just might answer honestly with his fingers deep inside her pussy and his thumb circling her clit. There was no reason she shouldn't have a few orgasms before he got his. He wanted her boneless and exhausted and sleeping in his arms.

"Anything."

"You haven't let me have this gorgeous little asshole for years, but you allowed me to plug you during scenes. Were you trying to taunt me? Were you trying to remind me of what I couldn't have?" He didn't think so. He thought it was for another reason, but he wanted to hear it from her.

"No," she said in a breathless voice. "No, Alex. I wouldn't do that. I let you plug me so I would stay trained. I did it because I always hoped we would be back here. I did it because it reminded me of how it felt to have you deep inside me, everywhere."

That was his wife. "I thought about it, too. I thought about being inside you, nothing forbidden. Nothing is going to come between us again. I promise you that." He was going to make sure of it. He reached for the lube, eager to prepare her. "I'm the Dom. I should have ordered you to come back to me."

She turned slightly, looking back, and he loved the little frown on her face. He loved the way she fought with him now. She fought to keep her place. It was easy to see she wasn't going to let him roll over her the way he used to and there was a piece of him that thrilled to it. She was going to challenge him, force him to see her side. This was what had been missing before, what they had needed to find. "Don't you pull the big bad Dom act with me."

He parted the cheeks of her ass, sighing a little at the sight of her rosette. Such a pretty little asshole. So small and tight and so about to be invaded. "You like the big bad Dom, angel."

She shivered a little as he dribbled lube on her asshole. "You needed me, too. You needed me to talk to you, but I just kept pushing. I should have thrown a fit and demanded that you pay attention to me instead of trying to top from the bottom."

He stopped. He felt a brilliant smile creasing his mouth up. A whole, beautiful world had just opened up in front of him. "You've been topping from the bottom for five years, Eve."

"Oh, shit," she cursed under her breath. "We should talk about this. There were psychological reasons for that."

He adored the way her skin flushed. He lubed up his middle finger and started a slow circle of that hole his dick was dying to get into. "Oh, baby, do you know how long and hard I'm going to punish you? I can't tell you what's going to happen to your ass when we get back to Sanctum. You are going to be the poster girl for submissive obedience."

A little laugh puffed from her mouth even as she stiffened slightly. "I think the word you're looking for is 'cautionary tale' and we should really talk about this. We need to talk about how things are going to work when we get back to Dallas. We've been apart for a long time. We should take things slow."

He growled a little. She wanted to talk, and he wanted

to be balls deep in her ass. He pressed his finger in slightly, just to the first knuckle. The little gasp Eve gave him went straight to his cock, making his balls pulse.

She wanted to know what would happen when they got back to Dallas? He could do that for her. He rimmed her gently, forcing her to open for him. "All right. We can take things slowly. When we get back, you'll have an hour or so before I move everything from your apartment to mine."

She groaned, her hands clutching the pillows in front of her. "That's not taking things slowly."

"It's far too slow for me." Another knuckle. Two deep and she was clenching at his finger. "If I had my way, I would call tonight and arrange for everything to be at my place when we get back. See, baby, I can totally compromise."

"That's not compromise." Her backside clenched as he slid another finger in. "God, Alex. It's been so long."

This was what he should have done the whole time. The next time he and Eve fought, they would talk about it—with his dick deep inside some part of her body. They would talk between kisses and fight while they fucked, but every minute they would hold on to each other. "Yes, it is compromise. I'm the Dom so I make up the definitions of words."

She laughed, shuddering as he scissored his fingers deep. "That's a new one. Any other new rules I should know about?"

So many new rules. "We're getting married again. And we're tearing up that dumbass contract. We'll negotiate a new one. You and me together, and you should know I'm going to push your every boundary. We'll go to the courthouse and then you can take a few days and look for a house because I really want a house again. Something nice, with bedrooms for kids."

She stopped, her voice a tiny rasp. "Alex, you know that won't happen."

"I do not." Doctors weren't always right, and they had only said that it might be difficult. He was done giving up on the things he wanted. He pulled his fingers out and used the wipes to clean off before lubing up his cock. "I only know that I love you, and I want a family with you. That family does not have to come out of your womb. If you want, we'll get a surrogate, but there are thousands of children out there who would be blessed to have you as a mother."

Eve would be a wonderful mother. He'd always seen her surrounded by family, their family.

"But you always wanted your own kids."

She was worried about that? "Oh, make no mistake, they will be mine. They will be ours. Biology does not make a family."

It didn't. The revelation hit him like a ton of bricks. He loved his mom and dad, but his brothers had always been distant. Ian and Sean were his real brothers, the ones he could always count on. They didn't need some mystical blood connection to build a family. They only needed each other and open hearts, and a will to dedicate themselves to their kids. Family, he'd discovered, was in the people a man collected along the way, the people who shared his life, like his precious wife.

"We can still have it, angel. We can still build a family."

Her hand came back, covering his. "Do you really think so, Alex?"

"I know it. I will make it happen. I won't ever give up."

He pressed in, pushing his cock past the muscles that tried to keep him out.

"I love you, Alex. I never stopped loving you." Eve pressed back against him. "And I missed this. I won't give up either."

He slid inside, her tight hole gripping him as he teared up. Just a little. Just enough to make the world hazy and beautiful and fresh again. She was here, really here with him. She was his partner.

He fucked into her, unable to hold back a second longer.

She called out his name as he dragged his cock out. The same muscles that fought to keep him out sucked at him, desperate to keep him inside.

So good. It was different from her pussy, the heat, the drag, the fight. Eve pushed back against him, gripping the headboard now. His sweet sub wasn't so submissive now. She fought for her pleasure, and he was more than willing to give it to her.

His balls drew up. A shiver went over his spine. She was too tight, too fucking good. He wouldn't last, but he would take her with him.

He let his hand slide forward, his thumb finding her clit. It was still slippery wet. He ground his palm against her as he went balls deep, his come shooting up from his testicles.

Eve clenched around him, her breath pounding from her lungs as she worked his cock and pressed her clit against his hand.

He filled her, fucking in and out until he had nothing left to give.

He fell forward, his cock slipping out.

Eve turned, catching his lips with hers. "My sweet Master."

He kissed her back. She was his everything, and he would never let her go again.

Chapter Thirteen

Eve stretched and glanced at the clock. Two a.m. Alex turned in his sleep, his big body moving as he reached for her pillow and slid an arm around it as though he was clutching her.

What the hell was she going to do with him? Could they really make it work this time? A million questions floated through her head, making it difficult to sleep. She grabbed her robe and slid it on before taking the file folders and walking out of the bedroom. She made her way to the kitchen and the gorgeous granite bar.

Which was already occupied.

"Can't sleep?" Sean asked. "I kind of thought you would be exhausted."

She groaned. She should have known they could hear. And it wasn't like they would be shy. "Tell me y'all didn't turn it into an event."

Adam snorted a little as he walked in from the balcony. "Sean made snacks and everything. Kristen found us and tried to get us to stop, but then she heard that little sizzling sound and she just shut up and asked for a beer. She resented the fact that she had to go back to the club."

"He brought a violet wand with him?" Sean asked.

She was pretty sure every cell in her body flushed with embarrassment. After the first round, Alex had been eager to play and he had, in fact, brought along a small, not too powerful violet wand. It emitted a little electrical charge against the skin that she happened to love, especially on her nipples. Alex had tied her down and tortured her, and apparently she'd been a little loud. "Alex likes to be prepared."

"A BDSM boy scout," Adam said with a grin. He looked off toward the back bedrooms, and his voice went low. "She knew exactly what she was hearing. Did you see that, Sean? Most people would think Taser, but no, her eyes actually dilated the minute she heard that sound. She was aroused by it."

Sean leaned in. "She's trained. I used my Dom voice on her a couple of times and I swear, she nearly went to her knees."

Eve placed the stack of files on the bar. "What does it matter if she's trained? And I thought you were starting to like her, Sean."

Sean's hands came up as though trying to stop an oncoming lecture. "I do like her. I actually think she's really cool, but sometimes I catch her watching me. I think she might be falling for me, and while it's perfectly understandable, I love my wife. I've made that very clear. I think what that girl is really longing for is a Dom."

"You don't know that she doesn't have one," Adam said. "But he's right. I've caught her staring at Sean for long periods of time. We really don't know a damn thing about her except that she's funny and can drink me under a table. Seriously, the girl can chug."

Sean shook his head. "Well, if she has a Dom, he's a crappy one because there's no way he would let her pull this shit alone. She nearly got caught earlier today. I had to step in or Chazz would have seen her sneaking into his office. As it was, she had to hide until he walked by. It's obvious to me that she's getting very impatient. I actually don't like the fact that she's back out there by herself. She believes in her own abilities too much."

"I don't know about that. Maybe she's not so great with the sneaky thing, but have you noticed how she moves?" Adam asked.

Eve had. "She's had some training."

"She's had a lot of training." Sean sighed and took a long tug off his beer. "But then again, she's written a lot of stories about the military. If I was in her position, I would take some Krav Maga classes, too."

"I've had self-defense," Eve added. "But I don't move like Kristen. She's very quiet."

"She's also got a couple of bullet wounds." Adam shrugged a little. "We share a bathroom. She doesn't lock it when she takes a shower. Her boobs are actually quite nice. Hey, Serena would appreciate them, too. I already told her I saw them and did not get an erection. Little Adam only responds to Serena now."

"I'm really fucking glad to hear that, asshole," Sean growled back.

God, she hoped she wasn't going to have to play referee. When Sean and his wife, Grace, had first gotten together, Adam had let it be known that he thought Grace would fit perfectly between him and Jake. Sean had not taken it well. But they had to be over that.

Adam gave Sean what she liked to think of as his "sad puppy" face. Adam sighed. "Did I ever mention how sorry I was to try to steal your woman? Cause I am. It would have been a huge mistake. Luckily, Grace has horrible taste in men."

Sean snorted. "I'm going to kill him, Eve."

She put a hand out. She needed to distract them and quickly. "Both of you stop. Sean, I've just had crazy, wild reunion sex with my husband for four hours. I'm hungry."

Sean smiled and his hand came out, covering hers. "You just called Alex your husband."

She hadn't even thought about it. "Yeah, well, he claims that the minute we land back in Dallas, I'm supposed to marry him, and we all know I'm a very good submissive."

Sean sighed, relief plain on his face. He hauled her off the chair and gave her a bone-cracking bear hug. "I'm so happy, Evie. I can't tell you how happy I am. He won't fuck up again. Ian and I will make damn sure of it."

She couldn't let him think she didn't know the score. "Well, it was my fault, too."

Sean settled her back into her chair and gave her a wink. "Absolutely, and your Master should have punished you for it. Lucky for you, I am not your Master, so I will feed you instead." He frowned. "I'm sure she's got some salad around here somewhere. Kristen actually seems more like a carnivore, though. I swear she's got a ton of meat in her freezer."

The last thing she needed was a salad. "Can you do a grilled cheese? Maybe with some ham. And if Kris has chocolate, I would love some."

Sex was hard work. She'd earned a little comfort food.

"Hallelujah! I think I saw some prosciutto." Sean strode to the fridge and started prepping.

"I'll take one, too," Adam said.

Sean never turned around, just flashed his middle finger as he went about his work. Adam ignored the rude gesture.

"He'll forgive me sometime," Adam said, staring down at the files. "So, whatcha looking at?"

She put a hand on the files. "This is the case the feds have against Evans."

And somewhere in there was a nice, fat report on her.

She took a long breath. It wouldn't hurt to read through it. She needed to do a whole new profile on the man. So much time had gone by that she needed to look through everything.

"I think he's in New York." Adam's quiet words sent a shiver up her spine.

"Think?"

He grabbed his computer and brought it up to the bar, his fingers flying across the keys in an instant. "I've been tracking the GPS you placed. Nice call on the shoe, by the way. Alex wouldn't think of the whole 'dry cleaning' thing. Does he wear anything that needs to be dry cleaned?"

Since he'd left the FBI, he really had reverted to his former jock wardrobe. "No. T-shirts, sweatpants, and jeans don't normally require much care. So my guy got to New York. What makes you think he's meeting with Evans?"

"This." He hit a key and a grainy picture came up. "When I realized he was walking on some of the busier streets, I thought I might be able to hack into the CCTV feeds there. Sure enough, this was caught as he was walking past one of the banks in midtown."

She stared at the screen. There was a crowd of people walking in the late-afternoon light, but she recognized one of the men from earlier in the day. His face was to the camera, but the man beside him was only in profile.

Closing her eyes against the wave of nausea she got, Eve was nearly transported back in time. Michael Evans. He was older, had cut most of his hair, but she knew that profile. She saw it in her nightmares. "That's him."

"Shit," Sean said. "I'll go wake up Alex."

Eve shook her head. "No. Give him a couple of hours. We can't do anything tonight. Let's see what Kristen finds out."

Sean stared at the screen, his hands on the bar. "He's really alive. Fuck. I hoped he'd managed to get himself horrifically murdered somewhere along the way."

There was a ding and the door opened. Kristen walked in, her red hair rumpled and a streak of blood on her face.

"What the hell?" Adam asked, standing up from his computer screen.

Kristen staggered to the couch. "It's nothing to worry about. I got into a little fight."

Eve rushed to the kitchen and wrapped some ice in a towel. She hurried back. Kristen was pulling back her hair. There was a nice knot on her forehead. "Is your cover blown?"

She took the towel. "I don't think so, but I have a dead bouncer in my trunk. He caught me coming out of Chazz's office. He thought I was trying to steal something. He made an offer to not turn me in."

Eve could guess what that had been. "So you jumped him when he got you alone for sex?"

"Is anything broken?" Sean asked.

Kristen shook her head. "I don't think so. He was a heavy fucker. I had to stuff him out a window so no one could see. It was really only my innate knowledge of pulleys and levers that saved my ass. Well, that, and a perfectly placed stiletto through his eye socket."

Adam's eyes widened. "You killed him with your heel?"

"No, dummy. I was talking about a knife. I told him I would do him in one of the private rooms. I have weapons hidden all over that club." She held the ice to her forehead. "Damn it. I promised myself I wouldn't kill anyone again. Jerk-faced asshole couldn't respect my fake need for vagina. No, he had to prove what a man he was. He promised he would turn me straight."

Sean smiled knowingly at her. "Which agency do you work for? Look, I've got my smiley face on so I'm not angry at all. But if you're trying to tell me you're a mild-mannered journalist who just happens to be able to shove a thin blade in precisely the right way and with the right amount of force to kill a man, then you don't have much respect for my intelligence. Are you domestic or foreign?"

Kristen closed her eyes. "Sean, I'm not what you think I am."

"He thinks you're Agency. I kind of do, too," Adam agreed.

"I am not a spy. I am no one's operative," Kristen said in a low voice. "I am not now, nor have I ever belonged to, any government agency and certainly not the CIA."

Eve kind of believed her. There was more than one reason to learn how to really defend oneself. "But you've been hurt before."

Kristen's eyes found hers. "Yes, in ways you can't imagine. I learned how to defend myself at a very young age. I had to. I don't hide weapons because some CIA handbook taught me to. I hide them because growing up I knew if I didn't have a way to defend myself, I would very likely not see another birthday, at least not one where I was whole. Can we move past my shitastic childhood and talk about what I found?"

Sean's jaw was a stubborn line. "Fine, but I'll figure you out and I probably won't be wearing my smiley face when I do. And I swear to god, if you hurt anyone on this team, I will make sure you pay."

"I'm sure your brother would be right behind you," she said absently.

"You know he would. Think about that before you

make your next move." Sean had gone positively arctic.

"You think I don't think about it every fucking day?"

Eve needed to chill them out before Sean and Kristen went after each other. Despite the fact that she didn't know a damn thing about the woman, she trusted Kristen. "What did you learn, sweetie?"

Kristen's eyebrows rose, and she turned to Eve. It was so easy to see the eager puppy on her face. She wanted to be one of the girls. She so deeply wanted friends. Eve watched as Kristen stopped herself, drawing her hands together and folding them on her lap. If Eve had to bet, she would say Kristen had wanted to reach out, to hold Eve's hand. "I got into Chazz's office. I knew I wouldn't have long. I got in. I looked at his calendar. I got out."

Eve moved toward her, offering her the affection she so clearly longed for. She held out her hand. "And what did you find?"

Kristen leaned forward, reaching for Eve's hand. "He's got the day after tomorrow circled. It says he's meeting with Mikey. We can get him, Eve. I'll help you. I'll be right there beside you."

Nothing in her eyes made Eve think she was lying. Eve threaded their fingers together. This was what Kristen so deeply desired, a sisterhood, a family. "All right. We'll wake Alex up early and let him know. We'll be ready for him."

She had a day to profile him, to figure out how best to go after him. She wouldn't sleep. It wasn't her job to be the avenger. It was her job to give Alex and Sean every bit of information they needed to know.

And Kristen. She just knew it. Kristen would be a warrior. Kristen needed to help.

Sean frowned. "All right then. Are you hungry?"

Kristen shrugged. "I could eat."

Sean shook his head and walked back into the kitchen.

Adam yelled after him. "Hey, you're willing to cook for the woman who won't tell us who she really is but not me?"

Sean didn't look back, just started buttering bread. "She didn't try to sleep with my wife."

Kristen shrugged. "I haven't seen her. Who knows? I might."

Sean just chuckled.

Kristen leaned in, whispering. "I really wouldn't. I really do still love the man I lost. I can't...I can't think of anyone else."

Eve smiled, squeezing her hand. "It's okay. You did...good." She gave Kristen's words back to her. She looked down at the file folders. "And thank you for these. I'm not looking forward to staring at the seventeen bombing victims, but I think it will be helpful."

Kristen frowned. "What do you mean seventeen? There were only sixteen folders."

Eve looked down at the folders in front of her, quickly counting them. Kristen was right. Sixteen folders. There were seventeen victims. Why did the FBI only have sixteen folders?

She moved back to the bar. "You didn't get them all."

Kristen was mistaken.

The redhead sat up, letting the ice pack down. "I took everything they had. If the FBI had a file, I hacked it."

"I know this case. There were seventeen dead. If you count my kidnapping, there should actually be twenty, but my folder that includes Leon and Tommy is considered ancillary."

"You're in there," Kristen said. "I just didn't count you among the dead. According to the FBI, there are sixteen dead from the bombings, two murdered agents and one rape and kidnapping victim. You."

Adam moved to his computer. "I'm on it."

She knew this case like the back of her hand. She knew the victims by heart. She played through them in her head. Brewer, Davies, Duncan, Foster, Clemmons, Johnson, Wilcox, Schroeder, Flynn, Betts, Gale, Hardison, Garcia, Kapoor, Ellig, Gilliland, and Foster.

The names were tattooed on her brain. Though she couldn't remember everything about each victim, she knew their names. Who was missing?

"There were only sixteen files." Kristen stood behind her, peering over her shoulder. "I pulled everything I could. Did I miss something?"

Garcia. There was no file for Garcia. "Uhm, I think you missed Carmen Garcia's file. She died in the last bombing. The one in DC."

It had been the bombing that forced Alex to make that fated move. Evans had bombed a free clinic that offered women healthcare. Four people had died in that bombing including a doctor who worked for nothing to make sure the women in the neighborhood had routine checkups and prenatal care. Dr. Kapoor's file was here. Where was Carmen Garcia's?

It was probably just an oversight. Files got lost sometimes. Though not typically in the computer age.

Kristen winced a little as she moved to one of Adam's three computers. "May I?"

Adam nodded, not looking up from his keyboard. "Sure. I'm going to hack into the fed's system. It could take me a minute or two. I'm going to route this system through another fifty so they'll have a hell of a time working the knot out. I don't want the feds on my doorstep."

"Don't you mean you don't want them on your doorstep

again?" Sean asked as he placed a perfectly golden sandwich in front of her.

Damn. She was hungry. Despite the way her every instinct was telling her something was wrong, her stomach rumbled. "I thought Adam didn't get caught anymore."

Adam shrugged. "There's always a way. No matter what a hacker does, if the investigator is tenacious enough, he'll find you. I just have to make it not worth their while."

"Shit." Kristen groaned as she looked down at the computer. "That will teach me to do all my research from government files. I pulled up the press on the last bombing. There she is. Carmen Garcia. Twenty-two years old. Pretty girl. She was a law student at Georgetown."

"That's right. I always thought it was odd that she was in that clinic. Her parents had money. She wasn't a scholarship student. She was from a fairly prominent family in San Antonio," Eve said. She hadn't fit the typical profile. Most of the victims were doctors or nurses or indigent women, women who had no other means of health care. "She would have to drive a long way to get to that particular clinic."

"She had a history of volunteer work," Kristen mused. "Maybe she was helping out."

"Her volunteer work all had to do with legal work and politics. The survivors didn't remember ever seeing her there before, and all the paperwork was lost in the fire. She had to be identified by dental records."

"I'm in." Adam got that focused look he had when he was working on a problem. This was Adam's world. Oh, he could shoot and wield a knife with the rest of them, but when Adam was at a computer, his magnificent brain processing, that was when he was at his deadliest.

Sean put a second plate in front of Adam, proving that

most of their animosity was for show. Or that Sean couldn't resist showing off because that was an amazing grilled cheese. Eve bit into hers and couldn't help but sigh. The man could cook. "As Kris would say, I didn't even poison it. Do you want fries with yours? You have a couple of potatoes I could fry up."

His eyes were hooded, a little wary, as he looked at Kristen, who shook her head slightly. "Nope. Just the sandwich, but brown bag it for me, please. Lugging Jersey Carl's corpse around made me a little queasy. Maybe after I find a place to dump his body I'll be ready for a snack. I was thinking of weighing him down a little and dumping him in the ocean. It's a nice night for it. There should be a current around here, right?"

"I'll check," Sean said, obviously resigned to being her accomplice. "Do you have a boat?"

"I do not have a boat, but I do have two good hands with which to borrow one without the owner knowing, so the glass is truly half full. I'll go clean up a little before we go. I know a little harbor down the road where the night guard is usually asleep by this point in time."

Sean started to clean up the kitchen as Kristen walked off.

"Are you all right with this?" Eve asked. Sean was a dad now. He might not want to become an accomplice to probably justifiable murder.

Adam shook his head. "Has she done this before? Why would she know about when the night guard at a harbor sleeps? Is she Dexter?"

Eve snorted a little. "She's not a serial killer."

Sean shook his head. "I don't think she is either, but she does seem to pay very close attention to her surroundings."

"If she grew up in an abusive household, she very likely

had to," Eve mused. "But really, are you all right? I could wake up Alex and we could go with her."

"Nah. I'd rather keep an eye on her. And I buy her story about Carl. I've only worked with the asshole for a week and I saw him harassing most of the waitresses. They're afraid of him. The kitchen staff, too. I think he's blackmailing some of the illegals, telling them he'll call in immigration if they don't turn over a cut to him. He was also carrying, so one less asshole we have to worry about. Maybe Chazz will lean more heavily on Alex now." Sean glanced back toward the hall where Kristen had disappeared. "She knows more than she's saying. One of us needs to get closer. She seems to like me."

She remembered the last time Sean got close to a female involved in an operation. They had a baby together. "Sean, you can't."

He rolled his eyes. "God, Eve, I'm not going to seduce her. I might top her a little, though. You can do that without ever touching a woman. She's hiding a lot behind her sarcasm. Maybe I can get her to open up a little, figure out what she's really doing here. What's wrong with you? I'm not the one who tries to screw around with women who don't belong to him."

Adam groaned. "I swear I would kill him if he wasn't such a good cook. He has the memory of an elephant." Adam's eyes went wide. "Got it. I pulled the files straight from the feds. Sixteen. No Carmen Garcia. Could they have classified it? Why would they do that?"

Eve had absolutely no idea.

"Why are you up?" Alex asked, walking out of their bedroom wearing nothing but a pair of sweats. Adam could keep his perfectly cut suits. She loved Alex just the way he was. He didn't need a suit to make her drool.

"Couldn't sleep." Nor could she help the little sigh that came out of her mouth. Such a lovely Master with his sleepy eyes and broad shoulders.

"Then I didn't do my job. Come back to bed, angel." He held his hand out. "I can't sleep without you."

And she just left everything. It would still be there in the morning. The fact that a file was missing was very likely a mistake on the government's part.

"Did I miss anything?" Alex asked.

Eve filled Alex in. "Adam thinks he's found Evans in New York. Kristen got a look at Chazz's day planner and thinks Evans is going to be here the day after tomorrow. Oh, and Kristen killed a bouncer."

"Was it Carl?" Alex asked, seeming perfectly fine with every single piece of news she'd given him.

"Yes." She really should have paid more attention to Carl.

"Good for Kris. Who's on corpse duty? Tell me she has the body."

Kristen stepped out of the hallway. She'd changed her clothes and was now wearing all black. "Of course. I'm not a tourist. It's in the back of my Navigator. Dude was heavy."

"I'll handle it, Alex," Sean said.

"And I'm on Evans." Adam was back to focusing on his computer. "I'm running some programs to see if I can figure out what name he's using. Kristen had found about four of them. Hopefully he's using one of those. We'll get him. You and Eve get some rest."

"So he's really coming here?" Alex asked, his hand tightening on hers.

Kristen nodded. "I told you I would give him to you on a silver platter."

"All right." He turned and started leading Eve back to

the bedroom.

"Alex?" She'd expected him to go into full-on commando mode, but he was walking away.

He pulled her into his arms. "No, Eve. No more talk about this. We'll figure it out in the morning. We'll sit down and talk it out. All right? I won't leave you out of the decision-making process, but you have to know I'll let his ass go if it's a choice between hauling him in or you getting hurt again."

He would choose her. Tears threatened again and she laid her head against his chest. She would always choose him. "Yes, Master."

"Kiss me."

She tilted her head up. The Master wasn't done with her yet.

Chapter Fourteen

In the low light just before dawn, Jesse checked the safety on his SIG. He'd decided to make it quick. Clean and easy. No fuss, no muss. The boss had called again, in an agitated state.

And Jesse hadn't told him everything. He hadn't told him what he'd witnessed.

Kristen. He'd watched as Kristen led that fucker Carl to one of the back rooms. He'd been surprised at just how much he'd hated that. It wasn't that he liked Kris. *Fuck.* It was impossible not to like Kris. She was one of those glowy people, the kind who could get the shit knocked out of them and get back up and still have a smile to show the world.

His heart had taken a little dive when he'd seen her with Carl. Carl was an ass. He treated all women like they were nothing but holes to stick his dick in. What the hell did she see in him? And wasn't she supposed to be all girl-on-girl action? Carl, with his copious body hair, was as far from feminine as it was possible to be.

He'd had to take a walk, grab a smoke. It felt like things were coming to a head. Chazz had informed him that the man who ran everything was coming in for a visit.

He'd overheard Chazz talking about the "farm" again. He mentioned it from time to time, but if Chazz was growing carrots and potatoes, Jesse wasn't aware of it.

"You'll get to meet the big boss," he'd said.

Like I didn't already know that, dumbass. You have no

idea who I am.

Jesse had just lit up, trying to think his way out of what he had to do.

That was when he'd seen Carl the Douchenozzle taking a header out the window. He'd wondered why Carl was leaving via window when there was a perfectly good front door. He'd giggled a little and then realized the dude was dead. He didn't move at all. Jesse knew what a dead body looked like. He knew it all too well.

Kris was awfully cool under pressure. He'd watched as she maneuvered Carl's body into the back of her SUV, all the while keeping track of who was coming and going. She'd even moved off to talk to one of the cocktail waitresses, probably to ensure that she didn't step into the scene of Kristen's crime.

So why hadn't he mentioned it to his boss?

For the same damn reason he was about to do what he was about to do.

Because he'd just found out that there were lines he couldn't step over.

He stared out at the gorgeous condo where his prey was staying. Another lie he'd been told. According to the lovely Kristen, everyone should be at her rundown little house in St. Augustine proper. But he'd followed her out to Palm Coast, driving along a lonely highway with his lights off so she wouldn't think she was being tailed. He'd followed her past the beach houses and Marine World. Well, he'd followed as far as he could. Once he'd crossed through the toll bridge, he'd come to a gate with a security guard.

He'd had to park his car and make his way around the security. It hadn't been easy, but they hadn't given him the call sign "Wraith" in his old unit for nothing. He hunkered down inside one of the gated lanais on the first floor. He wouldn't have known what building she was in if he hadn't been able to find her car.

He felt safe here. The windows were all dark and there were no little tables on this side, the inland side. As far as he could tell, the lanai went all the way around the back to the ocean side. These were seriously wealthy people.

What the fuck was she doing tending bar when she could afford this place?

About an hour after he'd found her, she'd left again with the big blond cook who looked like he could butcher more than a cow.

After they had driven away, Jesse had found Master A's vehicle, broken in, placed his equipment inside and then walked back to his hidey-hole. Jesse waited patiently. He was sure he was in the right place, watching the right door.

Just him and his gun.

The sun had come up an hour or so ago, roughly twenty minutes after Kristen and the cook had completed whatever their errand had been. From where he was sitting, he had a view of the door Kristen and the cook had disappeared into earlier. He would have taken a closer look, tried to peek inside, but there was a security camera on the door. It was the only one. Once the target was a few feet past the entryway, Jesse could act without the problem of prying eyes.

He had two roads to go down. Three, really. If Master A came out first or with the cook, he would pop them both and be done. If his target came out with one of the women, he would have a choice to make, but if the sub came out alone, he had a plan.

It was all about waiting now.

Waiting and figuring out how to salvage his career.

Or just accepting that he was a fuck up now and he

always had been.

What would his hero father think of him now? There was no way he would be proud, right? He would be like the rest. He would wonder why Jesse Murdoch's head was on his body when the rest of his team had met such a grisly fate.

Jesse closed his eyes because sometimes he could stop the visions if he thought of something else. Anything but that dank Iraqi prison, smelling of death and blood and piss. Anything but the way poor Alannah had looked at him right before the sword had severed her head from her body.

He'd cared for her and she'd hated him in that moment. She'd hated the fact that she was dying and he wasn't. She'd believed that he'd turned.

So did everyone else.

Losing this job would be the nail in his coffin, but by god, he would go out being true to himself.

The sun kept rising, but Jesse felt no warmth.

* * * *

"So what's the problem?" Alex asked, looking down at the computer screen. It was a mass of 1s and 0s and a bunch of shit that made no sense to him.

Adam yawned, stretching in the early morning light. Apparently he'd been up all night dealing with the horror of 1s and 0s. "It's weird. If this particular file had been classified, there would be something here I could find, but it's just gone. Someone deleted this file."

"Why the hell would they delete a file?" Alex couldn't understand it. "Do you think Evans did it?"

It was the only thing that made sense. The feds needed every single bit of information they could get. It was precious and to be hoarded like gold. How had they not seen it? Had they let this case go cold? No. He wouldn't believe it.

There was no way Warren allowed it to happen.

Adam shrugged. "I don't know, but someone did and they did it from inside the Bureau. If someone had done it from the outside, there would be footprints. I can't exactly figure out where the deletion comes from. This computer used to be registered to a Tommy Guinn, but now the system is deemed inactive."

Tommy. God. Tommy had died in the attack on Eve. "Can you tell what the date is?"

Adam pressed a few keys.

"March 15th. Does that date mean anything?" Adam asked.

It was ten days after he'd quit the Bureau. "Not really. I wasn't there anymore. I don't know. I need to call some of my contacts. I'll figure it out."

Adam stood. "Don't. Don't call them. Let's take a look at this on our own."

Alex sighed, closing his eyes. "You think this is an inside job."

"And you're too close to it."

Adam was right. "Okay. Let's go over all the reasons someone on the inside would delete that file. Get Sean out here. Eve is in the shower. She shouldn't be too long. We have a couple of hours before we have to be at the club. I want to think this through. Text Ian."

Ian was his damn sounding board. He needed Ian. *Damn it.* How the hell had Nelson picked the perfect time to separate him from Ian?

"Already did. He's going to Skype in soon. I'll put it through the big TV. He can yell at us in HD." Adam seemed relieved to have something to do. He started gathering wires and cords.

Alex looked down at the files. Was Carmen Garcia a rabbit hole he shouldn't go down? "What did you find out about her?"

Adam was attaching cords to the big TV in the living room. "Favorite daughter of a high-profile San Antonio family. Her father has been in the Texas state senate. Her brother played college ball for the Longhorns. She had damn near perfect LSATs. Picked Georgetown over Harvard. Not sure that was a great decision, but she wanted to be close to Washington according to the articles I read on her."

Why was she important? In all the years he'd spent with the Bureau, he'd never had a problem with someone deleting files. No. This was deliberate. It might be a rabbit hole when it came to Evans, but something about it was making his every instinct light up.

Sean walked out, yawning but already dressed for the day. He had his knives rolled up and in his left hand. "Jersey Carl is swimming with the fishes and hopefully catching a nice current toward the North Atlantic. I have to head in early. I'm going to talk to some of the dishwashers and see if I can get anything out of them about the upcoming meet spot. Chazz talks a lot, and he doesn't understand that most of these guys have picked up some English. He talks in front of them like they're not there. Call me if you need anything."

"Like breakfast?" Adam asked.

"Ain't happening today." Sean shut the door behind him.

Eve walked out of the back of the condo wearing pajama bottoms and a T-shirt that couldn't hide the fact that she wasn't wearing a bra. Her hair was up in a haphazard bun and she had little fuzzy pink flip-flops on her feet. She wore no makeup, and he'd never seen her more beautiful. Even after all the sex from the night before, his cock was at full attention the minute she entered a room. "Where did Sean go?"

"To get some information from his staff. He thinks they might know more than they're saying. What's your take on Carmen Garcia?" Alex asked, walking to the coffee maker to get it started.

"I don't know. There are only so many reasons a girl with her money and ties to the community would go to a free clinic if she wasn't volunteering. My bet is she didn't want her people to know she needed the services of an ob-gyn. She was pregnant. Whether she was looking for confirmation of the pregnancy or she was seeking to terminate it, we may never know."

"But why does it matter? Why delete her file?" He fumbled with the storage case at the bottom of the coffeemaker. It was completely empty. "Damn it, Adam."

"Sorry. I was up all night. I needed fuel." Adam was lost in a tangle of wires that ran from various computers.

Eve needed coffee. She was a little touchy until she'd had her morning joe. And now it was Alex's formal job again to make sure she got it. "I'll go buy some."

A soft hand touched his back and then he felt her all along his spine, her face resting against his shoulder blade. "Don't, babe. There's a common area downstairs. Kristen showed it to me. There's one of those single cup coffee makers. I'll go and make a cup."

"I can do it." Taking care of her was his job, and now that she was allowing him to, he intended to take it damn seriously.

She giggled a little. "Alex, you don't know how to work

one. I could be standing up here slowly dying of caffeine deficiency for hours. Besides, I could use the little walk to wake myself up. Someone tired me out last night."

He turned and had his lips on hers in a heartbeat. He tangled his hands in her hair, unloosing that bun, and gave her a proper good-morning kiss. "I'll tire you out again tonight, angel." He let his forehead rest against hers. "One way or another, this is all over in a couple of days."

If Evans showed, Alex would try to take him down. If he didn't, he was going to turn everything over to someone else because he didn't want Eve in danger and Eve wouldn't leave him, ergo he was off this case and soon.

Maybe it was time to let Ian just assassinate the fucker.

"I know." She got on her tiptoes. "I'll be back in a second. Why don't you make me some toast?"

He could do that. It was about all he could do in the kitchen, but he could use a toaster. "Okay."

She turned and started out of the condo. He heard the elevator ding as she went down.

He went to the fridge as his mind pondered the possibilities.

There had been an awful lot of chance that went Evans's way. He'd eluded capture multiple times when Alex should have had the man. Once, twice, he could deal with that, but he'd had prime information on Evans's movements right after the DC bombing. He'd found his hideout and Evans was gone, a cigarette still smoking in an ashtray as though he'd known exactly when to bail out.

And then there was the escape. He could still remember how he'd felt when Warren had called to tell him that Evans was on the loose.

Chazz had been in that jail. He'd been pulled out of the actual cell when the bedding was brought in, but he'd been housed with Evans for weeks. He very likely knew exactly how Evans had escaped.

He might know if there was a connection between Evans and Carmen Garcia.

He might know if there was a connection between Evans and someone on his old team.

Was he ready to go heavy on Chazz? Right before Evans got here?

Did he have a choice?

"You are deep in thought. Are you trying to cook the eggs with your brain?" Adam asked.

Alex turned to him. "I need you to look into the members of my old team. The ones who are still alive. You're looking for any connection between Carmen Garcia and anyone in the FBI."

Adam's eyes widened and he whistled a little. "You think someone on your team deleted that file."

"Who else could have done it?" It didn't make a lick of sense for someone on the outside to hack in and delete a file. "There's no point to it. Anyone who knows the case at all knows that there were seventeen victims. So why do it here?"

"No idea. All a person has to do is pull up any news article and the full list is right there. I checked with the local district attorneys and they all have the proper files." Adam stretched and yawned. "I'll get on it. I need hazard pay for this assignment. Every time I clean up one of Ian's little problems, another crops up. I got him off the no-fly list, but when I tried to book him a flight for the morning, all his credit cards are maxed out. He's been doing a lot of shopping online apparently. Did you know Ian likes high-end lingerie and wears a 36 double D? He's got several shipments from Neiman Marcus arriving tomorrow. And apparently he really has a thing for lacy boy shorts. How the hell am I going to tell him that?"

Alex snorted a little. "I'll tell him."

He turned back to his eggs. When he got back to Dallas, it looked like they would have a whole new issue to deal with.

"Guilt."

Alex turned the burner up and glanced back at Kristen, who had been the one to speak. "Guilt?"

Dressed for work in black pants and a club T-shirt, she looked no worse for her previous evening's work. "You asked why someone would do it. You couldn't come up with a possibility, but I can. Sometimes you erase things because you don't want a reminder of what you did wrong. It doesn't work. You can get rid of pictures and whatever and you still remember."

He scraped the eggs, scrambling them. "I'll buy that. I have Adam trying to make a connection."

"Good. When you find the connection, you'll know. It could be as simple as she was a friend and whoever deleted the file felt he or she had let her down. Sometimes we don't mean to hurt the people we love. Sometimes they just get caught in our crossfire and all we can do is pray they survive it. Maybe Carmen Garcia didn't survive it."

Or maybe it was something more sinister.

"I need to talk to Eve." Something she'd said the night before was playing through his brain. He had no idea how it connected to anything, but suddenly he needed to talk to her about what Warren had said to her on the night that Evans had taken her. She'd said something about Warren bringing him back to her.

Warren never mentioned going home. Warren had been steadfast at his side.

*We're going to take this fucker down together, buddy.
You and me.*

Maybe she'd been wrong. Maybe Warren had told her
he would make damn sure Alex got home. Warren was
talking about not letting him die and Eve took it as
physically bringing him home. Surely.

When Eve came back, he would clear it all up.

"Hey, where's my coffee?" Kristen asked. She rounded
on Adam. "You bastard. Do you know what I'm like without
coffee? Have you ever seen a badger? They look all cute and
cuddly until some dumbass smokes it from its hole and then
the claws and fangs are out. I'm about to grow claws and
fangs, Adam."

Adam held up his phone, dialing furiously. "Eve's
getting some from the common area. Look, I'll have her get
you some, too. Nice, badger. Good, badger. No smoke
here."

Kristen hissed his way.

Okay, someone really needed to get the girl some
coffee.

"It went to voice mail. Did Eve leave her phone up
here?" Adam asked.

"She always carries it." Something crawled up his
spine. Something was wrong.

Alex turned off the stove and walked to the door, every
instinct in him screaming that he should find his wife.

"What is it?" Kristen was right behind him.

He pressed the door to the elevator, the fountain behind
him not soothing at all now. *Let her be on her way up. The
doors are going to open and she'll be there with her cup of
coffee and I'll be a paranoid idiot.*

The doors slid open. No Eve. Just an empty elevator.
His heart seized just a little.

"Adam, hold down the fort. I'll be right back." He got into the elevator. "I just want to check on Eve."

Kristen hopped in before the door closed.

Alex took a long breath and prayed his instincts were wrong.

Chapter Fifteen

Eve breathed in the heavenly scent of coffee. This was what she needed. She needed to have a nice cup of coffee and a little breakfast and then she would be ready to work. She would sit on the couch in the living room, with its gorgeous views of the Atlantic, and snuggle unashamedly up to her husband and they would work through the problem.

Her husband. They'd gotten a divorce, but he'd always been her husband. He'd stayed close. He was just a man. Men were kind of dumb. She needed to remember that.

She was female, and that brought with it a certain amount of responsibility. She had to plainly state what she needed. Oh, it would be so much better if he would understand her needs, but his reasoning skills were hampered by a really large penis. She had to make adjustments.

Eve took a long breath. Oh, it felt so good to joke, even if only with herself.

The world was opening up again. It was like someone had pushed a button and suddenly she could see in color when the last several years had been a brutal black and white. Maybe, oh just maybe, she hadn't been completely shattered. Maybe she'd just been a little broken and she could put the pieces back together. She would be held together with hot glue and hope, but she was alive.

In the end, that was all that mattered.

She walked out of the little kitchen in the common area.

The floor was a lovely marble and everything about the building was elegant. She really loved it here. Perhaps she and Alex could get more than just a house in Dallas. Maybe they could find a lovely summer home. Or winter home. Or just a getaway house.

They had options.

She got to the end of the hall. The elevator was on her left, but she turned right, wanting to sit out by the pool that overlooked the Atlantic. At this time of the morning, she could watch dolphins playing. It was so peaceful. She pressed through the door. In this particular building, there were only two condos per level. All she had to do to reach the pool was to walk around the first floor's giant lanai. A little walkway led to the pool area, and at the back of the pool, she could shout up to their balcony and get Alex to join her. He would come down with her breakfast and they could watch the dolphins play and enjoy the gorgeous sunrise.

Or she could text him. Although throwing stuff at the window sounded like more fun. She walked outside even though she knew she couldn't get back in without help. She'd left her keys upstairs.

Master, please save your poor sub. She's locked out and can't get back in without her sweet Master.

Maybe she could get him in the hot tub. That would be fun.

The clean ocean air hit her, and she stopped for a moment, just breathing it in. Everything seemed possible again. A family. A life. Everything. It really was out there just waiting for her to decide she was brave enough to grab it.

She started to pass the lanai and it's pretty little private gate. The first floor was a rental, Kristen had mentioned.

Maybe they could take a look at it while they were here. The lanai looked huge, wrapping around the whole condo. It was like a kid run. She could just toss the kids out here and they would run themselves silly.

Kids. She and Alex could have babies. They didn't have to come out of her womb. They only needed her love for her to be a mother. Hers and Alex's. She could have a family.

She looked out over the parking lot and decided to just text. She'd never had a great throwing arm and the hurricane glass in the windows might just bounce anything she threw right back at her face. She pulled up Alex's number and started to text.

And then she heard the tiniest squeak.

She started to turn, but felt something press against her spine.

"Drop the phone, sweetheart."

She brought her leg up. She would bring her stiletto down on the bridge of his foot and start running, but her pink Ugg flip-flop did not have the same effect.

"Don't try that again. I'm doing you a favor, Amanda. I'm trying to save you, but if you scream or try anything else, I won't have another choice but to put a bullet in your spine."

She knew that raspy voice. "Jesse?"

His voice shook just the tiniest bit. "Yes, sweetheart. I'm not going to hurt you. God, I'm trying not to hurt you, but you have to understand that the mission is more important than you. If I can save you, I will. So we're going to move real slowly toward your car."

"I don't have my keys." She wasn't planning on driving anywhere.

"I don't need keys."

What to do? She took a deep breath and thought about

tossing the coffee in his face.

"Drop the cup or I'll shoot you."

Damn it. She kind of believed him. She let the cup drop, which was a shame because she needed that little bit of caffeine. "All right. The cup is gone."

He wasn't done. "Now the phone. Drop it."

She took a long breath and let the phone drop because that gun was pressed right against her back. It would split her spine in an instant. God, Alex was going to be so upset. Tears blurred her eyes. "Please don't do this."

His arm wound around her waist. "I don't want to. I know you won't believe this, but I really don't have a choice."

She had to stay calm. This wasn't like the last time, even though every cell in her body tried to tell her that it was. Her brain knew that Jesse Murdoch wasn't Michael Evans. He'd proven it by trying to explain himself. Evans had simply taken. Jesse was a different fish, and she had to play him another way. "You always have a choice."

She felt him sag a little. "No. You don't, honey. Sometimes every single choice a man has is a bad one. I hope you never find that out. I'm going to try really hard to make sure you're out of this. Now move. I know you're in the white SUV."

He'd been observant. Alex had rented a white SUV. It was parked close to the lanai. Now she wished they had parked farther away, in the garage, like they had the night they arrived.

"Put your wrists together."

She wasn't going to do that. She couldn't. She kicked out, but he caught her ankle easily, the SIG Sauer he was carrying coming against her gut.

"I'm not playing, sweetheart." His face was tortured, his

eyes narrowed. "I don't want to hurt you, but I have a mission. Don't make me knock you out. I'm not sure I wouldn't kill you, and I want to avoid that at all costs. All costs except my mission."

He slid a set of zip ties over her wrists and had her hands bound in an instant. He pressed her along, forcing her toward the SUV. *Damn.* She could see that he'd already managed to get the door open. It was slightly ajar. He was prepared.

"Why are you working for him?" She still had a chance to get through to him. Jesse Murdoch wasn't so far gone that he wouldn't listen to some sweet reason. After all, he hadn't killed her yet. The question was why.

Was he taking her to Evans?

"Because it's the right thing to do," he replied. "I could ask you the same thing, but I know the answer. Keep moving."

He opened the back door and shoved her inside. He zip tied her feet as easily as he had her hands.

"Right? You think it's right to work for him?" How long would Alex wait? He would notice she was missing, but how long would it be? And how would he react? Would this send him right back into his shell? She couldn't stand the thought of it.

"Master A isn't who you think he is." Jesse stared down at her while he pulled off his jacket. "I know you think he's a good guy, but a real man wouldn't hit you. A real man wouldn't show you off. You're a lovely woman. You deserve someone who really loves you."

Every word made her wonder what the hell this man was doing. A man who gave a damn about women wouldn't work for Evans. "I have a man who loves me. Please, don't do this. If you give me to your boss, he's going to hurt me.

Please. Take me back. You can make this right."

His blue eyes were just the slightest bit fanatical. "I am trying to do that even now. I know you can't see it, but I'm saving you. We're going to drive for a while and then I need you to be quiet. If I hear a loud word from your mouth, I'll have to knock you out. I don't want to hurt you. I don't want to be like every other man you've ever met. I'm not a fucking pervert. I'm not."

He slammed the back door, and she saw him moving into the front seat. He'd been damn sure of himself. He'd already moved his things into her car. A sniper rifle lay at the bottom of the floorboard. Who the hell was that for? Her blood chilled. Jesse said he was saving her from something. What the hell was he saving her from?

"I love him." She put her every emotion into those three words. If that sniper rifle was for Alex, then she had to try absolutely everything she could to save him.

"Because you don't know better." He was playing around under the dash. He proved just how good he was when the engine immediately purred to life. His face turned back and there was nothing but sympathy in his eyes. "One day you'll find someone worthy of you and you'll thank me."

"It's not going to be you?" His actions made her wonder if he hadn't fixated on her. His time in Iraq had obviously made him unstable, and sometimes unstable men fixated on a woman. He wasn't trying to hurt her. He seemed to be bent on saving her. She'd read his file. She searched her memory. A woman had been on his squad. Hannah? Alannah?

His mouth turned down. "I'm not capable of what you need. I'm…I'm just not good enough. But I am good enough to know that you deserve better and I can't just leave you to your fate, so I'm doing what I have to. I don't have to stop at the toll on the bridge on this side of the island, and there's no one out this early in the day. If I hear you making too much noise, I'll just gag you. That won't be pleasant for you, will it?"

She didn't bother to mention that she'd been gagged many times before. He was right. She didn't particularly like it. It really was a punishment.

He gunned the engine and put it in reverse.

"What are you going to do with the rifle back here?" Was there any way she could get it? He'd been smart to tie her hands behind her back. She couldn't even move her feet.

"I'm going to do what I need to do." His hands tightened on the wheel as he took a hard left and the car angled as they went up a hill and kept curving. She'd been here for a week and she knew this curve. It led to a circle at the top of the hill that overlooked the condo building.

There was a gorgeous bank of oleanders at the top of the hill, thick and tall. It would be the perfect cover for an assassin.

She could see it play out. Alex wouldn't wait long before he looked for her. She gave him five minutes tops before he realized she was taking far too long. He would come down the elevator and retrace her steps and then he would look outside. He would stand right outside the door, and he would be the perfect target. He would be so worried about her that he wouldn't take any defense. He would be vulnerable.

"Please don't shoot him." It was the off-season for tourists. One of the things she'd noticed was how few people were actually in the building. During her walk to the common area, she'd seen no one. The building had been quiet and empty.

She bet the roads were the same at this time of day.

There would be no crowds of people to scare Jesse away from what he obviously wanted to do.

He sat in the front seat of the car. She couldn't see his face, but his fist kept clenching and unclenching. "You don't understand because you're a civilian. You don't understand that sometimes things get dirty, but this is the right thing to do. This is the right thing to do."

He sounded like he was trying to convince himself. "It's not. It's murder."

"A soldier's job isn't black and white, and sometimes hard choices have to be made. I don't make decisions. I just follow orders." He took a long breath and reached into the back, grabbing the rifle. "No one's on the roads this early, and I doubt they would hear you if you screamed anyway. You can thrash about all you like because these windows have a nice tint on them, but you should save your strength. It's all going to be over in a few minutes and then we'll talk about how to set up your new life."

"Someone's going to see you." It was very unlikely, but she had to give him any reason to not do this. Her heart pounded, threatening to burst against her ribs. Alex. She couldn't lose him. She couldn't live in a world that didn't have Alex McKay in it. The very thought of his big body silenced forever played at her sanity.

He looked back in the SUV as he pulled up the hood on his black jacket. "People see what they want to see. They always do."

He slammed the door. She had a single look at him as he turned away. All anyone would see was a flash of a face. In this light, they wouldn't even be able to tell what his skin color was. He was wearing gloves. All a witness would be able to give was a vague height and weight and the fact that he drove away in the victim's SUV.

The victim. Oh, god. Alex was going to be the victim.

She couldn't lie here. *No. Fuck no.* She wasn't going to be submissive here. *No fucking way.* She couldn't reach anything with her hands, but she had her feet. She scooted down the leather seat and kicked off her shoes. Lying on her back, she found the door and the driver's side backseat console. He'd locked the doors. She felt for the buttons blindly. The way her feet were tied, she couldn't use her toes and her heels weren't exactly sensitive.

Nothing. Panic threatened.

She moved her foot down and tried again. Nothing. *Damn it.*

And then the ball of her foot hit metal. The door handle. Yes. A little to her right and there was the manual release. She pressed, her foot slipping a little, but she heard a beautiful click. She was running out of time. She needed to distract Jesse, needed to scream out to Alex.

She found the handle and managed to grasp it with her right toes. She pulled back hard and the door opened just the tiniest of bits.

She kicked out, adrenaline pumping through her system. Scooting along the seat, she felt her feet hit the ground.

And heard the one sound she didn't want to hear.

Gunfire cracked through the air.

"Alex!" She screamed with everything she had as she fell out onto the concrete. There was no way to balance, no way to stop herself from falling. She hit her head on the door as she fell and rolled, her shoulder striking the unforgiving road. Pain exploded along her skin, but she had only the briefest moment to process it before she was hauled up.

"Damn it, I didn't want to do it this way," Jesse said with a frown just before he brought the rifle down on her head.

The world went black even as she tried to call out for her husband one last time.

Chapter Sixteen

Alex stormed out of the elevator, his only thought on finding Eve.

"The common rooms are on your right." Kristen jogged to keep up with him. "No one can get her in this building, Alex. I made sure I picked a very secure location. No one can get in without a key fob."

There were so many ways around that it was silly. He stalked down the hall praying he would see Eve coming the other way. She would be in the common room messing around with the coffee maker. *Deep breath. Move.*

"And no one knows we're out here," Kristen argued.

"Someone could have easily followed us from the club."

"But we've been driving different cars and switching at the apartment in town. I had protocols in place. No one should be able to find us here."

If he'd been on the other side and new faces had shown up right around the time that Evans was scheduled to visit, he would have put a twenty-four hour ghost on them for a couple of days, but then Chazz was kind of an idiot.

"Here it is." Kristen pushed the door open.

It was a small kitchen, the scent of coffee still lingering in the air.

No Eve.

He checked in the trash. There was a single-use cup tossed into the can. It was a dark roast, exactly what Eve would have selected. She'd been here and now she wasn't.

"She went outside." She'd talked a lot last night about enjoying the mornings here. She loved the waves and the scent of the ocean. Which exit would she have used? The main exit was closest, but there was an exit just a few feet from the private elevator. It was closer to the building's pool and had a spectacular view of the ocean.

He was going to spank her ass red if she was sitting out on the patio sipping her coffee. *Please let her be sitting out on the patio sipping coffee. Please. Please.*

"You think she left? Alex, we should go and grab some ordnance," Kristen said, worry creeping into her tone. "Maybe something bad has happened. I'm not carrying."

Neither of them was carrying because he hadn't gotten dressed for the day, because he'd been too busy luxuriating in his wife to take care of her. "Call Adam. I'm going to search the grounds."

"Damn it," Kristen cursed behind him.

He made it to the side door and immediately saw something that set his heart to racing.

A cup on the ground, coffee spilled all over the concrete.

He pushed through the door, his eyes searching for Eve. "Eve!"

"Shit. McKay, let's get back inside." She had a cell in her hand. "Adam, Eve's not here. Turn on the locator to her cell phone now."

"Where's our SUV?" He looked out over the lot. He knew damn well where he'd parked last night, and the vehicle was gone. But Eve's keys were upstairs. She didn't have them on her. So where the hell was the car?

He forced himself to calm down. He needed his brain working, not pondering every bad possibility.

"Shit and fuckballs, is that her phone?" Kristen walked onto the lawn and bent down, picking something up. She turned, showing him the phone in her hand. Eve's phone. She wouldn't have just lost it.

"He made her get rid of it." And then it was easy to follow the bastard's line of thinking. "He's in the car we rented. Have Adam start a trace on the GPS. The rental company will have some way to track it down."

Kristen stepped out, speaking to Adam, but she had a hand over her brow as though trying to see in the distance. "Yes, get someone on it. And pull the feed from the CCTVs. At least we'll know when she stepped out of the building." Her arm came down in a quick motion. "Alex, drop!"

He saw it, but briefly, a little flash of light, the sun hitting the scope of a rifle and reflecting off of it.

He started to move, but there was a crack in the air. He needed to drop, but Kristen had moved faster than he had, and she covered his body.

Alex felt the bullet hit her, her frame jerking against his.

He put his arms under her and pulled her back, his hands going for his key fob. He had to get them out of the line of fire.

In the distance, he was almost certain he heard someone scream, but he couldn't make it out.

There was another flash and he ducked, covering Kristen's body as much as he could with his own. The bullet zinged past his ear, fire grazing along his skin. He covered her head with his hands.

"Fuck that hurts," Kristen said. "Oh, god. Oh, god I can't breathe."

Her words came out in tortured pants, and he could feel blood covering his arm.

He needed to run like a madman toward the man with

the gun. The man with the gun had Eve. Was she dead? Was her body lying somewhere just waiting for him to find it? Had Evans come in early and somehow discovered they were here? Was he back to finish the job?

The door behind him came open, and Alex felt two arms go under his own, pulling him back. He held onto Kristen, his hand on her wound.

"She's hit bad, Adam."

"Already called a bus. I heard the shot over her phone. Are you hit?" Adam's voice held none of his normal sarcasm. As always in a crisis, Adam became deeply competent.

"No, she jumped in front of me." Why the hell had she done that? She didn't have to. It was obvious who the fucker was going for, but this woman who didn't really know him had leapt to save his life.

"This is so much worse than the first time. First time, he was here." Kristen was talking nonsense as Alex moved her away from the glass door.

He heard a car screech away and knew, just fucking knew, that Eve was moving away from him. He needed to get to her, but he couldn't just run after them. It would give whoever had shot at him another chance and it would be Kristen's death sentence if he pulled his hand away now. He had to stop. He had to think. He had to trust that she would stay alive. "He's got Eve."

He laid Kristen down, twisting his body to keep his hand over her wound. Whatever happened, he couldn't dishonor his wife by allowing Kristen to die. Eve would have his fucking head.

She was alive. He would have felt it if she was dead. She lived and he would move heaven and earth to find her.

"I think her right lung is collapsed." Alex pressed down,

but he knew it wouldn't be enough. They needed to get that lung to inflate or she could die before the paramedics made it. And he had no idea how close the bullet was to her heart. One false move could nick something and she would bleed out on the floor, her unique flame doused.

Well, her loyalty had been proven beyond a shadow of a doubt.

"I'll be right back." Adam took off down the hall, leaving Alex alone with Kristen.

"Why did you do that?" Guilt was going to plague him. She'd taken a bullet meant for him.

Her skin paled past the normal ivory to something sallow and dull. "All for him. All for him."

A cold chill went up Alex's spine. The women in Evans's cult had a saying. They did it all for their lord.

"He doesn't want you dead. He wants you alive. He always wants you alive." She mumbled something he couldn't quite make out.

"Where is he?" He pressed down hard on her wound, and Kristen groaned. If she knew something about where his enemy was, he had to find it out.

"Love him. Love him." Her strength was fading.

"Where is he?" Had he been played? Had he been living with the fucking enemy?

Her hand came up, next to his, over her heart. "Here. Since the day I set eyes on him. He's been here. Tell him I did good. Tell him I was good. I was good for him. I was good. He can have a thousand other women, but I was his only true wife."

Oh, god, she was as insane as the rest of them. He should pull his hand back and let her bleed out.

But she might know who had Eve.

His brain churned, as wild as the ocean in a hurricane. If

Evans had just tried to take him out, why would Kristen throw herself in front of him?

How many factions was he fighting? Or was she just that crazy?

No. A calm came over him. If Kristen had been truly insane, Eve would have seen it.

"Are you working with Evans?" He checked himself. His wife's patient voice was working in his head, telling him to stay calm and sort through the problem. Nothing could be gained by killing Kristen.

Her eyes fluttered open. "What?"

"Evans. It's okay. He has a way with women."

A slightly drunken grin came over her. "Oh, he does. So beautiful. And he's such an asshole. Why do I love such an asshole?"

Footsteps pounded down the marbled hallway. Adam was coming back. Thank god. He ran down the hall, a box of plastic wrap in his hand. "The bullet's definitely in her lung. You can hear her trying to compensate. We need something that will form an airtight seal. Lift her shirt up. I need skin."

"You'll tell him I did good?" Her hands came up, but she was so weak.

Adam fell to his knees, pulling off a hefty piece of thin plastic. He caught Alex's eye and nodded.

Alex brought his hand up, and Adam immediately moved in, closing the wound. He brought the heel of his hand right over the bullet hole in her chest, and a low moan came out of Kristen's throat. Her eyes flared and then she passed out, going utterly limp in Alex's arms.

But her breathing sounded better.

"Can you take her?" Alex asked, his voice tense. Eve was gone and he'd very likely been sleeping in the home of his enemy. He needed to get to Sean. He needed to talk to

Chazz. A nice little chat that would end with Alex's gun up Chazz's anus and hopefully bring him some answers.

Adam moved into position. "What was she talking about?"

"I'm not sure, but she might be aligned with Evans." Although it didn't make sense. He tried to wrap his mind around it.

"No." Adam held his hand tight to her chest. "She cares about us. I don't know why, but she gives a damn."

She'd thrown her body in front of his, but someone— the same someone who had taken a shot at him—had taken Eve. If Evans was the one who had taken Eve and Evans was the one who wanted him alive, why would he have taken that shot?

Something else was at play and it had to do with that missing file.

He heard the sirens in the background. He needed to clear out or he would end up spending hours at the police station. He glanced to Adam. "Can you handle this?"

Adam nodded. "Yes. Call Serena and Jake. The police will try to take me in as a witness, but I have a plan to stay out of it. Tell Serena to get her sweet little self down here, and have Jake watch your back. Once I'm back up at the condo with my pregnant wife, who is likely going to need to lie down after all the trauma, I can get you the information you need. I walked out and found her this way. I'll handle the cops and I'll be back at my station before you know it. You need to go because there's blood on your shirt, and they will ask questions. Go and clean up. If Jake's not here by the time you need to leave, just take my car and he'll go to the club. Find Sean. I'll get you the info on the car and anything else I can find. She won't be gone long, Alex. You have a new team now."

"I want everything you can find on Carmen Garcia and my old team." He stood up, his gut somewhere in his knees. "Call Ian. Get him out here as soon as you can."

Ian would drive if he had to. If there was one thing he trusted in the world, it was that Ian Taggart had his back.

He glanced down at the woman who had just saved his life and wondered if she would pull through. The sirens were closer now and he let himself in the door, hopping on the elevator before the ambulance pulled up. Adam was right. He had very little time, and he couldn't get caught up in a police investigation. Kristen might have given her life to save his, and he wasn't going to question it right now.

Later he would ask all the relevant questions, but until she was conscious and able to talk, there was nothing she could do to help further. He had to make sure her sacrifice hadn't been in vain.

When he got to the condo, he changed and cleaned himself up. He called Jake to meet him. Sean was already in place.

They needed to talk to Chazz, and he was pretty sure Chazz wasn't going to be happy with how they talked to him.

As he waited impatiently, he glanced down at the notes Adam had pulled up on Carmen Garcia.

Just another victim, like his Eve. Just another life Michael Evans had wasted. She'd been a Georgetown student, chasing a career in the law and politics, working on political campaigns and going to parties.

Maybe getting pregnant by someone who had a lot to lose.

His fists clenched. Garcia had been young and attractive and a volunteer on campaigns. Which campaigns had she worked for? Who had the most to lose?

And who had ties to a man who could make it all look like an accident?

A new anger rolled in Alex's gut because he'd just figured out who had truly betrayed him.

* * * *

Pain. Her head ached as she started to come back to life. She groaned a little. Where was she? She tried to move her right hand, to bring it up to ease the pain in her skull, but it was tethered to the left.

She opened her eyes. How long had she been out? Light streamed in through a window, but it was a bit murky, the glass opaque. There was a couch under her, but she was pretty sure it had seen better days.

It was so quiet. So unlike the condo where she could always hear the ocean. The condo where she'd last seen her husband.

Everything came back in one horrific flash. He'd tied her up and then left her in the backseat of her own vehicle, and he'd moved into position to gain a kill shot. She'd heard one blast and then another.

"Please don't try to move. It will only make it worse," a now familiar voice said.

Jesse Murdoch. The man who had murdered her husband.

"You killed Alex."

Jesse stood over her, his hands held out. "I'm not so sure about that. I checked the police radio and monitored the hospital admissions. No male gunshot victims. I'm pretty sure I hit Kris."

And he didn't look happy about it. His eyes were sunken as though he hadn't slept for days. There was a grim line to his mouth and his face was marked with stubble. He ran a hand through his hair, and then his whole body twisted as he screamed.

The sound reverberated through the room, making Eve flinch back, but there was nowhere to go.

He finally stopped that tortured sound and his hands shook. "I'm sorry. I just fucked up again. I can't stop fucking up. Why can't I stop?"

He was a little bit crazy with a side of fucking nuts. And that was a professional opinion. But Alex was alive. She hoped she hid her smile. If Alex was alive then he would come for her, and she had to be ready. She needed to do anything she could to make his job easier, and that included talking Jesse Murdoch out of whatever plans he was coming up with now.

"Are you upset that you missed Alex or that you hit Kristen?" She scooted around, trying to sit up. He'd adjusted her, and now her hands were zip tied in front of her body. He seemed to have gotten rid of the one on her legs. She could move them freely now.

He moved toward her and for a minute, she was sure he was going to hit her, but he merely shoved a hand under her elbow and helped her to sit. A striking man, Jesse had sandy hair and blue eyes that went dark when he was emotional. She'd noticed it before. When he'd talked to her in the hallway that first day, his eyes had been almost like sapphires, but the day of the luncheon, they'd gone dark when one of the men had made a remark that he wasn't surprised to see Jesse at the club.

Because the man knew his past and thought he'd turned, she'd reasoned.

Jesse paced, still wearing a big hoodie even though the heat of the day was upon them. "I didn't mean to hurt Kris."

She hoped Kris was fine, but god, she was so glad it hadn't been Alex. "But it's fine to hurt Alex."

"He's a soldier. Soldiers get hit. It's what happens."

"This isn't war." She said the words, but then wondered if the war had ever ended for Jesse.

"You say that because you're a civilian." He took a long breath and seemed to attempt to gain some control. "I wonder if I killed her. I never killed a woman before. Not intentionally."

Oh, he wore his guilt right there on his sleeve. She needed to bring it out even more. Though it pained her, she needed to manipulate him. Something was off, and she had to find out what it was. "Are you talking about the woman in your unit?"

His eyes flared. "How did you know about that?"

"It was all over the news, Jesse. It was hard to miss. There was a woman who was captured with you."

"Alannah Tally." He whispered the name like it was a blessing, or perhaps a curse that had been following him.

He'd been close to her. "Was she your girlfriend?"

He shook his head, rubbing the scruff of his beard, his eyes far off. He glanced down at his cell phone as if it might save him. Not once did he react as he should, Eve noted. He was in the position of power. He could tell her to shut up or walk away, but once he decided he didn't have a handy excuse, he gave up. "I liked her a lot."

It was so lucky she spoke male. "So you slept with her, but you weren't in love with her."

He was a big man, but she noticed that he hid much of his bulk in the slump of his shoulders. "Yeah, something like that. She was a nice lady. She wasn't some slut."

And he was still defending her, as though the very act of sleeping with him put her at risk. Deep insecurities. She needed to play on them and soothe them. He was obviously a man who needed a soft voice in his life. And he responded to women. "I would never use that word, Jesse. Women don't often merely sleep with a man to scratch an itch. We tend to sleep with men we admire. She must have admired you."

His breath hitched. He stood again, that anxious pacing beginning. Two steps one way and then another three the other. Over and over, as though the pattern was ingrained in his head.

He was walking the length of his cell. She would bet that he'd paced that small enclosure so often during his imprisonment that now it was ingrained in him, a habit he couldn't break.

She could pull him back from Evans. She could bring him to their side.

"She didn't admire me in the end. She hated me. Did you see the video?" He stopped and seemed to force himself to be still. He patted his jacket down and came up with a cigarette and lighter. "I fucking hate these things, but it was the only thing they let me do. Did you see the tape?"

She shivered a little as he lit up, and the smell of cigarettes filled the air. "The one where she died?"

He took a long drag. He was twenty-seven, but she would have sworn he was fifty in that moment. "Yeah."

"Part of it." It had been all over the news, but they had cut out just before the killing blows had been delivered. Major news networks carried the story, but declined to show the grislier parts of the video. Of course, nothing was ever really contained on the Internet. She knew Ian had watched the video after the Agency had asked him to consult.

"They made me watch," Jesse explained. "They would get me high on heroin and then they would stand me up and force me to watch as they beheaded my brothers."

No wonder he was a little cuckoo. But he was still the reason she was tied up and he'd still tried to kill her husband. "They gave you heroin so you would look passive, as though you didn't really care or were even involved in the process."

"Yeah, I got that. I don't think Alannah did. None of them did. They all thought I'd turned. They hated me. I just wanted to make my dad proud, you know. I thought I could go into the Army and make something of myself."

She needed to make connections. He'd just given her a big one. "My husband was in the Army."

Jesse's brow furrowed. "Are you talking about Master A?"

And she needed to try to establish a little trust. "Don't prevaricate, Jesse. I suspect you know a lot about my husband. His name is Alex."

"Yeah, McKay. I figured that out."

"Did you know he was a decorated soldier? He served his country just like you."

His blond head shook shortly. "Not like me."

"Not exactly, but there are a lot of similarities. He's been trying to bring down your boss for a long time. Do you want to know why?"

Jesse's eyes narrowed, and he put the cigarette out. "How do you know about this? He talks to you about his work?"

Otherwise known as the "maybe you're not so innocent" question. She stepped lightly. "He values me."

"He beats you."

She was so done with this crap. Impatience got the best of her. "Mr. Murdoch, you seem to kill people for a living, so I don't think you have a right to look down on me for my sexual choices. What my husband and I do together is our business, but I will tell you he's never hurt me in a way I didn't find pleasurable. We're not all the same. We don't all enjoy vanilla sex. Some of us need more, and it doesn't always have to do with something that went wrong in our childhoods. I was built this way and there's nothing wrong with me. I enjoy dirty games and a certain level of pain when it comes from the man I love more than my own soul. I make no apologies for the love I make. I will not beg forgiveness for my differentness. I celebrate it. I fight for it."

He'd blushed a little the minute she'd mentioned the word sex. He ignored all but her last words. "Fight for it?"

Here was where she would get him. Evans had obviously been lying to him. The man had issues with women being hurt. The thought that he'd killed Kristen— god, she hoped that wasn't so—had torn him up. It was time to give him the truth about his boss. "I was raped and tortured by a man who used my lifestyle against me. He hurt me over and over and told me what a pervert I was, what a whore I was to want what I wanted."

He flushed again, running a hand through his hair. "I'm so sorry to hear that. I…I wouldn't wish that on anyone. I would think you would stay away from it."

"That was what he wanted. He wanted to take something precious from me, and I wouldn't let him." A well of strength seemed to have opened up inside her. She'd been a psychologist studying the human mind for most of her life, but she'd learned that while she could empathize, sometimes things had to be experienced to be fully understood.

She was only his victim as far as she allowed herself to be. She hadn't been in control of what Evans had done to her, but she was in control of how she reacted. She'd let that

322

monster take too many years from her. She wasn't going to allow him to take her husband, too.

He nodded and seemed to come to a decision. "Why is your husband doing this?"

Was it time for honesty? "He's been searching for the man who hurt me for years."

Jesse's fists clenched, his eyes tightened. "And this man is here?"

Yes, it was definitely time for honesty. He was on the hook. She just had to reel him in. He could be turned. She could make him an ally instead of an enemy. He could possibly lead them right to Evans. "Yes, Jesse. Your boss kidnapped me and raped and tortured me. Michael Evans did that, and he's hurt a lot of women. I don't know what he's told you, but he's lying. Alex was the FBI agent who took him down. He's working in the private sector now, but he still has connections. When we catch Evans, if he's alive at the end of it, we'll turn him over."

Jesse stood up, staring down at her. "That's impossible."

"No. Just read the news on him, Jesse. It's so simple. Look him up on the Internet. Michael Evans is a monster. He's a rapist and a terrorist, and he's running drugs through the club we're working at."

"I know. That's exactly why I've been hunting him. He's not my boss. I work for the FBI. Do you understand? I'm not the bad guy. I'm a fed, and you're a liar."

Her whole body went cold. "You're working for the SAC?"

He was working for Petty. Petty, who had called her half an hour before Michael Evans had kidnapped her. He'd told her he was bringing Alex home.

Petty, who had known where she was and how many

guards were watching her. He'd selected them himself.

Petty, who knew their house as well as his own. She'd always wondered how they had known exactly which windows to go through and how to move through the house.

There was a knock on the door. Jesse straightened up and took a long breath. "Now you'll see. That's Special Agent Petty. He's going to clear this up, and you're going to find out your husband has been lying to you."

The truth was almost too much to bear, but she couldn't question it now. She couldn't come up with a reason for Jesse to lie. But she could come up with one reason for Petty to lie. Carmen Garcia.

How far had their old friend gone?

"Does he know I'm here?" She practically hissed the question. He'd set Jesse on them, ordered the hit on Alex. "Does he know Alex isn't dead?"

He looked toward the door. "He knows I brought you in. I wasn't going to lie. He knows I was going to try to take McKay out earlier. I have to tell him now. I'll make him see reason about you."

"Don't answer that door, Jesse. He's done with you. He's about to have everything he wants and he won't need you anymore. Please don't answer it."

He shook his head as he approached the door. "We're the good guys."

The door opened, and Warren walked through. She hadn't seen him in years, had thought he was out of her life. "I just got your message. You didn't kill the woman?"

Jesse shook his head, moving deeper into the loft. "No, sir. I wanted to talk to you about that."

All of his attention was focused on Jesse. He didn't bother to look at her. Warren followed Jesse's every move. "But you carried out the attack on McKay? And now you have his woman prisoner?"

"Yes," Jesse began.

"Excellent." Petty reached into his coat and pulled out a nasty-looking gun. "Then your job is done, son."

"What?" The question came out on a shout. Jesse's hand went to his coat pocket, but he wasn't fast enough.

A little ping rang through the air, the silencer on the end of the gun doing its job. Jesse's big body jerked and then he looked over at her, his eyes going so sad as he fell to his knees and then forward. He hit the ground with a little quake.

"Eve, you really should have left well enough alone." Warren Petty finally turned his attention to her, stepping around Jesse's body. "Oh, well, at least I can now pay a debt that's been hanging over my head for years. Evans still wants you, dear. I think it's time he had you again."

He raised the gun, pointing it right at Jesse's head. A bullet to the heart obviously wasn't enough for Warren. Before he could fire, Eve ran at him, knocking him off guard. They tumbled together against the wall.

Eve jerked her body up. She had to get out the door.

"Not so fast." Warren put the gun to her head. "We're going to play this my way. Move. We're getting out of here."

She had no choice but to move along and pray Alex could find her in time.

Chapter Seventeen

Alex stepped up to the doors of Cuffs knowing damn well he was very likely a marked man. Whoever had taken that potshot at him today had to have reported back to Chazz. And that didn't mean a damn thing because he wasn't going down today. He was going to find his wife and get her back.

He gripped the doors and growled when he discovered they were locked.

He heard a lock slinking back and then the door opened. One of the big bouncers stood in the doorway, his massive shoulders blocking the way. Alex couldn't remember what his name was so he just thought of him as Massive Asshole.

Massive Asshole frowned. His Neanderthal-like looks didn't aid in his attractiveness. He looked like what he was—a hired killer. "You got fired. Chazz just called two minutes ago and said I'm not supposed to let you in."

Not supposed to let him in? What kind of pussy was Chazz? If it had been Alex, he would have had a kill-on-sight order out, not a "Hey, he got fired."

"I'm afraid I can't let the whole employment situation here stand. I need to talk to Chazz."

Massive Asshole's eyes tightened. His hand twitched to his side as though he was trying to make the decision on how to act. Maybe Chazz's orders had been a bit harsher, but MA wasn't a hardened killer. Not yet. Alex would use that to his advantage.

He kicked the door, shoving it against MA's enormous, very likely steroided-out chest. Alex would bet all of his strength had been gained in a gym.

"Hey!" MA lost his balance, proving that he had no real experience. "Man, you can't come in here."

Alex didn't hesitate. He didn't pause to talk to the fucker. He had one goal in his head, and no one was going to get in his way. Grabbing the guy by his shirt, Alex pulled his SIG, pointing it right at the middle of MA's head. "You should leave now. And if you call the cops, I will find you. You will wake up in the middle of the night and I'll be there standing over you. You won't go down fast. I'll make sure of it. Am I understood?"

Nope. The dude wasn't trained. Most trained operatives didn't piss themselves from one little threat and a gun to the forehead.

MA was out the door the minute Alex let go.

"I have your boy." Chazz stood at the top of the stairs, a gun in his hand. Unlike his bouncer, Chazz seemed fairly cool. He believed he had the upper hand.

He believed he had Sean. Alex wouldn't believe it until he saw it, though Sean hadn't answered his cell.

He needed to figure out how deep the shit was. And getting captured just might suit his plans since he needed to get taken to wherever Eve was.

Alex put his SIG on the floor and held up his hands. If they'd wanted to shoot him now, it would be done, but Alex had figured out there were two factions at hand. "Are you working for Evans or my old partner?"

Chazz frowned. "I work for Michael Evans, Mr. McKay. I'm his right-hand man."

He was Evans's flunkie, but it wouldn't pay to point that out now. "So he hasn't told you he's working with a fed?"

Chaos was his best friend.

"You're lying, but then you've been doing that to me this whole fucking time, haven't you. You and Kris. Where the fuck is she, anyway?" He started down the stairs just as two other bouncers showed up. They, like Massive Asshole, were big and dumb, but at least they had guns. They took up spots on either side of Alex.

"Kris was shot. She's probably dead. Are you telling me you didn't try to take me out earlier?" His brain raced with the possibilities. Chazz might not know he knew anything.

His cell phone buzzed in his pocket. Adam, he hoped. He prayed Adam had figured out who the shooter was. The ambulance had been loading Kristen in when Alex had slipped out of the building, taking Adam's ride. Adam had been playing the role of concerned bystander, explaining to the police that he had no idea what had happened, merely found the girl on the ground and tried to save her life.

And that was when Adam's wife proved to be an asset. Alex had stopped on the street just above the building and watched as she'd driven up like she owned the place, racing to her husband and hugging him. Serena had looked sweet and fragile, her hand on her belly to show off the baby growing there. Anything to keep Adam from getting taken to the station house for a statement when Alex needed him on that computer of his.

Alex had driven up the road and picked up Jake, secure that Adam would be there when they needed him.

Alex allowed the two bouncers to each get a hand on him, hauling him toward Chazz. Jake was outside, waiting for the signal that he was needed.

There were only three of them. Jake could take a nap, but before Alex could take everyone out, he needed to figure out where Sean was.

"Someone killed Kris?"

Shit. Chazz didn't know. He wasn't that great an actor. Evans wasn't keeping him in the loop. "Yeah, she took a bullet to the chest. She's dead."

Let him think that. Maybe Evans would be pissed that his girl got caught in the crossfire.

He wants you alive.

Kristen's face haunted him. Likely would for a long time. She'd seemed almost happy to have sacrificed for her lover.

Had Evans kept her out of the loop, too? Why else would she have disrupted his plans?

"Fuck. Mikey didn't order me to do that." Chazz nodded toward the back of the club. "But some of our friends alerted us to your presence here, McKay. Mikey would love to have a talk with you."

"Since he has my wife, I'd like to talk to him as well."

Again Chazz frowned, and Alex felt his gut tighten. "I don't know nothing about that either. I just got a call from the big guy and he's figured out that you're not who you said you were. I'm just going to keep you and your boy in there on ice until Mikey decides what to do with you. Bring him into the kitchens. We'll keep him with the other."

Alex followed along, making an inventory of the weapons on his body. He'd get his SIG back, but there was a semi in his right boot and a knife in his left. Jake's car was loaded down with ordnance under a false bottom in the trunk.

One of the very likely soon-to-be dead bouncer/meathead musclemen gave him a shove through the double doors of the kitchen. Three more of Chazz's bouncers were inside. They'd been ready and waiting apparently. Someone had tipped them off. He caught sight of Sean, making a careful but quick study of the kitchens. The line of stainless steel ovens and burner units were to his left, with two big refrigeration units on his right. The expo station sat between them. Someone had sent the rest of the staff home it looked like. They were alone in the big kitchen with nothing but the security staff.

Where was the kid? Alex looked at the bouncers but none of them was Jesse Murdoch.

"Hey, I've had a morning, brother." Sean sat at the back of the kitchen near a large prep space. The chair that held him was against a counter. It looked like he'd been jumped while he was working. His knife set was rolled out and there were piles of herbs and onions on the counter, precisely cut and portioned out. Sean sported a nice shiner and a couple of bruises. Why? How many assholes had they sent at him?

"I can see that. You look like you got taken down by a baseball team." They often used sports references to gain information. He couldn't just come out and ask Sean how many men were lurking around.

"More like an offensive line just before the snap," Sean shot back.

Seven then. Seven offensive players had to be on the line of scrimmage in football. Alex quickly counted. Six men were in the room with them and Massive Asshole had fled, likely into the waiting arms of Jake, who would be asking him the same types of questions.

Easy breezy.

"I should have known you would fuck this up," Alex told Sean. "You got tied up."

Sean's blue eyes closed briefly as though he couldn't stand the embarrassment. "Lost my best paring knife, too. It's been a shitty day. I'm ready to end it. I know everything

I need to know."

Nice. This was why he loved working with Sean. They communicated so well together. He quickly decoded the information Sean had imparted with a few bland sentences. Sean had managed to keep his three-inch blade and had already worked through the bindings. He was ready to go when Alex was.

"Get another chair for the new asshole," Chazz ordered. "We've got to keep him here until the boss tells us where to take him. It shouldn't be more than a couple of hours."

One of the bouncers walked out to do his boss's bidding.

"Their timetable moved up. Chazz got a phone call an hour ago," Sean said.

So that's why he'd allowed himself to be captured. With only seven untrained guys, there was no way Sean had been taken down in a fight.

"I didn't ask you to talk." Chazz took a long breath, and his eyes narrowed. "You know now that I have your friend here, I don't know that I need you anymore. I took you down because I thought I might need leverage if he showed up. Mikey said nothing about keeping you around. It might feel good to work one of you over. I got some issues to work out. He's probably going to close this club down now. We're going to have to move and all because you two are fuckwad cops."

"Is that what he said? And how did your boss find out?" Alex slightly shook his head, giving Sean the no-go sign. He brought two fingers up to his chest, scratching a little. *Two minutes to go.* He had a few things to discover before they got to the part where Chazz cried a lot and likely crapped his pants.

"That's none of your fucking business," Chazz shot

331

back.

"I'm not a cop."

Chazz snorted. "Really? And why should I believe you?"

"I used to be a cop, a fed actually. I used to work with the man who I believe is supplying your boss with information," Alex explained.

Sean's eyes went wide, but he stayed silent.

Alex stared at Chazz. "The question now is whether it's your boss or my former partner who took my wife."

Sean's whole body went tense.

"And who killed Kris," Alex announced.

Sean's face went red. "Are you fucking kidding me?"

Chazz shook his head. "I told you I didn't order that hit, but if the boss did, then the bitch needed killing."

"Alex," Sean hissed his name.

The thing with Kristen was going to kill him until he had an answer. He hoped she lived. "Yeah, go, but I need that idiot."

Sean moved with the grace of a natural predator. One minute he appeared to be all kinds of tied up, and the next he was on his feet, a knife in his hand. He tossed it through the air and reached back, grabbing two more off the counter. Before anyone could move, Sean had placed knives in three of their captors, two to the chest and a third seemed to have severed the bouncer's jugular. He went down clutching at the thing, pulling it out, sending blood across the floor.

Alex shoved his elbow into the man on his right's xiphoid process and just kept going, focusing the force of the punch through the man's chest with the intent of sending the delicate bone at the end of the sternum directly into his opponent's heart.

The man who had been holding him dropped to the

floor.

Alex turned to Chazz, who had backed up to the row of ovens. He held up his gun, but he couldn't mask the way his hand shook.

"Back up or I end this now," Chazz said. "I got more guys coming."

"He doesn't," Sean said. "He sent everyone away after he got that phone call. That was when his little goon squad hit."

Alex casually reached down and pulled his semiautomatic from his boot. Chazz kept staring between the two of them as if trying to decide which viper to shoot first. "And you decided to play with them?"

Sean shrugged, flipping over a large knife. He held it in his hand, tossing it casually and catching it again. "I thought I should play along. Is Kris really dead?"

"I don't know. I had to flee the scene. Adam was with her."

"I didn't kill her," Chazz said. "I didn't order a hit on anyone. Fuck, I don't make the rules here. I just keep my head down and do my time."

"Like you did in prison. Is that where Evans recruited you? He must have told you about me and yet you don't seem to remember my name."

"It's McKay. What does that have to do with anything?" Chazz asked.

"Alexander McKay. I was the SAC in charge of his case. I arrested him."

"Shit. He did your wife."

Alex fired, putting a bullet through Chazz's hand. Suddenly having a hole in his palm made it difficult for him to hold onto his weapon. It dropped to the floor as Chazz screamed and held his hand against his chest.

"You will speak of my wife with respect," Alex explained. "And you're going to help me find her."

Sean held up his really large knife. "Do you know what this is?"

Chazz had tears running down his face. "It's a knife."

Sean shook his head. "Oh no. This is a work of art. This is a seven-inch ceramic sushi knife. I've been playing around with it. The ceramic is just a step below diamonds on the hardness scale. This knife was made to debone a fish and make delicate, beautiful cuts. It's a little like me. It's very precise, but it can do some serious damage. Would you like me to filet you, Chazz?"

Chazz had gone sheet white. "I don't know nothing. Mike was supposed to come in a couple of days and spend some time at the farm, but then this morning he calls me and says I fucked up. He says that I let you in and I shouldn't have, and the only way to make up for it is to keep you here for him if you came in. He said he had someone smarter than me handling it, but this was the backup plan. I guess he thought you would come here if whoever was supposed to kill you failed. I'm supposed to put you all in lockdown."

Farm? He hadn't heard anything about a damn farm, but he had other questions for now. "Who exactly?"

Chazz's voice shook. He kept staring at the bodies around him. "You and the chef here and your women. I didn't know he was talking about your wife. I should have because he got that tone in his voice when he said 'women.' He always told me he shouldn't have let her go, but he made a deal, you see."

Oh now they were getting somewhere. "He made a deal?"

"Yeah. I don't know with who. I think it was the same guy who got him out of prison. That's all I fucking know.

He won't tell me where to pick him up. He just shows up on the doorstep with his bodyguards. I don't know where he stays neither."

The doors behind them knocked open and Jake strode in pushing the sixth man in front of him. "You lost one. And Adam called. Serena had a sudden pain and needed to lie down. The cops told him he could come in later and make his statement. He pulled from CCTVs all over the coast. He got a shot of someone driving your rental. It was ditched before he crossed the toll road, so he had to have had another vehicle waiting. Does the name Murdoch mean anything to you? And should I cap this guy or put him on ice?"

He would kill the little fucker. "Shove him in the freezer. We don't need more bodies to hide. Chazz, you are going to tell me absolutely everything you know about Jesse Murdoch, starting with where he lives."

He forced the panic down, forced himself to be strong. Eve needed him.

* * * *

Jesse bit back a cry. His lungs fucking ached. Goddamn bulletproof vest wasn't bulletproof enough. He'd put it on this morning because he had a protocol when it came to an operation.

And it was damn good, too, since he'd been shot by his own fucking boss.

He'd passed out from the shot. At point-blank range, the bullet might not have reached his heart, but it had damn straight knocked the wind out of him.

He had to find Master A...Alex McKay. He had to find the man he'd tried to kill.

335

Fuck fuck fuck fuck. He'd killed Kris and he hadn't had to. He'd fucked up again and he wasn't even sure why.

There was a loud bang as the door to his loft burst open.

Shit. They'd come back to finish the job. God, he couldn't breathe. The vest was too tight. He could feel something wet against his skin. *Damn it.* The round had been too close. Despite the Kevlar, he'd been hit. How far had the bullet gone in? How much time did he have left?

He'd wanted to do good. He let his head slip back down to the floor, the cool wood making him shiver. He'd just wanted to make his dad proud.

He'd tried by joining up. After Pawpaw died and the ranch had gone under, he'd just wanted to be able to hold his head up.

He thought about that gold star that sat on the mantle. His pawpaw had placed it there after his dad died.

That's what your daddy was. He was a star. Now people will tell you that stars are actors and singers, but they're wrong. Real stars are the people who set aside their own lives to do good. Like your daddy.

Twenty-seven years and he was still chasing his father's legacy. Still falling short.

Did his father know? God, he hoped there was some form of heaven and his father knew he'd never betrayed his country. He'd been stalwart. It was why they'd targeted him. He hadn't broken. He'd never given them anything past his name and rank and serial number, even when they'd shoved a hot poker into his chest. Even when he thought they would cut his cock off.

But they'd still found a way to break him. They'd taken his name. God, they had taken his name and his honor.

But no one got his soul.

"There's the little fucker. Shit."

336

He didn't have to look for McKay. McKay had found him.

"Is he dead?"

He could pretend. He could lie here and no one would know. And that would be cowardly. And he wasn't a fucking coward. He forced his head up. "He took her."

A shout exploded from his chest as he was turned over. McKay stared down at him and he would almost swear there were flames shooting out of his eyes. "Who? You tell me who the fuck you've been working for."

He forced the words out of his throat. God, he needed out of the vest. "Feds."

"Be more specific."

"SAC Petty. He contacted me a few months back and offered me an undercover job." At the time, Jesse had been fucking high on the offer. It was a way to get back in, back into the good guy's camp. He'd jumped at it. He'd been a fucking idiot.

"The feds don't go outside the house for undercover," a new voice said.

McKay hadn't come alone. Jesse forced himself to look around. There were two men with McKay. Sean Reilly, though who knew what his real name was, and a dark-haired man with a fierce frown.

"He's lying," Sean said. "Why would he lie about that?"

"Because he knows damn well I'll kill him when he tells me the truth," McKay pronounced.

Death. It was where he was heading anyway. He thought about it. He thought about it a lot. In his worst moments, he'd thought about eating his gun and calling it a day. He'd never really done anything worthwhile. He'd been such a burden his mom had left. She'd loved his dad, but she couldn't bring herself to love him, too. His pawpaw had to work to feed him when all he'd wanted to do was fish, but he couldn't afford to raise a kid on social security.

His dad hadn't even known him.

"Go ahead. Do it." In the end, he couldn't pull the trigger. But McKay could.

Alex McKay stopped, his brow furrowing. Funny word, furrowing. He laughed a little. Nothing left to do except laugh at how spectacularly meaningless his existence had been.

"Did you try to kill me?" McKay asked.

A simple answer. "Oh, yes."

"Why did you take my wife?"

Not so simple. "Couldn't hurt her. She was innocent. Wanted to save her from you. She told me off, though. Not as weak as I thought. It was a mistake. Everything's a mistake. Didn't mean to kill Kris. Just you."

McKay growled and let him drop, his head hitting the floor. God, everything ached. When would it stop?

"What reason did Petty give for killing me?" McKay asked, staring down at him like he was a bug who might still get stepped on.

There was no reason to hide anything now. He'd been played. He had no idea if McKay was a good guy or a bad guy. It simply no longer mattered. "He didn't have to give me a reason. He was in charge."

The chef got to one knee, blue eyes looking through Jesse. "What was your mission, soldier?"

"He's not…" McKay began.

Sean shook his head and McKay quieted. "What was your mission?"

Finally, a question he could answer. Every word made his chest ache, but he forced himself to speak. "I was supposed to infiltrate Evans's organization. My superior believed that St. Augustine was the most vulnerable of the eight clubs. He liked smaller cities. Said the law enforcement was lighter in smaller cities. I was supposed to get close to Chazz so I could report back on the group's activities. I figured out early on that they were trying to get an infrastructure in place to move drugs. They were also laundering money for cartels. I got word a couple of days ago that Evans was coming in. I called it in to my superior."

"Let me guess," McKay said. "He told you to wait and watch."

"Yeah. I was surprised. I thought bringing him in was the whole point."

McKay frowned. "And you never thought to look into the case yourself? You would have known my name if you had looked into the case. I was the original arresting officer."

"Hey, give him a break," Sean said.

"Why the fuck should I? As to that, why the hell are you treating him with kid gloves?"

"Because I was in the Army for years, man. You did your time and ran. Me and Jake know what it's like," Sean replied.

"You don't ask questions," the man who must be named Jake added. "You follow orders. It's possible that he thought he was doing the right thing. Petty took advantage of his training. He knew this kid wouldn't delve too deep. He would just follow orders."

God, that made him sound like an idiot, but it was true.

"Why you?" McKay asked. "There must be hundreds of ex-soldiers without jobs out there. Why pick you?"

Shame filled him. "Because Evans has ties to jihadists."

"And they all think you turned." McKay ran a hand over his head. "Fuck it, Petty always was smart. Where is my wife?"

He fucking wished he knew. "I told you he took her."

"Where?"

"I don't know." He searched his memory. He'd heard Petty say something to her as he'd fallen to the ground. "He said he had a debt to pay and she would do. Something about it hanging over his head for a long time. He was working with Evans, wasn't he?"

"Yeah." McKay took a step back, his cell in his hand. He turned away. "Adam, I need you to find every private airfield within fifty miles of this town. Look for anything you can find. Evans is coming in tonight."

He'd fucked up so badly. "Can I help?"

The big blond shook his head. "No. Not unless you have a tracking system on the fucker. How bad you hit? You wearing a vest?"

Jesse nodded. He couldn't be sure the other man wasn't just trying to gain info so he could shoot him, but it didn't matter.

Nothing fucking mattered.

He groaned as Sean and the guy who had been with Chazz a couple of nights back tried to help him out of his vest. Pain shot through him.

"That vest did its job. That's a heart shot," Sean said.

Jesse looked down. There was a tiny puncture wound right over his heart. His chest had a streak of blood from where the bullet had pierced his vest. If he hadn't become a paranoid freak, he would be dead. Like Kris.

Another woman he needed to atone for.

"Are you going to kill me or call the cops?" Jesse didn't really care. He just wanted to know what the next five minutes of his life would be like. "I'll confess about Kris."

"She's in surgery," Sean said. "Adam is monitoring the

situation. And we're not going to kill you. Believe it or not, I really do know what it means to be used by a superior. And Jake here was totally just a grunt. Adam's the brains of that operation. Jake would have shot first and asked questions never before Ian trained him."

"Fuck you, Sean. What he's not telling you is that he was my goddamn CO."

They were bitching at each other, but it was so easy to see that they were friends. All of his friends were dead or they'd turned away from him.

Kris was still alive. Thank god.

McKay came back, his face haggard. "There are nine potentials."

"Fuck," Sean said. "That's a lot. We need to split up."

Jesse forced his brain to work. He had to know something. What had Chazz talked about? Not all of it had made sense. He'd talked about going to the farm to pick up the big boss. "Is there anything about a farm?"

McKay checked his list. "Bartwell Farms has a private landing strip."

"That's it." It had to be.

"Fuck. That's what he meant. The little fucker said he didn't know anything. I hope Chazz freezes his balls off." McKay stopped. "If you're lying to me, you need to know that I will…"

Jesse could finish that sentence. "Do all kinds of things that will make me wish for death before you actually kill me. I get it. Now hear me. I swear on my father's honor that I am telling you the truth. I will do anything to make up for my mistakes. From what I can tell, Petty is alone and Chazz talked about the fact that Evans usually brought five guys with him. You need me."

McKay snorted. "I think I can handle it."

"I have an armory."

"Like I didn't come with guns." McKay started for the door. His cell trilled. "It's Adam."

He stepped outside, leaving Jesse alone with Sean and the one called Jake.

"Do you have a sniper rifle?" Sean asked. "We're good on handguns but we could use something with a scope. Alex isn't thinking."

"Alex probably doesn't want to have anything to do with the kid who nearly killed him," Jake mused.

But Jesse was already going for the rifle. He had more than one. His little piece-of-crap loft didn't have books or movies, but he had a metric shit ton of weapons and ammo. He opened the door to the closet he'd made into his own private supply shop.

Jake whistled. "Is that C-4? Are you fucking kidding me?"

Jesse shrugged. Everyone needed a hobby. "I like to be prepared, sir."

"We're not your superior officers, man. It's just Jake." Jake practically salivated. "Is that a fucking P90?"

Jake caressed the Belgian made submachine gun. It was highly restricted. Jesse had spent a lot of money buying it on the black market.

"You can take it. It might come in handy." God, he sounded like a five-year-old trying to make a friend.

Sean nabbed his SR-25 and an extra cartridge. "This should do it."

Jake sighed and Jesse would almost have sworn he whispered something to the P90 before moving away.

Alex opened the door again, his big body leaning into the room. "Adam has a line on that asshole we tagged. He just touched down here at Bartwell Farms."

A relieved grin came over Sean's face. "Don't you mean the asshole Evie tagged? You won't hear the end of this, man. Let's go get your girl."

"Thank god," Jake said, following.

They would leave him behind. He put a hand over the little hole that the bullet had left. His ribs ached, but that didn't matter. The three men were at the door, leaving him behind, and he did the one thing he hadn't done in years. Not through torture or death. Not when everyone he cared about had turned away had he said one little word.

"Please." It was his last chance.

McKay walked through the door. His voice floated back. "If you can make it to the car before I leave, I might think about using you as a human shield. And, Murdoch, if my wife is dead, I'll take you apart myself."

He got to the door, practically running to keep up.

Whatever happened, he would deserve it. One way or another.

Chapter Eighteen

Her wrists were bleeding and still she couldn't get them to slip out of the bonds.

"Come on, Eve. We need to move." Warren had been oddly polite ever since he'd shot Jesse. He reached for her hands and pulled her upright.

He'd knocked her out again. She was really damn sick of being rendered unconscious. Still, it gave her a realistic ploy. The longer she stayed away from Michael Evans, the better chance Alex had of catching up. She shook her head as though trying to clear it. "So woozy. What did you use on me?"

"Nothing that will kill you." He caught her arm under the elbow, stabilizing her. "Come on. You need to get out."

Slitting her eyes open, she could see that the afternoon sun was waning. Between Jesse knocking her out and Petty shoving a needle in her arm, the day had wasted away. She seemed to be in the back of a car. Her feet were untied, but her hands were still in the damn zip tie Jesse had placed them in. Where was she now? And how far behind was Alex?

"Evie, please." His voice had gone oddly soft. "Come on, honey. We have to move. His plane is already here."

He was trying to charm her to her own doom? Knowing that Evans was waiting for her didn't make her want to move any faster. She decided to play dumb. She put her hands to her head. "Who are you talking about?"

"You know who, Eve."

"I don't know why, Warren."

Warren Petty had gained some weight in the last few years, a paunch forming around his midsection. And time had not been kind to his hair. What he had left was rapidly going gray, but Eve could still see the bull-like strength in his meaty arms. "Does it matter?"

His eyes had shifted away as he asked the question. Guilt. He felt guilty. Which was a good thing since he was obviously guilty as hell.

He hauled her out of the car and Eve wished she still had her shoes. Somewhere along the way she'd lost them. The concrete was still hot from the day and up ahead she could see that the trail became rocky.

She forced herself to focus. A large metal building stood in front of her. In the distance, she could see another structure. This one seemed to be a large screened in area of some sort, perhaps attached to a resort or the back of a large family home. There might be people who could help her there.

A sign to her left welcomed her to Bartwell Farms and offered daily tours.

She needed to get to that farm. And that meant she needed to distract Warren.

"Was it because of Carmen?"

He stopped. "How do you know?"

"You erased her file because you can't stand to look at it. You have to know that someone will figure it out."

"I don't see why. I'm the SAC and I say the case is cold so no one needs to look at it." He pulled her along. "I really didn't want to drag you into this again, Eve. It's Alex's fault. He couldn't let go."

"Was she your lover?" She needed to keep him talking.

A little laugh huffed out of Warren's mouth as he moved along, forcing them both toward the building. "No. No. She wasn't my lover. She was a goddamn twenty-something kid. No. That's not my vice."

Realization hit. She remembered how flirty Warren's brother had always been. "But young women are Eddie's vice, aren't they?"

Edward Petty, senator from the great state of Oklahoma, the pride of his family, with a bright political future ahead of him. As long as no one discovered that he'd knocked up an intern.

"He can be a stupid fuck. She wasn't his first, but we managed to pay off the rest or scare the fuck out of them."

"But Carmen was pregnant."

Warren's face screwed up into a mask of distaste. "And the dumb bitch wouldn't get an abortion. I tried buying her off, but she actually had some family money behind her. The only thing that stopped her from talking right off was the fact that she didn't want to disappoint Daddy. Eddie had to convince her that he was going to divorce his wife and marry her. We had to buy some time."

But that would have ruined the senator's political chances. "Did you send her to that clinic?"

A horrible suspicion crept across her mind.

"It was out of the way."

Just how much was he guilty of? "It was exactly the kind of clinic Evans loved to hit. Tell me something, Warren, did you know he was going to hit there? Or did you suggest it?"

A flush stole across his face, and his hands tightened on her arm. "He's my brother. I couldn't let some stupid piece of ass come between him and the presidency. He's going to run next year. He'll run and he'll win."

Eve stopped, forcing him to as well. She hoped that someone, anyone, would walk by, but the place seemed deserted. "I deserve to know. I get the feeling I was used as payment."

Warren turned to her, exasperation plain on his face. "Fine. You want to know the whole truth? I sought him out. I made a fucking appointment with the man. I took a couple of my men. He brought a couple of his, and we made a deal. I would get Alex off his ass for a while in exchange for doing this little job for me. It had to be big. I couldn't just have her killed."

Because the media scrutiny on the death of an intern would likely have turned up the relationship with Edward Petty. The victim would have been the story. But by masking her death with others, she'd faded to the background, just another of Michael Evans's victims. "And he agreed to this?"

"Alex was close to figuring out his hiding place and the fact that he had some very important connections in the drug trade. I made sure Alex wasn't on top of his game. I wanted to get him thrown off the case, but Evans had another plan."

She knew exactly what that plan had been. "Evans wanted me."

"Evie, you have to know I hated it."

"Why? It was convenient. Tommy and Leon were the men you took with you, weren't they?" And they had known far too much. Warren had seen an easy way to get rid of them and to give Evans what he wanted.

So much betrayal.

"I didn't want to kill them," Petty said.

"So you found a way to let Evans do your killing again. Was he mad when Alex kept coming after him?" Alex hadn't done what Evans and Petty had expected of him. He hadn't retreated to take care of his wife. He'd rededicated himself to bringing in Evans.

"You have no idea. I've been dangling on his fucking strings for years now. When Alex called and started asking about him again, I knew I had to work fast. Alex is fucking everything up again. I had to get rid of a valuable asset, damn it."

She let logic lead her where it could. Alex really had upset Warren's carefully laid plans. Why else hire someone like Jesse for this job? He'd wanted to be free of Evans and he couldn't risk bringing him in. "Jesse was supposed to assassinate Evans for you."

"Of course not." He could deny it all day, but Eve didn't believe him.

He very likely had men like Jesse in all of the clubs, just waiting to take out Evans so Petty's secret would finally be safe.

He'd sacrificed so many people so his brother could rise through the ranks. Of course, he'd risen, too. By making his deal with Evans, he'd practically ensured that Alex would leave the Bureau, and that opened the way for Petty to slide into his spot.

"He raped me." Anger started to thrum through her system. "You ate at my house the night before you facilitated my rape."

He flushed again. "I had to protect my brother."

"Did you know what he would do? Did you sit there at my dinner table in my home and think about how he was going to assault me? I was friends with your wife. I was there when your youngest was born and you threw me to the wolves. Alex was your partner."

He snarled a little. "And Eddie is my brother. You can't talk your way out of this, Eve. You think that going over my crimes is going to make me see the light? I understand what a complete shit I am. I know it every day of my life. Sacrifices have to be made for great men. My brother is a great man. I'm so sorry, Eve, but I'm going to sacrifice you again."

He didn't hesitate this time. A look of terrible conviction furrowed his brow, and he hauled her along. She stumbled, hitting the ground, her knees scraping and pain exploding along her skin.

"Get the fuck up."

She bit back a cry against the agony in her legs. He jerked her up.

Eve opened her mouth to scream. Maybe someone would hear her. "Help!"

"It won't matter. The farm is closed. Do you think the livestock is going to help you?" Warren asked, his face nearly purple with the strain.

"No," a new voice said, the sound snaking through her. "She's doing it for me. Eve remembers how much I love to hear her scream. Hello, lover."

Michael Evans walked out of the double doors from the hangar building. He was older, thinner, still a monster. He moved over to her, and she couldn't help but try to get away. A primal fear took over. She pulled at the hold Warren had on her. Every bit of terror she'd gone through in those days with Evans bubbled to the surface.

He bore down on her, using his height to his advantage.

"Hello, whore. I missed you. I was so sad to have to give you up." He reached out for her.

Scream for me, you dirty whore.

She could still hear him yelling at her as he struck her with the razor-tipped flogger.

She flinched away, her voice leaving her. Panic

threatened. A muscle memory of the pain he'd given her flared, and she could feel the skin flaying off her back. She could feel the blood running down to her legs and feet. He hadn't cleaned her up. She would smell the coppery scent for hours.

And she could feel a soft kiss to each scar. A smooth hand covering hers as words were whispered into her ear.

I loved you then. I love you now. I will love you long after we're dead and gone.

A quiet voice took over. The screaming one didn't stand a chance against Alex's voice. She closed her eyes. He was with her. He was always with her.

Calm down. Be patient. What would her Master want?

He would want her to stay alive. And this time she knew that she could handle anything. She could take the pain and humiliation because Alex would hold her and love her and make her whole again.

And if he got lost, she would be strong enough to bring him back. The mistake she'd made the first time was in not telling her Master what she needed. More than anything, she needed him.

He was here. No matter what happened, he loved her.

And she would survive.

"Fuck you." He wouldn't get her submission. That belonged to the man who had earned it.

Evans's dark eyes narrowed. "You haven't aged well, whore. You seem to have forgotten your place. I will teach you again. Warren, bring her in. We're leaving in thirty minutes."

He turned and walked away as though he knew no one would ever disobey his commands.

"I'm sorry." But Warren forced her up.

"My husband is going to kill you." Eve limped along.

She was bleeding from her wrists and knees. It wasn't bad yet, just some scrapes and cuts. She had no doubt that she would bleed freely soon.

Warren stopped. "Jesse killed him."

It was time for a little truth. Jesse had seemed so sure. And she would have felt something if Alex was no longer walking the earth. "No. He failed. Alex is alive. I was there."

She hadn't watched it, but she'd heard how Jesse cursed.

"You're fucking lying, but even if you're not, it won't change a damn thing."

Alex being alive changed everything. "He won't stop until he finds me and kills you."

Warren seemed to think about it for a moment. "He's dead. Jesse wouldn't lie."

"You didn't give him a chance to lie. You just shot him. Alex is alive. Jesse failed."

He shook his head as though trying to grasp the concept. "Then I'll just have to be his friend again. When Evans takes you, I'll wait a couple of days and then I'll call him. I'll let him lean on me. I'll pretend to try to find you. He doesn't know anything."

Eve shook her head as Warren opened the door and shoved her in. "No. He'll figure it out. He has everything he needs to know. He knows someone erased a file at the FBI. He knows Carmen Garcia's name. He'll start checking into her. He'll put it together and he'll be at your doorstep one night. He won't be any more merciful with you than Evans was with me."

Warren hurried her along. "You were always the brains of that operation, Eve. Without you, Alex is just a big piece of meat. He's nothing without you. I saw the way he disintegrated the first time. He'll be worse now. He won't be able to think about anything except you, and I'll find someone to finally take him out. And Eddie will be safe. When he wins the White House, I'll have a place at his side. Like it should be."

She was dragged into the hanger. The building was large, easily housing a small Learjet. Evans had come up in the world. She counted eight men walking around the hanger, including one of the men who had watched her the other day in Chazz's office.

She felt a savage sense of satisfaction. Her Master was going to owe her big time. He was still wearing the same shoes, the very ones she'd attached the GPS to. Oh, she was never going to let him live that down.

And then she saw something that chilled her to the bone.

Stack after stack of what looked to be fertilizer lined the long walls of the hanger. Maybe she was wrong. Maybe it was something for the farm that seemed to be attached. They were stacked ten bags high and the hanger went on for thirty yards. There must have been hundreds and hundreds of bags. That many bags could be turned into a bomb of unimaginable force.

Evans walked up to her, holding his hands out as though inviting her to a great event. "Welcome, Eve. The last time we were together, I was a small operation. I think you'll find my brief time in prison has refined and refocused my passion. How do you like me now, whore?"

"Not any better than I did before." God, what was he going to do with all that fertilizer? She was afraid she knew damn well. And Warren was going to let it happen? She wasn't sure who was the bigger monster—Evans, who was a sociopath, or Warren, who knew better and still allowed it to happen.

Evans seemed to enjoy having an audience. "I've got bigger plans than before. Do you have any idea how long I've had to take to gather this much ammonium nitrate without the feds coming down on my ass? I've gathered it from all over the country, using all of my followers. McVeigh used forty fifty-pound bags in Oklahoma City. I have three hundred."

Three hundred bags of pure grade-A death when used in the most improper way. "I'm sure Warren here helped you hide that. How are you going to justify that, asshole? Do you know how many people he can kill with a bomb that big? Do you really think you can hide your ties to him forever?"

Evans grinned, a smile that on anyone else would indicate genuine joy. His joy was killing people and getting away with it. "I think that SAC Petty will continue to do what he needs to do. Or he'll lose everything. Besides, his brother plans to run on a law and order platform. I'm giving him something to rail against. Everyone wins, Eve."

Everyone except the people he killed. She knew who the true monster was. There was something deeply wrong with Michael Evans that began in his childhood. She'd studied him. His mother had fled her abusive husband, using a women's shelter to hide from him. But she'd left her son behind. Michael had grown up listening to his father rail against whores and turning his abuse on his son.

Warren had grown up wealthy, with parents who doted on him. He knew exactly what he was doing. Evans was sick and deserved to be put down, but Warren was simply greedy. There was no defense for him. "You're a traitor. Not just to your friends and your job. You're a traitor to your country. I will not stop until I out you and your brother."

"It won't work." Warren sounded like he was trying to

convince himself.

Evans walked up and put an arm around his partner in crime. "He's mine, Eve. He has been since the minute we met over coffee and discussed blowing up that clinic. He facilitated my exit from the United States federal penal system, and it's been a marriage made in heaven ever since. When he called me to let me know that Alexander had resurfaced, I was so excited. We have unfinished business. I heard about your divorce. So sad. I suppose he couldn't handle the fact that another man had his woman."

"I divorced him." And she'd been stupid to do it. She could see it now. She'd been weak. She was Alex's sub. It was her freaking job to tell her Dom what she needed. At the time, she'd been too scared to ask. She'd been scared of what he might say, but now she knew something she hadn't before. Love—real love—required courage. It required her to speak out. It required her to fight for it.

A strange light came into his eyes. He looked a little like a fallen angel. It wasn't hard to see why women flocked to him just based on his looks. But once he opened that mouth, he was the devil and she wondered if she hadn't just given him an in. "Because you wanted me. You wanted what only I can give you."

God, he was so wrong. Nausea built inside her. She didn't know how she would handle it if he managed to put a hand on her. "I hate you. You have to know that. I can't stand the thought of you. I love my Alex and we're getting remarried because I finally realized something."

He snarled a little. "And what is that, little whore?"

"I realized that he loves me no matter what. You gave me that. You forced me to realize something I might never have known. I might have gone to my grave wondering, but now I truly know. Most couples aren't tested the way you did us. We know now. You took years from us, but you don't get our forever. You can do anything you want, but I belong to him. My choice. I choose him. Always." And forever more. There wasn't time to worry. There was only time to love. She loved Alex. She wasn't going to fight it. It didn't matter if she was afraid. Her love was worth more than fear. Their relationship was worth fighting for. "It won't work. You can't break us. We went through your fire and we're stronger now."

Evans face had flushed as though he was anticipating the challenge. "Oh, but it will, dear. This time I will make sure you don't get back to him. I only let you go the first time because I thought he would be so worried about you, he would ignore me. I made the mistake of underestimating his real obsession. As long as I keep you away from him, he'll hunt for you and I can do my very important work."

"Alex will find me." He had to.

His hand came up, gesturing to the plane. "That airplane is going to take you to South America. You will disappear there. You'll spend a few months at my private apartment, and then I have other plans for you. I always hoped this day would come. Though it's a bit sudden, plans are already in place. Carlos?"

The man who had watched her spanking walked up, a leering smile on his face. "Hello, Amanda. Or should I call you Eve?"

You should call me the bitch who tagged you. He couldn't know it yet, but he was his boss's downfall. She kept quiet, not willing to engage any of them.

He reached out. She tried to back up, but Warren was behind her, keeping her from getting out of reach.

"I think you should be nice to me. Once Evans is done with you, I think he'll let me have you. I have a brothel in

Argentina. Your beauty will bring me much wealth." His hand dragged down the side of her face, chilling her. Only Warren's body blocked her from moving away.

She couldn't stand the thought. Every muscle in her body ached for Alex. *Please, please come for me. I need you, baby.*

"But not until I'm done," Evans said. "I think I'll let you stay alive long enough to see all of my plans bear fruit. You're mine until I give you away. I've set up a network I couldn't have dreamed of before. I really should thank your ex. When he shoved me in prison, he made a martyr. He brought me to a whole new world I never would have found if I hadn't been forced to run. I have everything I could possibly need. I have the feds on my side for once. And a senator in my pocket. Perhaps a president as well."

She needed a little chaos. "The SAC had a plant in your club here."

Warren's hand came out, catching her across the face. Fire licked along her skin. He'd smacked her and hard. "Keep your mouth shut, bitch. None of us wants to hear your lies."

"Maybe I would find her lies amusing," Evans said, his voice quiet.

She needed them at each other's throats. "Jesse Murdoch has been working for Warren."

Carlos frowned, staring Evans's way. "Murdoch is a believer in our friends' cause. I was assured of this. You assured me of this."

"Everyone is solid, Carlos. We don't need to call in our radical friends." Finally something seemed to jar his confidence.

"Check his financials." It was what Adam would do. "Warren's been paying him on the side. He intended to take you out. He was going to use Jesse to assassinate you so his secret was safe. You can't believe that the senator is really going to allow you to live. He can't run for president with this hanging over his head. And Warren could go to prison."

Evans stared at the SAC. "Or Warren could go somewhere far worse."

Warren was backing up, his hands lifted in denial. "She's trying to cause trouble between us."

"It's working, friend," Carlos said.

Eve edged away. Both men were so interested in Warren that they seemed to have forgotten her for a moment. She was close, so close to the exit. The other men were readying the plane.

"It is easy enough to check these financials," Carlos was saying.

"I didn't do it." Warren kept backing away, toward the airplane, and Evans and Carlos were tracking him like a predatory pack.

Eve felt the door at her back, the handle right below her waist. The highway was too far. She needed to make a break for the farm she'd seen. It was maybe two hundred yards away.

Warren was loudly arguing his innocence when she slipped outside.

Eve ran. She sprinted for everything she was worth. Keeping her balance was hard with her hands in front of her. Her cheek ached and she could feel a trickle of blood from where Warren had split her lip. In fact, she was bleeding from several places, but she kept running, praying there was a door into what looked like an arboretum. The structure ahead was screened in, perhaps to keep birds from the fruit trees. She had to hope there was a way in.

"Hey!"

She heard a man scream in the distance. This was all the head start she was going to get.

"Help! Help me!" Maybe someone was outside. The sign had claimed they had daily tours. The sun was starting to wane, but maybe there were stragglers.

A door! She caught sight of it and ran toward it. Just a few more feet. The ground beneath her had become soft, muddy. *Please be unlocked. Please. Please.*

Eve fumbled with the latch. The door came open and she slipped inside. With a heaving breath, she closed it and turned the lock. It wouldn't keep her pursuers out for long.

But they weren't running anymore. Four men were leisurely walking now, laughing as they moved toward her.

"When you're ready to come back, princess, let me know," one of the men yelled.

Eve turned, ready to run across the farm. She could hide somewhere.

A low hiss turned her blood to ice.

It wasn't a citrus farm. Mud and swamp and hundreds and hundreds of sleepy reptiles started to writhe and awaken around her.

It was an alligator farm, and Eve worried that she'd just become dinner.

Chapter Nineteen

Alex looked through the scoped rifle at the target up ahead.

"Do you see her?" Jake stood beside him as Sean and that dipshit Murdoch checked and rechecked the guns and ordnance.

"Not yet. I can't get a line on anyone. There's a single vehicle in the parking lot. Looks like a rental." Warren's most likely. Betrayal burned in Alex's gut and all he could think about was getting his hands around his ex-partner's throat and squeezing until he turned blue and his fucking eyes popped out. Or maybe he would just carve out Warren's eyeballs. And his tongue. And then he would take the fucker's cock and feed it to him. "Have Adam run the plate."

Jake got on the phone immediately, feeding Adam the information he needed. According to Adam, one plane, a Learjet 40, arrived roughly thirty minutes ago out of New York and immediately filed a flight plan for Mexico City.

They would be required to file a plan because they were leaving US airspace, and the choice of Mexico City was telling. Mexico City had a large airport. Once they arrived, Evans didn't have to worry about US government records, and he could move Eve around South America with very little trouble as long as the governmental wheels had been greased with cash.

Eve would be gone. Utterly untraceable.

Revenge would have to wait. "Getting Eve out is all that matters."

Sean took a place beside him. "So if you get a shot at Evans, you're not going to take it?"

Not if he had a second's concern. It twisted him up. The need to avenge her was right there, a fire in his belly, but he had to put her first this time. "I can't."

A savage grin crossed Sean's face. "I think you should let me do it. It's been a long time since I got to kill someone."

"You killed a couple of people not an hour ago."

Sean shrugged. "Fine, it's been a long time since I killed someone who mattered."

"Are we killing the fed, too?" Jake asked. "Adam said that sedan was rented by Warren Petty."

So this was the place. "As much as I hate to say it, we probably need the fed alive."

To question. For a really long time. He couldn't even bring himself to call Warren by his name. He was the fed, the man who had sentenced his wife to hell on earth.

"We need to get closer." Sean studied the scene.

"We need to make sure they don't take off. Murdoch, can I trust you with what will very likely end up being a suicide mission?"

Murdoch still looked a little pale, but he stepped up. Alex's first instinct was to shoot the big guy between the eyes, but then he'd actually looked at those eyes. Regret. Hollowness. Alex had seen that look in the mirror every day for five years. Maybe Sean was right and the kid really had been following orders, trying to redeem himself.

Why the hell else would Warren have left him for dead? He'd seen the wound on Murdoch's chest. That had been a kill shot, one he'd watched Warren take several times before over the course of his career.

"Yeah. Anything you need." Murdoch had turned into a needy puppy. But he was a needy puppy who seemed to be very comfortable with firearms.

"I need you to make sure that plane can't lift off." He couldn't risk Eve being taken out of the country.

Murdoch nodded. "Do you want me to kill the pilot or blow up the plane? I can do either. I brought some C4."

Of course he had. Sean and Jake's new puppy was a little deranged. "Don't blow up anything unless my wife is safe. Then go fucking crazy, man. But I need Evans alive."

He couldn't believe he was saying it, but Evans was the only one who could verify what Alex thought he knew—that Petty was dirty and his brother was potentially very dirty. Alex didn't buy that Petty was the one who had the affair with Carmen. Oh, but he knew Eddie. Eddie had always loved younger women, and Petty had spent most of his life covering for his brother.

This time he'd gone too far. Alex couldn't allow Eddie to run for the presidency. He had to take him down. For Eve. Because she would want him to do the right thing, and the right thing was to protect their country from a man who would abuse its highest power.

But damn he wanted to kill the fucker.

"Can I kill my boss?" Murdoch asked.

Again, he heard Eve's gentle voice. She would ask him to do his job, to be the law and not vengeance. Even when vengeance would feel so fucking good. But Eve was all that mattered now. "Not if we can take him alive. I think he'll look damn good in prison orange."

And he would likely make some new friends. Very intimate friends. Yes, prison might be better than killing Petty.

Where was his wife? God, he wasn't going to be able to breathe until he saw that she was alive.

"I can avoid the cameras." Murdoch said. He pointed to them. They seemed stationary. "I can hit the wheels as they roll out. They can't take off if I take out a couple of wheels."

"Do it. Jake, go with him." No one got a jump on Jake. And Jake could keep track of the puppy. "Use him as a human shield if you need to. And Murdoch, Warren Petty is not your boss anymore." He used the words the kid would understand. "I'm your commanding officer, and there will be fuck-all hell to pay if you fail in this operation."

"Yes, sir." Murdoch's hand started up as though the salute was ingrained in his very being. He managed to stop, but only just.

He and Jake started off across the field, moving with ease and avoiding the cameras.

"She's in there." Sean stood next to him. "She's alive. I know it. We need to get close enough to figure out how many men he has with him."

He needed to walk into that hangar and shoot up every single man who came between him and his wife. He brought the binoculars back up to his eyes, searching all around. There was the airplane hangar. It looked like it would hold one, maybe two planes. "Has Adam figured anything out about this place?"

Sean looked at his phone. Alex had asked Adam to text Sean with any information he could come up with. "It's a reptile farm. It looks like one of Evans's contacts bought it a couple of years back. They sell alligator skins to make shoes and bags. Along with all the creepy crawlies, they've got the airstrip and nine hundred acres of citrus and berry farm. Shit. According to Adam, Bartwell isn't selling fruit anymore, but they have bought a metric shit ton of fertilizer."

And fertilizer meant something to a man like Evans. It meant bombs and death and destruction. At least they knew what he'd been up to.

"We have to find his stash and figure out what his target was."

Sean's eyes widened. "If my math is right, he likely had more than one target. Even if we shut down this site, who knows how many more he has? This is bigger than just you and Eve. We can't let him get out of the country."

No. They couldn't, but he also couldn't kill him. "They have to have her inside the hangar. We need to sneak in, get her out, and then deal with the rest of the situation. Ian's calling in his contacts."

They had to go around the feds because he couldn't trust that Petty would have friends who could take out Evans before he could talk. Ian was trying to talk to some of his contacts at Homeland Security for backup, but for now they were on their own.

In the distance, he watched Jake and Murdoch approach the hangar. Jake turned around and held up two fingers. *Two cameras.* He clenched his fist. *Stationary.* The cameras only watched the doors, didn't swing or move to catch what was happening in the parking lot.

"I'm going in. Take a position." He gripped his SIG, checking the clip.

Sean stepped up beside him. "Uh, I think I should follow you. I'm not sending you in there alone."

He needed to make some things clear to his friend. "You're not sending me in there at all. This is my operation and I need you in a sniper position."

Sean's jaw firmed stubbornly. "I'll text Jake and get his ass back here."

Alex shook his head. There was no time. He needed them both to do the jobs he'd assigned them. "I can't trust Murdoch. Jake is the last line. I won't let that fucker leave with Eve. I'm going to try to sneak in and get Eve out. Then the rest of you can do what you need to do. I'll be taking care of my wife."

He had no idea what had already been done to her. Had Evans gotten his hands on her again? Had he beaten her? Raped her? His heart ached at the thought of his precious wife brutalized again, but he knew one thing would change this time. This time she would be in his arms and he would do whatever it took to bring her back to life. He would give up anything to hold her and love her again.

"Alex, you don't want to take down Evans yourself?"

He wanted to eviscerate the fucker. "Eve is the only important thing here."

Sean put a hand on his arm. "Get your wife. I'll take care of bringing in Evans and Petty. Alex?"

"Yeah?"

"When everything is out in the open, we can handle them both together."

A nice, quiet assassination. A little weekend project to share with his brothers. "Yeah."

He turned to the hangar. There looked to only be the one door on this side and no windows. It was very likely still open on the garage side. He would have to sneak in that way.

"Alex, uhm, I think Eve's already gotten away herself." Sean pointed to the northern side of the hanger where the field led down to the alligator farm.

Eve was sprinting across the grass still dressed in her pajamas, but her shoes were gone. He looked through the binoculars. She was bleeding, but she was alive.

He had to get to her. Where was she going?

He heard a loud yell and then four men ran out of the hangar, pursuing his wife.

"Take them out, Sean."

Sean gave him a predatory grin and then hoisted the scoped rifle up. "With pleasure. What the fuck is she doing? Does she know what that is?"

Alex's heart nearly stopped because his wife ran into the enclosure. She would be surrounded by vicious predators.

Without another thought in his head, Alex took off running.

* * * *

Eve's hands started to shake as she looked around. Nausea rolled. She really didn't like reptiles. Why the hell had someone willingly put a freaking pit of goddamn alligators right in the middle of a very nice field? Whoever did it, they were stupid, out-of-their-mind assholes who deserved to die and very slowly.

She held as still as possible as a gargantuan gator moved past her, his wicked looking claws sinking into the mud as it crawled to the pool portion of her own private hell. The late-afternoon sunlight shone on the creature and its pitch-black eyes. Those eyes were dead, nothing like life in them. It was an eating machine that had climbed right out of the dinosaur age.

She'd seen eyes like that before. Michael Evans had dead eyes, too.

"Hey, princess, do you like our little friends?"

Her pursuers stood just outside the enclosure. There were four of them, and now they appeared to be in no hurry to drag her back. These men were obviously Evans's thugs. They were dressed for work in jeans and T-shirts, one of which had an oil stain on the front. They had likely been pulled away from their mechanical duties to run down the prisoner.

"You know, I heard those gators like to feed at twilight," one said. He'd holstered his weapon, his hands on his hips as though just waiting for a show. "They get a little aggressive when they scent blood, too."

She had no idea what alligators would and wouldn't do. She'd never expected to be close to one.

A scream leapt from her throat as she felt something scaly scratch across the back of her leg. A gator's tail swished behind her as though she was a fly it was trying to warn away. She jumped, but came down hard on her ankle and fell in the mud, landing right in front of another monster.

A horrible hissing sound filled the air as the gator's jaws opened, and she could smell fetid, rotten air.

The men outside the enclosure laughed as she scrambled away.

They were everywhere. So many of them. Fear threatened to choke her, but she forced herself up. They weren't attacking. She tried to remember everything she could. These weren't wild alligators. They were used to being fed by hand. And they were used to easy meals.

She wasn't going to be an easy meal. The men sent to get her were betting on how long she would last before she begged them to save her.

She wasn't going to be an easy meal for any of them.

There had to be another exit. Following the perimeter, she found the primary door across the enclosure. Could she make it? Or would they just run around and grab her on the

other side? She was trapped and had no idea what to do.
Think, Eve.

There was a shed close to the door, and then she saw it,
the weapon she needed. There was an emergency phone on
the wall of the shed, likely in case one of the workers got in
trouble.

How fast could the police get out here? She wasn't sure
if it would help, but she wasn't going down without a fight.

"Eve, my darling, I must say, you look very attractive
all broken and bloody. You know it's my favorite look on
you, but it's time to get cleaned up. We're leaving in fifteen
minutes. You don't want to make your first appearance in
South America all covered in mud, do you? After all, my
slave's hygiene reflects on me."

Evans stood with his men now, Petty and Carlos beside
him. He stared at her with a possessive look on his face.

She had to get to that phone. Fifteen minutes. They
might not be able to save her, but at least Alex would know
which airstrip the plane had taken off from.

And then the man beside Evans jerked as a loud bang
cracked through the air. He fell to his knees as a red stain
bloomed next to the oil stain on his shirt.

"Fucking sniper!" Evans screamed and everyone turned,
guns in hand.

And that was when she saw him. Alex. He was running
around the backside of the enclosure, away from the gunfire
likely provided by Sean or Jake. Whoever was in sniper
position had the higher ground, and another one of Evans's
thugs went down, blood splattering against the screen of the
enclosure.

Rapid gunfire broke out, and the door slammed open.

She wasn't alone with the gators anymore. She had to
move. Evans, Petty, and Carlos were taking refuge in the

monster pit. Eve ran, trying to sidestep the gators. One hissed her way, but she kept moving, trying to get to the other door. Alex was running for it, and she had to get to him before they got to her.

"Stop right now, Eve!" Evans screamed her way.

"We have to get the fuck out of here." Panic sounded in Petty's voice. "Let her go."

"We can't let her go. You get her back or I swear to god, I'll kill you." Evans was on the ground, staying out of the line of fire.

Alex made it to the door first, kicking his way in. His big body stood in the doorway, his eyes searching for her. He laid down a couple of rounds, forcing the other men to hit the ground.

A high-pitched scream sounded through the enclosure. She glanced back at Carlos. He'd slipped and fell right into a pit of gators, and one seemed to have taken exception. There was a terrible huffing sound that Eve would have sworn she could feel vibrations from and then a nasty snap. "It's got my hand!"

He began screaming in rapid-fire Spanish.

Alex seemed to dance around the large reptiles. They were restless now. Even she could smell the blood in the air. Their tails had started to twitch, brushing this way and that. Hisses and growls seemed to permeate the very air around her.

Alex grabbed her hand, hauling her close. "Stay calm. If one gets hold of you, punch, kick, and scream. Go for the snout and the eyes."

He pressed her behind him as Evans walked up. Evans was holding a semiautomatic in his hand. "I see you came to get your bitch. You lied, Warren. I believe you mentioned Special Agent McKay was no longer with us."

Carlos kept screaming, but Warren seemed to have gotten his panic under control. "It's easy enough to remedy. You have to remember, he needs us alive. Don't you, Alex?"

Warren was coming up on their left side, Evans on their right.

Alex didn't say a word, merely tried to back up.

"I can't move." Her heels were against something scaly. "There's an alligator behind me."

She could feel it breathing against her skin, its huge body coming halfway up her calves.

If they couldn't back away, there was no escape.

"Yes, you're right. He needs one of us alive. Well, let's face facts." Evans had a shit-eating grin on his face. "He needs me alive. I'm the only one who can put your dear brother away. He doesn't want Edward Petty in the Oval Office now, does he? Petty here gave you up so nicely. I have to admit I was a bit surprised when he arrested me. I rather thought I was done for. And then he takes me to a little coffee shop and gives me his proposal."

She felt Alex tense. God, they were right. Without any evidence, Edward would just go on with his career. Tears threatened. Alex was standing in front of her, his big gorgeous body ready to take any bullet that came their way. He wouldn't give her up. And he couldn't help but try for justice.

Evans stared at them. He didn't move at all, a predator with his prey in his sights. "He would let me go if I did this one little job for him. Just one little clinic. He knew how much I hated them, you see. It all started to go wrong when women forgot their place. Clinics like that and those fucking shelters, they're the problem. I don't understand you, McKay. I think that's why I find you fascinating. You really should be on my side."

Eve took a long breath. She had to get them out of here. Very slowly, she brought her foot up and back, praying she could reach the other side of the gator. It seemed to have fallen asleep, unlike the rest of its brethren. They were all twitching and moving, but no, she had to back up to the lazy boy.

"Why on earth would I be on your side, you piece of shit?" Alex's free hand reached back, giving her something to balance on. He kept his attention moving between the two men.

"Because of your lifestyle," Evans replied. "McKay, you opened a whole world for me. In some ways, I truly do feel gratitude to you. I admit, I started to check out the lifestyle as a way to hurt you, but when I began training Eve, I realized that this was the life I was born to lead, one where women knew their place."

Alex growled his response. "Her place is at my side."

Evans shook his head. "Her place is at your feet, begging for your mercy. Women are weak. They need a man's guidance and without it, they fail. They're born whores, McKay. Everyone knows it. They aren't smart enough to know how to properly live. They're vain and ignorant. They require a Dom."

"Which just goes to show me you have no idea what it means to be a Dom. My submissive is also the goddess I worship. Her trust and love are gifts to me. One that I can never properly repay. Stay back, Warren." He shifted his firing arm toward Warren.

She wasn't going to let Evans's words get to her. He was a madman. Nothing he said meant a damn thing. Eve found the mud behind her and managed to step across the alligator's big body. "About a foot and a half, babe."

Alex jumped back as though his body could measure

distance perfectly. He landed in the mud, but he never took his eyes off the targets.

Evans sneered their way. "What a disappointment you are, McKay. She is lovely, but she is nothing but a vessel. If you were half the man I thought you were, you would have killed her. She gave it up. All I had to do was slap her around a couple of times and her thighs spread wide."

Humiliation flooded her.

"As she should have," Alex said, his voice choking a little. "She knew what her Master would want. Death before dishonor is for idiots. My wife had one job to do when you took her. She had one order to obey. Stay alive and come home to me. That's the difference between us, Evans. I don't need to be the only man who's had her body. I'm the only one who has her heart, and that's what matters. You know nothing about being a Dom or being a man. And you know fuck all about loving a woman."

His eyes narrowed. "I know that you need me, and either Petty or I are going to eventually take a shot at you. It's inevitable. Oh, look, I believe Carlos has finally bled out. What's going to happen when you take a couple of bullets to the gut? So why don't we make a deal?"

Fear gripped her at the thought of Alex bleeding among the hungry reptiles.

"I'm not making a deal with you," Alex said.

Evans took a step closer. "I think you will. I'll take Eve off your hands. She gets to live. You get to live, too. We begin our game all over again. The other option is that you both die here and now. Let me see if my partner can persuade you."

A shot rang through the air, and she felt Alex's body jolt as though struck by lightning. His arm came up, shifting around and firing.

371

Warren Petty gave a loud gasp and then Eve watched as he fell over into the pit, a hole in his head. He slipped under the surface.

God, Warren. He was a horrible human being, but she'd seen his children born.

Alex stumbled back into her, his weight slamming into her. She stayed on her feet, but only just.

"Alex?" Her heart stuck in her throat. She wrapped her arms around his waist and felt warm liquid begin to coat her skin. *Alex's blood. Oh, god. No. No. No.*

Alex fired, but his aim was off. *Because he has a bullet in his gut.* Eve bit back a scream as Evans pulled the trigger and Alex's body jerked, sending them both to the mud. She cradled him, trying to protect him, but he wouldn't let her.

"Stay alive, baby. Sean will come for you. Ian will come for you," he said. He seemed to have lost control of his arm. The second bullet had lodged into his shoulder. The SIG fell down, slipping into the mud. "Love you so much. Love you, baby. Forgive me."

"Don't you go." Her heart threatened to stop. He was right there. He was in her arms. He couldn't be dying. He couldn't be bleeding out in the mud and the dirt.

She couldn't live without him and that meant one thing. Eve had spent so much of her life allowing events and the actions of others to mold her world. She'd clung to her own submission because it was her nature. But she finally understood. She might be Alex McKay's submissive, but she was his woman, too, and he was not allowed to die. He was not allowed to leave her alone on this earth. A well of strength possessed her. She was the passive one, the observer. It had been her life for so long, but she was surrounded by women who never gave in.

She had Alex's strength, but she had her sisters'

strength, too.

Grace, who quietly fought for her place.

Serena, who never accepted less than a happy ending.

Avery, who refused to allow tragedy to mold her life.

And Kristen. Somehow Kristen had become her sister, too. Kristen had stepped in front of a bullet to save Alex. She was fierce in her will to do good.

They were all with her, a great sisterhood of strength.

"I guess it's just you and me again, Eve. I'll be the right Master for you." Evans stood over her.

Her Master needed her. The SIG had slid beside her. She finally knew the truth. She'd almost seen her own death, but the truth had evaded her. Now it was clear. Justice didn't really matter in that moment. Righteousness slipped away.

At the end of everything—there was only love. And it was worth fighting for.

Eve picked up the gun and fired without hesitation. No warning. No forethought. He was evil. He threatened someone good. And she was suddenly a warrior for good.

Michael Evans, terrorist, rapist, tormentor of women, stared down at the hole in his chest.

Eve fired again.

Evans fell to his knees, raising his gun.

Again, the kickback made her shudder, but she clicked again and again because justice didn't matter. Revenge didn't matter. Only her man mattered. He needed her.

"Sweetie, I'm pretty sure he's dead. Please stop shooting so I can get Alex out of here." Sean's voice penetrated her primal brain.

She dropped the gun. Sean was here. She could move from warrior to wife again. She placed her hand on Alex's stomach, trying so desperately to staunch the bleeding. Tears poured from her eyes, pain from her soul. "Please help him."

She could lose him. God, she'd just gotten him back. Tears poured from her eyes. She just couldn't lose him.

"I fucking hate reptiles." Sean kicked at a gator, pushing it back. He knelt down in the mud beside her. "Alex! Alex McKay! You wake the fuck up right goddamn now!"

She heard the door slam again and then Jake was suddenly in her line of sight. "Evie? Are you hit?"

She shook her head. "He wouldn't let them touch me."

Her husband. Her Master. Her Alex. He wouldn't let them get her. He'd sacrificed himself. God, he couldn't die.

Please. Please. Please. She made a thousand deals with the universe in that moment. Anything to let him live.

"We killed the rest. They tried to get here, but we got them. The area's secure, and we called a bus," Jake said.

An ambulance. Yes. They needed one of those. She held onto Alex. She noticed Jesse behind Jake, but it didn't really register.

Sean moved into position, pulling Alex off her body. "Keep those fucking monsters off me."

He put his hands over Alex's heart and pressed down five times before covering Alex's mouth and breathing in.

Eve scrambled up and prayed to the heavens.

Chapter Twenty

Dallas, TX
Eight weeks later

Sanctum looked more like a garden tonight than a dungeon, and the smell of jasmine permeated the whole club. Alex looked out over the space, a deep feeling of satisfaction in his soul. His second wedding was smaller than the first, but the people they loved surrounded them and that was all that mattered.

Eve laughed at something Grace said and Alex felt his whole body tighten. She was so beautiful she took his breath away. And she was his. A two-carat diamond sparkled on her left hand and there were more diamonds around her throat, a collar commemorating the trust and love and connection between them.

"Alex, this is the most beautiful wedding I've ever been to." Serena looked lovely in her bridesmaid dress, but he knew that look in her eyes.

"I'm not letting you interview me, Serena." He looked around for Adam or Jake. Serena had been like a dog with a bone since she'd found out the standoff with Michael Evans had taken place in an alligator pit. Apparently she thought it would make a great hook for a book.

"I just want to know how it felt, Alex. I could really use something like this for my next book. I need sights and sounds and smells and emotions." She placed a hand over her ever-growing belly and sighed. "I would hope after all the help I gave you that you could just tell me a few facts."

He thought about growling, but it was his wedding day and Serena had been helpful. "It was a mud pit filled with snapping alligators. It smelled like ass and not particularly clean ass. It smelled like ass that hadn't been washed ever. As for emotions, well, I kind of didn't want to get torn apart by alligators."

Like Warren had been. He felt a fierce smile cross his face. When they'd drained the pit, his former partner had been in pieces. There was justice in the world.

Simon stepped up to the bar, looking perfect in his tailored tux. Alex could practically hear the unattached subs drooling, but Simon ignored them, preferring to frown affectionately at Serena. "You giving him hell again, love?"

Serena sighed. "He won't talk about the gators. It makes me sad."

Simon ordered a vodka tonic and shook his head. "He's got PTSD."

Alex rolled his eyes. "I don't have PTSD. I've got regrets, though. The feds can link the fertilizer to Evans, and they have cell phone records of Warren calling Evans. But I can't bring down Warren's brother without witnesses."

It was the only damn thing he regretted about the whole affair.

The senator had held a large press conference apologizing for his brother's actions and accusing Warren of being the one who had the affair with Carmen Garcia. So far, everyone was buying it. The senator looked golden.

"He's a weasel," Serena said. "I'm not voting for him."

Jake walked up, holding his hand out to his wife. "None of us will be voting for him. Adam is going to dig up the dirt. We just have to be patient. Now, dance with me, baby."

He led Serena off, but Alex was still thinking about the problem of Senator Petty.

It was the only thing that had gone wrong. Well, maybe not the only thing.

"I also wish I knew where she went." Alex took a long drag off his ridiculously expensive Scotch. Apparently nearly dying in an alligator-filled bog opened up the purse strings because he'd gotten several bottles of increasingly old Glenlivet as gifts. And the fifty-year from Ian was past heavenly.

"Are you talking about the Kristen girl?" Simon asked. He'd sent a lovely batch of alcohol to Alex's new house. He would likely start a trend. A liquor bouquet.

"Yeah." He couldn't help but wonder where she'd gone. He'd woken up in the hospital, recovering from surgery, and one of the first things he'd felt was a deep gratitude because he could have been shot earlier in that day, before he'd had a chance to defend his wife. Kristen had made that happen. No matter why she'd done it, she'd saved Eve and that meant something to Alex. He'd asked about her just about everywhere he could and he'd gotten nowhere. She hadn't been back to her condo.

"Well, I'm intrigued. I have to admit it," Simon said. "Any girl who can wake up from major surgery, pull out her IVs, and walk out of the critical care unit is a female I'd like to meet. Not to mention the fact that she managed to avoid all the security cameras. We should seriously consider bringing her on the team. We need some females."

Kristen was a loose end, and he hated loose ends.

Alex took a long drink. He glanced around Sanctum, feeling a deep sense of relief. This was his home. He might have screwed up by killing the only two people who could have exposed a conspiracy, but these people had his back.

They were his family. "I don't know about that. I think she might have had ties to Evans."

God, he hoped he was proven wrong. It was a testament to how much he liked her that he really hoped he was fucking wrong.

"Alex, I told you that doesn't fit my profile." Eve walked up, and his heart damn near stopped. She was so fucking gorgeous in her leather miniskirt and bustier. She was wearing his collar...and his wedding ring. She was his everything. "Kristen was focused on living a good life, on doing what was right. She wasn't insane. She knew right from wrong and Evans was wrong."

Alex pulled his wife close. He had her back. Oh, sure, it had taken a couple of bullets to the chest, but she was in his arms and legally his, and he was fucking keeping her. His wife. His sub. His forever. "Sure, baby. If she comes back, I'll welcome her with open arms."

It wasn't an untrue statement. He still had no idea why Kristen had done what she did. After the events of alligator road, as Alex called it, Kristen had disappeared from the world. He'd tried to find her, but had not an ounce of luck.

And Eve had been so disappointed that she couldn't invite her to their second wedding.

If he did find out she was involved with Evans, he would do what he needed to in order to help Kristen get over her mental problems. He would support her because deep down, she was good.

Eve wrapped her arm around his waist. "I'm so happy to hear that because I know we're going to find her. She needs a family. Like Jesse."

Alex frowned, staring out at the dungeon Ryan had managed to turn into a dance floor. This was the second of two weddings he'd facilitated in his time here. Avery and

Liam had been joined here as well. Jesse Murdoch was doing some sort of standing, jerk-every-now-and-then dance with one of the subs. He was still a puppy dog with really sharp, slightly rancid teeth. But he'd taken out everyone in that hanger and allowed Jake and Sean to save his life, so Jesse Murdoch was one of the team for now.

Oddly, Simon had taken a shine to the kid and was showing him the ropes. They were two outsiders, clinging to each other just a little.

"I just hope we can find a way to prove what Eddie did." He'd known he would sacrifice justice to save his wife's life, but damn, he wanted both. He looked over the club and wished Ian hadn't walked out right after the marriage ceremony. He'd stayed just long enough to pass Alex the ring. Ian and Sean were his family. He needed to be stronger. He wouldn't let Ian pull away anymore. He would be a pain in his ass until they were close as hell again. He and Ian and Sean. They had grown up together.

When the bullets had hit him, he'd found an odd calm. He'd known that Ian and Sean really would take care of his wife because they were family.

He'd realized that his love for Eve spanned more than a lifetime.

He'd known that his love for her was endless and so was he. More than death. More than life. His love for her would last beyond anything so simple as breathing. He would find her again and again. She was his destiny.

"Hey!" Adam ran up, a brilliant smile on his face. "I have good news and bad news."

Serena and Jake were right there with him. Serena wrapped an arm around her man's neck. "The good news is gooder than the bad news is bad. Yeah, I'm a totally awesome writer!"

Jake gave her a kiss on the cheek. "We've all been desperate. Every computer in our house has been focused on one thing."

"No. Two things," Adam said with a grin. "I found the proof. It's why I sent Jake to Philly. Alex, this is our wedding present to you."

Jake handed him a thumb drive. "That fucker Evans taped the meeting. It's all here. Warren Petty agrees to give him free rein if he takes out Eddie's mistress. It's so simple. The minute this hits the tabloids, they'll demand a DNA test on the samples the medical examiner took from Carmen's fetus. He can't run from this. He's done, man. No White House. No more politics. It's finished. Adam got a mystery e-mail that led us to where Evans hid the tape. We found it in a locker at an Amtrak station in Philadelphia. I have no idea who sent it to us, but he or she is a fucking angel."

He squeezed Eve close. He couldn't seem to help it. From the moment he'd woken up in the hospital to her lovely face, he hadn't been able to let her go. He'd slept beside her that night, pulling on her until she'd given up and climbed into the hospital bed with him. He wouldn't spend a night apart from her. She was his heaven. "Adam can't run the source down?"

Adam frowned. "Whoever it is, he's good. I mean damn good, and I'm not so sure it's a 'he.' As a matter of fact, I wonder if it isn't Kris because I found something else out. You remember how I've been looking into the whole thing where Liam's security card was used?"

They'd discovered the break-in during the Evans case. Alex knew Ian had been pissed as shit and already fired the previous building security, but Adam and Jake had apparently kept to the case. Someone had stolen Liam's card, duped it, gotten it back to him and infiltrated the building. "Sure. Did you finally get the video?"

Adam pulled up his laptop, flipping the lid open. "Yeah. And even more than that, I found out there was a complaint lodged that evening."

Alex tightened his hold on Eve. She peered in, her arm around his waist. Her face briefly turned up, a little wink in her eyes. He knew her language.

I love you.

She'd saved him. In every way possible. She was his bridge to the real world. He kissed her cheek. "I love you, too, angel."

He would do it all again. He would shoot Warren and take those damn bullets because he knew damn straight his sub would take care of business. His woman was fierce.

The video file began to run, showing the time and date stamp. He recognized the hallway that led to the copy room. A slight figure walked down the hall. It was easy to tell it was a woman. She had nice curves and long, dark hair flowed down her back. The image was black and white.

"The complaint was from the floor below us," Adam said.

"The lawyers?" The law firm of Gledon, McCloud, and Johnson had the floor below them.

"The complaint was about music being played at a high volume," Jake explained. "Apparently a couple of the younger lawyers stayed late that night, and they had some complaints about the volume we were cranking the music at. The building manager is scared of Ian, so we hadn't actually received a reprimand. This person says we played Guns N' Roses over and over for an hour."

A shiver went up Alex's spine. Guns N' Roses? "Sweet Child O' Mine?"

It was what Ian had played every year, once a year, on

the anniversary of Charlotte's death. He played that one song about a thousand times and drank his weight in Scotch until he passed out and then ignored the problem for another year. What was the chance that someone breaking into their building would be listening to the same song?

Adam looked up. "Yeah. They were annoyed that it was the same song. Over and over."

Sometimes in an investigation, little things came together, seemingly random events that knitted into a greater tapestry, a complete picture that hadn't been there before. As Alex watched the tape, the world coalesced into something he understood.

The dark-haired figure walked into the copier room, but not before she turned, looked at the camera and winked. She blew the camera a kiss before disappearing into the copy room.

Oh yes, and they are so totally helpful when you want to get information but you don't want anyone to know you have it. Really, it's awesome. So the hard drive on a copy machine actually takes a picture of everything the copy machine scans.

Kristen had been thrilled to tell him how she'd pulled information off the machine.

Kristen knew everything about him and Eve and all the members of McKay-Taggart Security Services.

She'd put herself in front of him, taking a bullet meant for him, because someone wanted him alive. Someone she wanted to please.

Here. She'd put her hand over his, covering her heart. *Since the day I set eyes on him. He's been here. Tell him I did good. Tell him I was good. I was good for him. I was good. He can have a thousand other women, but I was his only true wife.*

Kristen was the woman on the tape. She came back out of the room, dancing a little as she stuffed a thumb drive into her uniform. She looked up and winked and smiled. Somehow that smile was beneficent, as though what she was about to do would help the whole world.

Why do I love such an asshole?

He'd thought the asshole was Evans, but there was no tie between Kristen White and Evans. In fact, there was no tie between the woman they thought was Kristen and the real Kristen White. Days after he'd been shot, Alex had gotten the report. Kristen White was a nice forty-two-year-old with two kids. She had retired from journalism a year before. Her husband ran a software development company. She didn't have red hair, but she told the story of a woman who had helped her out of a problem with the Russian mob who fit the description. She'd called her an angel.

This is so much worse than the first time. First time, he was here.

Kristen was smart enough to fake her death, strong enough to come back from it.

Had she spent the last five years trying to find a way to get her husband back?

"Why would someone break into our place?" Adam asked. "That's Kris. I can see it with my own eyes. Why would she do that?"

Because she wanted to make up for her crimes.

Because she wanted her man back and she needed information. She'd taken information on all of them and decided on a plan of attack—or in her case, a plan to protect and give. They were her present to Ian. Alex and Eve. By bringing them back together, giving them their chance at justice, she'd been trying to prove herself to Ian.

He pulled his cell phone, his heart racing.

He dialed Ian's number. Ian's world had crumbled five years before. Maybe tonight, he would get it back.

He held Eve's hand as he waited for Ian to answer. Sometimes the universe was kind and a man got a second chance.

His heart filled with love. His second chance pressed her body against his.

All was fucking right with the world.

* * * *

Ian Taggart looked down at the screen of his computer, every cell in his body coming to life. He stared at it. Just a couple of lines that might mean the world. There he was. So fucking long he'd looked for Eli Nelson and there he was. At least he was pretty damn sure this was the line on the son of a bitch he'd been waiting for. Hoping for. Praying for.

No fucking way.

There was a little piece of him—the "glass was half-empty and very likely poisoned" part of him—that wondered if he wasn't being optimistic. Those couple of lines of e-mail could be from anyone. He would know more when he had photographic proof, and the person in the e-mail had promised it would come. He should be patient, but that had never been his strong suit.

Kristen Priest. The e-mail had come from the same woman who had supposedly saved Alex's life. Why hadn't she used her real last name? It was White. Did she still consider herself undercover? Who the fuck was she and why couldn't they get a line on her? She was a ghost, and Ian didn't like ghosts.

This woman was playing an angle, but he would join the game if it meant finding Nelson.

384

Eli Nelson had nearly killed his sister-in-law. He'd had problems with Grace at first, but she was his blood now. She made his brother happy and she was his niece's mother. No one got to hurt Grace. Or his brothers. Or his country. Eli Nelson had threatened them all.

And possibly had a hand in killing Ian's wife. He was going down.

If Ian could just find the little fucker.

He'd become obsessed, and it wasn't just about Nelson. It was about the turns his life was taking.

He'd walked out of his best friend's reception because he couldn't stand there and watch everyone. The music had been playing and he'd just known he couldn't stay there. It was a pussy thing to do, but his whole team was happy and he was still aching over Charlotte—who was a manipulative liar and didn't deserve him. Or anyone.

Fucking Russian mob princess who had the sweetest smile.

Except he'd wondered recently what it meant to be a Russian mob princess. What had her life been like? He'd seen her scars. How much had she suffered before she'd died?

He could still see her looking up at him as he entered her. She hadn't been a virgin, but those kick-him-in-the-gonads eyes had opened up with wonder as he'd pressed his cock in for the first time. Fuck. He'd felt like a virgin when he'd made love to her.

It feels good. My Master, it feels so good. Please. Please teach me.

Teach her? She hadn't been talking about sex. She'd been talking about life.

God, he missed her.

No. He hated her. She'd lied. She'd fucking died. He

385

didn't need anyone. He needed vengeance in the form of one Eli Nelson.

And he might have just found it.

A single e-mail concerning an energy project in a small country close to India. Loa Mali, an island country. Eli Nelson was expanding his terrorist activities. He just had to run down Kristen whatever her name was and figure out what the hell she wanted.

She was using his team and he wouldn't put up with that.

His cell phone buzzed beside him. He looked down. Alex. A long sigh came out of his mouth. Alex was probably calling to ask him where he'd gone. He was the best man after all. Best man. Such a ridiculous phrase. He was hardly a man at all. He was a monster, and he proved it day after day.

He wouldn't worry Alex with his problems now. It was Alex's honeymoon. He'd just watched Alex and Eve renew the vows they'd made so long ago in a simple ceremony that had gotten to Ian far more than he was willing to admit.

He'd made vows to love Charlotte, and he'd been a motherfucking, led-by-his-cock idiot. Nothing he'd promised her had been false. He'd meant every stupid word. He'd meant to love and cherish her. He'd meant to die for her.

But she'd lied and played him like a moron.

And she'd died first. That hurt worst of all.

He could feel her in his arms, her sweet body a cooling corpse. He'd loved once and never again. Charlie was his woman, his soul's mate. She was a fucking righteous bitch, the perfect mate to his inner bastard, and now she was gone and he would be alone for the rest of his life.

But he didn't need a goddamn thing. He was a warrior.

He didn't need a permanent woman.

A chime went off.

Ian looked up, slightly startled. Someone was at his door? No one got to his door without setting off his perimeter alarms. He pressed a couple of buttons on his computer. Nothing. Why hadn't his security gone off?

He got up and walked to the door. His security was damn near perfect, but somehow the person who had knocked hadn't set off the alarm.

His cell phone trilled again. Alex. He loved Alex. Oh, he would never put it in those words, but Alex was his brother. He was thrilled that Alex and Eve were all "man and wife forever and shit" again, but he needed the night off. He'd managed to stand beside them, managed to watch Alex place a ring on her finger and a collar around her neck, but he'd slunk out of the reception. Everyone had a wife now. Sean was married with a kid. Liam had a wife and kid on the way. Fuck, even crazy Adam and Jake had managed to find someone and knock her up.

Alex had found his way home to Eve.

He'd found his true love and she'd died in his arms. Was it any wonder he kind of hoped he could horrifically murder whoever was on the other side of his door? It was all he had left. He set the phone aside. He wasn't going to answer it tonight.

He pulled his SIG, clicking the safety off. He looked at the monitor he kept by the door. It was fed by the camera he kept on his entryway. Female. Even in a dark hoodie and jeans, he could see her curves. She held her hands out, showing him she wasn't carrying, but her head was down. He kept his gun ready because he wasn't about to just trust that she wasn't armed.

He opened the door because, yeah, he was curious.

Someone had managed to get around his copious security system. Had she been sent by Eli Nelson? Was this the mysterious Kristen? Who the fuck else could it be? He had CCTV cameras and motion detectors and every other kind of security, and not a single alarm had gone off, just that one little bell, signaling someone was at his front door.

He stared at the figure in his doorway. Her head came up and he actually felt his heart start to pound. Five foot eight with killer curves. Red hair that reached past her shoulders. It had been black before, but the red looked good on her. And those eyes. God, he knew those eyes. He'd looked into them a hundred times and a hundred times, they had kicked him straight in the gut.

Master, I love you. I wish nothing more than to please my most precious Master.

She'd made him believe, with her shining eyes and her snarky wit and those curves that went on for days. She'd been so smart, so deadly, so damn good at her job. He'd known she was trouble from the minute he'd met her, but he hadn't been able to turn away.

She'd brought him to his knees because he'd died the day that she did.

His heart dropped to his toes.

"Hi," she said in a breathy voice.

"You're Kristen." Everything fell into place. Now he knew why she hadn't wanted him in Florida. She'd been the one to cause all the chaos. And he understood how she'd gotten past his security. No one was sneakier. "Hello, Charlotte."

Ian forced his legs to stay strong. After all, it wasn't every day his dead wife came back to life.

Ian Taggart and the whole McKay-Taggart Security team will return in *Love and Let Die*.

A Tragic Love Story

Charlotte Dennis's mission was clear: distract and misdirect CIA operative Ian Taggart by any means necessary. If she failed, she would never see her sister again. With her training, it should have been simple, but after one night in Ian's arms, she knew that saving her sister would mean losing the man of her dreams.

Ian was tracking a terrorist when he met the beautiful American daughter of a Russian mobster. His instincts told him Charlotte was trouble, but his body craved her like a drug and his heart would not be denied. She took his ring and his collar. For once he was truly happy. But as he closed in on his target, her betrayal cost him his mission while her sacrifice saved his life. As she died in his arms, Ian vowed he would never love again.

A Dangerous Reunion

For six years, Charlotte has thought of nothing but returning to her husband, her Master. Working in the shadows, she has devoted herself to earning a chance to reclaim her place in Ian's life. But forgiveness isn't a part of Ian's vocabulary.

Nothing is more important to Ian Taggart than his new mission. But the information he needs is firmly in the hands of the woman who betrayed him. To catch his most dangerous prey, Ian will have to let Charlotte back into his life. As the hunt takes them to some of the world's most exotic locations, the danger grows and their passion reignites.

Will Ian forgive his wayward submissive…or lose her again?

About Lexi Blake:

Lexi Blake lives in North Texas with her husband, three kids, and the laziest rescue dog in the world. She began writing at a young age, concentrating on plays and journalism. It wasn't until she started writing romance that she found success. She likes to find humor in the strangest places. Lexi believes in happy endings no matter how odd the couple, threesome or foursome may seem. She also writes contemporary western ménage as Sophie Oak.

Connect with Lexi online:

Facebook:
Lexi Blake

Twitter:
www.twitter.com/@authorlexiblake

Smashwords:
www.smashwords.com/profile/view/LexiBlake

Website:
www.LexiBlake.net

Other Books by Lexi Blake:

Masters And Mercenaries
The Dom Who Loved Me
The Men With The Golden Cuffs
A Dom Is Forever
On Her Master's Secret Service
Coming in 2013:
Love and Let Die

Coming Soon:
Leaving Camelot, Wild Western Nights, Book 1

Masters of Ménage by Shayla Black and Lexi Blake
Their Virgin Captive
Their Virgin's Secret
Their Virgin Concubine
Their Virgin Princess
Coming Soon:
Their Virgin Hostage

Their Virgin Hostage
Masters of Ménage, Book 5
By Shayla Black and Lexi Blake

Available June 2013

One Hostage Bride

Kinley Kohl agrees to marry wealthy Greg Jansen to save her family. Her wedding day should be the happiest of her life…except that she doesn't love him. And she can't help but wonder if she's making a mistake. Even so, she refuses to let her loved ones down. Then moments before her nuptials, she's kidnapped—and her whole life changes.

Three Determined Mercenaries

Dominic Anthony has waited years to avenge his sister's murder. He knows Greg Jansen is dirty, but he needs a witness to help prove his case. Jansen's new bride is the perfect hostage. Kinley Kohl will tell him everything…or else. But his two business partners aren't so sure. Law and Riley Anders worry that Kinley isn't as guilty as she seems. And Law suspects she might be the one woman who can handle them all.

From Target to Treasure

In the wilds of Alaska, the three men try to pry Kinley open, only to discover she's both stronger and more innocent than they imagined. Her sweet beauty melts their suspicion and steals their hearts. Together, they awaken her passion and brand her as their own. When danger strikes, the men realize they must save Kinley or lose the love of their lives forever.

Enjoy the following excerpts from Shayla Black, Cherise Sinclair, and Kallypso Masters.

Dangerous Boys and Their Toy

By Shayla Black
Available Now!

Trading orgasms for information isn't their usual way of doing business, but when a missing criminal-turned-star-witness and fifty grand are on the line, bounty hunter R. A. Thorn and Detective Cameron Martinez are prepared to put their bodies to the task and give gorgeous Brenna Sheridan everything she needs.

An exchange they never anticipated becomes an experience none can forget—or walk away from. Sexual hunger sizzles the threesome, but the stakes and danger rise as a mafia bad-ass stalks Brenna.

Soon, their "deal" is no longer about information—or sex. Emotions bind Brenna, Cam and Thorn together more tightly than they ever imagined as the men protect—and serve—the beloved woman neither can live without.

* * * *

"Detective," she cried. "Thorn broke in, tied me up in my sleep and fondled me without my permission."

"Not exactly true. I used the key under the flower pot on the front porch to let myself in, and I touched you with your permission—more or less. I asked you if you'd tell me what I wanted to know if I made you come, and you said yes."

"I didn't mean it."

"How was I supposed to know that? You were wet as

395

hell when I touched you. As far as I'm concerned our bargain still stands."

"Even if it did," Brenna argued. "You didn't make me come."

Thorn flushed red. "I came damn close. Besides, you didn't specify that I personally had to make you come, just that I had to make sure it happened. Cam will take care of the technicalities."

Cam sighed and opened his mouth to refute Thorn.

Brenna shot back, "He can't make me come, either."

Normally, Cameron would let such a comment slide off his back. He didn't have the chest-beating, macho caveman instincts Thorn possessed. But somehow, Brenna's bald statement riled him a touch.

"Actually, I think, under normal circumstances, I could. I'm a patient man willing to take the time to discover what my partner needs during sex." He cocked his head and stared at Brenna. An odd sort of longing crossed her face. He remembered the night by the pool, watching her frustrated attempt to orgasm. "But what you're talking about is deeper, right?" He crossed the room to sit on the bed beside her. "Have you ever had an orgasm?"

Brenna flushed twenty shades of red then turned away.

He took that to mean no.

An orgasm deficit to most would not be a huge tragedy. Through most of high school and college, Cameron had gone without. Too many people underfoot for self-pleasure. In his mostly white school, too many folks had been unwilling to get naked with someone half Apache, half Hispanic. In Arizona, that century and a half year-old prejudice against Indians and Mexicans still quietly lived on in more than a handful of people.

But Brenna... Her deficit wasn't a mere case of going

without. It was an inability, her shamed expression told him. And Cameron ached for her. What would it be like to be an adult and not know the joy of sexual satisfaction?

Tragedy.

"See? She's frigid," Thorn mouthed off.

Cameron whirled on him. "Has anyone ever told you what an enormous prick you are?"

Thorn grinned. "No, but I hear frequently what an enormous prick I have."

Cameron rolled his eyes then turned back to Brenna. "Ignore him. When the phrase son of a bitch was coined, they had Thorn in mind."

"You're not much better. Pinching me so hard it brought tears to my eyes."

So he had. Totally unlike him. This stupid plot of Thorn's wasn't getting them anywhere, but he may be onto something.

"Key." He held out his palm to Thorn.

"Ah, shit. Man, you're going to uncuff her? She looks hot, bound and ready."

She did. No refuting that. But Thorn couldn't see the long-term benefit of uncuffing Brenna beyond the short-term benefit the view provided his dick.

"I'd hate to have to arrest you. You'd have to call your brother to bail you out."

"Oh, hell no!" With another curse, Thorn slapped the key in Cam's palm. "You ruin all the fun, you know that?"

"I'm the original party pooper."

With a quick turn of his wrist and a few tugs, Brenna's wrists were free. He untied her ankles. Just as she would have leapt from the bed and reached for the robe on the floor beside it, Cameron placed a palm between her bare collarbones.

"Not just yet." Once he had her pinned to the bed, he said, "I am sincerely sorry that no man has taken the time or care with you to give you the pleasure you deserve. I'm sorry you have yet to figure out how to bring yourself to orgasm." He brushed a stray curl from her cheek. "I know it must bother you. You must feel somewhat left out and…defective."

Tears flooded Brenna's eyes, and Cameron sucked in a shocked breath. He'd hoped that he was close to the truth, but hadn't imagined that he was dead on. Her tears and pained expression said, however, that he was.

"It's okay," he whispered. "You're not. It's wrong for you to go on suffering needlessly. We will help you discover what you need to find fulfillment, if that's what you want. But…" Cameron sighed, hating what he had to say next. "Thorn is right. We need your help in return. Lawton worked with a man named Julio Marco and others to traffic humans across the border and sell them into slavery. I was Lawton's arresting officer. Thorn is his bail bondsman. We need Lawton to live up to his word to turn evidence for the state so the victims can have justice. He must come in and provide the testimony he promised. You're our only hope of finding him."

Brenna blinked. Tears ran down the sides of her face. Cameron hurt for her. She was clearly confused, didn't know who to trust or what to do. He understood.

Cameron thumbed her tears away. "I would never want to hurt you. I believe we can help you. In return, I hope you're willing to help us." He leaned down and placed a gossamer kiss across her trembling lips. "Will you?"

For more information visit www.shaylablack.com.

Club Shadowlands

By Cherise Sinclair
Available now!

Her car disabled during a tropical storm, Jessica Randall discovers the isolated house where she's sheltering is a private bondage club. At first shocked, she soon becomes aroused watching the interactions between the Doms and their subs. But she's a professional woman--an accountant-- and surely isn't a submissive . . . is she?

Master Z hasn't been so attracted to a woman in years. But the little sub who has wandered into his club intrigues him. She's intelligent. Reserved. Conservative. After he discovers her interest in BDSM, he can't resist tying her up and unleashing the passion she hides within.

* * * *

"What is your name?" Her new host's voice was deep, dark as the night outside.

"Jessica." She stepped back from his grip to get a better look at her savior. Smooth black hair, silvering at the temples, just touching his collar. Dark gray eyes with laugh lines at the corners. A lean, hard face with the shadow of a beard adding a hint of roughness. He wore tailored black slacks and a black silk shirt that outlined hard muscles underneath. If Ben was a Rottweiler, this guy was a jaguar, sleek and deadly.

"I'm sorry to have bothered—" she started.

Ben reappeared with a handful of golden clothing that

he thrust at her. "Here you go."

She took the garments, holding them out to keep from getting the fabric wet. "Thank you."

A faint smile creased the manager's cheek. "Your gratitude is premature, I fear. This is a private club."

"Oh. I'm sorry." Now what was she going to do?

"You have two choices. You may sit out here in the entryway with Ben until the storm passes. The forecast stated the winds and rain would die down around six or so in the morning, and you won't get a tow truck out on these country roads until then. Or you may sign papers and join the party for the night."

She looked around. The entry was a tiny room with a desk and one chair. Not heated. Ben gave her a dour look.

Sign something? She frowned. Then again, in this lawsuit-happy world, every place made a person sign releases, even to visit a fitness center. So she could sit here all night. Or…be with happy people and be warm. *No-brainer.* "I'd love to join the party."

"So impetuous," the manager murmured. "Ben, give her the paperwork. Once she signs—or not—she may use the dressing room to dry off and change."

"Yes, sir." Ben rummaged in a file box on the desk, pulled out some papers.

The manager tilted his head at Jessica. "I will see you later then."

Ben shoved three pages of papers at her and a pen. "Read the rules. Sign at the bottom." He scowled at her. "I'll get you a towel and clothes."

She started reading. *Rules of the Shadowlands.*

"Shadowlands. That's an unusual na—" she said, looking up. Both men had disappeared. Huh. She returned to reading, trying to focus her eyes. Such tiny print. Still, she

400

never signed anything without reading it.

Doors will open at...

Water pooled around her feet, and her teeth chattered so hard she had to clench her jaw. There was a dress code. Something about cleaning the equipment after use. Halfway down the second page, her eyes blurred. Her brain felt like icy slush. *Too cold—I can't do this.* This was just a club, after all; it wasn't like she was signing mortgage papers.

Turning to the last page, she scrawled her name and wrapped her arms around herself. *Can't get warm.*

Ben returned with some clothing and towels, then showed her into an opulent restroom off the entry. Glass-doored stalls along one side faced a mirrored wall with sinks and counters.

After dropping the borrowed clothing on the marble counter, she kicked her shoes off and tried to unbutton her shirt. Something moved on the wall. Startled, Jessica looked up and saw a short, pudgy woman with straggly blonde hair and a pale complexion blue with cold. After a second, she recognized herself. *Ew.* Surprising they'd even let her in the door.

In a horrible contrast with Jessica's appearance, a tall, slender, absolutely gorgeous woman walked into the restroom and gave her a scowl. "I'm supposed to help you with a shower."

Get naked in front of Miss Perfection? Not going to happen. "Thanks, b-b-b-but I'm all right." She forced the words past her chattering teeth. "I don't need help."

"Well!" With an annoyed huff, the woman left.

I was rude. Shouldn't have been rude. If only her brain would kick back into gear, she'd do better. She'd have to apologize. Later. If she ever got dried off and warm. She needed dry clothes. But, her hands were numb, shaking uncontrollably, and time after time, the buttons slipped from her stiff fingers. She couldn't even get her slacks off, and she was shuddering so hard her bones hurt.

"Dammit," she muttered and tried again.

The door opened. "Jessica, are you all right? Vanessa said—" The manager. "No, you are not all right." He stepped inside, a dark figure wavering in her blurry vision.

"Go away."

"And find you dead on the floor in an hour? I think not." Without waiting for her answer, he stripped her out of her clothes as one would a two-year-old, even peeling off her sodden bra and panties. His hands were hot, almost burning, against her chilled skin.

She was naked. As the thought percolated through her numb brain, she jerked away and grabbed at the dry clothing. His hand intercepted hers.

"No, pet." He plucked something from her hair, opening his hand to show muddy leaves. "You need to warm up and clean up. Shower."

He wrapped a hard arm around her waist and moved her into one of the glass-fronted stalls behind where she'd been standing. With his free hand, he turned on the water, and heavenly warm steam billowed up. He adjusted the temperature.

"In you go," he ordered. A hand on her bottom, he nudged her into the shower.

The water felt scalding hot against her frigid skin, and she gasped, then shivered, over and over, until her bones hurt. Finally, the heat began to penetrate, and the relief was so intense, she almost cried.

Some time after the last shuddering spasm, she realized the door of the stall was open. Arms crossed, the man leaned against the door frame, watching her with a slight smile on his lean face.

"I'm fine," she muttered, turning so her back was to him. "I can manage by myself."

"No, you obviously cannot," he said evenly. "Wash the mud out of your hair. The left dispenser has shampoo."

Mud in her hair. She'd totally forgotten; maybe she *did* need a keeper. After using the vanilla-scented shampoo, she let the water sluice through her hair. Brown water and twigs swirled down the drain. The water finally ran clear.

"Very good." The water shut off. Blocking the door, he rolled up his sleeves, displaying corded, muscular arms. She had the unhappy feeling he was going to keep helping her, and any protest would be ignored. He'd taken charge as easily as if she'd been one of the puppies at the shelter where she volunteered.

For more information, visit CheriseSinclair.com

Nobody's Angel (Rescue Me #2)

By Kallypso Masters
Available Now!

(Should be read after the introduction, Masters at Arms; this is not a stand-alone series)

Angelina was a bundle of nerves as she waited for Marc to return tonight for her punishment. He had so many more implements and devices he could employ this time. What would he use?

"Karla, would you walk through the club with me before Marc gets back? I want to see everything so I can know what to expect."

"Sure. Where should we start? The theme rooms?"

"No!" Angelina had to take a deep breath to decrease her anxiety. "I don't think I'm ready for that yet."

"How about the great room where I sing?"

She remembered the Dom in the Harley vest and the coiled whip. Maybe there was no safe place in the club. "I guess we could start there. Maybe you can describe some of the activities you've seen there."

A few minutes later, Karla flipped the lights on and the great room was illuminated before her. It looked so…normal without all the people in BDSM gear hanging around. She walked into the room filled with ottomans and tables. They were closer to the stage now than they had been the night she'd been here with Allen.

Angelina walked up to the center post and lifted up a cold, heavy chain with a leather cuff attached to it. Had the Dom in the Harley vest chained the blonde submissive here and used his whip on her? Still, she shivered when she thought about being restrained by them with Marc.

"Do the chains excite you, pet?"

The pit of Angelina's stomach dropped, and she turned loose of the chain as if it was suddenly on fire. It clanged against the center post and Angelina turned to find Marc standing in the entryway beside Karla. He wore black leather pants and a black leather vest, his chest bare, except for the tufts of hair over his heart. Dear Lord, her nipples hardened just looking at him.

His gaze went to her breasts. "Never mind. I can see your answer."

He stepped into the room and walked toward her like a wolf stalking its prey. Her heart pounded, curiously depriving her of oxygen that might have helped keep her mind from turning to mush. When he reached her, he stared until she squirmed in her skin, then took his knuckles and brushed them over her nipples, making them even more engorged. She hissed, gasping for air.

"Karla, Angelina won't be needing you for a while." He didn't even turn around to dismiss Karla. His gaze remained fixed on Angelina.

"Angie, will you be okay?"

No, never again. "Yes. I'll see you upstairs later." Karla was sweet to worry about her, but Marc wouldn't administer pain without pleasure. She wouldn't enjoy the first, but couldn't wait for the other.

"Did you miss me, pet?"

How should she answer that? Karla had kept her busy with unpacking and chatting, but Marc had dominated her thoughts all evening, mostly with her worrying about the scene to come.

"Answer me."

"Yes, Sir." Oh, God. She really had.

405

"Thank you for your honesty, pet. Now, strip."

Her eyes opened wider. Had she heard him correctly? She looked around to make sure Karla had left and that they were alone. They were, but someone could come in at any minute, couldn't they?

"I'm not sure..."

"I am. I said strip. Now. Or you'll add to the length of your discipline session."

"It's not a punishment?"

"No, pet. We're still training that mind and body of yours to submit. This is discipline."

Angelina sucked air into her lungs as she reached up to the vee of her blouse and began to slip each button through its hole, making her way downward to the hem. If this was how bad she felt to be disciplined, she hoped to never have to be punished. She spread the flaps open a bit and untied the peasant skirt belt, then shimmied the cotton over her hips until it pooled at her feet. She hadn't worn panties today, per Marc's explicit instructions before they left her house this morning. The cool air made it abundantly clear her pussy already was wet.

Marc motioned for her to continue. She reached up to spread open her blouse, pull it off her shoulders, and slip it down her arms to join the skirt on the floor. Her breasts were shielded in a skin-tone bustier that captured Marc's interest.

His hands reached up to cup her breasts, rolling her swollen nipples through the lace before he bent down to take one lace-covered peak between his teeth. He bit her with enough force to cause her knees to buckle. Marc caught her elbows to steady her.

"We can't have that, now, can we?"

Angelina wasn't sure what he meant, until he reached behind her and picked up the leather cuffs. "No! I'm not

406

ready for that!"

Marc smiled and took each of the cuffs off the chain and rubbed them over her nipples, teasing her with the brass buckles. The sensations were delicious.

"What is your safeword, pet?"

"Red, Sir."

"Do you trust me to stop when you say that word?"

Did she? She liked to think so, but how could she know unless she actually used the word?

"Pet, I hope to enjoy your gift of submission all week. Why would I do anything to jeopardize that on our first night? I think you know I will stop immediately if you use your safeword."

She did. Didn't she? Oh, God. She could do this. She really could. Angelina extended her hands to him, palms up.

"Good girl."

His praise melted away some of the ice in her veins. As she held her hands before him, he wrapped each wrist in one of the cuffs and fastened them with Velcro. So the buckles were just for show, as she would be if he strapped her to the post. He slipped his finger between the leather in the skin. "Not too tight?"

"No, Sir. It feels fine."

"Well, let's see if we can do better than fine." He hooked the two cuffs together and pulled her hands over her head and placed his other hand on her upper right arm to begin maneuvering her into place before the post.

I can do this. I can do this. Oh, God. I can't do this. I can't do this!

Angelina's chest rose and fell rapidly. "Yellow!"

Marc stopped moving, but still kept her hands high above her head. With his other hand, he trailed gently down the underside of her arm until he reached her breast and rubbed his knuckles against her rigid nipple.

"Tell me what you're thinking, pet."

"I don't think I can do this, Sir."

"What frightens you?"

"My hands over my head. That reminds me of…" *the one who shall remain nameless.*

"When you were restrained before, were your hands together or apart?"

"Apart, Sir."

"Were you restrained to a post like this?"

"No, Sir. To a St. Andrew's cross."

"Good. I want you to focus on how this experience is different from that earlier one, not the least difference being who your Dom is this time. Will you trust me to continue, Angelina?"

Her name always sounded so lyrical when he said it and calmed her down more than when he called her pet or other endearments. She took a deep breath. *This is Marc. He doesn't want to hurt you.*

"Yes, Sir. Thank you for slowing down for me."

He rolled her nipple. "Thank you for remembering to use 'yellow' to slow me down. Now, we will continue." He guided her backward. Would he turn her around to face the post? Oh, God. Then she wouldn't be able to see what he was doing. Just like when Allen…

"Relax, pet. You're almost there."

She felt the wooden beam press against the expanse of skin between her shoulder blades and the cheeks of her bare ass. She still wore the bustier, although, with its front hooks, he could remove it whenever he chose. Apparently, he liked having her wearing it. For now.

"Keep your hands here."

Was he going to do honor bondage again? That

wouldn't be so bad. Then she heard the rattle of chains and dread pooled in her lower abdomen. He knelt on one knee in front of her, the out-of-whack symbolism making her smile, and attached a leather cuff to each ankle.

After checking to make sure the bindings weren't too tight, he stood and walked to a wall where a variety of whips, paddles, and straps hung. He would remember she'd said no whips, wouldn't he? Before the concern became a full-blown panic, he bypassed them for a display of bars of varying lengths considering several before choosing one and bringing it back to her.

"Spread your legs. Wide." When she hesitated too long, he added, "Don't make me repeat my commands, pet."

The Rescue Me series is an ongoing saga that began in *Masters at Arms*, the Rescue Me series introduction, which is free at most Amazon online stores, Kobo, Apple iTunes/iBooks, Barnes & Noble, Smashwords, and All Romance eBooks. Because the characters return in significant roles in each other's books, the series should be read in order, as follows:

Masters at Arms
Nobody's Angel
Nobody's Hero
Nobody's Perfect

The next installment, *Somebody's Angel* (Rescue Me #5), should be available by late summer 2013.

For more information visit:
http://kallypsomasters.blogspot.com

CPSIA information can be obtained
at www.ICGtesting.com
Printed in the USA
FSOW01n1254220917
39084FS